Gao Xingjian

is the first Chinese recipient of the Nobel Prize for Literature. Born in 1940 in Jianxi province in eastern China, he studied in state schools, earned a university degree in French in Beijing, and embarked on a life of letters. Choosing exile in 1987, he settled in Paris, where he completed *Soul Mountain* two years later. In 1992 he was named a Chevalier de l'Ordre des Arts et des Lettres by the French government. He is a playwright and painter as well as a fiction writer and critic.

From the international reviews for *Soul Mountain*:

'Arguably [Gao's] finest work... *Soul Mountain* is a quirky, thick, playful monster of a book, a bit like what one might expect if Beckett or Ionesco had traveled in China and been steeped in Chinese myths. It is not easy to say what the novel is about – and yet the marvel is that somehow it is still both engaging and elegant.'   *New York Times*

'A rich soup of a book... One man's personal and philosophical odyssey evolves against the dramatic and vibrantly physical background of Central China's ancient forests. Part novel, part philosophical tract, the genius of *Soul Mountain* lies in its not attempting to offer any answers... It instead belongs to that curious genre of intellectual quest dominated by the great German writer WG Sebald. This search for self serves to set the book beyond cultures while also succeeding in presenting the Western reader with a wonderfully broad portrait of a country caught between the ancient and the modern in a most fundamental way.'   *Irish Times*

'Gao's flight to rural China to evade imprisonment inspired this dazzling autobiographical novel... Superficially, this epic picaresque resembles familiar western literary forms but its bedrock is utterly other.'   *Guardian*

'An original voice unlike any contemporary writing available in English... *Soul Mountain* is an extraordinary product of an imagination infused with European and Chinese cultures; an exploration of individual identity in a society that exalts the collective and a daring play with voice that plunders ancient Chinese myths, philos

Australian

GAO XINGJIAN, *Recueillement, 1997*
Ink on paper
15¼″ x 15½″ (38.5 x 39 cm)

SOUL
MOUNTAIN

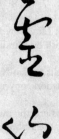

GAO XINGJIAN

Translated from the Chinese by Mabel Lee

This edition produced for The Book People Ltd,
Hall Wood Avenue, Haydock, St Helens WA11 9UL

Flamingo
An imprint of HarperCollins*Publishers*
77–85 Fulham Palace Road,
Hammersmith, London W6 8JB

Flamingo is a registered trade mark of
HarperCollins*Publishers* Limited

www.**fire**and**water**.com

Published by Flamingo 2001
1 3 5 7 9 8 6 4 2

First published as *Lingshan* in Taiwan by Lianjing Chubanshe in 1990
First published in English by Flamingo (Australia) in 2000

Cover image: Gao Xingjian and Flip Chalfant/The Image Bank

ISBN 0 00 768038 4

Printed and bound in China by Imago

Introduction

Gao Xingjian was born on 4 January 1940 in war-torn China soon after the beginning of the Japanese invasion. He completed secondary and tertiary studies in the People's Republic of China (established in 1949 after the Communist victory in the civil war against the Nationalists), graduating with a major in French from the Beijing Foreign Languages Institute in 1962. Gao Xingjian came to national and international prominence as a writer and critic during the early 1980s for his experimental works of drama, fiction and theory that contravened the guidelines established by the ideologues of the Chinese Communist Party. At the time, China was just beginning to emerge from the throes of the Cultural Revolution (1966–1976), a decade during which the self of the individual was virtually annihilated from intellectual and creative activities. Basic human instincts, sensitivities, thinking, perceptions and judgements were repressed and stunted, and extreme forms of socialist-realist and romantic-revolutionary representations of reality became the compulsory basis of all creative endeavours: literature and the arts therefore became representations of a distorted reality.

The end of the Cultural Revolution and the implementation of considerably more liberal policies meant that Gao Xingjian was able to publish, despite continuing aftershocks from those times. It also meant that he was able to travel abroad as a member of two writers' delegations – in 1979 to France, and in 1980 to Italy. From 1980 to 1987, he published short stories, novellas, critical essays and plays in various literary journals, as well as four books: *A Preliminary Discussion of the Art of Modern Fiction* (1981), a novella *A Pigeon Called Red Beak* (1985), *Collected Plays of Gao Xingjian* (1985), and *In Search of a Modern Form of Dramatic Representation* (1987). In addition, three of his plays were staged at the Beijing People's Art Theatre: *Absolute Signal* (1982), *Bus Stop* (1983) and *Wild Man* (1985). However, events in Gao Xingjian's life during those few years made him resolve to fully commit himself to the creative expression of his own reality, and no authority other than that of his self would again be allowed to dictate his judgements of that reality.

In 1987, when Gao Xingjian left China to take up a D.A.A.D fellowship in Germany, he did not intend to return. He had taken with him the most important thing in his life: the manuscript of a novel he had begun in Beijing in the summer of 1982. This novel was *Lingshan* which he subsequently completed in September 1989 in Paris (where he now resides and has French citizenship) and published in Taipei in 1990. G ran Malmqvist, whose translations of ten of Gao Xingjian's plays were published as a set by the Swedish Royal Dramatic Theatre in 1994, published the Swedish version of the novel as *Andarnas berg*, in 1992; and No l and Liliane Dutrait's French version, *La Montagne de l' me*, was published in 1995. For the English version, the title *Soul Mountain* has been used.

Soul Mountain is a literary response to the devastation of the self of the individual by the primitive human urge for the warmth and security of an other, or others, in other words by socialized life. The existence of an other resolves the problem of loneliness but brings with it anxieties for the individual, for inherent in any relationship is, inevitably, some form of power struggle. This is the existential dilemma confronting the individual, in relationships with parents, partners, family, friends and larger collective groups. Human history abounds with cases of the individual being induced by force or ideological persuasion to submit to the power of the collective; the surrender of the self to the collective eventually becomes habit, norm convention and tradition, and this phenomenon is not unique to any one culture.

In traditional China, the philosophy of Confucius was developed into an autocratic ideology alongside infrastructures that allowed it to permeate all levels of society, and the individual after birth was conditioned to be subservient to a clearly defined hierarchy of authorities. Unless intent on challenging those authorities and facing the consequences, nonconformists had the possibility of living the life of the recluse or taking temporary or long-term refuge in Buddhist monasteries or Daoist retreats, although as institutionalized orders, they too constitute collectives. Alternatively, the nonconformist could remain in conventional society and survive by feigning madness or could achieve freedom, transcendence and self-realization in literary and artistic creation. However, these options were gradually eroded in China from the early years of the twentieth century as self-sacrifice was promoted first in the name of patriotism and then also in the name of the communist revolution which promised equality and social justice. Self-sacrifice became an entrenched habit that facilitated, aided and abetted the extremes of social conformity demanded by the Cultural Revolution which was engineered by sophisticated modern strategies for ideological control. Writers and artists for whom creation was the expression of the self were relentlessly and effectively silenced.

During the 1960s and 1970s, Gao Xingjian's irrepressible urge for artistic self-expression resulted in several hundred works of prose, plays and poems. He was aware that what he wrote could not be published, and that even as unpublished works they could be used as evidence against him for failing to comply with prescribed guidelines. To hide his writings became increasingly difficult, and he finally burnt all of them during the height of the Cultural Revolution rather than face the consequences of having them found.

As noted above, Gao Xingjian was able to publish a substantial number of works during the 1980s, but not without considerable anxiety. The publication of *A Preliminary Discussion of the Art of Modern Fiction* in 1981 resulted in his being criticized for promoting modernist ideas borrowed from the decadent capitalist West and he was placed under surveillance. Nonetheless, his debut as a playwright occurred in 1982 and took Beijing by storm: *Absolute Signal* was staged over a hundred times to packed performances at the Beijing People's Arts Theatre. However, those were politically ambiguous times and in the following year, 1983, a ban was placed on the performance of *Bus Stop*, although one special performance was ordered so that criticisms could be written up. As the author, Gao Xingjian was singled out for criticism during the "oppose spiritual pollution" campaign of that year, and he was banned from publishing: a senior Party member had declared *Bus Stop* "the most pernicious work since the establishment of the People's Republic". It was at this time, during a routine health check, that he was diagnosed with lung cancer, the disease that had killed his father a couple of years earlier. He resigned himself to imminent death until a later X-ray revealed that a wrong diagnosis had been made. He returned from the transcendent tranquillity he had experienced at the brink of death to the reality of life and the rumour that he was to be sent to the notorious prison farms of Qinghai province. He made a quick decision to flee Beijing immediately, and taking an advance royalty on his proposed novel, he absconded to the remote forest regions of Sichuan province and then wandered along the Yangtze River from its source down to the coast. By the time the "oppose spiritual pollution" campaign had subsided and it was safe for his return to Beijing, he had travelled for ten months over 15,000 kilometres of China.

These events of 1983 form the autobiographical substance of *Soul Mountain*, the story of one man's quest for inner peace and freedom. Gao Xingjian's brush with death had dislodged many forgotten fragments of his past and he recaptures these as well as his emotional experience of confronting death in *Soul Mountain*. Keeping his whereabouts secret, his travels take him to the Qiang, Miao and the Yi districts located on the fringes of Han Chinese civilization and he considers their traditions and practices with the curiosity of an archaeologist, historian and writer. His excursions into several nature reserves allow him to ponder the individual's place in nature; and his visits to Buddhist and Daoist institutions confirm that these are not places for him. Although he admires the forest ranger living the life of a virtual recluse and the solitary Buddhist monk-cum-itinerant doctor, he realizes that he still craves the warmth of human society, despite its anxieties. For the author, who has an obsessive need for self-expression, *Soul Mountain* poses the question: when deprived of human communication, will not the individual be condemned to the existence of the Wild Man in the forests of Shennongjia, the Big Foot of America or the Yeti of the Himalayas?

The autobiographical dimensions of *Soul Mountain* are richly overlaid with an exploration of various forms of human relationships and their implications for the individual. A rigorous and critical analysis of the self of one man is achieved by dissecting the authorial self into the singular pronouns, "I", "you", "she" and "he", who together constitute the composite protagonist. On his solitary journey, the protagonist seeks to alleviate his acute loneliness and creates "you" so that he will have someone to talk to. The "you", who is a reflection of "I", naturally experiences the same loneliness and creates "she" for companionship. The creation of an unnamed "she" allows the author to project himself with immense freedom into the psyche of women. The lengthy journey draws the "you" and the "I" too closely together and reduces the analytical distance sought by the author, so he allows "you" to walk away, and the back of "you" walking away becomes "he" ... and there are yet further changes.

The author, on his long journey as a political refugee from Beijing, employs the strategy of storytelling to disperse his loneliness, and at the same time reconstructs his personal past as well the impact of the Cultural Revolution on both the human and physical ecology of China. Through the characters who are projections of his self, the author engages in intimate conversations with anonymous others to tell the stories of many different types of people who populate China, but yet who in the final analysis can be found in all societies and cultures.

Gao Xingjian is a writer with an artist's sensitivity and an intense and continuing curiosity for experimentation with language and other expressive forms; and he is acutely aware of the challenge to the writer, and to literary genres, in the visual-image-oriented world of modern times. Through the publication of the novel *Lingshan* in 1990, he has exorcised lingering remnants of homesickness and has succeeded in devoting himself singlemindedly to a creative life. Since 1987, full productions of his plays have been staged in Paris, Bordeaux, Avignon, Stockholm, Hamburg, New York, Taipei, Hong Kong, Vienna, Veroli, Poznan, Cluj, and have been performed in small theatres and workshops in Tokyo, Kobe, Edinburgh, Sydney, and B nin. However, since 1987, his only publication in China has been *Taowang* (Absconding), a play about three people who escape to a disused warehouse after the tanks roll into Tiananmen in the early hours of 4 June 1989. *Absconding* was reproduced in newspapers and magazines and criticized as a pornographic and immoral work fabricated by the writer Gao Xingjian who was not in Beijing at the time. On the other hand, the American group that had commissioned the play requested changes, insisting that the student demonstrators be portrayed as heroic figures. He declined to make any changes and withdrew the play. Living in Paris, Gao Xingjian mainly supports himself through painting the large black and white Chinese ink-paintings for which he is well known. To date he has held thirty solo exhibitions in various galleries throughout Europe, as well as Beijing (prior to 1987), New York, Taipei and Hong Kong; and his works have been collected in several galleries in Europe and America.

Most of Gao Xingjian's recent writings have been published in Chinese in Taipei and Hong Kong. A significant number of these have also been published in French, and are now beginning to appear in English. Some of his recent plays were first written in French and then Chinese. In 1992 Gao Xingjian was honoured by the French with the title of Chevalier de l'Ordre des Arts et des Lettres. His play in French *Le Somnambule* won the Prix Communaut français de Belgique in 1994, and his novel *La Montagne de l' me* was awarded the Prix du Nouvel An chinois by a French panel of judges in 1997. In early 2000, a second edition of *La Montagne de l' me* went into print simultaneously with the French version of his second novel, *Yige ren de shengjing* which was published last year in Taipei. No l and Liliane Dutrait's French version is called *Le Livre de seul homme*, my English version will be called *One Man's Bible*.

Mabel Lee
April 2000

Mabel Lee was born Mabel Hunt in Warialda, northern New South Wales, and attended Parramatta High School. A graduate of the University of Sydney (BA with First Class Honours and PhD), she was a member of the academic staff of her alma mater from 1966 until January 2000. She is co-editor of the University of Sydney East Asian Series which publishes the work of Australian scholars on Asia, and the University of Sydney World Literature Series which sees literature as an activity that is shared by all peoples of the world. Mabel Lee retains a close association with the University of Sydney as Honorary Associate Professor in Chinese Studies.

1

The old bus is a city reject. After shaking in it for twelve hours on the potholed highway since early morning, you arrive in this mountain county town in the South.

In the bus station, which is littered with ice-block wrappers and sugar cane scraps, you stand with your backpack and a bag and look around for a while. People are getting off the bus or walking past, men humping sacks and women carrying babies. A crowd of youths, unhampered by sacks or baskets, have their hands free. They take sunflower seeds out of their pockets, toss them one at a time into their mouths and spit out the shells. With a loud crack the kernels are expertly eaten. To be leisurely and carefree is endemic to the place. They are locals and life has made them like this, they have been here for many generations and you wouldn't need to go looking anywhere else for them. The earliest to leave the place travelled by river in black canopy boats and overland in hired carts, or by foot if they didn't have the money. Of course at that time there were no buses and no bus stations. Nowadays, as long as they are still able to travel, they flock back home, even from the other side of the Pacific, arriving in cars or big air-conditioned coaches. The rich, the famous and the nothing in particular all hurry back because they are getting old. After all, who doesn't love the home of their ancestors? They don't intend to stay so they walk around looking relaxed, talking and laughing loudly, and effusing fondness and affection for the place. When friends meet they don't just give a nod or a handshake in the meaningless ritual of city people, but rather they shout the person's name or thump him on the

1

back. Hugging is also common, but not for women. By the cement trough where the buses are washed, two young women hold hands as they chat. The women here have lovely voices and you can't help taking a second look. The one with her back to you is wearing an indigo-print headscarf. This type of scarf, and how it's tied, dates back many generations but is seldom seen these days. You find yourself walking towards them. The scarf is knotted under her chin and the two ends point up. She has a beautiful face. Her features are delicate, so is her slim body. You pass close by them. They have been holding hands all this time, both have red coarse hands and strong fingers. Both are probably recent brides back seeing relatives and friends, or visiting parents. Here, the word *xifu* means one's own daughter-in-law and using it like rustic Northerners to refer to any young married woman will immediately incur angry abuse. On the other hand, a married woman calls her own husband *laogong*, yet your *laogong* and my *laogong* are both used. People here speak with a unique intonation even though they are descendants of the same legendary emperor and are of the same culture and race.

You can't explain why you're here. It happened that you were on a train and this person mentioned a place called Lingshan. He was sitting opposite and your cup was next to his. As the train moved, the lids on the cups clattered against one another. If the lids kept on clattering or clattered and then stopped, that would have been the end of it. However, whenever you and he were about to separate the cups, the clattering would stop, and as soon as you and he looked away the clattering would start again. He and you reached out, but again the clattering stopped. The two of you laughed at the same instant, put the cups well apart, and started a conversation. You asked him where he was going.

"Lingshan."

"What?"

"Lingshan, *ling* meaning spirit or soul, and *shan* meaning mountain."

You'd been to lots of places, visited lots of famous mountains, but had never heard of this place.

2

Your friend opposite had closed his eyes and was dozing. Like anyone else, you couldn't help being curious and naturally wanted to know which famous places you'd missed on your travels. Also, you liked doing things properly and it was annoying that there was a place you've never even heard of. You asked him about the location of Lingshan.

"At the source of the You River," he said, opening his eyes.

You didn't know this You River either, but was embarrassed about asking and gave an ambiguous nod which could have meant either "I see, thanks" or "Oh, I know the place". This satisfied your desire for superiority, but not your curiosity. After a while you asked how to get there and the route up the mountain.

"Take the train to Wuyizhen, then go upstream by boat on the You River."

"What's there? Scenery? Temples? Historic sites?" you asked, trying to be casual.

"It's all virgin wilderness."

"Ancient forests?"

"Of course, but not just ancient forests."

"What about Wild Men?" you said, joking.

He laughed without any sarcasm, and didn't seem to be making fun of himself which intrigued you even more. You had to find out more about him.

"Are you an ecologist? A biologist? An anthropologist? An archaeologist?"

He shook his head each time then said, "I'm more interested in living people."

"So you're doing research on folk customs? You're a sociologist? An ethnographer? An ethnologist? A journalist, perhaps? An adventurer?"

"I'm an amateur in all of these."

The two of you started laughing.

"I'm an expert amateur in all of these!"

The laughing made you and him cheerful. He lit a cigarette and couldn't stop talking as he told you about the wonders of Lingshan.

3

Afterwards, at your request, he tore up his empty cigarette box and drew a map of the route up Lingshan.

In the North it is already late autumn but the summer heat hasn't completely subsided. Before sunset, it is still quite hot in the sun and sweat starts running down your back. You leave the station to have a look around. There's nothing nearby except for the little inn across the road. It's an old-style two-storey building with a wooden shopfront. Upstairs the floorboards creak badly but worse still is the grime on the pillow and sleeping mat. If you wanted to have a wash, you'd have to wait till it was dark to strip off and pour water over yourself in the damp and narrow courtyard. This is a stopover for the village peddlers and craftsmen.

It's well before dark, so there's plenty of time to find somewhere clean. You walk down the road looking around the little town, hoping to find some indication, a billboard or a poster, or just the name "Lingshan" to tell you you're on the right track and haven't been tricked into making this long excursion. You look everywhere but don't find anything. There were no tourists like you amongst the other passengers who got off the bus. Of course you're not *that* sort of tourist, it's just what you're wearing: strong sensible sports shoes and a backpack with shoulder straps, no-one else is dressed like you. But this isn't one of the tourist spots frequented by newlyweds and retirees. Those places have been transformed by tourism, coaches are parked everywhere and tourist maps are on sale. Tourist hats, tourist T-shirts, tourist singlets and tourist handkerchiefs printed with the name of the place are in all the little shops and stalls, and the name of the place is used in the trade names of all the "foreign exchange currency only" hotels for foreigners, the "locals with references only" hostels and sanatoriums, and of course the small private hotels competing for customers. You haven't come to enjoy yourself in one of those places on the sunny side of a mountain where people congregate just to look at and jostle one another and to add to the litter of melon rind, fruit peel, soft drink bottles, cans, cartons, sandwich wrappings and cigarette butts. Sooner or later this place will also boom but you're here before they put up the gaudy pavilions and terraces, before the reporters come with their cameras and before the celebrities come to put up plaques with their calligraphy. You can't help feeling rather pleased with yourself, and yet you're anxious. There's no sign of anything here for tourists, have you made a blunder? You're only going by the map on the cigarette box in your shirt pocket, what if the expert amateur you met on the train had only heard about the place on his travels? How do you know he wasn't just making it all up? You've never seen the place mentioned in travel accounts and it's not listed in the most up-to-date travel guides. Of course, it isn't hard to find places like Lingtai, Lingqiu, Lingyan and even Lingshan on provincial maps and you know very well that in the histories and classics, Lingshan appears in works dating back to the ancient shamanistic work *Classic of the Mountains and Seas* and the old geographical gazetteer *Annotated Water Classic*. It was also at Lingshan that Buddha enlightened the Venerable Mahakashyapa. You're not stupid, so just use your brains, first find this place Wuyizhen on the cigarette box, for this is how you'll get to Lingshan.

You return to the bus station and go into the waiting room. The busiest place in this small town is now deserted. The ticket window and the parcel window are boarded up from the inside so knocking is useless. There's no-one to ask so you can only go through the lists of stops above the ticket window: Zhang Village, Sandy Flat, Cement Factory, Old Hut, Golden Horse, Good Harvest, Flood Waters, Dragon Bay, Peach Blossom Hollow ... the names keep getting better, but the place you want isn't there. This is just a small town but there are several routes and quite a few buses go through. The busiest route, with five or six buses a day, is to Cement Factory but that's definitely not a tourist route. The route with the fewest buses, one a day, is sure to go to the furthest destination and it turns out that Wuyizhen is the last stop. There's nothing special about the name, it's just like any other place name and there's nothing magical about it. Still, you seem to have found one end of a hopeless tangle and while you're not ecstatic, you're certainly relieved. You'll need to buy a ticket in the morning an hour before departure and you know from experience that with mountain buses like this, which run once a day, just to get on will be a fight. Unless you're prepared to do battle, you'll just have to queue up early.

But, right now, you've lots of time, although your backpack's a nuisance. As you amble along the road timber trucks go by noisily sounding their horns. In the town the noise worsens as trucks, some with trailers, blast their horns and conductors hang out of windows loudly banging the sides of the buses to hasten the pedestrians off the road.

The old buildings on both sides stand flush with the road and all have wooden shopfronts. The downstairs is for business and upstairs there is washing hung out to dry – nappies, bras, underpants with patched crotches, floral-print bedspreads – like flags of all the nations, flaping in the noise and dust of the traffic. The concrete telegraph poles along the street are pasted at eye level with all sorts of posters. One for curing body odour catches your attention. This is not because you've got body odour but because of the fancy language and the words in brackets after "body odour".

> Body odour (known also as scent of the immortals)
> is a disgusting condition with an awful, nauseating
> smell. It often affects social relationships and can
> delay life's major event: marriage. It disadvantages
> young men and women at job interviews or when
> they try to enlist, therefore inflicting much suffering
> and anguish. By using a new total treatment, we can
> instantly eradicate the odour with a rate of up to
> 97.53% success. For joy in life and future happiness,
> we welcome you to come and rid yourself of it …

After that you come to a stone bridge: no body odour here, just a cool, refreshing breeze. The bridge spanning the broad river has a bitumen surface but the carved monkeys on the worn stone posts testify to its long history. You lean on the concrete railing and survey the township alongside the bridge. On both banks, black rooftops overlapping like fish-scales stretch endlessly into the distance. The valley opens out between two mountains where the upper areas of gold paddy fields are inlaid with clusters of green bamboos. The river is blue and clear as it trickles over the sandy shores, but close to the granite pylons dividing the current it becomes inky green and deep. Just past the hump of the bridge the rushing water churns loudly and white foam surfaces from whirlpools. The ten-metre-high stone embankment is stained with water levels – the new greyish-yellow lines were probably left by the recent summer floods. Can this be the You River? And does it flow down from Lingshan?

The sun is about to set. The bright orange disc is infused with light but there's no glare. You gaze into the distance at the hazy layers of jagged peaks where the two sides of the valley join. This ominous black image nibbles at the lower edges of the glowing sun which seems to be revolving. The sun turns a dark red, gentler, and projects brilliant gold reflections onto the entire bend of the river: the dark blue of the water fusing with the dazzling sunlight throbs and pulsates. As the red sphere seats itself in the valley it becomes serene, awesomely beautiful, and there are sounds. You hear them, elusive, distinctly reverberating from deep in your heart and radiating outwards until the sun seems to prop itself up on its toes, stumble, then sink into the black shadows of the mountains, scattering glowing colours throughout the sky. An evening wind blows noisily by your ears and cars drive past, as usual sounding their deafening horns. You cross the bridge and see there a new dedication stone with engraved characters painted in red: "Yongning Bridge. Built in the third year of the Kaiyuan reign period of the Song Dynasty and repaired in 1962. This stone was laid in 1983." It no doubt marks the beginning of the tourist industry here.

Two food stalls stand at the end of the bridge. In the one on the left you eat a bowl of bean curd, the smooth and tasty kind with all the right ingredients. Hawkers used to sell it in the streets and lanes but it completely disappeared for quite some years and has recently been revived as family enterprises. In the stall on the right you eat two delicious sesame-coated shallot pancakes, straight off the stove and piping-hot. Then at one of the stalls, you can't remember which, you eat a bowl of sweet *yuanxiao* dumplings broiled in rice wine. They are the size of large pearls. Of course, you're not as academic about food as Mr Ma the Second who toured West Lake, but you do have a hefty appetite nevertheless. You savour this food of your ancestors and listen to customers chatting with the proprietors. They're mostly locals and all know one another. You try using the mellifluous local accent to be friendly, you want to be one of them. You've lived in the city for a long time and need to feel that you have a hometown. You want a hometown so that you'll be able to return to your childhood to recollect long lost memories.

On this side of the bridge you eventually find an inn on an old cobblestone street. The wooden floors have been mopped and it's clean enough. You are given a small single room which has a plank bed covered with a bamboo mat. The cotton blanket is a suspicious grey – either it hasn't been washed properly or that's the original colour. You throw aside the greasy pillow from under the bamboo mat and luckily it's hot so you can do without the bedding. What you need right now is to off-load your luggage which has become quite heavy, wash off the dust and sweat, strip, and stretch yourself out on the bed.

There's shouting and yelling next door. They're gambling and you can hear them picking up and throwing down the cards. A timber partition separates you and, through the holes poked into the paper covering the cracks, you make out the blurred figures of some bare-chested men. You're not so tired that you can drop off to sleep just like that. You tap on the wall and instantly there's loud shouting next door. They're not shouting at you but amongst themselves – there are always winners and losers and it sounds as though the loser is trying to get out of paying. They're openly gambling in the inn despite the public security office notice on the wall prohibiting gambling and prostitution. You decide to see if the law works. You put on some clothes, go down the corridor and knock on the half-closed door. Your knocking makes no difference, they keep shouting and yelling inside and nobody takes any notice. So you push open the door and go in. The four men sitting around the bed in the middle of the room all turn to look at you. But it's you and not they who gets a rude shock. The men all have bits of paper stuck on their faces, on their foreheads, lips, noses and cheeks, and they look ugly and ridiculous. They aren't laughing and are glaring at you. You've butted in and they're clearly annoyed.

"Oh, you're playing cards," you say, putting on an apologetic look.

They go on playing. The long paper cards have red and black markings like mahjong and there's a Gate of Heaven and a Prison of Hell. The winner penalizes the loser by tearing off a strip of newspaper and sticking it on a designated spot. Whether this is a prank, a way of letting off steam, or a tally, is something agreed upon by the gamblers and there is no way for outsiders to know what it's all about.

You beat a retreat, go back to your room, lie down again, and see a thick mass of black specks around the light globe. Millions of mosquitoes are waiting for the light to go out so that they can come down and feast on your blood. You quickly let down the net and are enclosed in a narrow conical space, at the top of which is a bamboo hoop. It's been a long time since you've slept under a hoop like this, and you've long since passed the age of being able to stare at the hoop to lose yourself in reverie. Today, you can't know what traumas tomorrow will bring. You've learnt through experience everything you need to know. What else are you looking for? When a man gets to middle age shouldn't he look for a peaceful and stable existence, find a not-too-demanding sort of a job, stay in a mediocre position, become a husband and a father, set up a comfortable home, put money in the bank and add to it every month so there'll be something for old age and a little left over for the next generation?

2

It is in the Qiang region halfway up Qionglai Mountain, in the border areas of the Qinghai-Tibetan highlands and the Sichuan basin, that I witness a vestige of early human civilization – the worship of fire. Fire, the bringer of civilization, has been worshipped by the early ancestors of human beings everywhere. It is sacred. The old man is sitting in front of the fire drinking liquor from a bowl. Before each sip he puts a finger into it and flicks some on the charcoals which splutter noisily and send out blue sparks. It is only then that I perceive that I too am real.

"That's for the God of the Cooking Stove, it's thanks to him that we can eat and drink," he says.

The dancing light of the fire shines on his thin cheeks, the high bridge of his nose, and his cheekbones. He tells me he is of the Qiang nationality and that he's from Gengda village down the mountain. I can't ask straight out about demons and spirits, so I tell him I'm here to do some research on the folk songs of the mountain. Do traditional song masters and dancers still exist here? He says he's one of them. The men and women all used to form a circle around the fire and dance right through to daybreak, but later on it was banned.

"Why?" I know quite well but I ask. I'm being dishonest again.

"It was the Cultural Revolution. They said the songs were dirty so we turned to singing *Sayings of Mao Zedong* songs instead."

"And what about after that?" I persist in asking. This is becoming a habit.

"No-one sings those anymore. People are doing the dances again but not many of the young people can do them, I'm teaching the dances to some of them."

I ask him for a demonstration. Without any hesitation, he instantly gets to his feet and proceeds to dance and sing. His voice is low and rich, he's got a good voice. I'm sure he's Qiang even if the police in charge of the population register insist that he isn't. They think anyone claiming to be Tibetan or Qiang is trying to evade birth restrictions so they can have more children.

He sings song after song. He says he's a fun-loving person, and I believe him. When he finished up as village head, he went back to being one of the mountain people, an old mountain man who likes good fun, though unfortunately he is past the age for romance.

He also knows incantations, the kind hunters employ when they go into the mountains. They are called mountain blackmagic or hexes and he has no qualms about using them. He really believes they can drive wild animals into pits or get them to step into snares. They aren't used only on animals, they're also used against other human beings for revenge. A victim of mountain blackmagic won't be able to find his way out of the mountains. They are like the "demon walls" I heard about as a child: when a person has been travelling for some time at night in the mountains, a wall, a cliff or a deep river appears right in front of him, so that he can't go any further. If the spell isn't broken the person's feet don't move forward and even if he keeps walking, he stays exactly where he started off. Only at daybreak does he discover that he has been going around in circles. That's not so bad, the worst is when a person is led into a blind alley – that means death.

He intones strings of incantations. It's not slow and relaxed like when he is singing, but just *nan-nan-na-na* to a quick beat. I can't understand it at all but I can feel the mystical pull of the words and a demonic, powerful atmosphere instantly permeates the room, the inside of which is black from smoke. The glow of the flames licking the iron pot of mutton stew makes his eyes glint. This is all starkly real.

While you search for the route to Lingshan, I wander along the Yangtze River looking for this sort of reality. I had just gone through a crisis and then, on top of that, a doctor wrongly diagnosed me with lung cancer. Death was playing a joke on me but now that I've escaped the demon wall, I am secretly rejoicing. Life for me once again has a wonderful freshness. I should have left those contaminated surroundings long ago and returned to nature to look for this authentic life.

In those contaminated surroundings I was taught that life was the source of literature, that literature had to be faithful to life, faithful to real life. My mistake was that I had alienated myself from life and ended up turning my back on real life. Life is not the same as manifestations of life. Real life, or in other words the basic substance of life, should be the former and not the latter. I had gone against real life because I was simply stringing together life's manifestations, so of course I wasn't able to accurately portray life and in the end only succeeded in distorting reality.

I don't know whether I'm now on the right track but in any case I've extricated myself from the bustling literary world and have also escaped from my smoke-filled room. The books piled everywhere in that room were oppressive and stifling. They expounded all sorts of truths, historical truths to truths on how to be human. I couldn't see the point of so many truths but still got enmeshed in the net of those truths and was struggling hopelessly, like an insect caught in a spider's web. Fortunately, the doctor who gave the wrong diagnosis saved my life. He was quite frank and got me to compare the two chest X-rays taken on two separate occasions – a blurry shadow on the left lobe of the lung had spread along the second rib to the wall of the windpipe. It wouldn't help even to have the whole of the left lobe removed. The outcome was obvious. My father had died of lung cancer. He died within three months of it being discovered and it was this doctor who had correctly diagnosed it. I had faith in his medical expertise and he had faith in science. The chest X-rays taken at two different hospitals were identical, there was no possibility of a technical mistake. He also wrote an authorization for a sectional X-ray, the appointment was in two weeks' time. This was nothing to get worried about, it was just to determine the extent of the tumour. My father had this done before he died. The outcome would be the same whether or not I had the X-ray, it was nothing special. That I in fact would slip through the fingers of Death can only be put down to good luck. I believe in science but I also believe in fate.

I once saw a four-inch length of wood which had been collected in the Qiang region by an anthropologist during the 1930s. It was a carved statue of a person doing a handstand. The head had ink markings for the eyes, nose and mouth, and the word "longevity" had been written on the body. It was called "Wuchang Upside Down" and there was something oddly mischievous about it. I ask the Qiang retired village head whether such talismans are still around. He tells me these are called "old root". This wooden idol has to accompany the newborn from birth to death. At death it accompanies the corpse from the house and after the burial it is placed in the wilderness to allow the spirit to return to nature. I ask him if he can get me one so that I can carry it on me. He laughs and says these are what hunters tuck into their shirts to ward off evil spirits, they wouldn't be of any use to someone like me.

"Is there an old hunter who knows about this sort of magic and can take me hunting with him?" I ask.

"Grandpa Stone would be the best," he says after thinking about it.

"How can I find him?" I ask right away.

"He's in Grandpa Stone's Hut."

"Where's this Grandpa Stone's Hut?"

"Go another twenty *li* on to Silver Mine Gully then follow the creek right up to the end. There you'll find a stone hut."

"Is that the name of the place or do you mean the hut of Grandpa Stone?"

He says it's the name of the place, that there's in fact a stone hut, and that Grandpa Stone lives there.

"Can you take me to him?" I ask.

"He's dead. He lay down on his bed and died in his sleep. He was too old, he lived to well over ninety, some even say well over a hundred. In any case, nobody's sure about his age."

"Are any of his descendants still alive?"

"In my grandfather's generation and for as long as I can remember, he was always on his own."

"Without a wife?"

"He lived on his own in Silver Mine Gully. He lived high up the gully, in the solitary hut, alone. Oh, and that rifle of his is still hanging on the wall of the hut."

I ask him what he's trying to tell me.

He says Grandpa Stone was a great hunter, a hunter who was an expert in the magical arts. There are no hunters like that these days. Everyone knows that his rifle is hanging in the hut, that it never misses its target, but nobody dares to go and take it.

"Why?" I'm even more puzzled.

"The route into Silver Mine Gully is cut."

"There's no way through?"

"Not anymore. Earlier on people used to mine silver there, a firm from Chengdu hired a team of workers and they began mining. Later on, after the mine was looted, everyone just left, and the plank roads they had laid either broke up or rotted."

"When did all this happen?"

"When my grandfather was still alive, more than fifty years ago."

That would be about right, after all he's already retired and has become history, real history.

"So since then nobody's ever gone there?" I become even more intrigued.

"Hard to say, anyway it's hard to get there."

"And the hut has rotted?"

"Stone collapses, how can it rot?"

"I was talking about the ridgepole."

"Oh, quite right."

He doesn't want to take me there, nor does he want to find a hunter for me, so that's why he's leading me on like this, I think.

"Then how do you know the rifle's still hanging on the wall?" I ask, regardless.

"That's what everyone says, someone must've seen it. They all say that Grandpa Stone is incredible, his corpse hasn't rotted and wild animals don't dare to go near. He just lies there all stiff and emaciated, and his rifle is hanging there on the wall."

"Impossible," I declare. "With the high humidity up here in the mountain, the corpse would have rotted and the rifle would have turned into a pile of rust."

"I don't know. Anyway, people have been saying this for years." He refuses to give in and sticks to his story. The light of the fire dances in his eyes and I seem to detect a cunning streak in them.

"And you've never seen him?" I won't let him off.

"People who have seen him say that he seems to be asleep, that he's emaciated, and that the rifle is hanging there on the wall above his head," he says, unruffled. "He knew blackmagic. It's not just that people don't dare go there to steal his rifle, even animals don't dare to go near."

The hunter is already myth. To talk about a mixture of history and legend is how folk stories are born. Reality exists only through experience, and it must be personal experience. However, once related, even personal experience becomes a narrative. Reality can't be verified and doesn't need to be, that can be left for the "reality-of-life" experts to debate. What is important is life. Reality is simply that I am sitting by the fire in this room which is black with grime and smoke and that I see the light of the fire dancing in his eyes. Reality is myself, reality is only the perception of this instant and it can't be related to another person. All that needs to be said is that outside, a mist is enclosing the green-blue mountain in a haze and your heart is reverberating with the rushing water of a swift-flowing stream.

3

So you arrive in Wuyizhen, on a long and narrow street inlaid with black cobblestones, and walking along this cobblestone street with its deep single-wheel rut, you suddenly enter your childhood, you seem to have spent your childhood in an old mountain town like this. The one-wheel handcarts can no longer be seen and instead of the creak of jujube axles greased with bean oil, the streets are filled with the din of bicycle bells. Cyclists here need the skills of an acrobat. With heavy hessian bags slung across the saddle, they cause loud swearing as they weave through people with carrying poles or pulling wooden carts and the hawkers under the awnings. It is loud, colourful swearing which mingles with the general din of the hawkers' calls, bargaining, joking and laughing. You breathe in the smell of soya sauce pickles, boiled pork, raw hide, pine wood, dried rice stalks and lime as your eyes busily take in the narrow shopfronts lining the street with products of the South. There are soya bean shops, oil shops, rice shops, Chinese and Western medicine shops, silk and cotton shops, shoe shops, tea shops, butcher stalls, tailor shops, and shops selling stoves, rope, pottery, incense, candles and paper money. The shops, squashed up one against the other, are virtually unchanged from Qing Dynasty times. The smashed signboard of the Ever Prosperous Restaurant has been repaired and one of the flat-bottomed pans used for frying its speciality *guotie* dumplings is beaten like a gong to announce it is back in business. The wine banner is again hanging from the upstairs window of the First Class Delicacies Restaurant. The most imposing structure is the state-run department store, a newly renovated three-storey concrete building. A single display window is the size of one of the old shops but the insides of the glass windows look as if they have never been cleaned. The photographer's shop is eye-catching: photos of women in coquettish poses and wearing awful dresses are on display. They are all local beauties and not movie poster film stars from some place at the other end of the earth. This place really produces good-looking women, every one of them is stunning. They have their beautiful cheeks cupped in their hands and their eyes have alluring looks. They've been carefully coached by the photographer but they are garishly dressed. Enlargements and colour prints are available and there's a sign saying photos can be collected in twenty days, apparently they have to be developed in the city. Had fate not otherwise decreed, you could have been born in this town, grown up, and married here. You would have married a beautiful woman like one of these, who would long since have borne you sons and daughters. At this point, you smile and quickly move off in case people imagine you've taken a fancy to one of the women and start getting the wrong idea. And yet it is you who are carried away by your imagination. As you look up at the balconies above the shops with their curtained windows and pots of miniature trees and flowers, you can't help wondering about the people who live here. There's a big apartment with an iron padlock on the door – the pillars are now crooked but the carved eaves and railings which have fallen into disrepair indicate how imposing the place was at one time. The fates of its owners and their descendants fill you with curiosity. The shop at the side sells Hong Kong style dresses and jeans, and the stockings on show have a Western woman showing off her legs on the packaging. At the front door there's a gold-plated sign, "Ever New Technical Development Company", but it's not clear what sort of technical development it is. Further on is a shop with heaps of unprocessed lime, and further on still is probably a miller's and next to that a vacant allotment where rice noodles are drying on wires strung between posts. You turn back and go into a small lane next to the hot water urn of the tea stall, then turning a corner you are again lost in memories.

Within a half-closed door is a damp courtyard, overgrown with weeds, desolate and lonely, with piles of rubble in the corners. You recall the back courtyard with the crumbling wall of your childhood home. You were afraid but it had a fascination for you, for the fox fairies of story books came from there. After school, without fail, you would go off alone with some trepidation to have a look. You never saw a fox fairy but that feeling of mystery always lingered in your childhood memories. There is an old stone bench riddled with cracks and a well which is probably dry. The mid-autumn wind blows through the dry yellow weeds in the rubble and the sun is very bright. These homes with their courtyard doors shut tight all have their histories which are all like ancient stories. In winter, the north wind is howling through the lane, you are wearing new warm padded cloth shoes and are with other children stamping your feet by the wall. You can remember the words of the ditty:

> In moonlight thick as soup
> I ride out to burn incense
> For Luo Dajie who burnt to death
> For Dou Sanniang who died in a rage
> Sanniang picked beans
> But the pods were empty
> She married Master Ji
> But Master Ji was short
> So she married a crab
> The crab crossed a ditch
> Trod on an eel
> The eel complained
> It complained to a monk
> The monk said a prayer
> A prayer to Guanyin
> So Guanyin pissed
> The piss hit my son
> His belly hurt
> So I got an exorcist to dance

The dance didn't work
But still cost heaps of money

Pale withered weeds and lush green new sprouts in the roof-tiles quiver in the wind. How long is it since you've seen grass growing in roof-tiles? Your bare feet patter on the black cobblestone street with its deep single-wheel rut, you've run out of your childhood back into the present. The bare feet, the dirty black feet, patter right there in front of your eyes. It doesn't matter if you've never run barefoot, what is crucial is this image in your mind.

After a while you find your way out of the little lanes and make it back on the highway. This is where the bus from the county town turns around to go back. There's a bus station by the road with a ticket window and some benches inside, this is where you got off the bus earlier on. Diagonally across the road is an inn – a row of single-storey rooms – and the whitewashed brick wall has a sign "Good Rooms Within". It looks clean and you have to find somewhere to stay, so you go in. An old attendant is sweeping the corridor and you ask her if there's a room. She says yes. You ask her how much further is it to Lingshan. She gives you a cold look, this is a state-run inn, she's on a monthly state award wage and isn't generous with words.

"Number two," she says pointing with the broom handle to a room with the door open. You take your luggage in and notice there are two beds. On one there's someone lying on his back, one leg crossed over the other, with a copy of *Unofficial Record of the Flying Fox* in his hands. The title is written on the brown paper cover of the book, apparently on loan from a bookstall. You greet him and he puts down the book to give a friendly nod.

"Hello."

"Staying here?"

"Yes."

"Have a cigarette." He tosses you a cigarette.

"Thanks." You sit on the empty bed opposite. It happens that he wants to chat. "How long have you been here?"

"Ten or so days." He sits up and lights himself a cigarette.

"Here buying stock?" you ask, taking a guess.

"I'm here for timber."

"Is it easy getting timber here?"

"Have you got a quota?" he asks instead, starting to become interested.

"What quota?"

"A state-plan quota, of course."

"No."

"Then it's not easy to get." He lies down again.

"Is there a timber shortage even in this forest region?"

"There's timber around but prices are different." He can't be bothered, he can tell you're not in the game.

"Are you waiting for cheaper prices?"

"Yes," he responds indifferently, taking up his book again to read.

"You stock buyers really get to know about a lot of things." You have to flatter him so that you can ask him some questions.

"Not really." He becomes modest.

"The place Lingshan, do you know how to get there?"

He doesn't reply so you can only say you've come to do some sightseeing and is there anywhere worth seeing.

"There's a pavilion by the river. If you sit there you'll get a good view of the other side of the river."

"Enjoy your rest!" you say for want of something to say.

You leave your bags, find the attendant to register and set off. The wharf is at the end of the highway. The steps, made of long slabs of rock, go down steeply for more than ten metres and moored there are several black canopy boats with their bamboo poles up. The river isn't wide but the riverbed is, clearly it's not the rainy season. There is a boat on the opposite bank and people are getting on and getting off. The people on the stone steps are all waiting for it to come across.

Up from the wharf, on the embankment, there is a pavilion with upturned eaves and curling corners. The outside is lined with empty baskets and resting inside are farmers from the other side who were here for the market and have sold all of their goods. They are talking loudly and it sounds like the language used in the short stories of the Song Dynasty. The pavilion has been painted recently and under the eaves the dragon and phoenix design has been repainted and the two principal columns at the front are inscribed with the couplet:

> Sitting at rest know not to discuss the shortcomings of other people
> Setting out on a journey fully appreciate the beauty of the dragon river

You go around to look at the two columns at the back. These words are written there:

> On departing do not forget to heed the duckweed waters
> Turn back to gaze in wonder at Lingshan amongst the phoenixes

You're intrigued. The boat is probably about to arrive as the people resting and cooling off have got up and are rushing to shoulder their carrying poles. Only an old man is left sitting in the pavilion.

"Venerable elder, may I ask if these couplets ... "

"Are you asking about the couplets on the principal columns?" the old man corrects me.

"Yes, venerable master, might I ask who wrote the couplets on the principal columns?" you say with added reverence.

"The scholar Mr Chen Xianning!" His mouth opens wide, revealing sparse black teeth, as he enunciates each of the words with great precision.

"I don't know of him." You'd best be frank about your ignorance. "At which university does this gentleman teach?"

"People like you wouldn't know, of course. He lived more than a thousand years ago." The old man is contemptuous.

"Please don't make fun of me, venerable elder," you say, trying to stop him ridiculing you.

"You don't need glasses, can't you see?" he says pointing up to the beam at the top of the columns.

You look up and see on the beam which hasn't been repainted, these words written in vermilion:

> Erected during the Great Song Dynasty in the first
> month of spring in the tenth year of the Shaoxing
> reign period and repaired during the Great Qing
> Dynasty on the twenty-ninth day of the third month
> of the nineteenth year of the Qianlong reign period.

4

I set out from the hostel of the nature reserve and go back to the house of the Qiang retired village head. A big padlock is hanging on his door. This is the third time I've been back but again he's not there. It seems that this door which can lead me into that mystical world has closed for me.

I wander on in fine drizzling rain. It's been a long time since I have wandered about in this sort of misty rain. I pass by the Sleeping Dragon Village Hospital, it looks deserted. The forest is quiet but there is always a stream somewhere not too far away, for I can hear the sound of trickling water. It's been ages since I have had such freedom, I don't have to think about anything and I let my thoughts ramble. There's no-one on the highway, and no vehicles are in sight. As far as the eye can see it is a luxuriant green. It is the middle of spring.

The big deserted compound on the side of the road is probably the headquarters of the bandit chief Song Guotai mentioned by the reserve warden last night. Forty years ago, a single mountain road for horse caravans was the only access to this place. To the north it crossed the 5000-metre-high Balang Mountains into the Qinghai-Tibetan highlands and to the south it went through the Min River valley into the Sichuan basin. The opium smugglers from the South and the salt smugglers from the North all obediently put down money here to buy passage through. This was called showing proper respect. If there was a fuss and proper respect wasn't shown, it would be a case of arriving and not returning. They would all be sent to meet the King of Hell.

It is an old timber compound. The two big heavy wooden gates are wide open and inside, surrounded on three sides by two-storey buildings, is an overgrown courtyard big enough for a caravan of thirty or forty horses. Probably in those days, as soon as the gates were closed, the eaved balconies with their wooden railings would be thick with armed bandits so that caravans thinking of stopping the night would be trapped like turtles in a jar. Even if a shoot-out took place there wouldn't have been anywhere in the courtyard to escape the bullets.

There are two sets of stairs in the courtyard. I go up. The floorboards creak noisily and I deliberately tread heavily to show my presence. However the upstairs is deserted. One after another I push open the doors to empty rooms smelling of dust and mildew. Only a dirty grey towel hanging on a wire and an old worn shoe show that the place has been lived in, but probably some years ago. When the reserve was established the supply and marketing cooperative, local produce purchasing depot, grain and oil depot, veterinary clinic as well as the village administrative office and the personnel were all relocated in the narrow hundred metres of street built by the reserve administration where there is not a trace of Song Guotai's hundred or so men and their hundred or so rifles once housed in this compound. In those times they would lie on rush mats smoking opium and fondling their women. These women, who had been abducted, had to cook for them in the daytime and sleep in turn with them at night. At times, either because the loot wasn't shared equally or because of a woman, fights would break out and wild rioting probably took place on the floors of this very building.

"Only the bandit chief Song Guotai could keep them under control. This fellow was ruthless and cruel, and renowned for his cunning." The warden of the reserve does political work and he is eloquent and convincing. He says his lectures to university students here for practical work range from protection of the giant panda to patriotism and that his lectures can reduce the women students to tears.

He says that amongst the women the bandits abducted there was even a soldier of the Red Army. In 1936, during the Long March, when a regiment of the Red Army was passing through the Mao'ergai grasslands, one of the battalions was attacked by bandits. The ten or so girls of the laundry detachment were abducted and raped. The youngest was seventeen or eighteen and was the only one to survive. She was passed around several of the bandits and eventually an old Qiang man purchased her to be his wife. She lives in a nearby mountain flatland and can still recite the name of her battalion, regiment and company, as well as the name of her commanding officer who is now an important official. He's quite excited and says of course he can't talk about all these things to the students, then goes back to talking about the bandit chief Song Guotai.

This Song Guotai started out as a junior assistant, he says, for an opium merchant. When the merchant was killed by Big Brother Chen, the bandit chief who had taken over the district, he threw in his lot with the new boss. By wheeling and dealing he soon became Big Brother's confidante and had access to the small courtyard where Big Brother lived at the back of the compound. The small courtyard was later blown up by the Liberation Army in a mortar attack and is now a mass of trees and shrubs. But in those years it was really a Little Chongqing, a replica of the wartime capital, where Big Brother Chen and his harem debauched themselves on sex and liquor. The only man allowed to wait on him was Song Guotai. A caravan arrived from Ma'erkang full of bandits who had been eying this strip of territory where all you had to do was to sit there waiting for the loot to come to you. A fierce battle raged for two days with deaths and injuries to both sides, but before any clear victory or defeat, they held peace negotiations and sealed an agreement in blood. The gates were opened and the other party invited inside. Upstairs and downstairs two lots of bandits joined in finger-guessing games and drinking liquor. Actually it was Big Brother's plan to get the other side drunk so that he could deal with them swiftly. He got his mistresses to flit about from table to table with their breasts exposed. It wasn't just the other bandits, who of either side could resist? Everyone was rotten drunk. Only the two bandit chiefs were still sitting upright at the table. As pre-arranged, Big Brother snapped his fingers loudly and Song Guotai came to pour more liquor. In one swift action, faster than it takes to tell this, he snatched the rival bandit chief's machine gun from the table and one bullet each sent the pair sprawling, Big Brother included. Then he asked: Anyone who doesn't want to surrender? The bandits looked at one another, not one dared to utter so much as half a murmur of dissent. Song Guotai thereupon moved into Big Brother's little courtyard and all the mistresses came into his possession.

He tells all this with great drama, he isn't boasting when he says he has the women students in tears. He goes on to say that in 1950 they came into the mountains to exterminate the bandits. The little courtyard was surrounded by two companies of soldiers. At daybreak they shouted to the bandits to put down their weapons, change their wicked ways and reform, and warned that there was a blockade of several machine guns at the main gate so no-one should try to escape. It's as if he'd taken part in the battle himself.

"What happened then?" I ask.

"At first they stubbornly resisted so the little courtyard was bombarded with mortar. The surviving bandits threw down their guns and came out to surrender. Song Guotai was not amongst them. When a search was made of the little courtyard they only found a few weeping women huddled together. Everyone said the house had a secret tunnel which went up into the mountain but it was never found, and he has never shown up anywhere. It's over forty years now, some say he's still alive and others say he's dead but there's no real evidence, only theories." He sits back into the round cane chair and tapping his fingers on the edge where his hands are resting, he begins to analyse these theories.

"There are three theories about what happened to him. One is that after escaping he fled to another area, changed his name, and settled somewhere to work in the fields as a peasant. The second is that he could have been killed in the gun fight but the bandits wouldn't admit

It would be superstitious to believe what the mountain folk say: according to them the brothers fell foul of blackmagic. The two of them bumped into each other after going in a circle around the top of the mountain. There was a heavy mist. The elder brother saw his younger brother, mistook him for a bear, and shot him with his rifle. The elder brother had killed the younger brother. He went home during the night and lay his and his brother's rifles alongside one another by the bamboo gate of the pig pen so that his mother would see them when she got up to feed the pigs first thing in the morning. He didn't go inside the house but went back up the mountain to where his brother lay dead and slit his own throat."

I leave the empty upstairs and stand for a while in the courtyard big enough for a whole caravan of horses, then head back to the highway. There still is no sign of people or vehicles. I look at the dark green mountain enveloped in a haze of rain and mist on the opposite side. A steep greyish-white logging chute is over there and the vegetation has been totally ravaged. Earlier on, before the highway was put through, both sides of the mountain would have been covered in thickly-wooded forest. I am becoming obsessed with getting to the primeval forest at the back of the mountain and find myself drawn to it by some inexplicable force.

The light drizzle gets heavier and turns into a thin film which completely enshrouds the ridge, obscuring the mountain and gully even more. There is the rumble of thunder behind the mountain, muffled and indistinct. Suddenly, I realize that the noise of the river below the highway is much louder, there is a perpetual roar as it charges endlessly at great speed from the snowclad mountains to pour into the Min River. It possesses an intimidating and violent energy not found in rivers flowing over flat country.

5

It is by the pavilion that you encounter her. It is an undefinable longing, a vague hope, it is a chance meeting, a wonderful meeting. You come again at dusk to the riverside, the pounding of clothes being washed reverberates from the bottom of the pitted stone steps. She is standing near the pavilion and like you she is looking at the mountain on the other side. You can't take your eyes off her. She stands out in this small mountain village. Her figure, poise and enigmatic expression can't be found among the local people. You walk away but she lingers in your mind and when you return to the pavilion she is no longer there. It is already dark and in the pavilion a couple of cigarettes glow from time to time as they are smoked, people are there quietly talking and laughing. You can't see their faces, but from their voices you guess that there are probably two men and two women. They don't seem to be locals, who always talk loudly whether they're flirting or being aggressive. You go up and eavesdrop. It seems they are talking about what they have had to do to get away on this excursion: deceive their parents, lie to the head of the work unit, and think up all sorts of stories. Talking about it is such fun they can't stop cackling with laughter. You've already passed that age and don't have to be supervised by anyone, still you aren't having as much fun as they are. They probably arrived in the afternoon, but as you recall there's only the one morning bus from the county town. Anyway they probably have their own ways and means. She doesn't seem to be among them and didn't seem to be as cheerful as this crowd. You leave the pavilion and walk straight down along the river-bank. You no longer need to think about to it. Bandits have their own set of rules – they may be embroiled in a terrible fight amongst themselves but they won't divulge anything to an outsider. They have their own ethics, a code of bandit chivalry if you like, and yet on the other hand they are cruel and wicked. Bandits have two sides to them. The women had all been abducted but once they came into his lair, they became a part of the gang. They were abused by him and yet kept secrets for him." He is shaking his head not because he finds it incomprehensible but because he is moved by the complexity of the human world, it seems.

"Of course one can't dismiss the third possibility that he fled onto the mountain, couldn't get out, and starved to death."

"Do people get lost on the mountain and die there?" I ask.

"Of course, and not just the peasants from elsewhere who come to dig for medicinal herbs. There are even local hunters who have died on this mountain."

"Oh?" This is even more intriguing.

"Just last year a hunter went up the mountain and didn't come back for ten or so days. It was only then that his relatives sought out the village authorities, and we were notified. We contacted the forestry police and had them send us tracker dogs. We got them to sniff his clothes and carried out the search by following them. Afterwards we found him caught in a crack in the rocks. He had died there."

"How did he come to be stuck in the crack in the rocks?"

"Could've been anything, he probably panicked. He was hunting and hunting's prohibited in the reserve. There's also the case of a man killing his younger brother."

"How did this happen?"

"He mistook his brother for a bear. The brothers had gone into the mountain to lay traps. There's good money in musk. Laying traps has been modernized – a trap can be made with a small piece of wire pulled out of a steel construction cable and a person can lay several hundred in a day on the mountain. It's impossible for us to supervise an area of this size. They're all so greedy, it's hopeless. The brothers went into the mountain to lay traps and in the process were separated.

finding your way. There are several dozen houses by the river but only the last one, which sells cigarettes, liquor and toilet paper, has the half door-flap of the shop open. The cobblestone road swerves back towards the town and then there's a high wall. In the weak yellow streetlight on the right, through the dark doorway, is the village administrative office. The tall buildings and large courtyard with a watchtower must once have been the residence of a rich and powerful family at one time. Further on is a vegetable plot fenced off with broken bricks and opposite is a hospital. Two lanes up is a cinema, built just a few years back, and now showing a martial arts movie. You've been around this small town more than once so you don't need to go to see what time the evening session starts. The lane at the side of the hospital cuts through to the main street and comes out right opposite the big department store. You know all this perfectly, as if you're an old resident of the town. You could even act as a guide if anyone wanted one, and you desperately need to talk with someone.

You didn't think that after dark there'd be so many people about on this small street. Only the department store has the iron door shut and the grill up and padlocked in front of the windows. Most of the shops are still open but the stalls that were out during the day have been put away and replaced by small tables and chairs or bamboo bed planks. People are out on the street eating and chatting, inside the shops watching television as they eat and chat, and silhouetted on the curtains of upstairs windows moving about. Someone is playing a flute and there are small children crying and yelling – every household is making its own full-blast din. Songs popular a few years ago in the cities are playing on tape recorders – tenderness laced with petulant lyrics alongside the beat of heavy metal electronic music. People sit in their doorways chatting with people across the street and it is at this time that married women in singlet and shorts and plastic slippers take tubs of dirty bath water to pour into the street. Gangs of adolescent boys are everywhere, deliberately brushing against the young girls strolling hand in hand. Suddenly, you see her again, in front of a fruit stall. You walk more quickly, she's buying pomelos, which are just coming into season. You push in front and ask how much they cost. She touches the round unripe pomelo and walks off. You say, that's right, they're not ripe. You catch up to her. Like to join me? You seem to hear her agree, she even gives a nod which makes her hair shake. You had been nervous, terrified of a rebuff, you hadn't imagine she'd agree so spontaneously. You instantly relax and you keep pace with her.

Are you also here because of Lingshan? You should have been able to say something smarter than that. Her hair shakes again, then you begin to chat.

On your own?

She doesn't answer. The front of the hairdresser's shop is fitted with neon lights and you see her face. It's youthful and that slight weariness is distinctly attractive. You look at the women with their heads under the dryers and getting their hair done and say that modernization has been most rapid in this. She looks away, laughs, and you laugh with her. Her hair covers her shoulders and is black and shiny. You want to say, you have lovely hair, but think it would be going a bit too far, so you don't say it. You walk along with her, and don't say anything else. It's not that you don't want to get on closer terms with her but that you can't think of the right words to say. You can't help feeling embarrassed and want to get out of this dilemma as quickly as possible.

May I walk with you? Again, this is really a stupid thing to say.

You're really a funny person, you seem to hear her mumbling. She looks reproachful and yet approving. However you can tell she's trying to look cheerful, you must keep up with her quick steps. She's not a child and you're no teenager, you try flirting with her.

I can be your guide, you say, this was built in the Ming Dynasty and goes back at least five hundred years, you're talking about the heat-retaining wall behind the Chinese herbalist's shop, one of the flying eaves of the gable curls upwards out of the darkness into the star-lit sky. There's no moon tonight. In the Ming Dynasty, five hundred years ago, no, even just a few decades ago, to walk along this road at night you had to carry a lantern. If you don't believe me you only have to go off this main street and you'll be in pitch-black lanes. You don't even have to go back a few decades, just take twenty or thirty paces and you'll be back in those ancient times.

While chatting you come to the front of the First Class Fragrance Teahouse where there are adults and children standing along the wall. You stand on tiptoes to look inside and stay there as well. The narrow door leads into the long teahouse where all the square tables have been put away. On the rows of benches are the backs of craning heads and right in the middle is a square table draped with a yellow-bordered red cloth: a storyteller in a robe with wide sleeves is seated on a high stool behind it.

"The sun goes down, thick clouds hide the moon, and as usual the Snake Lord and his wife lead their pack of demons back to the Palace of Blue Vastness. On seeing the plump fair-skinned boys and girls and the lavish banquet of pork, beef and lamb, they are delighted. The Snake Lord says to his wife: This good fortune is due to you. Today's birthday celebration is magnificent. One of the demons says: Today being her Ladyship's birthday requires wind and string music and the Master of the Grotto has had to busy himself with these." Bang! He slams his wooden clapper on the table, "Indeed, lofty aspirations produce ideas!"

He puts aside the clapper and taking the drum stick strikes a few dull beats on the slack drum skin. In his other hand he takes up a tambourine threaded with metal bits which he slowly shakes so that it tinkles. Then in his old rasping voice he begins to explain:

"The Snake Lord gives instructions and in all four quarters are activities which immediately transform the Palace of Blue Vastness with colourful decorations and a medley of wind and string instruments." He suddenly raises his voice, "And, when the frog heard, it croaked loudly and the owl waved his conductor's baton." He deliberately imitates the recitation style used by TV performers and makes the audience roar with laughter.

You look at her and both of you laugh. This is the happy face you've been hoping for.

Shall we go in and sit down? You've found something to say. You lead her past wooden benches and peoples' legs, find a bench which isn't full and squeeze in. Just look at the storyteller trying to get the audience worked up. He's standing up and banging his clapper again, very loudly.

"The birthday salutations now begin! All the lesser demons —" he gaily hums as he turns to the left performing the actions of bowing with hands cupped together in salutation, then turns to the right to wave his hands and sing in the voice of the old seductress, "Thank you, thank you."

They've been telling this story for a thousand years, you say close to her ear.

And they'll still go on telling it. She seems to be your echo.

Will they go on telling it for another thousand years? you ask.

Mmm, she replies, pursing her lips like a cheeky child. You feel very happy.

"Let's go back to Chen Fatong. He makes it to the foot of Donggong Mountain in three days, a journey normally taking seven times seven equals forty-nine days, where he encounters the Daoist Wang. Fatong bows in salutation and says: I have a request of the Venerable Master. The Daoist Wang responds with a salutation and Fatong asks: May I ask where the Palace of Blue Vastness can be found? Why do you ask? The demons there are really fierce. Who would dare go there? My surname is Chen and my name, Fatong, means 'comprehending Buddha's laws'. I have come especially to capture the demons. The Daoist Master heaves a sigh and says, young boys and girls have just been sent there today, they may already be in the Snake Lord's belly. On hearing this, Fatong exclaims, I must go quickly to their rescue!"

Bang! You see the storyteller raising his drum stick in his right hand and rattling the tambourine in his left hand. His eyes open wide until they show the whites and as he recites a chant his whole body begins to shake ... You smell something, a subtle fragrance in the midst of the strong smell of tobacco and sweat, it's coming from her hair and from her. There is the cracking of melon seeds as people eat the seeds with their eyes fixed on the storyteller, who has donned a monk's robe. He is holding a magic sword in his right hand and a dragon's horn in his left and talking faster and faster, as if he is spitting out a string of pearls.

"Laying down three times the magic tablet, one–two–three, three troop-summoning amulets instantly muster the divine troops and the generals of Lu Mountain, Mao Mountain and Longhu Mountain, *o-ya-ya a-ha-ha da-gu-long-dong cang-ng-ya–ya–ya–wu-hu*. Emperor of Heaven, Emperor of Earth, I am the younger brother sent by the True Lord Emperor to exterminate demons. Holding the precious magical sword and treading on the wheel of wind and fire I wheel to the right and wheel to the left –"

She turns and stands up, you follow after her, stepping over people's legs. They all glare at you.

"Quick, quick, you've got your orders!"

A roar of laughter follows the two of you.

What's the matter?

Nothing.

Why didn't you want to stay?

I was feeling sick.

You're sick?

No, I feel better now, it's stuffy inside.

You walk outside and the people sitting on the street chatting look up at the two of you.

Should we look for somewhere quiet?

Yes.

You lead her around a corner into a small lane, the sound of people and the lights of the street fall behind you. There are no streetlights in the lane, just the weak glow coming from the windows of the houses. She slows down and you think back to what has just happened.

Don't you think you and I are like the demons being pursued?

She chuckles.

Then you and she can't stop laughing. She laughs so much that she doubles over. Her heels clatter noisily on the cobblestones. You emerge from the lane and before you are paddy fields bathed in faint glimmering light. In the hazy distance are a few buildings, you know it's the one middle school in town. A little further off are sprawling hills beneath the grey star-lit night sky. A breeze starts up, bringing ripples of cool air which sink into the clean fragrance of the paddy rice. You draw close to her shoulder, and she doesn't move away. Neither of you say anything but go wherever your feet take you along the greyish paths between the fields.

Enjoying yourself?

Yes.

Don't you think it's wonderful?

I don't know, I can't say, don't ask me.

You lean against her arm and she leans towards you, you look down to her, you can't see her features but you sense her small nose and you again smell that familiar warmth. Suddenly she comes to a halt.

Let's go back, she mutters.

Back where?

I have to get some rest.

I'll take you back.

I don't want anyone with me.

She is quite adamant.

Do you have relatives or friends here? Or are you here on your own?

She doesn't answer. You don't know where she's from nor where she's going back to. Still, you escort her to the main street and she walks off on her own, vanishing at the end of the street, as if in a story, as if in a dream.

6

In the 2500-metre giant panda observation compound at Haiba, water drips everywhere and my bedding is damp. I've spent two nights here. During the daytime I wear the padded clothes issued by the camp but still feel perpetually damp. The most comfortable time is in front of the fire drinking hot soup and eating. A big aluminum pot hangs on a metal wire from a rafter in the kitchen shed and the log in the stove isn't cut into sections but just burns its way down, sending up sparks two feet into the air and providing light. When we're sitting around the fire a squirrel always comes and sits by the shed rotating its round eyes. It's only at night that everyone gathers around and there's a bit of joking. By the end of the meal it's completely dark, the camp is surrounded by the pitch-black forest, everyone retreats into the shed and in the light of kerosene lamps is preoccupied with his own business.

They've been deep in the mountain all year and have said all they have to say, and there's no news. They hire a Qiang from Sleeping Dragon Pass, 2100 metres from Haiba and the last village after entering the mountain, to come every couple of days with a basket on his back filled with fresh vegetables and slabs of mutton or pork. The ranger station is even further off than the village. They only take turns to go down the mountain for a couple of days' leave every month or every few months, to go to the ranger station for a haircut, a bath and a good meal. Their normal days off accumulate and when the time comes they take the reserve car to Chengdu to see their girlfriends or go back to their homes in other cities. For them this is the way to live. They don't have newspapers and don't listen to radio broadcasts. Ronald Reagan, the economic reforms, inflation, the eradication of spiritual pollution, the Hundred Flowers Movie Award, etcetera, etcetera, etcetera – that noisy world is left to the cities, for them it's all too far away. However, a university graduate sent here to work just last year always has headphones on. It was only after I got close enough that I discovered he was learning English. And there's also a young man who reads by the kerosene lamp. Both are studying for research postgraduate exams so that they can get away from here. There's another man here who picks up wireless signals, locates and plots them onto an air navigation tracking chart. These are signals transmitted from giant pandas which have been captured, tagged with wireless neckbands and then returned to the forest.

The old botanist with me has already spent two days wandering around in the mountains; he's been in bed for some time but I can't tell whether or not he's asleep. I just can't get warm in this damp bedding and lying here fully clothed even my brain seems to have frozen, yet down the mountain it's May and the middle of spring. My hand comes upon a tick which has lodged itself on the inner part of my thigh. It must have crawled up my trouser leg during the day while I was walking through tall grass. It's the size of my little fingernail and as hard as a scab. I hold onto it and rub myself but can't pull it out. I know if I pull any harder it will break off and the head with the mouth which has a good bite on me will remain embedded and grow into my flesh. I get help from the camp worker in the bed next to me. He gets me to strip, gives my thigh a hard slap and squeezes out the blood-sucking little bastard. Tossed into the kerosene lamp it smells like the meat stuffing in a pancake. He promises to get me a bandage in the morning.

It's quiet both inside and outside the shed, but everywhere in the forest there is the sound of water dripping. A mountain wind blows from afar but doesn't reach the mountain and instead recedes and lingers noisily in faraway valleys. Afterwards the planks above me also start dripping and seem to drip right onto my quilt. Is there rain leaking through? Mindlessly, I get up. It's as damp inside as it is outside.

So let it just drip, drip, drip ... Later on, I hear a rifle discharge. It's clear but muffled and reverberates in the valley.

"Over there near White Cliff," someone says.

"Fuck. Poachers," another person swears.

Everyone is awake, or it might have been that no-one had been asleep.

"See what time it is."

"Five to twelve."

Then nobody says anything. It's as if they're waiting for another shot, but there isn't one. In the shattered yet suspended silence, there's only the dripping of water outside the shed and the reverberation of the wind imprisoned in the valleys. Then you seem to hear wild animals. This world belongs to wild animals but human beings persist in interfering with it. The enclosing darkness hides anxiety and restlessness, and this night seems to be even more perilous, awakening your phobia that you are being spied upon, stalked, about to be ambushed. You can't get the spiritual tranquillity you crave ...

"Beibei's here!"

"Who?"

"Beibei!" the university student yells.

It's total chaos in the shed and everyone's up and out of bed.

There's a loud snorting and grunting outside. It's the baby panda they saved when it came fossicking for food, sick and starving! They've been waiting for it to come, they were certain it would come. It had already been ten days and they'd been counting the days. They said it would definitely come before the new bamboo shoots started to sprout. And here is their pet, their treasure, clawing on the timber walls.

Someone opens the door a crack and slips out with a bucket of corn mush and the rest quickly troop out after him. In the murky night this huge dark grey thing lumbers about. Corn mush is quickly poured into a dish and this thing comes up to it, snorting and grunting noisily. The torches are all trained on this animal with black semicircles around its black eyes. This doesn't worry it at all, it's completely engrossed in eating and doesn't look up even once. They are madly taking photos so there's a constant glare of flashlights, and everyone takes a turn to go up to it, to call it, to tease it, and to touch its fur which is as hard as pig bristle. It looks up and everyone runs to take refuge back inside the shed. It is after all a wild animal and a healthy panda can wrestle a leopard. The first time it came it chewed up the aluminum container and ate it as well as the food, and then excreted a trail of undigested aluminum pellets which they had all followed. There was a journalist who kept going on about the giant panda being as cute as a pet cat and got into the enclosure to have his photo taken with his arms around one they'd caught in the ranger station at the foot of the mountain. He got his genitals torn off and was immediately driven to Chengdu, fighting for his life.

It eventually finishes eating and, grabbing a piece of sugar cane and chewing on it, saunters off towards the clumps of Cold Arrow Bamboos and bushes at the edge of the camp.

"I said Beibei would come today."

"It mostly comes at this time, round about two or three."

"I heard it snorting and grunting and scratching on the wall."

"It's good at begging for food, the cheeky devil."

"It was starving. It ate up everything in that big bucket."

"It's fatter. I touched it."

They are very excited and go into minute details – who was first to hear, who was first to open the door, how he saw it through the crack in the door, how it followed him, how it put its head into the bucket, how it sat down next to the pan, and how it really enjoyed eating. Someone even said he'd put sugar into the corn mush and that it likes eating sweet things! Normally they scarcely speak to one another but here they are talking about Beibei as if it's everyone's sweetheart.

I look at my watch, this whole episode took no more than ten minutes but they are raving on endlessly about it. They've got all the lamps on and some are even sitting up in bed. That's just the way it is, life is monotonous and lonely on the mountain and one needs this bit of comfort. From Beibei they go on to talking about Hanhan. The rifle shot earlier on had alarmed them. Hanhan came before Beibei and was killed by a peasant called Leng Zhizhong. They had been getting Hanhan's signals from the same location for a number of days and, thinking it was seriously ill, set out to look for it. Finally, under a fresh mound of earth in the forest they dug out Hanhan's carcass and its neckband which was still giving signals. They organized a search with tracker dogs and got to this Leng Zhizhong's house where they found the rolled up skin hanging under the eaves. Another panda with a neckband was Lili but its signal simply disappeared in the wilderness of the forest and was never again heard. There was no way of knowing whether it had been attacked by a leopard and its neckband chewed up or whether it had met a clever hunter who had smashed the neckband with his rifle butt.

Close to daybreak two shots sound from the lower part of the compound. Their muffled echoes reverberate in the valley for a long time, stubbornly lingering like smoke in the barrel of a rifle that's been fired.

7

You regret not fixing a time to see her again, you regret not chasing after her, you regret your lack of courage, not getting her to stay, not chatting her up, not being more forward, and that there will not be a wonderful liaison. To sum up, you regret losing the opportunity. You don't suffer from insomnia but you sleep badly the whole night. You're up early, think it's all ridiculous and luckily you hadn't been rash. That sort of rash behaviour damages one's self-esteem. But then you detest yourself for being too rational. You don't even know how to go about starting a romance, you're so weak you've lost your manliness, you've lost the ability to take the initiative. Afterwards, however, you decide to go to the riverside to try your luck.

So you're sitting in the pavilion just as the timber merchant had suggested, sitting in the pavilion and looking at the scenery on the other bank. From early morning it's busy at the crossing. The water level goes right up the sides of the ferry as people cram into it. As it docks, even before the ropes are tied, people fight to get ashore. People with big baskets on carrying poles and people pushing bicycles jostle one another, all shouting and swearing as they surge towards the town. The ferry shuttles back and forth and eventually brings across all the people from the other shore. This side of the crossing also turns quiet. Only you are left sitting in the pavilion, like an idiot, pretending to wait for an appointment which wasn't made, with a woman who came and vanished, just as if you're daydreaming. Could it be that you're bored, that you're fed up with your monotonous life devoid of passion and excitement and that you want to live again, to experience life again?

The river-bank is suddenly bustling with activity, this time they're all women. They crowd onto the stone steps by the water – some washing clothes and others washing vegetables and rice. A black canopy boat approaches and the fellow standing at the prow with the punt-pole shouts at the women. The women shout back but you can't tell whether they're flirting or quarrelling. Just then you see her again. You say you thought she'd come, that she'd return to the pavilion so you could tell her about its history. You say an old man sitting in the pavilion told you about it. He was wizened like firewood and as the words came from his parchment-like lips with a wheeze, he looked like a demon. She says she's terrified of demons so you say that his rasping voice was like the wind blowing onto high-voltage wires. You say there are town records dating back to the *Historical Records* and that in early times this crossing used to be called Yu Crossing. Legend has it that when Yu the Great quelled the floods, he crossed here. On the river-bank there used to be a round carved stone with seventeen barely discernible tadpole-like ancient ideograms on it. However, as no-one was able to decipher them, when stone was needed to build the bridge they dynamited it. Then they couldn't raise enough money and the bridge wasn't ever built. You show her the couplet written by the famous Song Dynasty scholar. The Lingshan you seek was known to men of ancient times, however the generations of villagers who have lived here since don't know the history of the place, don't know about themselves. If the lives of the many generations of inhabitants of these courtyards and apartments were written up in full, without leaving anything out or any fabrications, it would really amaze writers of fiction. You ask if she believes you. Take for example the old woman sitting on the doorsill and staring blankly ahead. Her teeth have all fallen out and her wrinkled face is like a salted turnip. She's like a mummy, there's no movement except in her dull, lustreless, sunken eyes. But in those times, she was radiant and beautiful. For several ten *li* around, she ranked as the number one or number two most beautiful woman and people who saw her couldn't help taking another look. But today who can imagine how she looked in those times, not to mention how sexy she looked after becoming the bandit's wife? In this town the bandit chief was called Second Master. Whether he came second amongst his siblings or was honoured with the nickname to get on good terms with him is of little consequence, but everyone in town, young or old, addressed him as Second Master, partly to curry favour but more out of fear. The courtyard beyond the doorsill she's sitting on isn't huge but there are a series of courtyards. Back then, gold coins were brought in big cane baskets from the black canopy boats to this courtyard. She's now staring blankly at the black canopy boats: long ago the old woman was kidnapped and taken onto one of these. At the time she was like those girls with long plaits washing clothes on the stone steps, only she had wooden clogs instead of plastic sandals, and came to the river with a basket to wash vegetables. A boat came alongside and before she realized what was happening two men had grabbed her by the arms and were dragging her into the boat. She didn't have time to call for help because cotton wadding had been stuffed into her mouth. Before the boat had travelled five *li* she had been raped in turn by several bandits. In these black canopy boats which have plied the river for a thousand years, once the woven bamboo canopy was drawn, it was possible to perpetrate such crimes in broad daylight. That night she lay naked on the bare deck boards, the next night she was lighting the stove to cook at the prow of the boat . . .

What will you talk about now? Will you talk about her and Second Master, how she became the bandit's wife? Or will you talk about why she is always sitting on the doorsill? Back then her eyes weren't dull like now and she always carried a woven bamboo container in her bosom and her hands were forever busily embroidering. Her plump white fingers would embroider mandarin ducks frolicking in the water or peacocks with their tails outspread. She coiled her black plaits onto the top of her head and held them with a jade and silver hair-clasp, painted her eyebrows and trimmed the hairline around her face, but no-one dared to suggest that she was attractive. People around her, of course, knew that the container had coloured silk threads on top and a pair of loaded shiny black revolvers underneath. If soldiers boarded while the boat was moored, these delicate hands which embroidered would shoot them down one at a time. While this took place, the elusive Second Master would be sure to be at home fast asleep. Second Master took a fancy to the woman and had kept her for himself, so she followed the womanly virtue of following the man she had married. Didn't anyone in the town ever report them? Well, even rabbits don't eat the grass growing close to the burrow. Then, miraculously, she assumed a life of her own. As for the once famous bandit chief Second Master, whose fighting prowess was unchallenged by all the bandits prowling the roadways or waterways, in the end he was killed by this woman. How? Second Master was cruel but this woman was worse – men are no match for women when it comes to being cruel. If you don't believe me you can ask Mr Wu the teacher in the town middle school. He's been commissioned by the new tourist office of the county to compile a chronicle of the customs, history, and stories of Wuyizhen. The director of the tourist office is the uncle of the wife of Wu's nephew, otherwise he wouldn't have got the job. People born and brought up in the locality all have stories to tell and he's not the only one in town who can write. Who doesn't want to go down in the annals of history and moreover be able to draw advance overtime payments as well as a writer's fee? Wu is a local from a family which has been influential for generations. The clan genealogy mounted on yellow silk, confiscated and publicly burnt during the Cultural Revolution, was twelve feet long. His ancestors enjoyed power and high positions as Leader of Court Gentlemen during the reign of Emperor Wu of the Han Dynasty and as Hanlin Academician during the reign of the Guangxu Emperor of the Qing Dynasty. However in his father's generation they ran into the land reforms and the re-allocation of land and, burdened by their landlord classification, suffered decades of misfortune. Now however, his elder brother, an overseas professor on the verge of retirement with whom he'd lost contact, arrived in a car to visit his hometown accompanied by the local county head and with a colour television for him. As a result the cadres in town started showing him respect. Don't talk about all this. All right, I'll talk about the rebellion of the Long Hairs – the Taipings. At night they came along and torched half of the main street. Previously, the main street of the town ran along the river-bank from the wharf. The present bus station is located at the end of the main street, on the old site of the Dragon King Temple. Before the Dragon King Temple was reduced to a heap of rubble, on the fifteenth day of the lunar New Year, the evening of the Lantern Festival, the best view of the lanterns was from the opera stage of the Dragon King Temple. The lantern dragons from the four villages along the river congregated there – teams of men wearing red, yellow, blue, white or black turbans depending on the dragon they performed with. At the sound of the gongs and drums, the heads in the crowd thronging the streets begin to move to the beat. The shops along the river all have their bamboo poles out with red packets of cash dangling from them, everyone wants good business during the year. The red packets of old man Qian in the rice shop diagonally opposite the Dragon King Temple are the most lucrative and two strings of five hundred crackers hang from his upstairs window. It's among exploding crackers and in a sea of light that the lantern performers demonstrate their prowess. One after the other, the dragons wheel and somersault: it's hardest for the performers manipulating the dragon's head or holding the embroidered ball. And while I'm telling you this, two dragons appear – the red one from Gulaicun in the village and the black one from town led by Wu Guizi. Don't go on with this story, don't. But you do, and go on to tell about the black dragon and about Wu Guizi, the great performer everyone in town knows. The young women are all besotted with him and if they see him they call out, Guizi, come in for some tea, or they bring him a bowl of liquor. Improper behaviour! What? You go on with your story. Wu Guizi, performing in the lead, approaches with the black dragon. He's covered in sweat and in front of the Dragon King Temple unbuttons his vest and tosses it to someone he knows in the crowd. There's a black dragon tattoo on his chest and the youngsters on the street shout their approval. At this point, the red dragon from Gulaicun comes onto the scene from the other end of the street. Twenty or so youths of the same build, each charged with strength and energy, have also come to contest the first prize at old man Qian's rice shop. Neither team will yield and both begin to perform at the same time. The red and the black dragons are lanterns lit by candles and two fiery dragons are seen prancing amongst the heads and feet of the crowd, suddenly rearing their heads and wagging their tails. Wu Guizi is performing with a ball of fire, somersaulting bare-chested on the cobblestones and turning the black dragon into a fiery circle. The red dragon also puts on a good performance – following the embroidered ball closely, it thrusts forward and back like a centipede biting into some living thing. Just as the two strings of five hundred small crackers finish, the employees let off a few bungers. The two teams of contestants, panting and dripping with sweat like eels coming out of water, charge up to grab the red packet hanging from the pole next to the counter. In one bound, it is seized by a youth from Gulaicun. How could Wu Guizi and his team take this humiliation? Loud swearing between the two teams replaces the sound of crackers and then the black and red dragons are embroiled in a fight. The onlookers can't tell who started it but in any case both had been itching for a fight, and this his how fights often start. As usual the children and women start screaming and women who had been standing on stools at doorways to watch the fun grab their children and retreat indoors. The stools they leave behind turn into vicious weapons for both sides. The town does have a policeman but on a festival day like this people would be buying him drinks or else he'd be hanging around mahjong tables watching people play to find pretexts for extracting bribes … preserving public order isn't free of charge after all. Civil disturbances of this nature don't involve the law. The fight results in one death in the black dragon team and two in the red dragon team, and that's not counting little Yingzi's big brother who was watching. Three of his ribs were broken when, for no reason at all, someone knocked him down and stomped on him. Luckily, they managed to save his life by using dogskin plaster, a family prescription from Pockmark Tang's which is next door to Joy of Spring Hall, the brothel with the red lanterns hanging outside. You've made it all up and it's a story you could go on telling, except that she doesn't want to listen.

8

In the maple and linden forest in the lower part of the camp, the old botanist who came with me onto the mountain discovers a giant metasequoia. It is a living fern fossil more than forty metres high, a solitary remnant of the ice age a million years ago, but if I look right up to the tips of the gleaming branches some tiny new leaves can be seen. There's a huge cavernous hole in the trunk which could be a panda's den. He tells me to climb in and have a look, saying that if it did belong to a panda it would only be inside during winter. I do as he says. The walls are covered in moss. The inside and outside of this huge tree has a green fuzz growing on it and the gnarled roots are like dragons and snakes crawling everywhere over a large area of shrubs and bushes.

"Now here's primitive ecology for you, young man," he says striking his mountaineering pick on the trunk of the metasequoia. He calls everyone in the camp young man. He's at least sixty, in excellent health, and gets around everywhere on the mountain using his mountaineering pick as a walking stick.

"They've cut down every tree that can be sold for timber. If it were not for this tree cave this would have gone too. Strictly speaking, there are no primary forests here. At most these would be secondary growth forests," he says, quite moved.

He's here collecting specimens of Cold Arrow Bamboo, the food of the giant panda. I go with him into a clump of dead Cold Arrow Bamboos which are the height of a man, but there isn't a single live bamboo plant to be found. He says it takes a full sixty years for the

Cold Arrow Bamboo to go through the cycle of flowering, seeding, dying and for the seeds to sprout, grow, and flower. According to Buddhist teachings on transmigration this would be exactly one *kalpa*.

"Man follows earth, earth follows sky, sky follows the way, the way follows nature," he proclaims loudly. "Don't commit actions which go against the basic character of nature, don't commit acts which should not be committed."

"Then what scientific value is there in saving the giant panda?" I ask.

"It's symbolic, it's a sort of reassurance – people need to deceive themselves. We're preoccupied with saving a species which no longer has the capacity for survival and yet on the other hand we're charging ahead and destroying the very environment for the survival of the human species itself. Look at the Min River you came along on your way in here, the forests on both sides have been stripped bare. The Min River has turned into a black muddy river but the Yangtze is much worse yet they are going to block off the river and construct a dam in the Three Gorges! Of course it's romantic to indulge in wild fantasy but the place lies on a geological fault and has many documented records of landslides throughout its history. Needless to say, blocking off the river and putting up a dam will destroy the entire ecology of the Yangtze River basin but if it leads to earthquakes the population of hundreds of millions living in the middle and lower reaches of the Yangtze will become fish and turtles! Of course no-one will listen to an old man like me, but when people assault nature like this nature inevitably takes revenge!"

I go with him through the forest, surrounded by waist-high cyrtomiums – their leaves grow out in circles and they look like huge funnels. Of an even deeper green is the edible tulip, which has seven leaves growing out in a circle. There's an all-pervading dampness everywhere.

I can't help asking, "Are there snakes in the undergrowth?"

"It's not the season yet, it's only in early summer when it gets warmer that they're quite vicious."

"What about wild animals?"

"It's people and not animals that are frightening!" He tells me that as a young man he encountered three tigers on the same day. The mother and her cub walked off right past him and then the male came up to confront him. They looked at one another and when he looked away the tiger walked off. "Tigers generally don't attack people but people are stalking tigers everywhere. In South China tigers are already extinct. If you come upon a tiger nowadays you can count yourself lucky," he says sardonically.

"Then what about the tiger-bone liquor on sale everywhere?" I ask.

"It's fake! Even museums can't get hold of tiger bones, and over the past ten or so years not a single tiger skin has been purchased in the whole country. A person in some village in Fujian province had a tiger skeleton but it turned out to be something put together from pig and dog bones!" He roars with laughter and has to lean on his mountaineering pick to catch his breath.

"In my lifetime," he continues, "I've barely escaped with my life a few times but not from the claws of wild animals. Once I was captured by bandits who demanded one gold bar as ransom, thinking I was the offspring of some wealthy family. They had no way of knowing I was a poor student in the mountains doing research and that even the watch I was wearing had been borrowed from a friend. The next time was during a Japanese air raid. A bomb fell onto the house I was living in. It smashed the roof and sent tiles flying everywhere but it didn't explode. Another time was later on when an accusation was brought against me and I was labelled a rightist and sent to a prison farm. Those were difficult times, there was nothing to eat, my body bloated up with beri-beri and I almost died. Young man, nature is not frightening, it's people who are frightening! You just need to get to know nature and it will become friendly. This creature known as man is of course highly intelligent, he's capable of manufacturing almost anything from rumours to test-tube babies and yet he destroys two to three species every day. This is the absurdity of man."

He's the only person in the camp I can have a conversation with, maybe it's because we're both from the world of hustle and bustle.

The others are in the mountains all year long, they have grown silent like the trees, and seldom speak. A few days later he went down the mountain to go home. It's frustrating not being able to engage the others in conversation. I know that they only think of me as an inquisitive tourist. But why have I come to this mountain? Is it to experience life in a scientific research camp such as this? What does this sort of experience mean to me? If it's just to get away from the problems I was experiencing, there are easier ways. Then maybe it's to find another sort of life. To leave far behind the unbearably perplexing world of human beings. If I'm trying to be a recluse why do I need to interact with other people? Not knowing what one is looking for is pure agony. Too much analytical thinking, too much logic, too many meanings! Life has no logic, so why does there have to be logic to explain what it means? Also, what is logic? I think I need to break away from analytical thinking, this is the cause of all my anxieties.

I ask Wu (the one who removed the tick for me) if there are other ancient forests in the vicinity.

He says they used to be all around.

I say this is indeed so but I want to know where I'll now be able to find one.

"Then go to White Rock, we've laid a track to it," he says.

I ask if it's the track in the lower part of the camp leading into a valley. The upper part of the valley is a bare cliff and from a distance it looks like a white rock sticking out of a green sea of forest.

He nods to say yes.

I've been there. The forest looks quite forbidding and the creek is full of huge black trunks which the current didn't carry down.

"It's also been logged," I say.

"That was before the reserve was established," he explains.

"But does the reserve have ancient forests which haven't been desecrated by workers?"

"Of course. You'll have to go to Zheng River."

"Can I get there?"

"Not you. Even with all our equipment and provisions we can't get into the central area, it's a huge gully with very difficult terrain! And there are 5000- to 6000-metre snowclad mountains all around."

"How can I get to see this genuine ancient forest?"

"The closest spot would be at 11M 12M." He's referring to numbers on the aviation maps they use here. "But you wouldn't be able to get there on your own."

He says last year two university graduates who'd just been assigned to work here set off with a bag of biscuits and a compass thinking they'd have no problems. They couldn't get back that night. It wasn't until the fourth day that one of them finally managed to crawl back onto the highway and was sighted by a truck convoy on its way to Qinghai. They went back down the valley to search for the other who was already unconscious from lack of food. He warns that I absolutely must not go off too far on my own and that if I really want to go and have a look at the forest I'll have to wait until someone goes to 11M 12M to collect the signals on giant panda activity.

9

Are you in some sort of trouble? you say, teasing her.

What makes you say that?

It's obvious, a young woman coming to a place like this on her own.

Aren't you also on your own?

This is a habit of mine, I like wandering around on my own, it lets me think about lots of things. But a young woman like you ...

Come on, it's not just you men who think.

I'm not saying that you don't think.

Actually, some men don't think at all!

You seem to be in some sort of trouble.

Anyone can think, but that doesn't necessarily mean they're in trouble.

I'm not trying to pick a fight.

Me neither.

I'd like to help.

Wait until I need it.

Don't you need it now?

Thanks, no. I just need to be alone, I don't want anyone upsetting me.

So something is worrying you.

Whatever you say.

You're suffering from depression.

You're making too much of it.

Then you admit something is worrying you.

Everyone has worries.

But you're looking for worries.

What makes you say that?

It doesn't take a great deal of education.

You're so glib.

As long as it doesn't offend you.

That's not the same as liking it.

Nevertheless, she doesn't refuse your suggestion to go for a stroll along the river. You need to prove you are still attractive to women. She goes with you along the embankment, upstream. You need to search for happiness and she needs to search for suffering.

She says she doesn't dare look down. You say you know she's afraid.

Of what?

Water.

She starts laughing loudly but you can tell she's putting it on.

But you don't dare jump, you say, deliberately going to the edge. Below the steep embankment is the surging river.

What if I jump? she says.

I'll jump in and save you. You know if you say this you'll make her happy.

She says she feels dizzy, that it'd be easy to jump. She'd only have to close her eyes. Dying like this would be intoxicating and virtually painless. You say a young woman just like her from the city jumped into the river. She was younger and more na ve. You're not saying she's complicated, just that people today aren't significantly more intelligent than they were yesterday and yesterday is right there in front of you and me. You say it was a moonless night and the river looked darker and deeper. The wife of the ferryman Hunchback Wang Tou said afterwards that she had shoved Wang Tou and told him she heard the chain of the cable rattling. She said if only she'd got up and had a look then. Later, she heard sobbing and thought it was the wind. The sobbing must have been quite loud. It was late at night and everyone was asleep. The dogs weren't barking so she thought it couldn't have been someone trying to steal the boat and fell asleep again. While she was half asleep the sobbing continued for quite some time and even when she woke up she could still hear it. The wife of Hunchback Wang Tou said if someone had been there, the girl wouldn't have taken her own life. She blamed her husband for sleeping too soundly. Usually it was like this: if there was an emergency and someone wanted to cross the river at night, they would knock on the window and shout out. What she couldn't understand was why the girl was rattling the chains if she wanted to kill herself. Could it have been that she was trying to get the ferry to the county town so that she could get back to her parents in the city? She could have taken the noon bus from the county town. She must have been trying to avoid being found out. No-one could say for sure what she was thinking before she died. Anyway, she was a perfectly good student who had been sent from the city to work on the fields in this village. She had neither family nor friends here and was raped by the party secretary. At dawn thirty *li* downstream at Xiashapu, she was fished out by loggers. The upper part of her body was bare, her shirt must have caught on a branch in a bend of the river. She had left her sports shoes neatly on that rock. Later on, "Yu Crossing" was carved into the rock and painted in red and the tourists all climb on it to have their photos taken. It's only the inscription that remains and the spirit which had suffered an unjust death has been completely forgotten. Are you listening? you ask.

Go on, she replies softly.

People used to die at this spot all the time, you say, and they were very often children and women. Children would dive off the rock in summer, the ones who didn't re-surface were said to have been trying to die and had been reclaimed by parents of another life. Those forced into taking their own lives are always women – defenceless young students sent here from the city, young women who had been maltreated by mothers-in-law and husbands. Many pretty young girls have also suicided. Before the schoolteacher Mr Wu started doing his research on the town, Yu Crossing was known to the villagers as Grieving Ghost Cliff and grown-ups would always worry if their children went swimming there. Some say at midnight the ghost of a woman in white always appears. She is always singing a song they can't identify but which sounds something like a village children's song or a beggar girl's flower-drum song. Of course, this is all superstition, people often frighten themselves with what they say. In fact there's an aquatic bird here which the locals call a blue head and the academics call a blue bird, you can find references to it in Tang Dynasty poetry. Blue heads have long flowing hair according to the villagers. You must have seen them, they're not very big and have a silver-blue body and two long dark blue plumes on the head. They're alert, agile, and lovely to look at. She always rests in the shade under the embankment or by the thick bamboos near the bank of the river, and looks about nonchalantly. You can enjoy looking at her for as long as you like but if you make a move, she flies off. The blue head in this village is not the mythological blue bird which took food to the Queen Mother of the West as mentioned in the *Classic of the Mountains and Seas,* but it does have an aura of magic nonetheless. You tell her that this blue bird is like a woman, of course there are also stupid women but you're talking about feminine intelligence, feminine sensuality. Women who fall deeply in love really suffer – men want women for pleasure, husbands want their wives to manage the home and cook, and parents want the son's wife to continue the family line. None of these are for love. Then you start talking about Mamei. She listens intently. You say Mamei was driven to suicide in this river, this is what people say. She nods and listens child-like, so beautifully child-like.

You say Mamei was betrothed but she disappeared when the mother-in-law came to fetch her. She ran away with her lover, a young village fellow.

Was he a lantern dragon dancer? she asks.

The lantern dragon team involved in the fighting in town was from Gulaicun downstream, this young fellow's family was from Wangnian, fifty *li* upstream. He was lower than her in the clan hierarchy but was a fine youngster. Mamei's lover had neither the money nor the means, his family had only two *mu* of dry land and nine portions of paddy field. In this area, people won't starve if they work hard and have strong limbs. Of course that's as long as there are no natural disasters and no rampaging soldiers, when these occur it's not unknown for eighty to ninety per cent of the villagers to die. Now back to Mamei. For her lover to marry such a pretty and clever girl as Mamei, this bit of property wasn't enough. A girl like Mamei came at a specified price: a pair of silver bracelets for the deposit, a betrothal gift of eight boxes of cakes and a dowry of two cartloads of gilded wardrobes and chests. The person who paid this price lived in Shuigang, behind what is now the photographer's shop. The old house has long since changed owners, but we're talking about the owner at that time. His wife kept giving birth to daughters and because he had his mind set on having a son, this wealthy man decided to take a secondary wife. It so happened that Mamei's mother was an intelligent widow who had worked out her daughter's future: it was better for her to become the secondary wife of a rich man than to spend her life working in the fields with a poor man. An agreement was made through a go-between. As there would not be a bridal sedan, the required sets of clothing for both the bride and her mother were to be provided. A date to fetch the girl was fixed but during the night she ran away. She just bundled up a few clothes, and in the middle of the night tapped on her lover's window to get him to come outside. They burned with passion and she gave herself to him right there. Then, wiping the tears from their eyes, they pledged themselves to one another and agreed to run away into the mountains to eke out a living. Arm in arm they arrived at the river crossing and looked at the surging waves. However the lad vacillated and said he'd have to go home to fetch an axe and a few work tools. He was discovered by his parents. The father beat the unfilial boy with a length of wood and the mother was heartbroken but couldn't bear to have her son leave home. In the prolonged chaos of the father's beating and the mother's weeping it was soon daybreak. The ferryman who was up early said he had seen a girl with a bundle. Then there was a heavy mist and as it became light, the morning mist from the river became thicker so that even the sun turned into a ball of dark red burning charcoal. The ferryman doubled his guard: bumping into another boat wouldn't be too serious but there would be a disaster if they were rammed by a timber-float. There were crowds on the bank on their way to the markets, these markets which have been going for at least three thousand years. Amongst those on their way to these markets there were inevitably people who heard a shout which was instantly stifled in the mist. Then there was the sound of thrashing in the water. Some with sharper ears said they heard it more than once, but everyone just went on talking and nothing could be heard clearly. This is really a bustling crossing, otherwise Yu the Great wouldn't have decided to make his crossing here. The boat was laden with vegetables, charcoal, grain, sweet potatoes, mushrooms, chrysanthemums, edible fungus, tea, eggs, people and pigs, so that the punt-pole curved and the waterline came to the top of the sides of the boat. The rock called Grieving Ghost Cliff was just a grey shadow in the white mist of the river. Some women prattled about hearing the cawing of a crow early in the morning. It's a bad omen to hear a crow cawing. A black crow was cawing as it circled in the sky, it must have detected the aura of someone dying. When people are about to die, before they actually die, they give off an aura of death. It's something like an aura of bad luck which can't be detected by the eyes and ears, and can only be sensed.

Do I have an aura of bad luck? she asks.

You just make it hard for yourself, you have a masochistic streak. You're deliberately teasing her.

Hardly, living is such agony!

You then hear her screaming again.

10

The moss on the trunks, the branches overhead, the hair-like pine lichen hanging between the branches, even the air, everything, is dripping. Big bright, transparent drops of water, drop after drop, slowly drip onto my face, down my neck, icy cold. I tread on thick, soft, downy moss, layer upon layer of it. It grows parasitically on the dead trunks of huge fallen trees, grows and dies, dies and grows, so that with every step my sodden shoes squelch. My hat, hair, down-lined jacket and trousers are wet through, my singlet is soaked in sweat and clings to me. Only my belly feels slightly warm.

He has stopped just up ahead but doesn't turn around, the three-section metal aerial at the back of his head is still swaying. As soon as I clamber over a mass of fallen trees and get close, he takes off again before I have time to catch my breath. He is not tall and is lean and agile like a monkey. He thinks it's too much trouble to zigzag and I have no choice but to make my way straight up the mountain. Since setting out from the camp early in the morning, we've been going for two hours without a break and he hasn't spoken so much as a sentence to me. It seems he's using this strategy to put me off, thinking I'll find it's too hard and turn back. I struggle desperately to follow close behind but the distance between us keeps widening, so from time to time he stops and waits for me. While I catch my breath he puts up the aerial, dons his earphones, tracks the signals and makes a record in his notebook.

Weather equipment has been installed in a clearing. He inspects it, takes notes, and tells me the humidity is already at saturation point.

These are his first words to me all this time and may count as a sign of friendship. A little further on he beckons me to follow him into a clump of dead Cold Arrow Bamboos. Standing there is a big pen fenced with round wooden stakes taller than a man. The bolt isn't in place and the gate is open. The pen is for trapping the pandas which are shot with an anaesthetic rifle, tagged with a transmitter neckband, and then released. He points to the camera I've got hanging on my neck. I hand it to him and he takes a photo of me outside the pen, thankfully not inside it.

Going through the gloomy linden and maple groves, mountain birds trill in the nearby flowering catalpa bushes so there's no sense of loneliness. Then at an altitude of two thousand seven or eight hundred metres we come into a conifer belt – patches of scattered light gradually appear and giant black hemlocks soar up, their branches arched like open umbrellas. However, at a height of thirty or forty metres they are surpassed by grey-brown dragon spruce which soar to heights of fifty or sixty metres and are majestic with their peaked crowns of grey-green new leaves. There is no longer any undergrowth and it's possible to see quite a distance. In between the thick spruce and hemlock trunks are some round alpine azaleas. They are about four metres high and covered in masses of moist red flowers. The branches bow with the weight and, as if unable to cope with this abundance of beauty, scatter huge flowers beneath to quietly display their enduring beauty. This unadorned splendour and beauty in nature fills me with another sort of indescribable sadness. It is a sadness which is purely mine and not something inherent in nature.

Up ahead and down below are huge dead trees which have been snapped by the assault of the elements. To pass by these towering crippled remains reduces me to an inner silence and the lust to express which keeps tormenting me, in the presence of this awesome splendour, is stripped of words.

A cuckoo which I can't see is calling – it's further up then down below, to the left then to the right. It somehow keeps circling around me, as if it's trying to make me lose my bearings, and seems to be calling out: Brother wait for me! Brother wait for me! This brings to my mind the story of the two brothers who went into the forest to sow sesame seeds. In the story the stepmother wanted to get rid of the son of the first wife but fate rebounded upon the person of her own son. I also think of the two university graduates who got lost. A feeling of disquiet grips me.

He comes to a sudden halt, raises an arm to signal me, and I rush over to him. He pulls me down hard. I crouch there with him and start to get tense: then I see through a gap between the trees two large grey-white speckled birds with red feet running on the slope. When I make a quiet move, the pervading silence is instantly shattered by a disturbance in the air.

"Snow cocks," he says.

In barely an instant the air seemingly congeals again and the lively grey-white speckled snow cocks with red feet seem never to have existed, making me feel that I am hallucinating, for before my eyes there are only the huge unmoving trees of the forest. My passing through here at this moment, even my very existence, is ephemeral to the point of meaninglessness.

He is friendlier and no longer leaves me too far behind, he goes for a bit, stops, and waits for me to catch up. The distance between us shortens but still we don't talk. Afterwards, he stops to look at his watch and then turns to look up at the increasing patches of sunlight. He sniffs at the air, climbs up a slope and puts out a hand to pull me up.

I am puffing and panting when we finally come to an undulating plateau. Before us lies a monotone of undiluted fir forest.

"We're more than three thousand metres up, aren't we?" I ask.

He confirms this with a nod then runs to a tree on a high part of the plateau, looks back, puts on his earphones, pulls up the aerial, and rotates in all directions. I also look all around and notice the surrounding trees are of the same girth, equidistant from one another, equally straight, branch out at the same height, and are all equally fine specimens. There are no broken trunks, the trees that have died have fallen down whole, none are exempt from rigorous natural selection.

There are no pine lichens, no clumps of Cold Arrow Bamboo, no small bushes. The spaces between the trees are quite large so that it's brighter and one can see quite far. Some distance away is a white azalea bush which stuns me with its stately beauty. It has an ethereal purity and freshness and as I get closer, it seems to get taller – it is swathed in clusters of flowers with petals larger and thicker than those of the red azaleas I saw earlier. Lush white flowers are scattered beneath the bush. They have not begun to wither and are so charged with life that they exude a lust to exhibit themselves. This is pristine natural beauty. It is irrepressible, seeks no reward, and is without goal, a beauty derived neither from symbolism nor metaphor and needing neither analogies nor associations. This white azalea with the purity of snow and the lustre of jade keeps re-appearing but it is always a solitary bush and appears and disappears, here and there, among the slender cold fir trees, like the tireless hidden cuckoo which captivates one's soul and keeps leading one towards it. I take deep breaths of the pure air of the forest, inhaling and exhaling is effortless and I feel the very depths of my soul being cleansed. The air penetrates to the soles of my feet, and my body and mind seem to enter nature's grand cycle. I achieve a sense of joyful freedom such as I have never before experienced.

A drifting mist comes, just one metre off the ground, and spreads out right before me. As I retreat, I scoop it into my hands, it is like the smoke from a stove. I start running but I am too slow. It brushes past and everything in sight becomes blurred. It suddenly disappears but the cloudy mist following behind is much more distinct, coming as drifts of swirling balls. I back away from it without realizing I am going around in a circle with it but on a slope I manage to escape from it. I turn around to suddenly discover that right below is a deep ravine. A range of magnificent indigo mountains is directly opposite, their peaks covered in white clouds, thick layers of billowing churning clouds. In the ravine, a few wisps of smoke-like cloud are rapidly dispersing. The white line below must be the rushing waters of the river flowing through the middle of the dark forest ravine. This is not the river I passed a few days ago coming into the mountains where there was a stockade village, stretches of cultivated land, and where from the mountain above there was an exquisite view of the cable bridge slung between two cliffs. This gloomy ravine is dark forest and jagged rocks, utterly devoid of anything from the human world. Looking at it sends chills down my spine.

The sun comes out, suddenly illuminating the mountain range opposite. The air is so rarefied that the pine forests beneath the layers of cloud instantly turn a wonderful green which drives me into an ecstatic frenzy. It is as if a song is emerging from the depths of my soul and as the light changes there are sudden changes of colour. I run and jump about, struggling to photograph the transformations of the clouds.

A grey-white cloudy mist sneaks up behind me again, completely ignoring ditches, hollows, fallen trees. I can't get ahead of it and it unhurriedly catches up. It encloses me in its midst: images vanish from my eyes and everything is a hazy blur. But in my mind fragments of the images I have just seen linger. While in this predicament a ray of sunlight comes down over my head, illuminating the moss under my feet. Only then do I discover that underfoot is yet another strange organic plant world. It too has mountain ranges, forests, and low shrubs, and all of these sparkle brilliantly, and are a beautiful green. The moment I crouch down it is here again, that all-pervading obscuring mist and, as if by magic, instantly, everything is a grey-black blurred totality.

I stand up, at a loss, and just wait there. I shout out but there is no reply. I shout out again but hear my own muffled trembling voice immediately vanish without even echoing. I am instantly filled with terror. This terror ascends from my feet and my blood freezes. I call out again, but again there is no reply. All around me are only the black shapes of the fir trees and they are all exactly the same, the hollows and slopes are all the same. I run, shout out, suddenly lurching from one side to the other, I am deranged. I must immediately calm down, return to the original spot, no, I must get my bearings. But in every direction are towering grey-black trees, I can't distinguish anything, I have seen everything before, yet it seems I haven't. The blood vessels in my forehead start throbbing. Clearly, nature is toying with me, toying with this unbelieving, unfearing, supercilious, insignificant being.

Hey – Hello – Hey – I yell out. I did not ask the name of the person who brought me into the mountains so I can only hysterically shout out like this, like a wild animal, and the sound makes my hair stand on end. I used to think there were echoes in mountain forests, even the most wretched and lonely of echoes wouldn't be as terrifying as this absence of echoes. Echoes here are absorbed by the heavy mists and the humidity-laden atmosphere. I realize that my shouting probably doesn't transmit and I sink into utter despair.

The grey sky silhouettes a strangely-shaped tree. The sloping trunk branches into two parts, both similar in girth and both growing straight up without further branching. It is leafless, bare, dead, and looks like a giant fish-spear pointing into the sky. This is what makes it unique. Having got here, I would be at the edge of the forest, so below the edge of the forest should be that dark ravine, at this moment enshrouded in heavy mist, a path straight to death. But I can't leave this tree, it's the only sign I can recognize. I scour my memory for sights I saw along the way. I have first to find identifiable images like this and not a string of images in a state of flux. I seem to recall a few and try to arrange them into sequence to serve as signposts I can follow back. But what I recall is useless, like a deck of shuffled cards and the more I try to arrange some sort of order the more scrambled it all becomes. I am absolutely exhausted and can only sit myself down on the wet moss.

I have become separated from my guide just like that, lost in the three thousand metres of ancient forest in the 12M band of the aviation chart. I don't have the chart on me, nor do I have a compass. The only thing I find in my pockets is a handful of sweets given to me a few days ago by the old botanist who has already gone down the mountain. At the time he was passing on to me what had been his experience – when you go into the mountains it's best to take along some sweets in case you happen to get lost. I count how many I have in my trouser pocket: there are seven. I can only wait for my guide to come and find me.

The stories I have heard over the past few days of people dying in the mountains all transform into bouts of terror which envelop me. At this moment I am like a fish which has fallen into terror's net, impaled upon this giant fish-spear. Futile to struggle while impaled upon the fish-spear: it will take a miracle to change my fate. But haven't I been waiting for this or that sort of miracle all of my life?

11

She says, later she says, she really wants to die, it would be so easy. She would stand on the high embankment, close her eyes and just jump! But if she landed on the steps of the embankment, it would be awful, she doesn't dare imagine the sight of dying horribly with her brains splattered everywhere – it would be ghastly. Her death must be beautiful so that people will feel sorry for her, pity her, and weep for her.

She says she would go along the embankment upstream, find a sandy bay and walk from the foot of the embankment into the river. Of course she wouldn't be noticed and no-one would know, she would walk into the dark river at night. She wouldn't take off her shoes, she doesn't want to leave anything behind. She would just walk into the river with her shoes on, one step at a time, right into the water. By the time the water was waist high, even before it came up to her chest and breathing was hard, the fast-flowing river would suddenly have sucked her into the current and she wouldn't be able to resurface. She would be powerless, and even if she struggled, the instinct to live wouldn't be able to save her. At most her arms and legs would thrash about in the water for a while but it would all be quick, painless: it would be over before there was time for any pain. She would not shout. That would be futile, if she shouted she would immediately choke with water and nobody would hear anyway, much less rescue her. Thus her superfluous life would be totally obliterated. As she cannot eliminate her suffering, there is no choice but to let death resolve it. This act would resolve many things. It would be neat and it would be death with dignity, that is if she could really die with dignity like this. After dying, if her bloated corpse washed onto a sandbank downstream and started to rot in the sun, swarms of flies would settle on it. She feels sick again. Nothing is more nauseating than death. She can't get rid of the nausea.

She says nobody knows her, nobody knows her name, even the name she wrote in the hotel register is false. She says nobody in her family would be able to track her down, nobody would think she would come to a small mountain town like this. But she could imagine how it would be with her parents. Her stepmother would telephone the hospital where she works, sounding all choked up as if she had the 'flu and even as if she were crying. Naturally she would only be doing this after her father had pleaded with her. She knows if she dies her stepmother wouldn't really weep. She is just a burden to the family, her stepmother has her own son who is already a young man. If she spends the night at home her younger brother has to put up a wire bed in the corridor to sleep. They have their eyes on her room and can't wait for her to get married. She really doesn't like staying in the hospital because the dormitories for the night nurses always reek of antiseptic. All day long it is white sheets, white robes, white mosquito nets, white masks: only the eyes beneath the eyebrows are one's own. Alcohol, pincers, tweezers, the clatter of scissors and scalpels, hands constantly being washed and arms soaking in antiseptic until the skin bleaches – first the shine goes, then the colour of the blood. The skin on the hands of people who work all year round in operating theatres is like white wax. One day she will lie there with a pair of bloodless hands on the river-bank, crawling with flies. She feels sick again. She hates her work and her family, including her father. If there are disagreements, her stepmother only has to raise her voice and her father has no opinion. Why don't you shut up? Even if he objects he wouldn't dare say so. Then tell me, what have you done with all your money? You're going senile early, how can I let you hold onto any money? A single sentence can bring forth ten from my stepmother and she always talks so loudly. So he never says anything. He once touched her legs. He started touching and feeling her under the table. Her stepmother and younger brother were not at home, there were just the two of them, he had had too much to drink. She forgave him. But can't forgive him for being so useless, she hates him for being so weak. She doesn't have a father she can respect, a masculine father she can depend on, can be proud of. She wanted to leave this home long ago and have a little home of her own, but this is so disgusting. She takes a condom out of her trouser pocket. For him she had regularly taken the pill and he didn't ever have to worry. She couldn't say it was love at first sight but he was the first man bold enough to seek her love. He kissed her and she began to think about him. They bumped into each other again and made a date. He wanted her and she gave herself, breathlessly, intoxicated. She was in a daze, her heart was pounding, she was afraid yet willing. It was all so natural, good, beautiful, shy, and pure. She says she knew she wanted to love him, that he loved her. Later she would become his wife. And in the future she would become a mother, a little mother. But it made her vomit. She says it wasn't because she was pregnant. After he made love to her, she felt this thing in his back trouser pocket. He didn't want her to take it out but she took it out anyway. It made her vomit. That day after work, she hadn't gone back to the dormitory and hadn't eaten but had hurried to his place. Without letting her catch her breath, the moment she was in the door, he began kissing her and immediately made love to her. He said youth should be enjoyed, love should be enjoyed, enjoyed to the full. In his embrace, she agreed. They wouldn't have children right away so they could enjoy themselves for a few years free of worries, earn some money and travel. They wouldn't set up a home yet, they only needed a room like this which he already had. As long as she had him they would be wild, unrestrained, for ever and ever ... before she could appreciate all this, she felt sick. She couldn't stop the nausea and kept vomiting up bitter bile. Then she wept, became hysterical and cursed men! But she loves him, that is once loved him, but this is in the past. She loved the smell of sweat in his singlets, even after they had been washed she could smell it. But he was not worth loving, he could casually do this with any woman, men are filthy like this! The life she had just started had become soiled. It was like the sheets in her little hotel, all sorts of people sleep on them, they aren't changed and washed and reek of men's sweat. She should never have come to such a place!

Then where will you go? you ask.

She says she doesn't know, she herself can't understand how it was she had come here alone. Then she says she wanted to find somewhere like this where no-one knew her so that she could walk alone along the embankment upstream, not think about anything, just keep walking until she was exhausted and dropped dead on the road . . .

You say she's a spoilt child.

I'm not! She says no-one understands her and it's the same with you.

You ask if she will go across the river with you. Over there on the other shore is Lingshan where wonderful things can be seen, where suffering and pain can be forgotten, and where one can find freedom. You try hard to entice her.

She says she told her family the hospital had organized an excursion and told the hospital her father was ill and she had to look after him, and so she has leave for a few days.

You say she's really cunning.

She says she's not stupid.

12

Before this long trip, after being diagnosed with lung cancer by the doctor, all I could do every day was to go to the park on the outskirts of the city. People said it was only in the parks that the air was slightly better in the polluted city and naturally the air was better still in the parks on the outskirts. The hill by the city wall used to be a crematorium and cemetery, and had only in recent years been turned into a park. However, the new residential area already extended to the foot of the hill which was once a cemetery, and if a fence wasn't put up soon, the living would be building houses right onto the hill and encroaching on their domain.

At the top of the hill was a desolate strip strewn with stone slabs left behind by the stone masons. Every morning elderly people from all around came to practise Taijiquan boxing or to stroll in the fresh air with their cages of pet birds. However, by nine o'clock or so when the sun was overhead they picked up their cages and went home. I could then be alone, in peace and quiet, and would take from my pocket *The Book of Changes with Zhou Commentary*. After reading for a while, the warm autumn sun would make me drowsy and I would stretch out on a stone slab and, with the book as a pillow, quietly begin reciting the hexagram which I had just read. In the glare of the sun, a bright blue image of the sign of that hexagram would float on my red eyelids.

I hadn't originally intended to do any reading, what if I did read one book more or one book less, whether I read or not wouldn't make a difference, I'd still be waiting to get cremated. It was a sheer coincidence that I was reading *The Book of Changes with Zhou*

Commentary. A childhood friend who heard of my illness came to see me and asked if there was anything he could do for me. Then he brought up the topic of *qigong*. He'd heard of people using *qigong* to cure lung cancer, he also said he knew someone who practised a form of *qigong* related to the Eight Trigrams and he urged me to take it up. I understood what he was getting at. Even at that stage, I should make some sort of effort. So I asked if he could get me a copy of *The Book of Changes* as I hadn't read it. Two days later, he turned up with a copy of *The Book of Changes with Corrections to the Zhou Commentary*. Deeply moved, I took it and went on to say that when we were children I thought he'd taken the mouth organ I'd bought, wrongly accused him of taking it, and then found it. I asked if he still remembered. There was a smile on his plump round face. He was uncomfortable and said there wasn't any point in bringing this up. It was he who was embarrassed and not me. He clearly remembered yet he was being so kind to me. It then occurred to me that I had committed wrongdoings for which people did not hold grudges against me. Was this repentance? Was this the psychological state of a person facing imminent death?

I didn't know whether, during my lifetime, others had wronged me more or I had wronged others more. I knew however that there were people such as my deceased mother who really loved me, and people such as my estranged wife who really hated me, but was there any need to settle accounts in the few days left to me? For those I had wronged my death could count as a sort of compensation and for those who had wronged me I was powerless to do anything. Life is probably a tangle of love and hate permanently knotted together. Could it have any other significance? But to hastily end it just like this was too soon. I realized that I had not lived properly. If I did have another lifetime, I would definitely live it differently, but this would require a miracle.

I didn't believe in miracles, just like I didn't believe in fate, but when one is desperate, isn't a miracle all that could be hoped for?

Fifteen days later I arrived at the hospital for my X-ray appointment. My younger brother was anxious and insisted, against my wishes, on coming with me. I didn't like showing my emotions to people close to me. If I were on my own it would be easier to control myself, but I couldn't change his mind and he came anyway. A classmate from middle school was at the hospital and he took me straight to the head doctor of the X-ray section.

The head doctor as usual was wearing his glasses and sitting in his swivel chair. He read the diagnosis on my medical record, examined the two chest X-rays and said that an X-ray from the side would have to be taken. He immediately wrote a note for another X-ray, and said the wet X-ray should be brought to him as soon as the image had developed.

The autumn sun was splendid. It was cold inside and sitting there looking through the window at the sun shining on the grass, I thought it was even more wonderful. I had never looked at the sunshine this way before. After the side position X-ray, I sat looking at the sunshine outside while waiting by the darkroom for the film to develop. The sunshine outside the window was actually too distant from me, I should have been thinking about what was immediately to take place right here. But did I need to think a lot about that? My situation was like that of a murderer with cast-iron evidence against him waiting for the judge to pass the death sentence. All I could hope for was a miracle. Didn't the two damn chest X-rays taken by two separate hospitals at two different times provide the evidence for condemning me to death?

I didn't know when it was, I wasn't even aware of it, probably it was while I was staring out of the window at the sunshine, that I heard myself silently intoning, take refuge in Namo Amitofu, Buddha. I had been doing this for quite some time. It seemed I had already been praying from the time I put on my clothes and left the execution chamber, the X-ray room with the equipment for raising and lowering patients as they lay there.

In the past, I would certainly have considered it preposterous to think that one day I would be praying. I used to be filled with pity when I saw old people in temples burning incense, kneeling in prayer, and quietly intoning Namo Amitofu. My pity was quite different from sympathy. If I were to verbalize this reaction, it would probably be: Ah! Pitiful wretches, they're old and if their insignificant wishes aren't realized, they pray that they will be realized in their hearts. However I thought it was ridiculous for a robust young man or a pretty young woman to be praying and whenever I heard young devotees intoning Namo Amitofu I would want to laugh, and clearly not without malice. I couldn't understand how people in the prime of life could do such a stupid thing but now I have prayed, prayed devoutly, and from the depths of my heart. Fate is unyielding and humans are so frail and weak. In the face of misfortune man is nothing.

While awaiting the pronouncement of the death sentence, I was in this state of nothingness, looking at the autumn sun outside the window, silently intoning Namo Amitofu, over and over, in my heart.

My old schoolmate, who couldn't wait any longer, knocked and went into the darkroom. My brother followed him in but was sent out and had to stand by the window where the X-rays came out. Soon my schoolmate also came out and went to the window to wait. They had transferred their concern for the prisoner to the documentation of his sentence, an inappropriate metaphor. Like an onlooker who had nothing to do with it, I watched as they went into the darkroom, keeping in my heart Namo Amitofu which I silently intoned over and over again. Then, suddenly I heard them shouting out in surprise:

"What?"

"Nothing?"

"Check again!"

"There's only been this one side chest X-ray all afternoon." The response from the darkroom was unfriendly.

The two of them pegged the X-ray onto a frame and held it up for inspection. The darkroom technician also came out, looked at it, made an offhand remark, then dismissed them.

Buddha said rejoice. Buddha said rejoice first replaced Namo Amitofu, then turned into more common expressions of sheer joy and elation. This was my initial psychological reaction after I had extricated myself from despair, I was really lucky. I had been blessed by Buddha and a miracle had taken place. But my joy was furtive, I did not dare to appear hasty.

I was still anxious and took the wet X-ray for verification by the head doctor with the glasses.

He looked at the X-ray and threw up both of his arms in grand theatrical style.

"Isn't this wonderful?"

"Do I still have to have that done?" I was asking about the final X-ray.

"Still have to have what done?" he berated me, he saved people's lives and had this sort of authority.

He then got me to stand in front of an X-ray machine with a projector screen and told me to take a deep breath, breathe out, turn around, turn to the left, turn to the right.

"You can see it for yourself," he said, pointing to the screen. "Have a look, have a look."

Actually I didn't seen anything clearly, my brain was like a great blob of paste and the only thing I saw on the screen was a blurry rib cage.

"There's nothing there, is there?" he loudly berated me as if I were deliberately being a nuisance.

"But then how can those other X-rays be explained?" I couldn't stop myself asking.

"If there's nothing there, there's nothing there, it's just vanished. How can it be explained? Colds and lung inflammation can cause a shadow and when you get better, the shadow disappears."

But I hadn't asked him about a person's state of mind. Could that cause a shadow?

"Go and live properly, young man." He swivelled his chair around, dismissing me.

He was right, I had won a new lease of life, I was younger than a new-born baby.

My brother rushed off on his bicycle, he had a meeting to attend.

The sunshine was mine again, mine again to enjoy. My schoolmate and I sat on chairs by the grass and started discussing fate. It is when there is no need to discuss fate that people talk more about fate.

"Fate's a strange thing," he said, "a purely chance phenomenon. The possible arrangement of the chromosomes can be worked out, but can it be worked out prior to falling into the womb on a particular occasion?" He talked on endlessly. He was studying genetic engineering but the findings of the experiments he wrote up in his dissertation differed from those of his supervisor who was the head of the department. When called up for a discussion with the party general-secretary of the department, he had an argument, and after graduating he was sent to raise deer on a deer-breeding farm on the Daxinganling Plateau of Inner Mongolia.

Later on, after many setbacks, he managed to get a teaching position in a newly-established university in Tangshan. However, how could it have been forseen that he would be labelled the claws and teeth of anti-revolutionary black group elements and hauled out for public criticism. He suffered for almost ten years before the verdict "case unsubstantiated" was declared.

He was transferred out of Tianjin just ten days before the big earthquake of 1976. Those who had trumped up the case against him were crushed to death in a building which collapsed, it was in the middle of the night and not one of them escaped.

"Within the dark chaos, naturally there is fate!" he said.

For me, however, what I had to ponder was this: How should I change this life for which I had just won a reprieve?

13

A village lies up ahead. At the bottom of the terraced fields and the mountain, the same black bricks and tiles dot the riverside. A stream flowing right in front of the village is spanned by a long flat slab of rock. Once again you see a black cobblestone street with a deep single-wheel rut leading into the village. And again you hear the patter of bare feet on the stones, as wet footprints guide you into the village. Again, just like the one in your childhood, it's a small lane with mud-splashed cobblestones. You discover through gaps in the cobblestones that the lapping stream flows under the street. At the gate of each house a flagstone has been lifted so that the water can be used for washing and scrubbing, and bits of green vegetable float along the glistening ripples. Behind the front gates you make out the noisy pecking and flapping of chickens squabbling over food in the courtyards. There is no-one in the lane, there are no children, nor are there any dogs about. It is strangely quiet.

The sun over the tops of the houses shines onto a whitewashed heat-retaining wall and produces a lot of glare, but it's quite cool in the lane. A mirror flashes from a lintel, the Eight Trigrams are etched around the border. When you go up and stand under the eave by the door you notice that this Eight Trigram mirror is directed at the curled roof of the heat-retaining wall opposite to deflect the evil forces emanating from it. However if you position yourself here to take a photograph, the visual contrast of colours – the golden glow of the wall in the intense sunlight, the grey-blue shadows of the lane and the black cobblestones on the road – is pleasing and gives a sense of tranquillity, while the broken tiles on the curled roof and the cracks in the brick wall evoke a feeling of nostalgia. If you reposition yourself you can photograph the door, the Eight Trigram mirror and the stone threshold, worn and shiny from the bottoms of the little children who have sat upon it, all with great authenticity yet showing no trace of the animosity existing for generations between the families living in the two houses.

You tell barbaric and terrifying tales and I don't want to hear them, she says.

Then what would you like to hear about?

Talk about nice people and nice happenings.

Shall I talk about the *zhuhuapo*?

I don't want to hear about shamans.

A *zhuhuapo* isn't the same as a shaman, shamans are wicked old women. A *zhuhuapo* is a beautiful young woman.

Like Second Master's bandit wife. I don't want to hear cruel stories like that.

A *zhuhuapo* is charming and kind hearted.

She's walking in leather shoes on moss-covered rocks and you say she doesn't have a hope of getting very far, so she lets you hold her hand. You've warned her but she slips. You grab her and draw her into your arms, saying you didn't do this on purpose. She says you're bad and frowns but there's the hint of a smile at the corners of her tightly pursed lips. You can't restrain yourself and you kiss her, her lips relax and surprise you with their tenderness. You enjoy her warmth and fragrance and say that this often happens in the mountains. She entices you and you succumb and she nestles in your arms, closes her eyes.

All right, tell me then.

Tell you what?

Tell me about the *zhuhuapo*.

They specialize in enticing men where the road suddenly bends on the dark side of mountains, often in pavilions on mountain tops ...

Have you ever seen one?

Of course. She was sitting sedately on the stone bench of a pavilion built on a mountain road so that the road ran between the two stone benches of the pavilion. To go through you had to pass her. She was a young mountain woman wearing a pale blue fine-weave cotton jacket with knot-buttons running down the ribs to the waist and white binding on the collar and sleeves. A wax-dyed cloth was wound intricately into a turban on her head. You involuntarily slowed down and sat yourself on the stone bench opposite. Without turning, she casually looked you over. Her black eyebrows had been drawn with a charred willow twig and her thin lips pouted. She knew quite well that she was alluring and didn't try to hide it. When eyes flash so provocatively it is inevitably the man who feels awkward. Anyway it was you who felt uncomfortable first and you got up to leave. But on this mountain road on the dark side of the mountain with no-one is sight, she immediately cast a spell over you. Of course you know that you must show more respect than love to this seductive and beautiful *zhuhuapo* and that while you can want her you mustn't dare be rash. You say that you heard this from stone masons who were on the mountain gathering rocks. You spent a whole night drinking and talking about women with them in their work shed. You say that you couldn't take her to such a place to stay overnight, if a woman went it would be certain disaster, only a *zhuhuapo* could keep those stone masons in check. They said that *zhuhuapo* know the meridian points of the body, an art handed down over many generations and that their delicate hands can cure complicated illnesses which men can't, from infantile convulsions to paralysis. People also rely on their clever tongues to arrange and explain matters about marriage, death, birth and sex. When these wild flowers are encountered in the mountains they may be admired but not plucked. They said once there were three blood brothers who scoffed at this. They came upon a *zhuhuapo* on a mountain road and had a wicked idea. Couldn't we three brothers deal with one woman? They talked it over, then with a shout rushed up and dragged the *zhuhuapo* off to a cave. She was a woman after all and couldn't get away from these three big fellows. After the two older ones had finished, it came to the youngest brother's turn. The *zhuhuapo* pleaded with him – good and evil bring good and evil retribution, you're young, don't copy their wicked behaviour. If you listen to me and let me escape I'll tell you a secret recipe which you will find useful later on. When you've made enough money you will be able to marry a young woman and enjoy a happy life. The lad wasn't sure if he believed her or not but he was young and, distressed at seeing the woman in such a wretched state, he let her go.

Did you rape her or did you also let her go? she asks.

You say you got up and started to walk away but couldn't resist taking another look and saw the other side of her face. She had a red camellia in her hair. Light flashed from the tips of her eyebrows and the corners of her lips, and suddenly it was as if a bolt of lightning had lit up the dark mountain and valley. Your heart was on fire and started to pound, and you immediately realized you had run into a *zhuhuapo*. She was sitting adroitly there right in front of you, her firm breasts protruding under her light blue fine-weave cotton jacket. She had in the crook of her arm a bamboo basket covered with a new floral hand towel and the paper flowers pasted on her new blue cotton shoes stood out as clearly as papercut silhouettes on a window.

Come here! She beckons.

She is sitting on a rock holding her high-heel shoes in her hands and carefully testing the round pebbles with a bare foot. Her white toes wriggling in the clear stream are like plump little grubs. You don't know how it began but suddenly you are pressing her head against the green undergrowth on the bank. She sits up and you find the hook to her bra at the back and her perfect round white breasts glow in the noon sun. You see her stiff pink nipples and the fine blue veins below them. She calls out softly as her feet slide into the water. A black coloured bird with white toes, a shrike, is standing in the middle of the stream on a grey-brown rock. The rock is perfectly round just like a woman's breast. The sides of the rock reflect the rippling light of the water. Both of you slide into the water. She's upset about her skirt getting wet, not about herself, and her moist eyes sparkle like the sun's rays reflected in the stream. You have finally captured her, a stubborn struggling wild animal, and she suddenly turns docile in your arms and begins to silently weep.

The black shrike with white toes looks from one side to the other, sticking up its tail as its waxy red beak moves up and down. As soon as you approach, it flies off, skimming the water's surface and settling on a rock ahead. It turns to look back defiantly at you, nodding its head and wagging its tail. It challenges you to approach and then flies off, but not far, and is again waiting there for you, chirping in a quiet, shrill voice. This black spirit, it's her.

Who?

Her ghost.

Who is she?

You say she's dead. Those bastards took her out at night for a swim in the river. When they got back they said she was missing. It was all lies but this was their story. They even said there could be an autopsy and if we didn't believe them, a forensic expert could be called in. Her parents wouldn't agree to an autopsy, they couldn't take it. When their daughter died she was just sixteen. At the time you were younger than her but you knew this had all been planned. You knew they had got her to go out with them at night before, baled her up under the bridge pylons, took turns on her then later met to swap stories about their experiences. They laughed at you for being stupid and not having a go at tasting and feeling her. They had planned to get her. More than once you heard them talking dirty and mentioning her by name. You told her on the quiet she should be careful about going out with them at night, and she told you she was terrified of them. But she didn't dare refuse and went with them. She was frightened but weren't you also afraid? You coward! Those bastards harmed her but didn't dare own up to it. But you didn't dare expose them and for many years she has remained in your heart like a nightmare. Her wronged ghost will give you no peace, and appears in various manifestations, but how she looked as she emerged from under the bridge pylons that time remains unchanged. She is always in front of you, this chirping black spirit, this shrike with white toes and a red beak. You pull on chaste fronds and grab at willow roots in the cracks of the rocks to clamber ashore.

She calls out.

What's up?

I've sprained my ankle.

You can't go climbing mountains in high heels.

I hadn't planned on climbing mountains.

But now that you're in the mountains, be ready to suffer.

14

Outside the upstairs widow of the old house in a twisting narrow lane are rooftops sloping at all angles, running in all directions, all adjoining and stretching into the distance as far as the eye can see. Shoes are airing in the sun on the roof-tiles below the window of a little apartment poking up between two roof ridges. The room has a carved timber bed with a mosquito net and a red wooden wardrobe with a round mirror; a cane chair is next to the window and there is a bench by the door. She gets me to sit on the narrow bench. There is nowhere to move in the small room. I met her a couple of nights ago at the home of a journalist friend and we were all smoking, drinking and chatting. She wasn't put off when it came to crude jokes and in this small mountain town, she seemed to be quite up to date. When we later discussed my request, my friend said, you'll need a woman to take you there. She agreed straightaway and has now brought me here.

She whispers into my ear in the local dialect, quickly alerting me. "When she arrives you must ask for incense. You must ask for incense and also kneel and prostrate yourself three times. This ritual must be observed." Her voice and movements have reverted completely to that of the local women. Squashed next to her on this narrow bench, I suddenly feel quite uncomfortable. In this small county town where everyone knows everyone else couples come to places like this for illicit sex if they're having an affair. I detect the acrid smell of preserved vegetables. Yet the room is immaculate, the floorboards in the middle of the room have been scrubbed so clean that the original colour of the timber can be seen and the wallpaper behind the door is spotless. There isn't the space here for an urn to preserve vegetables.

Her hair brushes against my face, as she says in my ear, "She's here."

A fat, barely middle-aged woman comes in, followed by an old woman. The fat woman takes off her apron and straightens her dress which has faded from washing but is clean. She has just finished cooking downstairs. The slight and gaunt old woman who follows her into the room nods to me.

My friend immediately reminds me, "Go with her."

I get to my feet and follow her to the side of the stairs where she opens an inconspicuous little door and goes in. It is a tiny room where there is a table with an incense altar dedicated to the two Daoist deities, the Venerable Lord Superior and the Great Emperor of Light, and to the bodhisattva Guanyin. Below the incense altar are offerings of cakes, fruit, water and liquor. On the wooden walls hang red banners with black borders and jagged yellow pennants, all bearing words to invoke good fortune and to dispel misfortune. Sunlight streams in through a transparent roof-tile and smoke from a single stick of incense slowly rises in the ray of light, creating an atmosphere which prohibits speech. Only then do I realize why my friend has been whispering since we came in. From a slot under the incense altar, the old woman takes out a bundle of thin incense sticks wrapped in yellow paper. As instructed earlier by my friend, I immediately put one *yuan* into the woman's hand, take the incense sticks, light them from the burning paper she has put a match to in the censer, and holding them in both hands kneel on the rush cushion in front of the altar to reverently perform three prostrations. The old woman smacks her sunken lips to show her approval of my devoutness, takes the incense sticks from me and puts them into the incense altar in three lots.

When I return to the room, the fat woman has prepared herself and is sitting sedately in the cane chair, her eyes closed. She is apparently the spirit medium. The old woman sits down on the far side of the bed to say something to her in a low voice, then turns to ask my friend the zodiac sign of my birth. I tell her my birthday according to the solar calendar. I can't remember the exact date according to the lunar calendar, although I can work it out. The old woman also asks the hour of my birth and I say both of my parents are dead and there is no way of finding out. The old woman is obviously worried and has a quiet discussion with the medium. The medium says something which I understand to mean it doesn't matter, then puts her hands on her knees, closes her eyes, and begins to meditate. On the roof-tiles outside the window where she is sitting, a pigeon settles and starts cooing. The band of shining purple feathers around its neck puff out and I realize it is a male pigeon performing his mating ritual. The medium however suddenly inhales and the bird flies off.

I always feel sad when I see roof-tiles, the fish-scale overlapping shapes always conjure up childhood memories. I recall rainy weather, rainy weather when, drops of transparent water clinging to it, the spider web in the corner of the room trembles in the wind. This sets me thinking about why I have come into the world. Roof-tiles have the power of making me weak and making me succumb to inertia. I want to cry but I have already lost the ability to cry.

The medium burps a couple of times: the spirit must be attaching itself to her. She keeps burping, she has so much gas that I can't repress the urge to burp as well, however I don't dare and keep it bottled inside – I don't want to break our rapport and give her the idea that I've come to cause trouble and make fun of her. I am sincere in mind and heart although I don't really believe it all. She can't stop burping, and more and more frequently. Her whole body starts to convulse and she doesn't seem to be faking it. She is convulsing, I think, probably as a result of *qigong* during meditation. Her body is shaking and her fingers suddenly start jabbing into the air, that is to say, at *me*. She has her eyes still tightly closed and the fingers of both hands all stretching out, but the two index fingers are clearly pointing at me. My back is against the timber wall and there is no place to retreat, I can only brace myself. I don't dare look at my friend who would certainly be more reverent than me, even if she has brought me to have my fortune told. The cane chair creaks noisily with the shaking of the woman's fat body. She is barely comprehensible as she intones incantations. She is saying something like: Within the Lingtong Chamber of Efficacy of the Queen Mother of the West and the Lords of Heaven and Earth, grows a pine tree with the power to turn the wheels of Heaven and Earth and to entirely slaughter bovine demons and snake spirits. She speaks faster and faster, and with greater urgency. This really takes considerable practice and I judge that she is fully qualified. The old woman puts her ear up next to her and after listening, says with a grave expression, "It is an unlucky year for you, you should be careful!"

The medium goes on babbling but is totally incomprehensible. The old woman again explains, "She says you have encountered the White Tiger Star!"

I've heard of White Tiger referring to a very sexy woman and that if you get involved with her it is difficult to extricate yourself. I'm actually quite keen to have the good fortune of getting involved with such a woman but what concerns me is whether I'll be able to escape from my bad luck.

The old woman shakes her head, "It will be difficult to escape from your dangerous predicament."

I don't seem to be a lucky person, nothing lucky has ever happened to me. What I hope for is never realized and what I do not hope for often materializes. I've had countless disasters in my life, I've had involvements and troubles with women, that's right, I've even been threatened, although not always by women. I don't have real conflicts of interest with anyone, I don't think I'm an obstacle to anyone and only hope no-one will be an obstacle for me.

"Great calamities and disasters are imminent, you are surrounded by the tiny people," the old woman adds.

I know about the tiny people, they are described in the compendium of ancient Daoist writings called the *Daozang*. These naked tiny people known as "triple corpses" live as parasites in human bodies, hiding in the throat and thriving on the person's mucous. When the person is dozing they sneak away to the Heavenly Court to report to the Heavenly Emperor on the wrongdoings of the person.

The old woman adds that a violent person with bloody eyes wants to punish me and that even with incense and prayers I won't be able to escape.

The fat woman slides off the cane chair onto the floor and is rolling about on the floorboards. This must be why the floors are scrubbed so clean. I immediately feel that my impure thoughts have invoked her curses. She keeps cursing me, saying that there are as many as nine White Tigers surrounding me.

"Then can I be saved?" I ask, looking at her.

She is frothing at the mouth and the whites of her eyes are turned upwards – she has a horrible expression on her face. All of this is induced by self-hypnosis and she is already in a state of hysteria. There isn't enough space for her to roll about in the room and her body bumps into my feet. I hastily pull them back, stand up, and looking at this woman's fat body wildly rolling about I am gripped with fear – I don't know if it's fear of my own destiny or fear brought upon me by her curses. I have spent money to make fun of her and will eventually be punished. People's relationships with one another are really frightening.

The medium is still babbling away and I turn to ask the old woman what it all means. She shakes her head but doesn't explain. I see the fat convulsing body at my feet gradually humping its back and slowly recoiling to the foot of the cane chair like an injured animal. People in fact are animals and can be quite savage when injured. And it is madness for his wretched person to allow himself to be terrorized. When people go mad they torment themselves with their own madness, it seems.

She heaves a long sigh and there is a low rumbling in her throat, something like the growling of an animal. With her eyes still closed, she gropes about and gets to her feet. The old woman rushes to support her and to help her into the cane chair. I really think she has had an attack of hysteria.

She had correctly sensed that I had come for a bit of fun and she wanted revenge, so she cursed me. It is the friend who brought me who is even more alarmed and she asks the old woman if a session can be arranged for her to burn incense and to pray for me. The old woman asks the medium who mutters something, her eyes still closed.

"She says such a session won't help."

"What if I buy extra incense?" I ask.

My friend then asks the old woman how much it would cost. The old woman says twenty *yuan*. I would spend this amount on a meal for my friends, this is for myself and I immediately agree. The old woman discusses it with the medium and replies, "Even if you do this, it's not going to help."

"Does this mean there's no way for me to escape my bad luck?" I ask.

The old woman relates what I've said and the medium mumbles something again. The old woman says, "That remains to be seen."

What remains to be seen? How devout I am?

The cooing of the pigeon outside comes through the window. I think it's already pounced on its mate. But here I am, still unable to get a reprieve.

15

The dark cypress at the entrance to the village has been lashed by frost and the leaves have turned a deep red. Beneath it, a man with an ashen face is leaning on a hoe. You ask him the name of the village. His eyes look right at you but he doesn't reply. You turn to her and say the fellow is a grave robber. She bursts out laughing. Once past him she says in your ear, he's got mercury poisoning. You say he stayed in the crypt too long. There were two of them, the other one died from mercury poisoning but he survived.

You say his great-grandfather did this all his life and his great-grandfather's great-grandfather was also in the profession. With this profession if one's ancestors have been in it, it's hard to wash one's hands of it. Unlike opium smoking which results in the ruin of families and the squandering of property, grave robbing can bring huge profits for no capital. If a person is hard-hearted and is good at it, if there's a good haul, generations afterwards will become addicted. You feel wonderful talking to her like this. She's holding your hand, docile and compliant.

You say that in the time of his great-grandfather's great-grandfather's great-grandfather, the Qianlong Emperor made a tour of the area. Naturally enough, the local officials wanted to win favour and busied themselves choosing local beauties and collecting the treasures of former dynasties for the emperor. The father of his great-grandfather's great-grandfather's great-grandfather had only two *mu* of poor ancestral land which he worked during the farming season. In the off-season he would boil up a few catties of sugar, add colouring, and make candy men which he'd take in the baskets of his carrying pole to hawk around the towns and villages in the area. He made a whistle the shape of a little boy's penis and Pigsy carrying his wife on his back, but could he earn much from these? The great-grandfather's great-grandfather's great-grandfather whose name was Li the Third liked to roam around all day – he wasn't interested in learning to make candy men but he *was* interested in carrying a wife on his back. Whenever he saw women he'd go over to chat with them. The villagers all called him Skin Leak. One day a snake-medicine doctor arrived in the village. He had a cloth sack for snakes on his back and carried a bamboo tube, a crowbar and an iron hook as he set off to poke among the graves. It looked like fun so Li the Third went along with the doctor and helped to carry his tools. The doctor gave him a snake pill which looked like a black bean and told him to keep it in his mouth: it was very sweet but it was cooling and quenched the thirst. After going along with him for a couple of weeks it was clear that snake catching was a front and that the man actually dug up graves. It happened that the snake doctor was looking for an assistant and this was how Li the Third started getting rich.

When Li the Third came back to the village he was wearing a black satin skullcap with a jade button on the top. It was old cheap stuff he'd got from Pockmark Chen's pawnshop in Wuyizhen (this was before the old street of the town was torched by the Long Hairs). He was proud and cocky, or as the villagers put it was starting to show his mettle, and soon afterwards people were coming around to raise the matter of marriage with his father. However, he married a young widow and people didn't know whether it was the young widow who had seduced him or whether he'd got the young widow into his clutches. Anyway, sticking up a thumb he'd boast that he, Li the Third, had visited the Joy of Spring Hall with the red lanterns in Wuyizhen. After all he'd disposed of a shiny silver ingot. He said nothing about the ingot being black from soaking in the lime and sulphur of the grave and that he had to work hard scrubbing it clean with the side of his shoe.

The grave was on a rocky hill two *li* east of Roosting Phoenix Slope and was discovered by his mentor who noticed rain water running into a hole after a heavy bout of rain. As they poked around it became larger and after they had been digging from noon till almost dark, it was big enough for a person to go in, and of course it was he who had to go in first. He crawled and crawled and, fuck, fell right in, scaring him half out of his wits. In the mud and slush he came across quite a few pots and jars and, all in one go, smashed the whole lot. There was a bronze mirror he took from a wooden coffin which had rotted into a sloppy mess like soya-bean pulp. It was shiny and didn't have a spot of green tarnish, just the thing for the women to use when they combed their hair. He said if he was telling even half of a lie his mother was a bitch. Unfortunately his mentor, that old bastard, took everything and only gave him a bag of silver. He'd had a raw deal but was wiser for it, now he too could work out the entrance to a grave.

You arrive at the Li Family Ancestral Temple in the village. An ancient stone tablet carved with cranes, deer, pines and plum blossoms is set into the newly built buttress above the front doors. You push open the unlatched doors and immediately hear an elderly voice ask what you are doing. You say you've come to look around. A short, well-fed old man emerges from a room in the corridor. It would seem being the caretaker of the ancestral temple is quite a good job.

The old man says the place isn't open to outsiders and with these words starts pushing you out. You say your surname is Li and you're a member of the clan. You've been abroad and are now back visiting your native village. He wrinkles his bushy white eyebrows and looks you over from head to toe. You ask if he knows that earlier on there was a grave robber in the village. The lines on his face deepen and you wince at his expression, most memories can't help being painful. You can't tell if he's sifting through memories or trying to recognize you. In any case, it's awkward looking at his contorted old face. He mumbles to himself for some time, not daring to rashly believe this clan member wearing sports shoes instead of hemp shoes. After a while he blurts: Isn't he dead? It's not clear who is dead but he probably means the father, not the sons and grandsons.

You tell him the descendants of the Li family abroad are all rich through a stroke of good luck. He gapes at this, moves aside, bows, and reverently leads you into the hall of the ancestral temple. He seems to be an old servant of the family. He used to wear black oil-cloth shoes and was keeper of the keys, he is referring to the time before the temple was converted into a primary school. It has now been restored to the family and the primary school has been shifted elsewhere.

He points at the horizontal tablet. It looks like an archaeological relic and the lacquer is peeling off, nevertheless the full implication of the calligraphy in regular script is quite clear: "Illustrious Ancestors of the Glorious Clan." The iron hook under the tablet is for hanging the clan genealogy but that's kept by the father of the village head and normally it isn't brought out.

You say it's mounted on yellow silk and looks like the central scroll for a main hall. He says, quite right, quite right. In the land reform period when it was burnt, a new one was secretly made and hidden upstairs. Later on when people's things were confiscated, the floorboards were ripped up and it was found and burnt again. The present one was made by the father of the primary schoolteacher Mao Wa'er, according to what the three Li brothers managed to piece together. Mao Wa'er already has an eight-year-old daughter and she wants to have another child. Don't people now have to carry out family planning? If there's a second child it means not just a penalty but also that an identity card won't be issued! You say, is that so? You also say you'd like to have a look at the family genealogy. He says it's sure to have you there, it's sure to have you there, everyone in the village with the surname Li has been put in. He adds that there are only three families with other surnames in the village. These are families where there have been marriages with women of the Li family, otherwise they wouldn't want to stay on in the village. But people with other surnames remain people with other surnames, also women are not entered in the genealogy.

You say you know all this. The founder of the Tang Dynasty, Li Shimin, had the surname Li before he became emperor. While the Li clan of the village doesn't claim to be related to the imperial family, our ancestors do include generals and ministers of war and not just grave robbers.

Leaving the temple you find yourself surrounded by a group of children who have sprung out of nowhere. They trail along after you and when you say they're like a pack of arse worms, they break out into stupid cackling. You hold up your camera and they scurry off. The leader of the pack holds his ground and says you don't have film in the camera and you can check by opening it up. The child is quite bright, he has a slight build and is like a pike in water leading this pack of small fry.

"Hey, what's worth seeing around here?" you ask.

"The opera stage," he answers.

"What opera stage?"

They run into a small lane. You follow them. A foundation stone on the corner house of the lane bears a carved inscription: "Be as bold as the rocks of Mount Tai." You've never been able to work out the precise meaning of these words and even now perhaps no-one can say for sure what they mean. In any case there are associations with memories of your childhood. In this empty narrow lane, wide enough only for a person carrying a pole with a single bucket, you again hear the loud patter of bare feet on wet cobblestones.

As you emerge at the end of the lane suddenly before you is a drying lot spread with rice stalks which fill the air with the clean sweet smell of freshly cut rice. On the far side of the drying lot there really is an old opera stage. The framework consists of full-length logs and the actual stage platform, which is half the height of a person, is stacked with bundles of rice stalks. This pack of little monkeys is climbing up the posts, jumping down to the drying lot, and tumbling about in the piles of rice stalks.

The four posts of this open air stage hold up a large roof with upturned eaves and protruding corners. The crossbeams must once have been used to hang flags, lanterns, and the ropes used by the performers. The posts and crossbeams were once lacquered but have already peeled.

Here, operas have been performed, heads have been cut off, meetings and celebrations have been held; people have also knelt and kowtowed here. At harvest time it is filled with piles of rice straw and children are always climbing up and down on it. The children who used to climb up and down here are now old or have died. It's not clear who of those who have died have got into the genealogy. Is the genealogy put together from memory like the original one? Whether or not the genealogy exists finally makes little difference, if one doesn't travel afar one will still have to work in the fields in order to eat. What remain are only children and rice stalks.

There is a temple opposite the opera stage. Newly rebuilt on the rubble of the demolished old site, it is once again colourful and imposing. Two door gods, one green and one red, are painted on the vermilion main doors, and each holds a sword and an axe and has eyes like bronze bells. There is writing in black ink on the whitewashed wall: Huaguang Temple has been rebuilt with contributions from the people listed below. So-and-so one hundred *yuan*, so-and-so one hundred and twenty *yuan*, so-and-so fifty *yuan*, so-and-so sixty *yuan*, so-and-so two hundred *yuan* ...The last item is: Announced by representatives of the old, middle-aged and young of Lingyan.

You walk in. At the feet of Emperor Huaguang is a row of old women, some standing and some kneeling, all dressed in black tops and black trousers, and all toothless. As the ones kneeling stand up the ones standing kneel down, they are all scrambling to burn incense and pray. Emperor Huaguang has a smooth wide face with a square chin, a lucky face, and in the curling smoke of the incense looks even more benevolent. The brush, ink and inkstone in front of him on the long table make him look like a civil official carrying out public business. Above the offering table with its candle holders and incense burners hangs a red cloth with the words "Protect the Nation and Succour the People" embroidered with brightly-coloured silk threads. The black tablet above the curtains and canopy is inscribed with the words:

"Communion with Heaven Makes Wishes Come True." Alongside these words, but much smaller, are the words: "Presented by the People of Lingyan." But you can't make out the date of this antique.

Still, you've confirmed that there is a place called Lingyan and you think this wonderful place must really exist, proving that you haven't made a mistake by charging off to find Lingshan.

You ask these old women. Their sunken mouths make hissing sounds but none of them can say clearly how to get to Lingyan.

"Is it next to this village?"

"Shishisisi ..."

"Not far from this village?"

"Sisixixi ... "

"Go around a bend?"

"Xixiqiqi ... "

"Go another two *li*?"

"Qiqixixi ..."

"Five *li*?"

"Xixiqiqi ... "

"Not five *li* but seven *li*?"

"Xishiqishixishisi ... "

Is there a stone bridge? No stone bridge? Follow the creek in? Would it be better to go along the main road? It will take longer travelling by the main road? After making some detours you will understand in your heart? Once you understand in your heart you will find it as soon as you look for it? The important thing is to be sincere of heart? If your heart is sincere then your wish will be granted? Whether or not your wish is granted depends on your fate and lucky people don't need to search for it? This means that if you wear old iron shoes you won't find it anywhere and to look would be a total waste of time! Are you saying that this Lingyan is just an insensate rock? If I don't say that, what should I say? If I don't say that, is it because I shouldn't say it or because I can't say it? That is entirely up to you, she will be what you want her to be, if you think she is beautiful she will be beautiful, if there is evil in your heart you will only see demons.

16

I arrive at Lingyan shortly before night fall after walking the whole day on mountain roads. I have come in through a long and narrow valley, the two sides of which are brown sheer rock cliffs with only some patches of dark green moss growing where there is a trickle of water. The last rays of the setting sun on the ridge at the end of the valley are red, like sheets of flames.

Behind the metasequoia forest at the foot of the cliff there is a monastery built beneath the thousand-year-old ginkgo trees. It has been converted into a hostel which also takes tourists. I go through the gate. The ground is strewn with pale yellow leaves from the ginkgo trees and there doesn't seem to be anyone around. I look around downstairs and have to go out to the back courtyard on the left before I find a cook there scrubbing pots. I ask him for something to eat but without looking up he says it's past meal time.

"What time does dinner finish here?" I ask.

"Six o'clock."

I show him my watch, it's only 5.40.

"It's no use talking to me, go find the person in charge. I only cook to meal coupons." He continues scrubbing his pots.

I make another round of this huge empty building with winding corridors but still can't find anyone, so I shout out: "Hey, is anyone on duty here?" After I shout a few times, there is a lethargic response, then footsteps, and an attendant in a regulation white jacket appears in the corridor. He takes the money for the room and a deposit for the meals and the key, opens a room and hands me the key, then leaves. Dinner is a dish of left-over vegetables and some egg soup which is quite cold. I regret not having stayed the night in the young girl's house.

It was after leaving Dragon Pond that I met her on the mountain road. It was two or three o'clock in the afternoon and the mid-autumn sun was still quite strong. She was walking slowly up ahead with two big bundles of bracken on her carrying pole. She was wearing a floral shirt and trousers and her shirt clung with sweat to the hollow of her spine. Her back was rigid and only her hips and legs moved. I was walking close behind her. She heard me coming and turned her metal-tipped pole to let me pass, but the big bundles of bracken on the pole blocked the narrow road.

"It doesn't matter, just keep going," I said to her.

Afterwards we came to a small creek and she put down the pole to take a rest. It was then that I saw her flushed cheeks with wet hairs clinging at the sides. She had thick lips. Her face was that of a child, but she had large breasts.

I asked her how old she was. She said she was sixteen, without the bashfulness of a country girl meeting a stranger.

"Aren't you afraid of walking along mountain roads all on your own? There's no-one around, not even a village in sight."

She glanced at her carrying pole with the metal tip and said, "When I set out on my own on the mountain road, I only need to take a pole. I use it to fend off wolves."

She said her home was not far off, that it was just down in the hollow.

I asked if she still went to school.

She said she had been to primary school, now it was her younger brother's turn.

I asked why her father didn't let her go on with her schooling?

She said her father's dead.

I asked who else was in the family.

She said there was her mother.

I said her load probably weighed a hundred and ten catties.

She said there was no firewood around so they had to use bracken for fuel.

She let me walk in front. Just over the rise I saw by the road a solitary house with a tiled roof on the slope.

"That's my home with the plum tree growing in front," she said.

The leaves of the tree have almost all fallen and the remaining few orange-red leaves trembled on the smooth, purplish-crimson branches.

"This plum tree of ours is quite odd. It blossomed in spring, then again in autumn. The snow-white plum flowers all only dropped a few days ago. But this wasn't like in spring, this time there wasn't a single fruit," she said.

When we got to her house she wanted me to go in to have some tea. I went up the stone steps and sat on the millstone at the front door. She took the bundles of bracken on her pole to the back of the house.

Before long she had removed the latch of the door and re-emerged from the hall with an earthenware pot to pour tea into a large blue-rimmed bowl. The pot had probably been sitting in the hot ashes of the stove as the tea was piping hot.

Propped up in the coir bed of the hostel, I feel quite cold. The window is closed but in this upstairs room the walls are timber and the cold air comes through, it is after all a mid-autumn night in the mountains. I again recall her pouring the tea for me, her looking at me and laughing as she saw me taking the bowl in both hands. Her lips parted and I noticed her lower lip was very thick, as if it were swollen. She was still wearing her sweat-soaked shirt.

"You'll catch a cold like that," I said to her.

"That only happens with you city people, I wash in cold water even in winter. Won't you stay the night here?" She saw me give a start and quickly added, "In summer there are lots of tourists around and we take in lodgers."

Her eyes persuaded me to follow her inside. Part of the timber wall of the hall was covered with a Fan Lihua colour picture story. I seem to have heard the story when I was young but couldn't remember what it was about.

"Do you like reading fiction?" I asked, referring to stories with episodes like these.

"I'm keen on listening to opera."

I knew she was referring to the opera programs on radio.

"Would you like to give your face a wash? Should I bring you a basin of hot water?" she asked.

I said there was no need, I could go to the kitchen. She immediately took me to the kitchen, got a washbasin and deftly scooped water from the urn to scrub and rinse it, then ladled hot water from the pot on the stove. She brought it over and, looking at me, said, "Have a look at the room, it's clean."

I had succumbed to her sultry eyes and had already decided to stay.

"Who is it?" A woman's dull voice came from the other side of the timber wall.

"It's a guest, Mother," she answered loudly. Then, turning to me, she said, "She's ill, she's been bedridden for over a year."

I took the hot towel she handed me. She went into the room and I heard them quietly talking. Washing my face brought me to my senses and taking my backpack I went outside and sat down on the millstone in the courtyard.

"What's the cost?" I asked her when she came out.

"Nothing."

I took a handful of coins from my pocket and thrust them into her hand. She frowned and stared at me. I got to the road and after I'd gone some distance, looked back. She was still standing by the millstone, clutching the handful of coins.

I need to find someone I can to talk to. I get out of bed and start moving around in the room. There are noises on the floorboards next door. I knock on the wall and ask, "Is someone there?"

"Who is it?" comes a man's deep voice.

"Are you also here touring the mountains?" I ask.

"No, I'm here working," he says after briefly hesitating.

"Can I disturb you for a while?"

"Go ahead."

I go outside and knock on his door. He opens it. Some sketches for oil paintings are on the table and windowsill. He hasn't trimmed his hair and beard for some time, but then maybe that's his style.

"It's really cold!" I say.

"It'd be good if we could get hold of some liquor, but there's no-one there in the shop," he says.

"It's a hell of a place!" I swear.

"But the women here," he says, showing me a sketch of a woman with thick lips, "are really sexy."

"Are you talking about the lips?"

"It's sensuality devoid of evil."

"Do you believe that sensuality is devoid of evil?" I ask.

"All women are sensual but they always give a sense of goodness, and this is essential to art," he says.

"Then don't you believe in the existence of beauty which is not devoid of evil?"

"That's just man deceiving himself," he says curtly.

"Wouldn't you like to go out for a walk to see the mountain at night?" I ask.

"Of course, of course," he says, "except you can't see a thing out there. I've already been." He scrutinizes those thick lips.

I walk into the courtyard. The giant ginkgo trees rising from the gully block the electric lights in front of the building, turning the leaves stark white. I look around. The cliffs at the back and the sky vanish in the night mist which the lights have turned grey. Only the eaves of the building lit by the lights can be seen. Locked in this strange light, I am overcome by a slight dizziness.

The gate is already shut. I find the latch and open it. Once outside, I am instantly plunged into darkness. A nearby spring gurgles.

I look back after taking a few steps, the lights under the cliff are dim and grey-blue cloudy mists swirl around the mountain peak. Somewhere in the deep gully is the trembling chirping of a cricket. The gurgling of the spring intensifies and subsides. It sounds like the wind, but the wind is threading its way through the gully enshrouded in darkness.

A damp mist spreads over the valley and the trunks of the distant ginkgo trees silhouetted by the light become gentler. It is then that the shape of the mountain gradually manifests itself. I descend into the deep valley embraced by sheer cliffs. Behind the black mountain is a faint glow but all around me a thick darkness gradually closes in.

I look up. Looming high above and looking down menacingly on me is a monstrous black form. I make out the huge head of a bald eagle which protrudes in the middle of it. The wings are folded but it looks as if it is about to take off. I can only hold my breath under the huge talons and wings of this fierce mountain deity.

Further on, I enter the forest of towering metasequoias. I can see nothing at all. The darkness is so palpable that it is a wall and I'm sure if I take another step I'll crash into it. Instinctively, I turn around. Behind, between the shadows of the trees, is the faint glow of the electric lights – a haziness, like a tangled mass of consciousness, like elusive far-away memories. It is as if I am somewhere observing the destination from which I have come. There is no road, the tangled mass of unerased consciousness floats around before my eyes.

I put out my hand to verify my existence, but I can't see it. It is only when I flick my lighter that I see my arm is raised too high, as if I were holding a flame torch. The lighter goes out even though there's no wind. The surrounding darkness becomes even thicker, boundless. Even the intermittent chirping of the autumn insects becomes mute. My ears fill with darkness, primitive darkness. So it was that man came to worship the power of fire, and thus overcame his inner fear of darkness.

I flick my lighter again but the weak dancing flame is immediately extinguished by an invisible, formless wind. In this wild darkness terror gradually consumes me, making me lose my belief in myself and my memory of direction. If you go on you will plunge into an abyss, I say to myself. I immediately turn back but I am not on the road. I try taking a few steps. A belt of weak light, like a fence among the trees, appears briefly then vanishes. I discover that I am already in the forest on the left of the road, the road should be on my right. I get my bearings, grope. I should first find that grey-black towering eagle rock.

A sprawling hazy mist hangs like a curtain of smoke to the ground, a few spots of light glimmer in it. I eventually get back to the foot of the oppressive, black, towering eagle rock only to suddenly discover that the grey-white chest in between the two folded wings is like an old woman draped in a cloak. There is no trace of kindness in her and she seems to be a shaman. Her head is bowed and her withered body can be seen under her cloak. At the foot of her cloak kneels a naked woman, and you can feel the gully down her spine. She is down on both knees desperately beseeching the demon in the black cloak. Her hands are clasped so her arms are away from her upper body and her naked torso is even more clearly revealed. Her features can't be seen but the profile of the right side of her face is quite beautiful.

Her long hair falls onto her left shoulder and arm. The front of her body is now clearer. Still on her knees, she is sitting back on her calves, her head bowed: she is a young girl, is utterly terrified, and seems to be praying, pleading. She is constantly transforming. She now reverts to the young woman, the woman with hands clasped in prayer, but as soon as you look away she becomes the young girl again, and the lines of her body are even more beautiful. The curve of the left profile of her breast appears fleetingly, then can no longer be seen.

Once inside the gate, the darkness completely vanishes and I am back in the hazy grey of the electric lights. The leaves left on the old ginkgo trees growing in the gully are devoid of colour in the glow of the lights. Only the illuminated corridor and eaves are clearly defined.

17

You come to the end of the village. A middle-aged woman with an apron tied over her long gown squats by the creek in front of her door, gutting fish no bigger than a finger. The blade of her knife flashes in the glow of a pine torch burning by the creek. Further on are darkening mountain shadows and only the peak shows some slight traces of the setting sun. There are no more houses in sight. You turn back, perhaps it is the pine torch which draws you there. You go up and ask if you can stay the night.

"People often stop here for the night." The woman understands what you want, glances at your companion but doesn't ask any questions. She puts down the knife, wipes her hands on her apron and goes into the house. She lights the oil lamp in the hall and brings it along. You follow behind, the floorboards creaking beneath your feet. Upstairs is the clean smell of paddy straw, freshly harvested.

"It's empty up here, I'll fetch some bedding. It gets cold in the mountains at night." The woman puts the lamp on the windowsill and goes downstairs.

She says she won't stay downstairs, she says she's afraid. And she won't stay in the same room as you, she says she's afraid of that too. So you leave the lamp for her, kick the paddy straw piled on the floor, and go to the adjoining room. You say you don't like sleeping on plank beds but like rolling about in straw. She says she will sleep with her head next to yours so you will be able to talk through the wall. The wooden partition doesn't go right to the ceiling and you can see the circle of light projected onto the rafters in her room.

"This is unique," you say.

She asks for some hot water when the woman of the house returns with the bedding.

The woman brings her a small wooden pail of hot water. Afterwards you hear her latching the door.

You strip to the waist, throw a small towel over your shoulder and go downstairs. There is no light, probably the only kerosene lamp in the house is upstairs in her room. In the kitchen, you see the woman of the house by the stove. Her expressionless face, lit by the light of the open stove, is gentler. The burning straw crackles and you can smell the aroma of cooking rice.

You take a bucket and go down to the creek. The last remnants of sunset on the mountain vanish and the haziness of dusk descends. There are spots of light in the clear rippling water – the stars are out. A few frogs are croaking.

Opposite, deep in the mountain shadows, you hear children laughing on the other side of the creek. Paddy fields are over there. You seem to see a threshing lot in the mountain shadows, and the children are probably playing hide and seek. In the thick dark mountain shadows, separated by paddy fields, a big girl is laughing on the threshing lot. It's her, she's in the darkness opposite: a forgotten past is re-lived as one of that crowd of children one day recalls his childhood. One day the squeaky voice of the boy screaming cheeky nonsense thickened, became throaty and deep, and his bare feet pattering on the stones of the threshing lot left wet footprints as he departed from childhood to enter the big wide world. You hear the patter of bare feet on black cobblestones. A child by a pond is using his grandmother's embroidery frame for a tugboat. At a shout from his grandmother he turns and runs off, the patter of his bare feet resounding on the cobblestones. Once again you see the back of her, her single long black plait, in a small lane. In the wet lanes of Wuyizhen the winter wind is icy. She has a bucket of water on a carrying pole and is walking with quick short steps on the cobblestones as the bucket presses on her young frail shoulder, straining her body down to the waist. The water in the bucket wobbles and splashes the black cobblestones as she comes to a halt when you call out to her. She turns to smile at you then goes on walking with more quick short steps. She is wearing purplish-red cloth shoes. In the darkness children are laughing and shouting. Their voices are loud, even if you can't make out what it is they are shouting, and there seem to be layers of echoes. It is in this instant that everything comes back to life, Yaya . . .

In an instant your childhood memories become stark and vivid. The roar of dive-bombing planes, then black wings suddenly swoop up and fly into the distance. You are huddled in your mother's arms under a small sour date tree and the thorns on the branches have torn her cotton jacket, showing her plump arms. Then it's your wet nurse. She's carrying you. You like her cuddling you, she's got big floppy breasts. She sprinkles salt on rice *guoba* toasted a delicious crunchy golden brown for you. You love spending time in her kitchen. The bright red eyes in the dark belong to the pair of white rabbits you kept. One of them was mauled in the cage by a weasel and the other one disappeared. You later found it floating in the urine pot in the lavatory in the back courtyard, its fur all dirty. In the back courtyard there was a tree growing in a heap of broken tiles and bricks, the tiles had moss growing on them. You could only see as high up as the branch which came to the top of the wall, so you didn't know what it looked like after it grew over the wall. You only knew if you stood on your toes you could reach a hole in the trunk, and you used to throw stones into it. People said trees have feelings and tree demons are sensitive just like people and don't like being tickled. If you poked something into the hole of the trunk, the tree would shake all over laughing, just like when you tickled her under the arms and she immediately pulled away and laughed until she was out of breath. You can always remember the time she lost a tooth: "Toothless, toothless, her name is Yaya!" She was furious with you for calling her toothless and went off in a huff. Dirt spews up like a pall of black smoke and rains down on everyone's head, your mother scrambles to her feet, feels you, you're all right. But then you hear a long shrill wail, it's another woman:

it doesn't sound human. Next you are being shaken about on endless mountain roads in a tarpaulin-covered truck, squashed between the grown-ups' legs and the luggage, rain is dripping off the end of your nose. Mother's cunt, everyone down to push the truck. The wheels are spinning in the mud, splashing everyone in the face. Mother's cunt, you say imitating the driver, this is the first bit of swearing you've picked up, you're swearing because the mud has pulled off your shoe. Yaya ... The shouting of the children is still coming from the threshing lot, they are laughing and yelling as they chase one another about. But your childhood no longer exists, and all that confront you are the dark shadows of the mountain ...

You come to her door and beg her to open it. She says stop making a fuss, leave things as they are, she feels good now. She needs peace, to be free of desire, she needs time, she needs to forget, she needs understanding not love, she needs to find someone she can pour out her heart to. She hopes you won't ruin this good relationship, she's just starting to trust you, she says she wants to keep travelling with you, to go right to Lingshan. There's plenty of time for getting together but definitely not right now. She asks you to forgive her, she doesn't want to, and she can't.

You say it's something else. You've found a faint light coming through a crack in the wall. Someone else is upstairs apart from the two of you. You ask her to come and have a look.

She says no! Stop trying to trick her, stop frightening her like this.

You say there's a light flickering in a crack in the wall. You're quite sure there's another room behind the wall. You come out of your room and stumble through the straw on the floorboards. You can touch the tiles of the sloping roof when you put up an arm, and further on you have to bend down.

"There's a small door," you say, feeling your way in the dark.

"What do you see?" She stays in her room.

"Nothing, it's solid timber, without any joins, oh, and there's a lock."

"It's really scary," you hear her say from the other side of the door.

You go back to your room and find that by putting a big bamboo tub upside-down onto a pile of straw you can stand on it and climb onto a rafter.

"Quick, what can you see?" she asks anxiously.

"An oil lamp burning in a small altar," you say. "The altar is fixed to the gable and there's a memorial tablet inside. The woman of the house must be a shaman and this is where she summons back the spirits of the dead. The spirits of living persons are possessed and they go into a trance, then the ghosts of the dead attach themselves to these persons and speak through their lips."

"Stop it!" she pleads. You hear her sliding against the wall onto the floor.

You say the woman wasn't always a shaman, when she was young she was the same as everyone else, just like any other women of her age. But when she was about twenty, when she needed to be passionately loved by a man, her husband was crushed to death.

"How did he die?" she asks quietly.

You say he went off at night with a cousin to illegally cut camphor in the forest of a neighbouring village. The tree was about to fall when he somehow tripped on a root and lost his bearings. The tree was creaking loudly and he should have run away from it but instead ran towards it, right where it fell. He was pulverized before he could yell out.

"Are you listening?" you ask.

"Yes," she says.

You say the husband's cousin was frightened out of his wits and absconded, not daring to report the accident. The woman saw the hessian shoes hanging on the carrying pole of a man bringing charcoal down from the mountain, he was calling as he went for someone to identify a corpse. How could she not recognize the red string woven into the soles and heels of the hessian shoes she had made with her own hands? She collapsed and kept banging her head on the ground. She was frothing at the mouth as she rolled around, shouting: Let all the ghosts of the dead and the wronged all come back, let them all come back!

"I also want to shout," she says.

"Then shout."

"I can't."

Her voice is pitifully muffled. You earnestly call out to her but she keeps saying no from the other side of the wall. Still, she wants you to go on talking.

"What about?"

"Her, the mad woman."

You say the women of the village couldn't subdue her. It took several men sitting on her and twisting her arms before they managed to tie her up. From then on she became crazy and always predicted the calamities which would befall the village. She predicted that Ximao's mother would become a widow and it really happened.

"I want revenge too."

"On whom? That boyfriend of yours? Or on the woman who's having an affair with him? Do you want him to discard her after he's had his fun with her? Like he treated you?"

"He said he loved me, that he was only having a fling with her."

"Is she younger? Is she prettier than you?"

"She's got a face full of freckles and a big mouth!"

"Is she more sexy than you?"

"He said she was uninhibited, that she'd do anything, he wanted me to be like her!"

"How?"

"Don't be inquisitive!"

"Then you know about all that went on between the two of them?"

"Yes."

"Then did she know all that went on between the two of you?"

"Oh, stop talking about that."

"Then what shall I talk about? Shall I talk about the shaman?"

"I really want revenge!"

"Just like the shaman?"

"How did she get revenge?"

106

"All the women were frightened of her curses but all the men liked chatting with her. She seduced them and then discarded them. Later on she powdered her face, installed an altar, and openly invoked ghosts and spirits. Everyone was terrified of her."

"Why did she do this?"

"You have to know that at the age of six she was betrothed to an unborn child in the womb – her husband in the belly of her mother-in-law. At twelve she entered her husband's home as a bride, when her husband was still a snotty-nosed boy. Once, right on these floorboards upstairs she was raped in the straw by her father-in-law. At the time she was just fourteen. Thereafter, she was terrified whenever there was no-one else in the house but the father-in-law and her. Later on, she tried cuddling her young husband but the boy only bit her nipples. It was hard waiting years until her husband could shoulder a carrying pole, chop wood, use the plough, and eventually reach manhood and know that he loved her. Then he was crushed to death. The parents-in-law were old and were totally dependent upon her to manage the fields and the household, and they didn't dare to exercise any restraints on her as long as she didn't re-marry. Both parents-in-law are now dead and the woman really believes she can communicate with the spirits. Her blessings can bring good fortune and her curses can bring disaster, so it's reasonable for her to charge people incense money. What is most amazing is that she got a ten-year-old girl to go into a trance, then got the girl's long-dead grandmother, whom the girl had never seen, to speak through the child's mouth. The people who saw this were petrified . . ."

"Come over, I'm frightened," she pleads.

18

On the day I arrive on the shores of Caohai, where the Wu River begins, it is overcast and bitterly cold. Recently, a small building has been constructed on the shores of the lake – it is the new ranger station of the reserve. The rock foundations have been built up high and it stands in isolation in this vast stretch of swampland. The little road to it is nothing more than slushy soft mud. The lake has receded a considerable distance but what was once lake still has a few sparse reeds growing here and there. I go up the stone stairs at the side of the building where there are several rooms with the windows open and plenty of natural light. Specimens of birds, fish and crawling insects are piled up everywhere.

The chief ranger is a large man with a broad face. He plugs in the electric heater, makes tea in a big enamel pot, sits on the heater and invites me to warm myself and have some tea.

He says ten or so years ago, for several hundred kilometres around this high plateau lake, the mountains were covered in forests. Twenty years ago the thick black forests came to the shores of the lake and people often encountered tigers. Now these bald hills have been stripped bare and there is a shortage of firewood for cooking, not to mention heating. Especially during the past ten years, spring and winter have become intensely cold. Frost comes early and in spring there are severe droughts. During the Cultural Revolution, the new county revolutionary committee resolved to implement a new initiative: draining off the water and converting it into fields. They mobilized one hundred thousand civilian workers from the county, blasted scores of drainage channels, and built retaining walls to reclaim this part of the lake for cultivation. But it wasn't so easy to dry out a lake bed which had been saturated for several million years. That year there was a tornado over the lake and the locals said the Black Dragon of Caohai couldn't stay and had flown away. The lake is now only one third of what it used to be and the surrounding area is all swampland which defies drying off or being restored to its original state.

A powerful telescope has been installed at the window and the water several kilometres away is a dazzling white expanse through the lens. What the naked eye sees as a slight shadow turns out to be a boat. Two people are standing at the prow but their faces are indistinct. Another at the stern is moving about and seems to be casting a net.

"It's impossible to guard such a large area of lake. By the time you get there, they'll have slipped off long ago," he says.

"Are there plenty of fish in the lake?" I ask.

"It's easy to haul in hundreds and thousands of catties of fish. The problem is they're still using explosives. People are so greedy, it's hopeless." He is the chief ranger of the reserve and he is shaking his head.

He says that during the 1950s a man with an overseas PhD came here voluntarily from Shanghai, all full of enthusiasm. He brought along with him four biology and marine life graduates and set up a wildlife breeding station on the shores of Caohai where he successfully bred coypu, ermine, speckle-headed geese and several species of fish and aquatic birds. However, he offended some peasant poachers and one day when he was passing a corn field he was ambushed and blindfolded. They tied a basket of corn around his neck, accused him of stealing the corn, and beat him until he coughed up blood. The county committee cadres wouldn't stand up for an intellectual and the old man died without regaining consciousness. The breeding station disbanded and the coypu were divided amongst the various units of the county committee and eaten.

"Does he have any family?" I ask.

"No-one seems to know, the students who worked with him were transferred long ago to teach in universities in Chongqing and Guiyang."

"Hasn't anyone taken an interest in the matter since then?"

He says it was only when the county was sorting some old archives that they discovered ten or so of his notebooks. They contain many accounts of the ecology of Caohai. His research is meticulously detailed and he writes well. If I am interested he can show these to me.

There is a hollow sound like an old person with a racking cough coming from somewhere.

"What's that noise?" I ask.

"Cranes," he says.

He takes me downstairs. In the basement breeding room behind an iron fence is a one-metre high red-headed black neck crane and a few grey cranes. From time to time they make a hollow cry. He says the black neck crane injured its foot and was captured for treatment. The grey cranes are fledglings born this year and they were brought here from the nest before they could fly. In late autumn, flocks of cranes used to come here for the winter and were seen everywhere amongst the reeds and in the fields. Later on they were hunted near to extinction. Following the establishment of the reserve, the year before last more than sixty turned up, and last year more than three hundred black neck cranes flew here, and even a larger number of grey cranes. It's only the red-headed cranes that haven't started coming back.

I ask if I can go onto the lake. He says if the sun comes out tomorrow he'll pump up the rubber dinghy and go out on the lake with me. Today the wind's too strong and it's too cold.

I take my leave, and stroll towards the lake.

I follow a track on the slope of the mountain and come to a small village of seven or eight houses. The rafters and the supports are all made of stone. The only trees are the few growing in people's courtyards and in front of houses – the trunks are slender, no bigger than a rice bowl. Some decades ago, I imagine the dark forest must have come right up to this village.

I go down to the edge of the lake and walk on the earth embankment between the slushy mud. It is too cold to take off my shoes but as I go further on, the embankment gets softer and the mud sticking to my shoes gets thicker. Just ahead, the solid land comes to an end. At the water's edge is a boat and a boy. He is holding a small bucket and a fishing rod. I want to reach him, and get him to take the boat out onto the water.

"Will you take the boat out onto the lake?" He is barefoot, his trousers are rolled up above his knees and he looks to be thirteen or fourteen. But his eyes ignore me and are looking right over my head past me. I turn around and see someone waving to him from the village some distance away. The person is wearing a colourful jacket and looks to be a girl. I take another step towards the boy. My shoes sink right into the mud.

"Ai — yi — ya — yo —" The shouting in the distance is incomprehensible but the voice is clear and beautiful. She must be calling him. The boy with the fishing rod dashes off right past me.

It will be very hard to go any further but having reached the lake I have to get onto it to have a look. The boat is at most ten steps away, I just need to get one foot onto where the boy was standing, the mud there is clearly more solid, and I'll be able to get into the boat. A bamboo punt-pole is at the prow and I can already see aquatic birds skimming the water between the reeds. They are probably wild ducks and they seem to be calling. A wind has risen from shore and I can hear the distant shouting of the two children but not the calls of the nearby birds.

I think, if I can punt the boat out of the reeds I'll get to this broad expanse of water and I'll be able to drift about all alone in the middle of this lonely plateau lake. I won't have to talk to anyone. It wouldn't be bad at all to just vanish into this lake and mountain scenery where lake and sky unite.

I pull up a foot and take another step. I sink deep into the mud right up to my calf. I don't dare shift my weight onto my front leg for I know if it goes above my knee, I won't have a chance of pulling myself out of the mire. I don't dare try to move my back leg. I can neither go forward nor backward and am in an embarrassing dilemma. This is of course an absurd situation but at issue is not the absurdity but the fact that as no-one has seen me, no-one is laughing, and I won't be rescued which is worse.

Maybe they'll see me in the upstairs telescope of the little ranger station, just like I had seen people on the boat. But I would just be a meaningless figure moving about, they wouldn't be able to see my face. Even if they adjusted the lens, they'd only think I was some peasant taking the boat out to get a bit of extra income.

On the lonely lake, even the aquatic birds have gone. The dazzling surface of the water imperceptibly grows hazy, twilight emanates from the reeds and the cold rises from underfoot. I am chilled all over, there are no cicadas chirping, no frogs croaking. Can this possibly be the primitive loneliness devoid of all meaning that I seek?

19

On this chilly late-autumn night, dense heavy darkness encloses a totality of primitive chaos; indistinguishable are sky and earth, trees and rocks, and needless to say the road; you can only stay transfixed, lean forward, put out both arms to grope, to grope in this thick dark night; you hear it in motion, it is not the wind in motion but this darkness which is devoid of top bottom left right distance and sequence; you are wholly fused with this chaos, conscious only that you once possessed the outline of a body, but that this outline in your consciousness is rapidly vanishing; a light emanates from your body, dim like a candle in the darkness, a flame with light but no warmth, a cold light which fills your body, transcending the outline of your body and the outline of your body in your mind; you draw it into your arms, strive to guard this ball of light, this icy transparent consciousness; you need this sensitivity, you strive to protect it; a tranquil lake appears before you, on the other shore is a wood with trees which have shed all their leaves and trees which haven't shed all their leaves; the yellow leaves on the tall poplar and the two small pale yellow leaves on the black branches of the date tree tremble; bright red tallow trees, some thick and some sparse, are like balls of mist; there are no ripples on the lake, only reflections, clear and distinct, rich colours, many shades ranging from dark red to bright red to orange to light yellow to inky green, to greyish-brown, to bluish-white; on careful scrutiny these suddenly fade, turning into different shades of grey, black, white, like an old faded black and white photograph; vivid images lie before your eyes but instead of standing on the ground you are in another dimension, staring with bated breath at the images of your own mind; it is so tranquil, disturbingly tranquil, you feel it is a dream; there is no need to be anxious but you can't help being anxious because it is too strangely tranquil.

You ask if she can see the images.

She says yes.

You ask whether she can see the boat.

She says the boat makes the lake look even more tranquil.

You suddenly hear her breathing, reach out to touch her, your hand wanders over her body, she stops you, you grab her wrist, pull her to you, she turns around, curls up into your arms, you smell the warmth of her hair, look for her lips, she struggles to get away, her warm body is alive, her breathing quickens, her heart beneath your hand is pounding.

You say you want the boat to sink.

She says the boat is already full of water.

You part her and enter her moist body.

She knew it would be like this, she sighs, her body going limp, as if she has no bones.

You want her to say she's a fish!

No!

You want her to say she's free.

Ah, no.

You want her to sink, you want her to forget everything.

She says she's afraid.

You ask what she's afraid of!

She says she doesn't know, then says she's afraid of darkness, afraid of sinking.

Flushed cheeks and leaping flames are suddenly swallowed in darkness, bodies are twisting and turning, she tells you not so rough, she calls out you're hurting! She struggles, calls you an animal! She has been stalked, hunted, torn apart, devoured. Ah ... this dense palpable darkness, primordial chaos, no sky no ground, no space, no time, no existence, no non-existence, no existence and no non-existence; non-existence exists so there is non-existence of existence; non-existence of existence exists so there is non-existence of non-existence; burning charcoal, moist eye, open cave, vapours rising, burning lips, deep growls; human and animal invoking primitive darkness; forest tiger in agony, lusting; flames rise, she screams and weeps; the animal bites, roars and, possessed by spirits, jumps and leaps, circling the fire which burns brighter and brighter, ephemeral flames, without form. In the mist-filled cave a fierce battle rages, pouncing, shrieking, jumping, howling, strangling and devouring ... The stealer of fire escapes, the torch recedes into the distance, goes deeper into the darkness, grows smaller and smaller, until a flame no bigger than a bean sways in the cold breeze and finally goes out.

I'm terrified, she says.

What are you terrified of? you ask.

I'm not terrified of anything but I want to say that I'm terrified.

Silly child,

The other shore,

What are you saying?

You don't understand,

Do you love me?

I don't know,

Do you hate me?

I don't know,

Haven't you ever?

I only knew that sooner or later there would be this day,

Are you happy?

I'm yours, speak to me tenderly, tell me about the darkness,

Pangu wielded his great sky-cleaving axe,

Don't talk about Pangu,

What shall I talk about?

Talk about the boat,

The boat was about to sink,

Was about to sink but didn't,

Did it sink in the end?

I don't know.

You're really a child.

Tell me a story,

When the great flood broke out, only a small boat was left in the world, a brother and his younger sister were in the boat, they couldn't bear the loneliness and huddled close together, only the flesh of the other was real, could verify one's own existence,

You love me,

The girl was seduced by the snake,

The snake is my big brother.

20

I am taken by an Yi singer to several of the Yi camps in the mountain range behind Caohai. Further into the mountains, the hills are rounder and the forests more luxuriant. There is a primitive femininity about them.

The Yi women have dark skin, a high nose bridge and long eyes and they are very beautiful. They seldom look directly at a stranger and should they encounter one on a narrow mountain road, they keep their eyes down, say nothing, and stand aside to make way.

My singer guide sings many Yi songs for me. They all seem to be sad and tearful outpourings, even the love songs.

> When the moon is out,
> Don't take a torch with you,
> If you take a torch with you,
> The moon will be heartbroken.
> When vegetables are in flower,
> Don't take a basket to cut vegetables,
> If you shoulder a basket to cut vegetables,
> The vegetable flowers will be heartbroken.
> If you are pledged to a girl who loves you,
> Don't fancy another,
> If you fancy another,
> The girl will be heartbroken.

He tells me that marriages are still fully arranged by parents among the Yi people. Young people who fall in love can only meet secretly in the mountains. If they are found out, the parents must bring them home. In the past they were put to death.

> A pigeon and a chicken search for food together,
> The chicken has an owner but the pigeon does not,
> If the owner of the chicken takes the chicken home,
> The pigeon is left all alone.
> A girl and a boy play together,
> The girl has an owner but the boy does not,
> If the owner of the girl takes her home,
> The boy is left all alone.

He can't sing these love songs in front of his wife and children at home and comes to the hostel where I am staying in the county village. With the door of my room closed, he softly sings these in the Yi language and translates them for me.

He wears a long gown with a wide waistband and has a thin face and sad eyes. These are his translations of the songs into the Han-Chinese language and the sincerity of the words flow straight from his heart. He is a natural poet.

He says he's old but there is little difference in our ages. He says he can't hope to achieve anything for himself which I find surprising. He says he's the father of two children, a twelve-year-old daughter and a seventeen-year-old son and that he has to work for his children. Later, I go to his home in the mountain stockade. The pig pen is connected to the main room and they keep two pigs. The open hearth is in the middle of the house and the bed in the inner room is covered with a grimy, thin, tattered and old cotton-wadding quilt. His wife has some illness so life for him is a heavy burden.

He also takes me to see a *bimo*, an Yi priest. We pass through several dark, narrow passageways and arrive at a small courtyard with a single gate and a single leaf door. He pushes open the gate, calls out and, when a loud male voice immediately answers, he opens the door and tells me to go in. A man in a long blue gown at the table near the window stands up. He is wearing a wide waistband and a black turban.

Speaking in the Yi language, he introduces me to the *bimo*, then tells me about him. The *bimo* is from a big clan in a place called Kele, high up in the mountains. He was brought down to perform ritual practices for the Yi people living in the county town. He is fifty-three. His eyes look unblinkingly at me. They are bright and clear but there is no communication. While fixed on me what they see is somewhere else, some other forest or a spiritual world.

I sit down at the table opposite the *bimo* and the singer explains why I have come. He is copying out an Yi scripture and is writing with a brush just like the Han Chinese. He nods after listening, wipes the brush in the ink box, puts the cap on the brush and covers the ink box. Then, placing squarely in front of him the book of brush-written text on yellowing fibre paper, he turns to the beginning of a chapter and suddenly begins to sing in a resounding voice. His voice is too loud for the small room. He starts on a high even pitch, then fluctuates between three to five on the scale, which instantly transports one to the flat embankments of the highlands. His voice must really carry a long distance.

Behind him, outside the window of this chilly room, the sunlight is bright and produces a glare on the dirt ground of the courtyard. A rooster cocks its head, as if listening attentively, but getting used to it is no longer startled and puts its head down to peck on the ground again. It seems that chanting scriptures should be like this.

I ask the singer what the priest is singing. He tells me it is a funeral dirge written in the ancient Yi language and he doesn't understand it too well. I had asked him earlier about marriage and funeral practices, and especially if there would be an opportunity for me to see a funeral such as he had described, as nowadays to see the splendour of such an event is quite difficult. The sustained rising and falling crescendo of the high pitched singing of the *bimo* rises from the throat, hits the back palate, passes through the nasal cavity causing it to resonate, and then charges out through his forehead. His *qi* energy is fully developed but is showing signs of aging. Listening to him sing, I seem to see the crowds of a funeral procession: people beating gongs and drums, blowing the *suona*, carrying flags on poles, paper people, and paper horses. The women are riding on horses and the men have rifles which they fire along the way.

And I see the spirit house of woven bamboo pasted with coloured paper on top of the coffin and the surrounding wall made of branches. At the grave site a number of pyres are burning and each of the families of the clan of the deceased sit around one of these. The flames burn higher and higher as the sound of the dirge cuts through the night air. The people there leap and dance, beat drums and gongs, and fire rifles. People come weeping and wailing into the world. That they should make a big commotion before leaving, actually, is in keeping with their innate nature.

These practices are not unique to the Yi people in the mountain stockades of the highlands. Vestiges of these rituals are still to be found throughout the vast delta of the Yangtze but, generally, they have become vulgarized and have lost the original meaning of this great commotion. Fengdu, in Sichuan province, is known as the City of Ghosts and is the original location of the ancient Ba people. Recently, at the funeral of the father of the manager of a department store in the county town, they had a spirit house decked with strips of paper on the coffin. The bicycles of people who had come for the funeral lined one side of the gate and the other side was piled with wreathes, paper people and paper horses. By the road three tables of musicians took turns playing right through the night but the grieving relatives, friends and associates didn't sing the dirges or do the funeral dances and instead played poker at the card tables which filled the courtyard. When I tried to take a photograph of these contemporary funeral practices my camera was seized by the manager who demanded to see my credentials.

There are still plenty of people who can sing the dirges. In the Jingzhou and Jiangling regions where the Chu people originate, the dirges have been transmitted to the present. They are known also as tub-beating songs and are performed with wine libations by village Daoists. Documented evidence of this can be found in the *Zhuangzi*. When

Zhuangzi was in mourning for his wife he beat on a tub and sang, treating mourning as a joyous event. His singing, I expect, was very loud.

Recent research on the Yi people has advanced evidence that Fuxi, the first ancestor of the Han people, had the tiger totem of the Yi people. There are vestiges of the tiger totem everywhere among the Ba people and in the Chu region. A Han Dynasty brick excavated in Sichuan province has an engraving of the Queen Mother of the West which is definitely a tigress with a human face. In this Yi singer's mountain stockade, by the fence of woven chaste tree branches, I saw two children crawling about and playing. Both were wearing cloth hats embroidered with red tiger heads similar in style to the tiger head hats which I saw on children in the mountain regions of southern Jiangxi province and southern Anhui province. Even the clever and intelligent Jiangsu and Zhejiang people, who originate from the ancient Wu and Yue kingdoms in the lower reaches of the Yangtze, retain a fear of tigresses. Could it be that the totem worship of the tiger in matrilineal societies exists in people's subconscious memory? History is bewildering: it is only the singing of the *bimo* which is loud and clear.

I ask the singer whether he can give me a rough translation of the text. He says it points out the way to the nether world for the spirit of the dead person, tells of the deities of Heaven and the deities of the four directions, tells of the deities of the mountains and the deities of the rivers, and finally tells of where our ancestors have come from. By following the route indicated, the spirit of the deceased will be able to return to his ancestral land.

I also ask the *bimo* how many rifles were used at the largest funeral he had conducted. He stops to think, then, with the singer translating, says one hundred. However, he has seen a funeral with as many as twelve hundred rifles. This was the funeral of a chieftain's family: his father had conducted the funeral. At the time, he was only fifteen and had gone with his father to help. They are a hereditary *bimo* family.

A Yi cadre from the village enthusiastically secures a small jeep to take me to Yancang to see the enormous ancient "facing heaven" grave of a Yi king. It is a fifty-metre-high circular mound with a concave top.

During the time when people all went crazy about bringing land under cultivation for the sake of the revolution, they tore down the stones from the three-storey grave surrounds and reduced them to lime. They even dug up and smashed all the earthenware urns containing the remains and planted corn at the top of the bald mound. Now all that is left are a few desolate stunted bushes and the wind. Yi scholarship has shown that the graves of the ancient Ba kingdom documented in the Han Dynasty work *Record of the Kingdom of Huayang* are similar to these "facing heaven" graves of the Yi people. In both cases they originate in the practices of ancestor worship and the observing of celestial phenomena.

In his opinion, the ancestors of the Yi people come from the Aba region of north-west Sichuan province and share a common ancestry with the ancient Qiang people. This was where Yu the Great was born and he was a descendant of the Qiang people: I agree with him. The skin, facial features and stature of the Qiang and Yi people are very similar, I have just come from that region, I say, and I can testify to this. He pats me on the shoulder and immediately invites me home to drink and we become friends. I ask whether the Yi people have to drink blood in liquor when they form a friendship. He says yes, that a rooster has to be killed and its blood dripped into the liquor. However as he already has the rooster cooking in the pot you will have to wait for it to cook, then eat it with the liquor. He has a daughter who's just gone to Beijing to attend university and he asks me to help look after her. Also, he's written a film script based on an ancient orally-transmitted Yi epic: of course, it's a tragic story. He says if I can help him find a filmmaker, he can organize a team of Yi horsemen for the film. I hazard a guess that he is a Black Yi: the Black Yi used to be the slave-owning aristocracy. He doesn't deny this. He says last year when he was in the Daliang Mountains a local Yi cadre turned out to have a common ancestor ten or so, or several ten, I've forgotten which, generations ago.

I ask him whether in the past clan classifications of Yi society were very strict, for example, if men and women of the same clan married or had a sexual relationship were both parties put to death? If maternal cousins married or had a sexual relationship were they punished by death? If a White Yi slave and a woman of the Black Yi aristocracy had a sexual relationship, was the man put to death and the woman forced to suicide?

He says, "Yes, but didn't you Han people ever have these sorts of things?"

After thinking about it, yes.

I've heard that the death by suicide sentences were hanging, taking poison, slitting the stomach, drowning and jumping over a cliff, and that the death by execution sentences were strangulation, beating, being tied to a rock and drowned, being pushed over a cliff, or being killed with a sword or spear. I ask if this was the case.

He says, "That's more or less correct, but wasn't it the same with you Han people?"

As soon as I thought about it, in fact, yes.

I also ask him whether there were cruel punishments such as chopping off the heels, chopping off fingers, gouging out the eyes, piercing the eyes, slicing off the ears and spiking the nose.

He says, "We had all these, but of course in the past. They aren't much different from what happened during the Cultural Revolution."

I think this is in fact the case and I cease to be shocked.

He says that in the Daliang Mountains he met a Nationalist officer who said, "I am a graduate of the Huangpu Military Academy, of such and such a year and from such and such a class, I was field officer of such and such a unit, of such and such a division of the Nationalist Army." He was taken prisoner by a chieftain forty years ago and made a slave. He escaped but was recaptured, taken in manacles to the marketplace, and sold to another slave owner for forty taels of silver. Afterwards when the Communist Party came, he already had slave status and no-one knew of his former background, so he escaped several political campaigns. It is only now when they are talking about cooperation between the Nationalist Party and the Communist Party that he has spoken about his past history. The county officials wanted to give him the title of committee member for political cooperation, but he declined.

He's already over seventy and has five children borne to him by the two slaves his master allocated him when he was a slave. He fathered nine children but four died. The man still lives in the mountains and doesn't want to find out what happened to his former wife and children. He asks if I write fiction – he can give me the story for nothing.

After dinner when I emerge from his house it is pitch-black in the little street. There are no street lights and between the eaves on both sides there is just a narrow strip of grey night sky. If it hadn't been a market day during the daytime, Yi turbans and Miao headscarfs would be thronging the streets. There's not much difference between this street and those of little towns elsewhere.

On my way back to the hostel I pass the movie theatre. I don't know if a film is in session right now but a bright light beams on the voluptuous breasts and seductive eyes on a poster. The film probably contains either "women" or "love" in the title. It's still early and I don't feel like going back to the empty room with four beds so I make a detour to the home of a friend I had made after coming here. He had studied archaeology at university and for some reason was sent here. I didn't ask him about it and he couldn't be bothered complaining, and simply said anyway he didn't have a doctorate.

According to him, the Yi people are mostly located in the delta regions of the Jinsha River and its tributary the Yagong River. Their earliest ancestors are the Qiang people. During the Shang and Zhou Dynasties, when the slave system crumbled on the Central Plains, their ancestors gradually moved southwards and came here. Later, during the Warring States period, when the kingdoms of Qin and Chu went into battle and seized the territory of Qianzhong, the six ancestors divided into groups and moved further south to Yunnan. This is recorded in the ancient Yi text *Record of the Yi in the South West* and cannot be refuted. However, last year at Caohai he discovered over a hundred Palaeolithic stone artefacts. Later on, at the same site, he discovered Neolithic artefacts ground into shapes very similar to the stone artefacts unearthed at Hemudu in the lower reaches of the Yangtze. In the neighbouring county of Hezhang he also discovered an ancient site of a criss-cross style building. Hence he maintains that during the Neolithic period this place was connected with the culture of the ancestors of the White Yue people.

Thinking I'd come to look at stone artefacts, he brings out a basketful of rocks from under his child's bed. We look at one another and burst out laughing.

"I didn't come for rocks," I say.

"You're right, there's something more important than rocks, come, let's have something to drink!" He immediately puts the basket into a corner behind the door and calls out to his wife, "Bring us some liquor!"

I say I have just been drinking.

He says, "It doesn't matter, you can drink as much as you like, and then just bed down here!"

He seems to be Sichuanese. His Sichuan accent draws me closer to him and I start talking with him in Sichuan dialect. His wife instantly prepares a few dishes which bring out the full richness of the liquor. He is in high spirits and begins to hold forth on various topics – from the dragon bones he'd bought from a fish hawker which turned out to be a stegodon fossil unearthed in the marsh at Caohai to how local cadres could hold a meeting for a whole morning to discuss whether or not to buy an abacus.

"Before buying it, they had to scorch it to see if the beads were cow horn or dyed wood!"

"To see if it was authentic!"

He and I kill ourselves laughing until our bellies hurt. It is a wonderful, happy occasion.

When I leave his home my feet feel a lightness which is rare for this high plateau. I know that I have had the right amount of liquor, I am at eight-tenths of my capacity. Afterwards I remember I forgot to take from the basket the stone axe which had once been used by the descendant of someone with the surname Yuan. At the time he had pointed to the basket behind the door and shouted, "Take as many as you like. These magical treasures are the legacies of our ancestors!"

21

She says she's afraid of rats, even hearing them running on the floorboards terrifies her. And she is afraid of snakes. There are snakes everywhere on this mountain, she's afraid of spotted snakes slithering down from the rafters and getting into the bed, she wants you to hold her tight, she says she is afraid of the loneliness.

She says she wants to hear your voice, that your voice is reassuring. And she wants to pillow her head on your arm, this gives her something to lean on. She wants to listen to you talking, go on talking, don't stop talking, so that she will not feel lonely.

She says she wants to hear you tell her stories, she wants to know how Second Master came to take possession of the girl abducted by the bandits on the river-bank outside her house. How did the girl submit to Second Master and become the bandit chief's wife? Afterwards how did Second Master die by her hand?

She says she doesn't want to hear the story about the girl from the city who jumped into the river. Don't talk about the bloated naked corpse pulled out of the water, she won't think about suicide anymore, and she doesn't want to hear the story about the ribs being stomped on and broken in the dragon lantern competition. She has seen too much blood in the operating theatre of the hospital. She says she wants to listen to interesting stories like the one about the *zhuhuapo*, but you mustn't tell violent stories.

She asks if you have done this with other girls. She isn't asking about what sort of things you have done with other women but about tricking girls to come with you into the mountains, is she the first?

You ask her to say but she says how would she know? You ask her to guess, she says she wouldn't be able to guess and that even if you had you wouldn't tell her. Also, she doesn't want to know, she realizes she has come of her own volition, so if she has been tricked she has brought it upon herself. She says she wants nothing of you at this moment except that you understand her, care about her, love her.

She says the first time she was penetrated, he was very rough. She isn't talking about you but about that boyfriend of hers who didn't care about her at all. At that time she was totally passive, demanded nothing, and felt no excitement at all. He had frantically pulled up her skirt ... she had one foot against the floor all through it. He was utterly selfish, a swine who just wanted to rape her. Of course she had been willing. But it was very uncomfortable and he made her hurt awfully. She knew it would hurt, it was like fulfilling a duty, so that he would love her and marry her.

She says when she did it with him, there was no ecstasy and that when she saw his semen running down her legs, she vomited. Afterwards, each time the smell would immediately make her want to vomit. She says she was purely something for him to discharge his lust into, and whenever that thing of his touched her she would feel disgusted with her own body.

She says this is the first time she has ever indulged herself, the first time she has used her body to love a man. She did not vomit, she is grateful to you, grateful that you have given her this kind of joy. She says she will get her revenge on him like this, get revenge on that boyfriend of hers, she will tell him she has slept with another man. A man a lot older than her, a man who knew how to enjoy her and in turn gave her enjoyment.

She says she knew it would be like this, that she would let you enter her. And she knew all her defence stratagems had been to deceive herself. But why did she punish herself like that? Why didn't she just enjoy it? She says you have given her life, given her hope, she wants to go on living, and once again has desire.

She also says that as a child, her family had a dog which liked to nuzzle her with its wet nose to wake her up, sometimes it would even jump onto her bed. She loved putting her arms around this dog. Her mother who was still alive then, said that dogs had fleas and she wouldn't let the dog into her bedroom. Once she had a red rash all over her body and her mother said she had been bitten by fleas from the dog. Afterwards people weren't allowed to keep dogs in the city and when she wasn't home the dog-catching squad took away the dog and killed it. She wept and didn't eat dinner. She feels at the time she was very kind-hearted. She can't understand why people in the world are so wicked. Why is there such lack of sympathy between people? She says she can't understand why she is saying all this.

You ask her to go on talking.

She says she can't understand why, it's as if flood gates have opened and she can't stop talking.

You say she is doing very well.

She says she never wants to grow up and yet she also wants to grow up. She wants to be loved, wants everyone to look at her, but she's afraid of men's looks. She thinks men's looks are always salacious. When they look at someone they aren't looking at the person's beauty, they are looking at something else.

You say you're a man.

You're an exception, she says, you make her feel relaxed, she wants to be in your embrace.

You ask if she thinks you are salacious.

Don't talk like that, she says. She doesn't think you are, she likes you. Everything about you is so endearing, she says she now knows what it is to be living. But she says at times she is frightened and thinks life is a bottomless hole.

She thinks no-one really loves her, and if no-one loves her what meaning is there to living? She says this is what really frightens her. But a man's love is so selfish, they always want to possess you, but what do they give in return?

Men do give, you say.

But only what they want to.

But don't women also find men indispensable? You say it was Heaven's will that joined the male and the female as the two parts of the grindstone, this is the innate nature of human beings. You say there's no need to be afraid of anything.

She says you're getting her excited.

You ask surely she is enjoying it?

As long as it's so natural, she says.

Come, accept with all your body and heart. You arouse her.

Ah, she says she wants to sing.

You ask her what she wants to sing.

To sing of you and me, she says.

Sing whatever you like, you urge her to sing loudly.

She wants you to caress her.

You say you want her to abandon herself.

She wants you to kiss her nipples . . .

You are kissing her.

She says she also loves your body, nothing of your body is frightening anymore. She will do whatever you want her to do, oh, she says she wants to see you enter her body.

You say she has become a real woman.

Yes, she says, a woman owned by a man, she says she doesn't know what nonsense she's talking, she says she has never enjoyed herself like this before, she says she's drifting on a boat and doesn't know where she's drifting, she is no longer in control. Let it drift, on the black sea, she and you, no, there is only her, she's not really afraid but she feels terribly empty, she wants to die, death is seductive, she wants to fall into the sea, let the black sea drown her, she needs you, the warmth of your body, even your oppressiveness gives her a sense of security, she asks if you're aware of it, that she desperately *needs*!

Need a man? You bait her.

Yes, I need a man's love, need to be owned. She says, yes, she longs to be owned, she wants to abandon herself, forget everything, ah, she is grateful to you, she was anxious the first time, yes, she says she wanted to, she knew she wanted to, but she panicked, didn't know what to do, she wanted to cry, she wanted to scream, she wanted to be carried away by a storm in the wilds, to be stripped naked by it, to be flailed with a branch until her flesh was torn apart, to succumb to the pain, to be ripped apart by wild animals! She says she saw her, that wanton woman dressed in black, fondling her own breasts, that smile on her face, the way she walked swinging her hips, a licentious woman, she says, you don't understand, you don't understand this, you don't understand anything, you simpleton!

22

I get on a bus from the Yi nationality district on the Yunnan–Guizhou border, arrive in Shuicheng, and spend most of the day waiting for the train. The station is some distance from the county town and the whole area is neither town nor farm villages and gives me a sense of instability. This is especially so when I see, in what looks like a street, this couplet: "If children are playing outside the window, the people inside and outside are safe." It is pasted on the windowsill of an old house whose rafters and supports have gone black with age. I no longer seem to be walking forward but am returning to my childhood, moving backwards on my heels. It's as if I haven't gone through the war, haven't gone through the revolution, haven't gone through the endless sessions of struggle-meetings, haven't gone through the criticisms and counter-criticisms and the about-turn but not quite about-turn reforms of the present. It's as if my parents are not dead and I haven't endured any sufferings. It is in fact before I have grown up and I am moved to the verge of tears.

Afterwards, I sit myself down on a pile of logs which has been unloaded alongside the railway tracks to reflect on the happenings in my life. A woman about thirty or so who seems distressed comes up to me. She asks me to help her buy a train ticket. She probably knew I wasn't a local when she heard me talking just now at the ticket window in the railway station. She tells me she wants to go to Beijing to file a lawsuit but doesn't have the money for a ticket. I ask her what sort of lawsuit she intends to file. She talks at length without making it any clearer but it amounted to an unjust trial which had resulted in someone bringing about her husband's death. Up to now no-one has accepted responsibility and she hasn't received a cent of compensation. I give her one *yuan* and send her off, then go some distance further on to sit by the river where I spend several hours looking at the scenery on the opposite bank.

Some time after eight o'clock at night I eventually arrive in Anshun. I must first get a locker to deposit my backpack which has become quite heavy. I have in it a Han Dynasty brick with a design on it. I came across it in Hezhang where peasants were constructing pig pens with bricks taken from the Han Dynasty tombs. The lights are on in the locker deposit window but there's no-one there. After I knock on the window for some time, an attendant emerges, pins a ticket on my backpack, takes the money, puts the bag on an empty shelf, and goes inside again. The big waiting room is empty and it doesn't look anything like a station. Stations usually have people noisily milling around, sitting on their haunches by walls, lying on benches, sitting on luggage, or just wandering about, and there are always people selling or re-selling things to make a bit of money. Leaving this deserted station, I hear my own footsteps.

Dark grey clouds speed overhead but the night sky is bright. The high glow of sunset and the low dark clouds are richly coloured. Round mountains rise from the plains directly ahead. The tops of the mountains on this high plateau are like voluptuous breasts, but close up, they are huge and somewhat oppressive. I don't know whether it's because of the clouds speeding overhead but I have the sensation that the ground slopes and I have one long leg and one short leg ... and I haven't even been drinking! This night in Anshun gives me this odd sort of feeling.

I find a small inn opposite the railway station and in the semi-darkness I can't make out how the building is constructed but the room is like a pigeon cage and my head seems to be touching the ceiling. It's a room fit only for lying down.

I go out onto the street which is lined with places to eat with tables on the pavement. There is a blaze of electric lights but strangely there are no customers about. It's a crazy night and suddenly I am uneasy about eating here. However, at a square table some twenty or thirty metres away there are two customers, so I sit down at the table opposite and order a bowl of rice noodles with beef and chillies.

The two men are both rather gaunt. One is guarding a pewter wine jar and the other has one foot on the bench. Each has a small patterned wine bowl in his hand but they don't seem to have ordered any food. The ends of the single chopstick each holds touch and, in the same instant, one says "Dried prawns!" and the other says "Carrying pole!". Neither wins and the chopsticks separate. They are playing "Execute Drinking Orders". When both have psyched themselves up, the ends of the chopsticks meet again. One says "Carrying pole!" the other says "Dog!". The pole hits the dog so the one who said dog loses. The winner takes the stopper off the wine jar and pours a little liquor into the small patterned wine bowl in the hand of his opponent. The loser drinks it in one gulp and the ends of the chopsticks touch again. Their slow and meticulous movements make me wonder if they aren't immortals. However, looking carefully, I see that they are very ordinary people. Anyway, I expect immortals probably play "Execute Drinking Orders" just like this.

I finish eating the rice noodles and beef, get up and leave. I can still hear them playing and on this deserted street they sound very loud.

I come to an old street. The old houses on both sides are about to collapse and the eaves come right out over the road. The further I go the narrower the road becomes and the eaves of the houses on both sides virtually join. There are clear signs of imminent collapse. At every doorway is a stall with some things to sell, a few bottles of liquor, a few pomelos and small amounts of dried fruit, or some items of clothing which hang there, swaying like hanged corpses. The street is endlessly long, as if it goes through to the other end of the world. My deceased maternal grandmother seems to have brought me here, I recall that she took me out to buy a spinning top. The big boy next door had a top which filled me with envy but normally this particular toy was only on sale around the Spring Festival and even toy counters in the big shops didn't have them. My maternal grandmother had to take me to the Temple of the City God in the south of the city but there they only had performing monkeys and people practising martial arts. It was only in places where they sold dogskin medicinal plasters that tops might be found. I recall that when I went to the Temple of the City God to buy a top that I had gone along this kind of street. It's been a long time since I've played with this humble toy: the more you hit it the faster it spins. But none of the people on this street sell tops, the merchandise on show is all much the same and the more you look the more uninteresting it all is. Who actually comes to buy at all these shops? Do they really do business or is it all for show? Do they have proper jobs as well? Or does every household open up a shop, like some years ago every household used to paste up Old Mao's sayings to make their doorways look more impressive?

Later on, I somehow make a turn and come onto another big street. Here they are all regular government shops but they are already closed for the night – when they can do good business, they're not open. Nevertheless the street is thronging with people. The young women are particularly eye-catching. They are all wearing lipstick, walking noisily in high heels, and wearing sleeveless, body-hugging, low-cut, gaudy Hong Kong dresses which either have been smuggled in or else bought after being resold profitably many times over. They are not on their way to a nightclub but they look as if they have dates.

Coming to a crossroads, it is even more crowded and it seems that all the inhabitants of the city have come out and are all casually walking in the middle of the road. No cars are in sight and it's as if this wide road has been built for pedestrians and not vehicles. Judging by the size of this crossroads and the style of the houses on the street, I gather that I must be at the Big Ten of the city. The cities of this high plateau usually refer to the city centre as the Big Ten but it is dark here compared with the bright lights of the shops in the small winding lane. Maybe there's a shortage of electricity or maybe the shift workers forgot to put on the street lights, who knows? I make use of the light shining from a window and go right up to look at the road sign. It in fact reads "Big Ten" and it is quite certain this is the square in the centre of the city, the place where ceremonies and parades are held.

I hear the sound of chuckling coming from the darkness on the pavement. Puzzled, I go up to look and discover that people are sitting, one next to the other, all along the wall. I stoop to get a better look and see that they are all old people, several hundred of them, and they look to be neither meditating nor demonstrating. They are chatting, laughing and singing. There is the squeaking of strings from an untuned *huqin* resting on someone's knees: the cloth on his knees makes this *huqin* master look more like a cobbler mending shoes. The person next to him is leaning against the wall and singing the tune, "At the Drumbeat of the Five Watches" which counts each of the five watches from night to dawn and tells about a besotted girl waiting for her lover. The old people all around listen entranced. The intriguing thing is that they are not all men, there are also old women, all with huddled shoulders and bent backs, like so many shadows. However, their coughing is very loud, but the coughing seems to be coming from people made of paper. Someone is quietly talking, as if talking in sleep, or one could say talking just for oneself. However, there is the sound of laughter in reply. On eavesdropping, it turns out to be an old man earnestly flirting with an old woman. What sort of wood did elder brother fetch from the mountains? What sort of shoes did younger sister embroider with her hands? One asks and the other replies as in the singing of mountain love songs. Perhaps they are using the darkness of the night to transform the Big Ten into a singing stadium of their youth, or perhaps this was the very place where they flirted and talked of love in their youth. There is more than one old couple singing love songs, and there are even more earnestly chatting and laughing. I can't understand what they are saying or why they are having so much fun, only they can understand the hissing which comes through their sparse teeth. I wonder if I am dreaming and look carefully to see if these are real people. I pinch my thigh through my trousers and it does hurt, so I'm not mistaken. After coming to this high plateau I have been travelling from north to south, tomorrow I will catch the early long distance bus and go further south to Huangguoshu. In the waterfall there I will wash away these strange images and will have no doubts about the reality of my surroundings and myself.

On the way to the waterfall at Huangguoshu, I arrive at Longgong. Small colourful sightseeing boats drift on the mirror surface of the unfathomably deep water. The sightseers scrambling onto the boats don't seem to notice the hole by the crack in the heavily wooded cliff and on reaching this spot the smooth water pours thunderously into it. It is only after getting to the foot of the mountain where the mountain torrent roars as it charges out that one realizes how dangerous it is. The sightseeing boats however sometimes row as close as three to five metres from the hole, it is like playing a game before a drowning disaster. This is all in broad daylight but while I am sitting in the boat I can't help wondering about this sort of reality.

Along the road, the rapids sending forth white spray in the abundant mountain streams, the round mountain tops and the clear sky are simply too bright, and the slate rooftops shimmer in the sunlight. The lines are clear and distinct, like the colour paintings executed in the *gongbi* style. Shaking up and down in the speeding bus on the mountain road induces a sense of loss of gravity. I seem to levitate. I don't know where I'm drifting, and I don't know what it is that I am searching for.

23

You say you had a dream, just now, while you were asleep on her. She says yes, it lasted only a moment, she even spoke to you, you didn't seem to be fully asleep. She says she touched you while you were dreaming, she could feel you pulsating, for just a minute. You say yes, an instant ago everything was so vivid. You feel the warmth of her breasts, the heaving of her abdomen. She says she held you and felt you pulsating. You say you saw a black sea rising, its flat surface slowly, inexorably, towering up. When it was upon you, the horizon between the sky and the sea was squeezed to nothing and the black sea occupied the whole of your vision. She says you were asleep pressed against her breasts. You say you felt her breasts swelling, like a black tide, a surging tide, like surging lust, growing higher and higher, wanting to engulf you, you say it was disturbing. She says, you were nestled in my arms, like a sweet child, but you began to fiercely pulsate. You say you felt somehow oppressed, the swelling, inexorably spreading tide turned into a huge flat rippleless tide surging towards you, flat and smooth like black satin without sides spilling endlessly then turning into a black waterfall, pouring down from somewhere high out of sight and plummeting unobstructed into a bottomless abyss. She says you're really silly, let me caress you. You say you saw a black sea, a tide rising from the flat surface, swelling, spreading, occupying the whole of your vision, broaching no resistance. You were in my arms, she says, it was me embracing you with my warmth, you know it was my breasts, my breasts swelling. You say it wasn't. She says it was, it was me holding you, feeling you pulsate more and more fiercely. You say, in the surging black tide, there was a silver eel, moist, smooth, swimming like a flash of lightning, it too was totally swallowed by the black tide. She says she saw it, felt it. Afterwards, on the beach, after the tide finally subsided, there remained only an endless stretch, flat and covered with fine sand. As the tide receded, leaving only froth, you saw black human bodies kneeling, sprawling, entwined, writhing, humped over one another, turning and twisting together, then goring one another, soundlessly on the vast beach, where there was not even the sound of the wind, twisting and entwining, rising and falling, heads and feet, arms and legs inextricably intertwined, like black walruses but not completely, rolling, rising and falling, then again rolling, rising, falling. She says she felt you fiercely pulsating then going quiet, then pulsating again, then going quiet, she felt all this. You say you saw the bodies of human-like sea animals or animal-like humans, black, sleek bodies with a sheen like black satin yet like moist fur, twisting, rising and then falling, all the time rolling, all the time inextricably entwined so it was impossible to tell whether they were goring or slaughtering one another, there was no sound, not the slightest sound, you saw it so vividly, on the desolate beach where there was not even the sound of the wind, far away, twisting, rolling bodies, soundless. She says it was you pulsating, pulsating fiercely, growing quiet, resting, again pulsating and again growing quiet. You say you saw black sleek bodies of human-like sea animals or animal-like humans, gleaming with a sheen, like black satin yet like moist fur, twisting and rolling, rising then falling, all the time inextricably entwined, never stopping, slowly, idling, goring or slaughtering one another, you saw all this vividly, on the flat beach, in some far away place, they were clearly rolling about. She says you were lying on her, pressed against her breasts, like a sweet child, and you were sweating all over. You say you had a dream, just now, while you were lying on her. She says it was only for a minute, she heard your breathing next to her ear. You say you saw it so vividly, you can still see it, the black rising surface of the sea slowly, inexorably surging towards you, you are disturbed. She says you silly child, you don't understand anything.

But you say you really saw it so clearly, just surging towards you, occupying your whole vision, that endless black tide, surging, inexorably, soundlessly, smooth like black satin spilling yet like a waterfall, black, unobstructed, without spray, falling into the depths of the darkness, you saw it all. She says her breasts were pressed hard against you, your back was covered in sweat. That smooth black wall looming up and pouring down was disturbing, you instinctively closed your eyes and while aware of your own existence, helplessly allowed it to pour irretrievably away, you saw everything, you saw nothing, the sea tilted, you fell in and floated up, black animals, goring or slaughtering one another, forever twisting, desolate beach, no wind. Cradled in her arms, the physical contact makes you recall all these minute details but you cannot go through it all again. She says she wants to feel you pulsating again, she wants to, and she also wants the soundless battle of those twisting human animals to be a slaughter, moving entwined, on the vast flat beach with fine sand and with only froth remaining, she wants, and she still wants. When the black tide recedes, what remains on the beach?

24

It is a carved wooden mask of an animal head with a human face, two horns protrude from the top of the head and alongside these are a pair of smaller, sharp horns, so it cannot represent a domestic cow or goat. It would have to be some wild animal, the demonic aura of the face definitely doesn't have a deer-like docility and the places for docile deer's eyes have no eyeballs and instead are two round gaping holes, eye sockets jutting out. Beneath the brow bone is a deep furrow, the forehead is pointed, and incisions radiating upwards from the centre of the forehead and the brow bone make the eye sockets even more prominent. It is thus that the eyes terrify the enemy, which is precisely how it is when beast and man confront each other.

When the mask is worn, the eyes in the darkness would shine with an animal glow through the gaping holes in the protruding eye sockets. Especially with the lower eye sockets hollowed out into two black crescent-shaped furrows pointing upwards, it looks even more evil. The nose, lips, cheekbones and chin, all executed with delicate precision, are those of an old man with a sunken mouth. The cleft on the chin has not been forgotten and the dry, shrunken skin clearly shows the bone structure. The lines of the prominent bone structure have been carved with simplicity and forcefulness, so it is not just an old man but one exuding a spirit of determination. At both sides of the tightly pursed lips are two carved sharp fangs running right up to the sides of the nostrils. The nostrils are flared and produce a definite look of scorn and derision. The teeth haven't fallen out from old age but the front teeth have been knocked out and fitted with fangs. The two small holes at the corners of the tightly pursed mouth probably once had tufts of tiger whiskers sticking out from them. This very intelligent human face is at the same time full of animal savagery.

The sides of the nostrils, the corners of the mouth, the upper and lower lips, the cheekbones, the forehead and the middle of the forehead indicate that the carver had a sound knowledge of the human head. Looking at it closely again, it is only the eye sockets and pointed forehead that are exaggerated, the thrust of the carving of the flesh gives it a sort of tenseness. Without the tiger whiskers, it is a replica of the face of primitive man with markings on it. Their understanding of nature and the self is fully encompassed in the round black holes of the eye sockets. The two holes at the corners of the mouth reveal nature's scorn for man and show man's fear of nature. The face also accurately expresses the animal nature in human beings and the fear of this animal nature within themselves.

Man cannot cast off this mask, it is a projection of his own flesh and spirit. He can no longer remove from his own face this mask which has already grown like skin and flesh so he is always startled as if disbelieving this is himself, but this is in fact himself. He cannot remove this mask, and this is agony. But having manifested itself as his mask, it cannot be obliterated, because the mask is a replica of himself. It has no will of its own, or one could say it has a will but no means of expression and so prefers not to have a will. Therefore it has left man with an eternal face with which he can examine himself in amazement.

This is indeed a masterpiece. I found it amongst the holdings of a museum in Guiyang, at the time it was closed for renovations. Through the help of friends, I got letters of introduction, then had an acquaintance phone on some pretext which eventually moved the deputy director of the museum. He is a good-natured cadre, quite fat, and always holding a mug of tea in his hand. I think he is already quite advanced in years and probably near retirement. He got someone to open two big storerooms for me so that I could go through the shelves piled with bronze weapons and assorted earthenware pots. This was of course magnanimous treatment but I didn't discover anything memorable. So taking advantage of his good nature, I made a second visit. He told me they had too many artefacts and he didn't know what I really wanted to see and suggested I look through the catalogues. Fortunately, a small photograph was attached to each of the cards. In the file for religious and superstitious items, I found this set of exorcist masks. He said these were locked away and have never been displayed, if I really wanted to see them there were certain procedures to be followed and a time would have to be fixed. I went again for a third visit. This good-natured director has a big crate brought out for me. As the items are taken out one by one, I am terror-stricken.

Altogether there are more than twenty masks, it seems that they were confiscated as superstitious objects by the Public Security Bureau at the beginning of the fifties. Some people at the time had in fact performed a good deed. Instead of their being chopped up and used as firewood, they were delivered to the museum and so avoided the ravages of the Cultural Revolution. According to the museum archaeologist these were made at the end of the Qing Dynasty. The colour has mostly peeled off and the remaining bits of coloured lacquer have gone black and dull. The card indicated that the masks had been collected in Huangping and Tianzhu counties in the upper reaches of the Wushui and Qingshui rivers, a region inhabited by a mixture of Han, Miao, Tong and Tujia nationalities. I subsequently travel to these places.

25

In the orange-yellow sunlight of early morning, the mountain scenery is fresh and the air is clean, and it doesn't seem that you've had a sleepless night. You have your arm around soft gentle shoulders and her head is resting on you. You don't know whether or not she is the woman you dreamt of during the night, and can't tell which of them is more real, you only know that right now she has willingly come with you and isn't worried about where you are taking her.

Following the mountain road you come to a slope which turns out to be flat embankments, layer upon layer of broad terraced fields. Here stand two stone pillars which in former years must have been a gateway and nearby there are the remains of stone lions and stone drums. You say this had once been an imposing family. Going through the memorial gate you find courtyard after courtyard, the whole compound extending over one *li*, but it is now all paddy field.

When the Long Hairs – the Taipings – revolted, did they come across from Wuyizhen and torch all of this? she asks.

You say the fire came later. First it was when Second Master of the main branch of the family became a court official. He was promoted to minister for punishments then suddenly was implicated in a salt smuggling case. In fact, rather than corruption and breaking the law, it was a case of the emperor being addle-headed and stupidly believing the eunuchs that he was plotting with the empress dowager's family to usurp power. The outcome was that the whole family was hauled out and beheaded. In this big household of three hundred, some of the women were allocated to officials as servants and the rest, even babies were slaughtered. This was really to be without progeny, so how could this compound avoid being razed?

Or the story could go like this. If the stone tortoise half-buried far away over there counts as part of the same group of buildings as the stone gate, drums and lions, this area wouldn't have been living quarters but would have been graves. Of course this tomb with a passage stretching for one *li* would have been quite splendid. However this is hard to verify as the stone epitaph on the back of the tortoise was taken away by a peasant family and smashed up for a millstone during the time of the land reforms. The stone base was left buried in the fields: it was solid and too heavy to be put to good use because it would have been too hard to shift. Now this tomb obviously wouldn't have been for burying ordinary folk, and village gentry with even larger estates wouldn't have dared to make such a display of extravagance unless they were nobles or high officials.

It must have been a person who played a meritorious role in the founding of the Ming Dynasty, someone who had joined Zhu Yuanzhang's rebellion to drive off the Tartars. However most of the meritorious officials who helped to establish the dynasty failed to die a peaceful death. To be able to die of old age and be put to rest with a lavish funeral required exceptional talent. The owner of this tomb saw loyal generals of the emperor murdered one by one and spent his days in fear. He plucked up the courage to present the emperor with a petition for retirement, saying: Peace and prosperity have been achieved in the empire, the Imperial Grace reigns supreme and civil officials and generals fill the court. This insignificant subject lacks talent and is past half of a hundred years of age. His aged mother has spent her life all alone and years of hard work have resulted in illness. As not many years remain, he hangs up his cap of office to return to the village to fulfil his filial duties. By the time the petition had been conveyed to the emperor, he had already left the capital. The emperor was moved and of course handsomely rewarded him and on the man's death gave personal instructions for the building of this enormous tomb to commend him to later generations.

There could also be another version of the story. It varies significantly from the historical records, and is closer to *biji* fiction. According to this version, when the owner of the tomb saw the emperor purging the old guard purportedly to rectify court policies, he used the pretext of hastening to his father's funeral to relinquish his powers and flee to his village. Afterwards he feigned madness and refused to see outsiders. The emperor couldn't allay his suspicions and despatched an officer of the palace guards who after crossing many mountains to get there, found the gates bolted. He announced that he had come to convey instructions from the emperor and forthwith charged in. Suddenly, the man crawled out on all fours from an inner room and came barking like a dog at him. The investigator looked on in disbelief and ordered him to get dressed and present himself at the capital. However, the man promptly went off, sniffed at a heap of dog shit by the wall and put down his head to eat it up. The palace guard could do nothing but report back to the emperor. It was only then that the emperor's suspicions were allayed and when the man died, he presented him with a lavish burial. In fact the heap of dog shit was ground sesame seeds mixed with molasses made by his favourite maidservant, but how could the emperor have known this?

The county produced a village scholar who was determined to make a name for himself. After spending half his life in the civil service examination halls, finally at the age of fifty-two he managed to get his name on the list of successful candidates, albeit amongst the names at the bottom of the list. After that he spent all his days waiting for an appointment, or even half of an appointment, in the bureaucracy. Unknown to him his unmarried daughter was embroiled in a romance with one of her young maternal uncles and was pregnant. The silly girl thought that by taking bezoar she could induce an abortion and instead had diarrhoea for two months. She got thinner while her belly got bigger. Eventually her parents found out and there was utter chaos. To salvage the family reputation the old man bestowed death upon her in the same manner as emperors would deal with corrupt officials and rebels – he had his unchaste daughter nailed alive into a coffin.

This news spread far and wide and reached the county town where the magistrate, who was worried by the lack of morality in the locality and lived in constant fear of losing his black satin cap of office, seized upon the incident as being typical. He reported it to the provincial government which in turn reported it to the court.

The emperor, in the embrace of his favourite concubines, had for a long time not bothered with trifling court matters. However, one day when he was feeling bored he thought to ask about the common people. The court officials reported this interesting news item and when the emperor heard he gave an involuntary sigh: This is indeed a family of moral virtue. The words of the imperial sigh, of great import and immediacy, were conveyed to the provincial government. The governor immediately wrote instructions: There can be no delay with what the emperor has decreed. Erect a tablet and hang it high up to inform villagers far and wide. A fast horse took the despatch to the county yamen. The magistrate quickly sounded the gongs and got into his sedan chair, preceded by an official runner shouting to clear people off the road. How could this venal old Confucian scholar not be moved to tears as he knelt to hear the emperor's decree. The magistrate then sternly declared: Each of the Emperor's words, "Family of Moral Virtue", is precious, now hasten to set up a memorial arch so that they will be recorded in perpetuity and never forgotten! His virtuous action had moved heaven and earth and brought honour and glory to his ancestors and the whole clan. The old man purchased on credit tens of baskets of grain to hire workers to prepare slabs of stone, and day and night he supervised the meticulous carving of the words. He laboured for half of the year and before the winter solstice, when the work was completed, he laid out a feast for his neighbours to show his gratitude. At the end of the year when the accounts were finalized, needless to say, the whole year's income had been used to pay off debts, but he was still short by forty ounces of stamped silver ingots and seventeen strings of cash for the interest. He then caught a chill, became bedridden, barely managed to hang on through the first month of the New Year and died just before the planting of the new grain seedlings.

This memorial arch still stands at the east entrance to the village and lazy herd boys always hitch the ropes of the cows on them when they sneak off. However, when the director of the revolutionary committee came to inspect the countryside he found the wording on the horizontal tablet between the pillars quite inappropriate and had the secretary inform the local village secretary. It was changed to: "In Agriculture Learn From Dazhai", and the couplet on the stone pillars: "Loyalty and Filial Piety Long Transmitted in the Family" and "Poetry and History Long Continuing for Many Generations" was changed to the slogans "Plant Fields for the Revolution" and "For the Greater Community not the Individual". Who could have imagined that the Dazhai model would later be called bogus, that the fields would be returned to peasant ownership, that those who worked more would get more, and that nobody would pay any attention to the writing on the memorial arch? The more clever of the descendants of the family have gone into business and become rich, how could they spare the time to think about changing it all back?

At the back of the arch, at the door of the first house, an old woman sits pounding in a wooden bucket with a stick. A sandy coloured dog comes and hangs around, sniffing here and there. The old woman holds up the stick and savagely berates it: "I'll burn you to death with the chilli if you don't get lost!"

Anyway, you are not a sandy coloured dog, so you keep walking up, and address her.

"Venerable elder, are you making chilli sauce?"

The old woman neither says yes or no, just looks up at you then puts down her head and goes on pounding the fresh chilli in the bucket.

"Could you please tell me if there's a place called Lingyan here?" You know that to ask her about a far away place like Lingshan would be a waste of time. You say you've come from a village called Mengjia down below, and people there say there's a place called Lingyan up this way.

It is only then that she stops pounding to look the two of you over, especially scrutinizing her and then turning to you.

"Are the two of you wishing for a son?" she asks in an odd way.

She gives you a tug on the quiet. You've made a stupid blunder, so you go on to ask, "What's Lingyan got to do with wishing for a son?"

"What's it got to do with it?" The old woman raises her voice. "It's a place women go to. They only go there to burn incense when they haven't given birth to a son!" The old woman can't stop cackling, it's as if someone is tickling her. "So the young woman here is wishing for a son?" The old woman turns to caustically confront her.

"We're sightseeing. We want to have a look everywhere," you are obliged to explain.

"What's there to see in this village? It was just the same a few days ago. Several couples from the city tormented the whole village with the havoc they created!"

"What did they do?" you can't help asking.

"They brought along this electric box and made the mountains ring with the wailing of ghosts and the howling of wolves. They had their arms around one another right on the threshing square and they were all wriggling their bottoms. It was really wicked!"

"Oh, were they looking for Lingyan too?" You are becoming interested.

"Why do you keep asking about that demon-infested place Lingyan? Didn't I tell you just now? That's where women go to burn incense when they want to have a son."

"Why can't men go there?"

"If you're not afraid of evil vapours then go. Who's stopping you?"

She gives you a tug, but you say you still can't understand.

"Then get yourself splashed with blood!" You can't tell if the old woman is warning you or cursing you.

"She's saying it's taboo for men," she explains to you.

You say there are no taboos.

"She's talking about menstrual blood," she whispers in your ear, warning you to leave right away.

"What's so special about menstrual blood?" You say even dog's blood doesn't worry you. "Let's go and see what this Lingyan really is."

She says forget it and says she doesn't want to go. You ask why she's afraid, she says she's afraid of what the old woman is saying.

"There aren't all these regulations, let's go!" you say to her, and then ask the old woman how to get there.

"Wicked people, let the demons get the pair of you!" the old woman says to your back, this time cursing.

She says she's afraid, she has a premonition of something bad. You ask if she's afraid she will meet a shaman. You tell her that in this mountain village all the old women are shamans and all the young women are seductresses.

"Does that mean I am too?" she asks you.

"Why not? Aren't you a woman?"

"Then you're a demon!" she counters.

"All men are demons in women's eyes."

"Then am I the companion of a demon?" she asks sticking up her chin.

"A demon with a seductress," you say.

She chuckles and looks happy, but she pleads with you not to go to such a place.

"What could happen?" you stop and ask her. "Will it bring misfortune? Will it bring disaster? What's there to be frightened about?"

She snuggles against you and says as long as she's with you she will be all right. But you can tell there is already a black shadow in her heart. You strive to dispel it and deliberately talk loudly.

26

I don't know if you have ever observed this strange thing, the self. Often the more you look the more it doesn't seem to be like it, and the more you look the more it isn't it. It's just like when one is lying on the grass and staring at a cloud – at first it's like a camel, then like a woman, and when you look again it becomes an old man with a long beard, but this doesn't last because clouds are transforming every instant.

Suppose you use a lavatory in an old house and you happen to look at the water stains on the walls – every day you go there are changes in the stains. First you see a face, when you look again it's a dog dragging a sausage, afterwards it turns into a tree, there is a woman under the tree and she's sitting on a skinny horse. After a couple of weeks, or perhaps after several months, one morning, you are constipated and you suddenly find that the stain is in fact still a face.

When you are lying on the bed looking at the ceiling, the light projected onto the white ceiling too can undergo many transformations. If you concentrate on looking at yourself, you will find that your self will gradually separate from the self you are familiar with and multiply into many startling forms. So if I have to make a summary of myself, it terrifies me. I don't know which of the many faces represents me more and the more closely I look the clearer the transformations become, and finally only bewilderment remains.

You could wait, wait until the stain on the wall again turns into a human face, or you could hope, hope that it would one day turn out to have a particular form. But in my experience, it grows and grows but often not as you wish and moreover, mostly, contrary to what you wish. It is a monster child which you find impossible to accept, yet ultimately it was born of the self and has to be accepted.

I once looked at the photo of me on the monthly bus ticket I had thrown on the table. At first I thought I had a charming smile, then I thought the smile at the corners of the eyes was rather of scorn, arrogance and indifference, all deriving from self-love, self-adoration, and a sense of superiority. But there was also an anxiety which betrayed acute loneliness, and fleeting snatches of terror – certainly not a winner – and a bitterness which stifled the common smile of unthinking happiness and doubted that sort of happiness. This was very scary, it was like a void, a sense of falling without somewhere to land, and I didn't want to go on looking at the photo.

After that I went about observing other people, but whenever I observed other people I found this detestable omniscient self of mine interfering, and to this day there is not one face it hasn't interfered with. This is a serious problem, for when I am scrutinizing someone else, I am at the same time scrutinizing myself. I search for faces I like, or expressions I can tolerate, so I can't get rid of myself. I can't find people with whom I can identify, I search without success, everywhere: in railway waiting rooms, in train carriages, on boats, in food shops and parks, and even when out walking on the streets, I am always trying to capture a familiar face or a familiar build, or looking for some sign which can call up submerged memories. When I am observing others I always treat the other person as a mirror for looking inwardly at myself. The observations are inevitably affected by my state of mind at a particular time. Even when I am observing a woman, my senses react to her and my experiences and imagination are activated in making a judgement. My understanding of others, including women, is actually superficial and arbitrary. Women I like are inevitably illusions I have created to delude myself, and this is my tragedy. As a result, my relationships with women inevitably fail. On the other hand, if I were a woman and living with a man, this would also be a worry. The problem is the awakened self in the inner mind, this is the monster which torments me no end. People love the self yet mutilate the self. Arrogance, pride, complacency or anxiety, jealousy and hatred, all spring from this. The self is in fact the source of mankind's misery. So, does this unhappy conclusion mean that the awakened self should therefore be killed?

Thus Buddha told the boddhisatva: the myriad phenomena are vanity, the absence of phenomena is also vanity.

27

She says she wants to return to the carefree time of her childhood, when she went to school with her hair combed and perfectly plaited by her maternal grandmother, and everyone used to say her shiny long plaits were beautiful. After her grandmother died, she didn't wear her hair in plaits anymore but in protest cut it short so that it couldn't even be put into two bunches which was the style in the Red Guard period. At the time a neighbour had reported her father and he was locked up in the building where he worked and not allowed to go home. Her mother took him a change of clothes every two weeks, but she was never allowed to go along. Afterwards she and her mother were forced to go to a farming village as she didn't have the right qualifications to be a Red Guard. She says the happiest time in her life was when she had long plaits. Her maternal grandmother was like an old cat, always dozing by her side, and she felt secure.

She says she is old, she means her heart is old and nothing can excite her. Before, she would weep copious tears straight from her heart over nothing, it was effortless and soothing.

She says she had a girlfriend called Lingling and that they were good friends from childhood days. She was always so sweet, she would only have to look at you, and a dimple would appear on her face. Now she is a mother and she has become lethargic, talks in a monotone, and slurs her speech like she's half asleep. But when she was a girl she used to chatter like a sparrow and together they would talk nonsense all day without stopping. She says Lingling wanted to be outside playing all the time. But, she says, whenever it started raining she would become morose and say I want to strangle you: she would press hard on my neck and it really hurt.

One summer night, sitting by the lake, looking at the sky, she told Lingling she wanted to snuggle and Lingling said she wanted to be a little mother. They giggled and jostled one another, it was before the moon came out. She asks if you know the night sky is grey-blue when the moon is about to come out, oh, the moon gliding out of its corona, she asks if you have ever seen it, surging and billowing then spreading flat like a rolling mist. She says they even heard the sound of the moon flowing over the tops of the trees which looked like rippling waterweeds in a flowing stream, and they both wept. Their tears welled up like the waters of a spring, like the flowing of the moonlight, and their hearts felt sublime. Lingling's hair, she can feel it even now, brushed lightly against her face, their cheeks were pressed together and they were both flushed. There is a type of lotus, she says, not the water lily or the common lotus, it's smaller than a lotus and bigger than a water lily. It opens at night and its gold and red stamens glow in the dark. The pink petals are fleshy, like Lingling's ears when she was young but without the fine hairs, and they are shiny like the nails of her small hands, ah, at that time her trimmed long nails were like sea shells. However, the pink petals are not bright, they are thick like ears and tremble as they slowly open.

You say you see it, you see the petals trembling as they slowly open, the velvety gold stamens at the centre, also trembling. Yes, she says. You hold her hands. No, don't, she says, she wants you to listen to her. She says she feels solemn, it's something you wouldn't understand. But this doesn't mean you're not willing to understand, nor that you're not willing to understand her. She says this solemn feeling has a sacred and pure music. She adores the Holy Mother, the way the Holy Mother holds the Child, her eyes looking down, the delicate fingers of her gentle hands. She says she too wants to be a mother, to nurse her baby, a pure, warm, plump life, sucking her milk. It is a pure feeling, do you understand? You say you are trying to understand. That means you don't, you are so dense, she says.

154

She says a thick layer of curtain hangs there, then layer upon layer, and walking inside is like gliding, as one lightly pushes apart the silk velvety black-green curtains and passes through, not necessarily seeing anyone, threading one's way between rippling curtains. There are no sounds, all sound is absorbed by the curtains. Only a single note, a pure note, slowly wafts through, filtered by the curtains so that there are no impurities. In the darkness there is a source emitting a gentle light which gives a subtle glow to places it flows over.

She says she had a beautiful paternal aunt who often used to walk about the house in front of her wearing just a bra and a pair of scanty briefs. She always wanted to go up and touch her bare thighs but didn't ever dare. She says at the time she was just a skinny child and thought she'd never grow up beautiful like her aunt. Her aunt was surrounded by boyfriends and regularly received a number of love letters all at the one time. She was a performer and had quite a lot of men courting her, she always said they bored her but she actually liked them. Afterwards she married an officer in the army who kept a strict watch over her – if she got home a bit late he'd interrogate her, and he even struck her. She says at the time she really couldn't understand why her aunt didn't leave him and put an end to that sort of abuse.

She also says she once was in love with a teacher, he taught her class mathematics, yes, it was purely childish infatuation. She adored listening to the sound of his voice when he was teaching. Mathematics was dry and boring but because she loved his deep voice she was very conscientious in her work. Once she got a mark of eighty-nine for an exam and started crying. When the marked papers were handed back she broke into tears when she got hers. The teacher took it back and said he'd have another look at it. He re-marked it and gave her a few more marks but she said she didn't want them, she didn't want them, threw the exam paper on the floor and couldn't stop bawling in front of the whole class. This was quite disgraceful and after that she ignored him, refusing even to say hello. After the summer vacation, he no longer took this class of hers but she still thought of him, she liked his deep voice, that deep rich voice.

28

A red streamer stretches across the road on the Shiqian to Jiangkou highway. The bus I am on is intercepted by a small van and boarded by a man and a woman, each with red armbands: wearing a red armband gives people a special status and they can become intimidating. I thought they were chasing or arresting someone but luckily it turns out that they are only checking if people have tickets – they are inspectors from the Highways Management Department.

Soon after the bus started, at the first stop, the driver had checked the tickets. A peasant tried to slip away but the driver shut the door on his hemp sack, forcing him to pay ten *yuan* for a ticket before the sack was thrown off the bus. Then, ignoring the peasant's swearing and cursing, the driver put his foot on the accelerator. The bus started moving and the peasant had to quickly jump out of the way. As there are not many buses in mountain districts, sitting at the steering wheel confers supreme authority and the passengers can't conceal their hostility.

None of us imagined that the couple wearing red armbands would be even more overbearing than the driver. The man seizes a passenger's ticket and crooks a finger to summon the driver, "Get down, get down!"

The driver meekly gets off the bus. The woman writes out a ticket fining him three hundred *yuan*, a hundred times more than the three *yuan* ticket he had missed tearing a corner off. One thing will overcome another: this principle isn't restricted to the natural world, it applies also to the human world.

At first we hear the driver outside the bus explaining that he doesn't know the passenger and couldn't possibly re-sell the ticket, then he starts arguing with the inspectors. Either because the driver's income is more than theirs under the new work contract system or else to show the might of their red armbands, they are quite inflexible and stick rigidly to the rules. After ranting and raving, the driver puts on a forlorn look and desperately pleads with them. This goes on for a full hour and the bus still can't go. The persons giving the fine and the person fined have forgotten about the passengers locked in the bus who all this time have been undergoing punishment by being cooked in the blazing sun! Their hostility towards the driver gradually transforms into a hatred for the red armbands. It is only when everyone starts knocking on the windows and shouting their protests that the woman realizes they are targeting her. She quickly tears off the ticket and thrusts it into the driver's hand and the man signals with the little flag for the inspection van to drive over. Finally, they get in and depart, leaving behind a trail of dust in a show of might.

However, the driver squats on his haunches and refuses to get up. The passengers poke their heads out of the windows and of course say nice things to him to make him feel better. Another half hour passes and they gradually lose patience and start yelling and shouting at him. At this, he reluctantly gets on the bus.

Before long we come to a village. No-one is getting on or off but the bus pulls up, the front and back doors open, and the driver jumps out of the cabin and says, "All out, all out! We're not going on, the bus has to refuel." He then goes off on his own. At first the passengers stay on the bus complaining, but as no-one is there to take any notice, one by one they get out.

At the side of the highway, apart from the little restaurant, there is only a small shop for cigarettes, alcohol and odds and ends. It has an awning and also sells tea.

The sun is already moving towards the west and it is scorching hot even under the awning. I drink two bowls of cold tea one after the other but still the bus hasn't refuelled and there is no sign of the driver.

Oddly, all the passengers who were drinking tea under the awning or resting under the trees have wandered off.

I go into the little restaurant to look for them but there are only empty square tables and wooden stools, I can't work out where everyone has gone. I go looking in the kitchen and find the driver there with two plates of saut ed vegetables and a bottle of liquor on the table in front of him. The proprietor is sitting there with him and chatting.

"What time will the bus be going?" I ask in a justifiably unfriendly manner.

"Tomorrow at six in the morning," he answers, also not in a particularly friendly manner.

"Why?"

"Can't you see I'm drinking alcohol?" he asks me instead.

"Look, I didn't fine you. You're upset but you shouldn't be taking it out on the passengers, you know," I say, restraining my temper.

"Do you know there's a penalty for driving after drinking alcohol?" He reeks of alcohol and looks totally irresponsible. As I look at the beady eyes under his furrowed brows as he eats, I am seized by an indefinable rage and have the urge to grab the bottle and smash it over his head. I quickly leave the restaurant.

When I go back to the highway and see the empty bus by the road, I suddenly realize that there isn't in fact any rationality in the human world. If I hadn't got on the bus, wouldn't I have avoided all this stress? There would have been no driver, no passengers, no ticket inspectors and no fine. But the problem is I still have to find somewhere to spend the night.

I go back to the tea stall and see a fellow passenger is there.

"The damn bus isn't going," I say.

"I know," he says.

"Where are you spending the night?"

"I'm trying to find somewhere."

"Where have all the passengers gone?" I ask.

He says they're locals, they always have somewhere to go and time is of little consequence for them, a day earlier or a day later doesn't matter. However, he has to get to the county town by this evening so that he can go into the mountains early the next morning. He's been sent by the Guiyang Zoo which had received a telegram from Yinhong county saying the peasants had caught this half-bird-half-fish creature up in the mountains. If he goes any later this creature might die.

"So be it, if it dies," I say. "Can they fine you?"

"It's not that," he says. "You don't understand."

I say it's impossible to understand the world.

He says he's talking about this half-bird-half-fish creature, not about the world.

I say there's no great difference between this half-bird-half-fish creature and the world.

He takes out the telegram and shows it to me. It says, "The villagers of this county have caught alive a strange creature that is half bird and half fish. Come as quickly as possible to identify it." He also says the zoo once got a telegram saying that a forty- or fifty-catty giant salamander had been washed down a mountain stream, but by the time the person despatched arrived the fish not only had died but had been divided up and eaten by the villagers. It was impossible to reconstruct the corpse, so a specimen couldn't be made. This time he will wait on the highway to see if he can get a lift from a passing vehicle.

I stand with him for quite a while on the highway. A few trucks drive past and time after time he waves the telegram, but no-one takes any notice. It's not my mission to save this half-bird-half-fish creature or the world, so why am I here eating dust? I may as well go into the restaurant to have something to eat.

I ask the woman who brings out the food if I can stay the night. She seems to think I'm asking her if she's taking customers and, glaring at me, says, "Can't you see? This is a restaurant!"

I swear a silent oath to myself that I will not get on that bus again, but there is at least a hundred kilometres to go and it will take at least two days on foot. I go back to the highway, the person from the zoo is no longer there. I wonder if he got a lift.

The sun is about to set and the benches at the tea stall have been taken inside. The pounding of drums comes from below the highway – something must be happening. I look down at the bottom of the slope and before me are the tiled roofs of houses with cobblestoned spaces in between. Further on are layers of paddy fields, the early crop has been harvested and in some of the fields the black soil has been ploughed.

I walk down the slope, following the sound of the drums. A peasant goes by along the embankment with his trouser legs rolled up, his calves covered in mud. A little further on a child is leading a water buffalo on a rope towards a pond near the village. I look at the smoke rising from the chimneys over the rooftops below and a peacefulness rises in my heart.

I stop to listen to the sound of the drums from the village. There is no driver, no inspectors with red armbands, no infuriating bus and no telegram to go as quickly as possible to identify this half-bird-half-fish creature: everything belongs to nature. I think back to those years when I had to work as a peasant in the villages, if things hadn't changed later on, wouldn't I still be working in the fields just like them? I would also be up to the calves in mud, after work I wouldn't bother to wash, and I would no doubt be without my present anxieties. Nothing could be more natural than the evening scene of smoke from chimneys, tiled rooftops, and the near and yet distant sound of drums.

The drumbeats repeat *nan-nan na-na* over and over and seem to be telling a wordless legend. The colour of the water and the glow of the sky, the blackened rooftops, the pale grey cobblestones vaguely visible in the courtyards between the houses, the soil warmed by the sun, the snorting of water buffaloes, the sound of garrulous talk coming from the houses, the evening breeze, the rustling of the leaves on the trees above, the smell of the paddy hay and the cow sheds, the sound of water swilling, the creaking of a door hinge or a wooden pulley over a well, the chirping of sparrows and the cooing somewhere of a pair of pigeons nesting, the shrill voices of women or children, the feeling of sadness and the chirping of winged insects, the soil underfoot dry and hard on the surface but crumbling and loose underneath, submerged lust and the thirst for happiness, tremors in the mind induced by the sound of the drums, the desire to be barefoot and sitting on a doorsill worn black and shiny by all the people who have sat upon it, all suddenly converge.

29

The shaman of Tianmenguan has sent someone to the carpenter's yard to get the old man to make the head of the Goddess Tianluo. The shaman will come in person on the twenty-seventh day of the twelfth month to invite the goddess to receive offerings at his altar. The messenger has brought a live goose as a deposit and the work is to be completed on schedule. The old man will then be given a jar of rice wine and half of a pig's head which will be plenty to see him through to the New Year. The old man is petrified and realizes that he doesn't have many days. The Goddess Guanyin rules over the living and the Goddess Tianluo rules over the dead: the goddess is coming to hasten the end of his life.

Over the past few years, apart from the carpentry work, he has made quite a number of carvings. For people's homes he has made the god of wealth, the laughing arhat, the monk gatherer of vegetarian food, and the honest judge; for the exorcist performance troupe he has carved a whole set of masks: the half-man-half-god Zhang the Clearer of Mountains, the half-man-half-animal horse general, and half-man-half-demon goblins; and for people from outside the mountains he has carved the crooked mouthed Qin boy for them to amuse themselves. He has also carved the Goddess Guanyin but no-one has ever asked him to carve the malevolent Goddess Tianluo who controls people's fates. The goddess has come to take his life. How could he have been so muddle-headed as to agree? He blames himself for getting too old, for being too greedy. As long as people will pay he carves anything they want. Everyone thinks his carvings are like the real thing, one can tell at a glance it's the god of wealth, the clever official, the laughing arhat, the monk gatherer of vegetarian food, the honest judge, the impetuous general who clears mountains, the horse general, the goblins, or the Goddess Guanyin. He has never seen the Goddess Guanyin, he only knows she is the goddess who brings sons. A woman came from outside the mountains with two lengths of red cloth and a bundle of incense. She had heard that the rock where the mountain people made offerings to their ancestors was efficacious, so she came to the mountains to pray for a son. When she saw he could make figures of divinities, she asked him to make her a Guanyin and stayed the night in his house. She was up early, very happy, and took with her the Guanyin he'd spent the whole night carving for her. However, he has never made the Goddess Tianluo because no-one has ever asked him and because this malevolent spirit is only worshipped at the altars of shamans. He can't stop shivering and breaks out in a cold sweat all over: he knows that the Goddess Tianluo has already attached herself to his body and is just waiting to take his life.

He clambers onto a pile of timber to get the piece of little-leaf box airing on a cross beam. This wood has a very fine grain and won't warp or crack, he has kept this piece for some years because he didn't want to use it on something ordinary. After reaching for the wood, he slips and the whole pile of timber collapses. He is frightened out of his wits but his mind is lucid and, clutching the wood, he sits on the gnarled maple root he uses for chopping hay in the shed. For a small job like this usually he only needs to think a little, then he'd be ready to start. Shavings would start curling up the blade and when he blew it off the face would appear, it was easy. However he hasn't ever carved the Goddess Tianluo and clutching the piece of wood, he sits there in a daze shivering and feeling chilly spasms shooting through his body. Finally, he puts down the piece of wood, goes into the house, and sits by the fire on the round stump which is black with grease and smoke and shiny from being sat upon. He fears it's really the end for him and that he won't get through to the end of the year. On the twenty-seventh of the twelfth month, not waiting until the fifteenth of the first month, he stops breathing. It had been decided that he should not be permitted to pass through the New Year.

He had committed too many wrongdoings, she says.

Did the Goddess Tianluo say so?

Yes, she said he wasn't a good old man, he was an old man who wasn't content with his lot.

Maybe.

He knew in his heart how many wrongdoings he had committed.

Did he seduce the woman who came to pray for a son?

The woman was a slut, she was quite willing.

Then it doesn't count as a wrongdoing, does it?

It can be left out of the count.

Then his wrongdoing was—

He raped a mute girl.

In his shed?

He didn't dare do that, it was while he was away working. These itinerant craftsmen are out on their own all year round and earn quite a bit of money through their trade. It's not hard for them to find a woman to sleep with as there are plenty of wanton women about who want money. But he shouldn't have taken advantage of a mute girl. He raped her, played with her, and then discarded her.

When the Goddess Tianluo came to take his life, was it this mute girl who came into his mind?

Of course. She appeared before his eyes and he couldn't get rid of her.

Was it retribution?

Yes. Any woman who has been taken advantage of will hunger for revenge! While she lives, and if she can track down the person, she will gouge out his eyes and curse him violently, invoking demons to banish him to the eighteenth level of Hell so that he can be horribly tortured! But this girl was a mute and couldn't talk. She was pregnant, driven from home, and reduced to being a prostitute and beggar, rotten flesh despised by everyone. Before that she was quite pretty and could have married an honest farmer, had a normal married life, a home to keep

164

out the wind and rain, given birth to sons and daughters, and at death a coffin.

He wouldn't have been thinking all this, he would only have been thinking of himself.

But her eyes stare unrelentlingly at him.

The eyes of the Goddess Tianluo.

The eyes of the mute girl who couldn't talk.

Her eyes full of terror as he raped her?

Eyes full of revenge!

Eyes full of pleading.

She couldn't plead, she wept and tore at her own hair.

She was stupefied, dazed ...

No, she called out—

But no-one could understand her *yi-yi ya-ya*, they all laughed at her. He mingled with the crowd and also laughed.

Of course!

Of course at the time he knew no fear and he was even quite proud of himself, he didn't think he could be tracked down.

Fate would avenge her!

She will be here soon, the Goddess Tianluo. He pokes at the coals and she appears in the sparks and smoke.

His eyes close tightly and old tears flow.

Don't beautify him!

Smoke brings tears to anyone's eyes. He uses his hand, which is as rough as dry firewood, to wipe off a gob of snot, then shuffles into the shed. He takes the piece of little-leaf box and his axe and, squatting on the gnarled maple root, whittles away until dark. Then taking the piece of wood into the house he sits down on the round stump next to the fire. He clamps it between his legs and feels it with his calloused hands: he knows this will be his last carving and he is terrified he will not finish in time. He must finish before daybreak, and he knows that as soon as it is light the picture in his mind will vanish and that his fingers will lose their feeling. Her eyes, her lips, her upper lip is taut as she shakes her head. Her ear lobes are soft and fleshy and should be wearing big earrings, her flesh is tense but it is rich and supple, her face is smooth and elegant, her nose is straight and not snubbed. He thrusts his hand down under her tightly buttoned collar . . .

In the early morning, villagers on their way to shop for the New Year at the Luofengpo markets passed by his house and called out to him but there was no reply. The front door was wide open and there was the smell of something burning. They went in and saw him slumped in front of the fire, dead. Some said he had a stroke and others said he had burnt to death. At his feet was the head of the Goddess Tianluo he had carved. She is wearing a crown of twigs from the chaste tree. From each of the four small holes on the crown protrudes a tortoise's head which also looks like an animal crouched in the hole with its head poking out. Her eyelids droop as if in sleep, the bridge of her delicate nose joins with the elegant bones of her brow and there is a slight wrinkling between the brows. The thin lips of her small mouth are tightly pursed as if scornful of human existence and the eyes which can barely be seen emit cold indifference. Her eyebrows, eyes, nose, lips, cheeks, lower jaw and even her long delicate neck all reveal a young girl's fragile beauty. Only the ear lobes, from which hang copper earrings in the shape of spears, are big, voluptuous and sensual. Her neck however is tightly wrapped in the matching sides of her high collar. The Goddess Tianluo was later installed in the shaman's altar at Tianmenguan.

30

I've long heard many stories about the renowned and deadly Qichun snake. The villagers commonly call it the "five-steps dragon" and say that if bitten by it man or animal will drop dead before taking five steps, or that if one goes within five steps of where it is one will have trouble escaping with one's life. This must be the derivation of the saying, "The powerful dragon cannot overcome the snake on the ground." People say it's not like other venomous snakes. Even the deadly cobra can easily be detected – when it's about to strike, it will rear its head, stiffen its body and hiss to frighten its adversary. So, if encountered, a person can defend himself by throwing to its side whatever one happens to be holding or if empty-handed one can throw the hat from one's head or a shoe one is wearing. When it attacks what has been thrown, one can slip away. However eight to nine out of ten encountering a Qichun snake will have been attacked before detecting it.

In southern Anhui province I hear many myths and legends about the Qichun snake. They know battle strategy and spin a web, finer than a spider's, over the plants in their territory, and as soon as this is bumped by some living animal, the snake strikes like a flash of lightning. It's therefore not surprising that in areas where the Qichun snake is found there are all sorts of incantations which they say will give protection when silently intoned. However, the mountain people do not tell these to outsiders. When mountain people go into the mountains for firewood they always strap on leggings or else put on long canvas socks. People from the county town who seldom go into the mountains make the stories sound even more harrowing. They warn that if I encounter a Qichun snake, even if I am wearing leather shoes it will bite right through them; I will need to carry snake antidote, though ordinary snake antidotes won't work with Qichun snakes.

On the highway from Tunqi to Anqing, I pass through Shitai. At the food stall by the bus stop, I encounter a peasant who had lost a hand. He says he chopped it off himself after it had been bitten by a Qichun snake. He is one of the rare cases of someone surviving an attack. The soft straw hat he is wearing is woven from the pith of the rice-paper plant, it is a dress hat with a narrow rim. This type of hat is normally worn only by peasants who work the wharves, and peasants who wear these hats generally have seen a lot and know a lot. I order a bowl of soup noodles at the stall under the white cotton awning by the highway. The peasant is sitting opposite and holding his chopsticks in his left hand. The stump of his right arm keeps swaying in front of me and makes eating difficult. I correctly guess he might like to chat.

"Older brother," I ask him, "I've paid for your bowl of noodles along with mine. If you wouldn't mind, could you tell me how you injured your arm?"

He then starts to tell me about what had happened. He says he had gone into the mountains to look for Qi wood.

"Look for what?"

"Qi wood — eating it prevents jealousy. That wife of mine really drives me crazy, if another woman so much as says one sentence to me she starts throwing bowls about. I went to get Qi wood to brew a soup for her."

"Is this Qi wood a folk prescription?" I ask.

"No." Beneath the dress hat woven from the pith of the rice-paper plant, his big mouth opens wide, showing one gold tooth as he chuckles. It is then that I realize he is having me on.

He says a few of them had gone to chop trees to burn charcoal, at that time it was not like it is nowadays when doing business is all the fashion. If mountain people wanted to get an extra bit of spending money most of them went in for burning charcoal. You could steal timber and sell it for a profit but the timber was under the surveillance of the people in the production brigade and if you were caught it was a criminal offence. He didn't go in for doing things that were illegal. But even with burning charcoal, you had to know how to make it. He only went after white oak: the charcoal burns with a silver flame and it produces a metallic ring when you strike it. If you can produce it, a basket of this metallic charcoal will fetch double the price. I let him talk on, in any case it was the price of a bowl of noodles.

He says he was holding an axe and walking on ahead while his friends were still smoking and chatting down below. He had just bent down when he felt a cold chill rise from the soles of his feet and he knew instantly something was wrong. He says men are the same as dogs. If a dog out on its own sniffs a leopard it will stop in its tracks so scared that it will whimper like a kitten. He says at the time his legs just went soft: no matter how tough a man is, if he encounters a Qichun snake, that's the end of him. And right there, he saw this thing coiled on a rock under the branches of a chaste tree, it was mostly grey and drawn almost into a ball, in the middle of which was this head sticking up. Faster than it would take to say it, he chopped at it but instantly his hand turned ice cold and a jarring spasm went right through his body as if he'd had an electric shock. Everything went black before his eyes, even the sun became dark, it was eerie. The sound of the wind, birds and insects vanished, the colour of the gloomy sky darkened and the sun and the trees glowed with a chilly light. Maybe it was because his brain was still working, or that he was fast, or that he wasn't meant to die or that he was lucky that he took the axe in his left hand and chopped off his right hand. Then holding his back rigid in a *qigong* stance, he went down on his haunches and pressed his left thumb onto the artery of his right arm above the elbow. He says the blood which gushed out sizzled on the stones, immediately lost its redness, and turned into a pale yellow froth! Afterwards, his friends carried him back to the village. They also brought back the hand he'd chopped off. It had turned black: the fingernails, skin and flesh were black and streaked with purple. What remained of his arm also started turning black and it was only by using every sort of snake antidote that the poison was arrested.

I say, "You're really strong-minded."

He says if he'd baulked or that he'd been bitten an inch or so higher, he'd have been dead. "To lose a hand to save one's life, how could I quibble over it? Even a praying mantis will shed a claw to save itself."

"But it's an insect," I say.

"So what if it's an insect? Humans can't be inferior to insects. Foxes have bitten off a leg to get out of a trap, surely humans can't be less intelligent than foxes." He slaps a ten *yuan* note on the table, he doesn't want me to pay for his noodles. He says he's doing some buying and selling now and isn't making less than an educated person like me.

I keep watching out for Qichun snakes as I go on my journey, then on the road to Fanjing Mountain, in a village called Wenxiao or Shichang, I see dried Qichun snakes tied in coils in the ceiling drying area of a trading depot. They were just as the Tang Dynasty scholar Liu Zongyuan had described them: "Black body with a white pattern." This is a valuable Chinese medicine which is highly effective for relaxing muscular tension, aiding blood circulation, getting rid of rheumatism, and getting rid of colds. It fetches a high price so there are always brave fellows willing to risk their lives for it.

Liu Zongyuan considered this thing to be more dangerous than a tiger and went on to talk about harsh governments being more savage than tigers. He was a provincial governor whereas I am one of the common people. He was a scholar-official and in his lifetime he put worrying about the concerns of the world first, whereas I am wandering everywhere concerned only with my own life.

Just seeing these processed coils of dried snake isn't enough, I am keen to see a live one, to know how to identify it, so that I will know how to guard against it.

It is not until I reach the foot of Fanjing Mountain, the kingdom of this snake, that I see two of them. They had been confiscated from poachers and were kept in a wire cage at a ranger inspection station on the reserve. I finally get a proper look at them.

The scientific name is the beaked Pallas pit viper. Both are more than two metres long, not as thick as a small wrist but with a small tail section which is thinner. The body is a nondescript grey-brown with a grey-white triangular pattern, so it also has the common name of chessboard snake. They don't appear dangerous, and coiled on a rock would just look like a clump of soil. But if one looks closely, the rough dull brown triangular head has a scaly upturned-hook beak and a pair of small, pitiful, and lacklustre eyes. It has a comical greedy look reminiscent of the clownish Seventh Rank Sesame Official in traditional opera. However it doesn't rely on its eyes to attack its prey. Between the eyes and the nostrils is an indentation which is a unique temperature sensor. This is sensitive to infra-red rays and can detect temperature changes to one-twentieth of a degree within a radius of three metres. If an animal with a body temperature higher than its own approaches, it can stalk and attack it with precision. I learn all about this from a snake-bite researcher on the reserve afterwards when I go to Wuyi Mountain.

It is also on this road, in the upper reaches of the Chen River tributary of the Yuan River, in the still unpolluted and abundant flow of the Jin River, that the water is limpid. The boy cowherders pissing in the water are swept off by the fast-flowing current and are screaming. It is several hundred metres before they are hauled up onto the river-bank: the sounds carry clearly. Below the highway, a young girl is bathing naked at the water's edge. When she sees vehicles drive past on the highway, she stands there like a white egret, moving only her neck to stare. In the strong noon sun, the sunlight on the water is dazzling. Of course all this has nothing much to do with Qichun snakes.

31

She is laughing loudly. You ask her why she's laughing and she says she's happy but she knows she's not at all happy and is just trying to look happy. She doesn't want to let on that she's actually unhappy.

She says once she was walking along a main street and saw a man chasing after a trolley bus which had just driven off. He was walking on the toes of one foot, half running and half hopping, and shouting at the top of his voice. It turned out that when he was getting off the bus one of his shoes got caught in the door. He must have been a peasant from out of town. From the time she was a child her teachers had taught her not to make fun of peasants and when she grew up her mother warned her not to laugh stupidly in front of men. But she just couldn't help laughing aloud. When she laughed like this people always stared at her and it was only afterwards that she learnt when she laughed like this it was inviting, and men of wicked intent thought she was flirting. Men always look differently at women, even if it's not your intention it is wrongly interpreted as such.

She says the very first time she gave herself, it was to a man she didn't love at all. When he mounted her and took her he didn't know she was still a virgin and asked why she was crying. She said it wasn't because she couldn't stand the pain but because she pitied herself. He attempted to help her wipe away her tears but these weren't for him, so she pushed him away. She buttoned up her shirt and tried to tidy her messed-up hair in the mirror, she didn't want his help, he would only make it worse. He had enjoyed himself on her, he had taken advantage of a moment's weakness.

She couldn't say he had forced himself upon her. He had invited her to his room for lunch. She went, had a cup of liquor, felt a bit happy but not really happy, and began laughing like this.

She says she doesn't completely blame him. At the time she only wanted to see what would happen and drank in one gulp the half cup of liquor he had poured for her. She felt a bit dizzy, she hadn't imagined the liquor was so potent. She was aware that her face was burning and that she was laughing inanely. Then he kissed her, pushed her onto the bed, no, she didn't resist, she even knew when he was pulling up her skirt.

He was her teacher and she was a student, and this sort of thing shouldn't have happened. She could hear footsteps coming and going in the corridor outside the room, people were always talking, people always have so many totally meaningless things to say. It was midday and people were coming back to their dormitories after lunch in the canteen, and she could hear them clearly. In these surroundings it was like being a thief and she felt thoroughly ashamed. Animal, animal, she said to herself.

Afterwards she opened the door of the room and left, chest out and head held high. As soon as she got to the stairs, someone called out her name, and she says at the time she blushed, it was as if her skirt had been pulled up and she was wearing nothing underneath. Fortunately the lighting was poor on the stairs. It turned out to be a classmate who had just come in and wanted her to go with her to see this teacher about choosing courses for the following semester. She made the excuse that she was rushing to a movie and didn't have time, then went off. But she will always remember the sound of being called, she says her heart almost leapt from her chest. Even when she was being taken, her heart didn't pound as fiercely as it did then. In the end she got her revenge, in the end she took revenge, took revenge for all those years of anxiety and fear, she avenged herself. She says on the sports field that day the sun had a harsh glare, and in the sunlight there was a heart-rending scream, like a razor blade scratching on glass.

You ask who she is.

She says, her, and starts laughing loudly again.

You become apprehensive.

She urges you not to be like this. She says she is just telling a story, she heard it from a friend. She was a student from a medical college who had come to the operating theatre for practical experience. Afterwards they became friends and talked to one another about everything.

You don't believe her.

Why is it all right for you to tell stories but not for her?

You ask her to go on.

She says she's finished.

You say her story ended too abruptly.

She says she can't tell mysteries like you, and moreover you've told lots of stories and she's only just started.

Then go on telling it, you say.

She says she's lost interest and doesn't want to go on telling it.

She's a fox spirit, you say after some thought.

It's not only men who lust.

Of course. It's the same with women, you say.

Why can't women do what men can? It's natural to all human beings.

You say you're not censuring women, you're only saying she's a fox spirit.

There's nothing bad about fox spirits.

You say you're not criticizing them, you're just talking about them.

Then talk about them.

Talk about what?

If you want to talk about fox spirits then talk about them, she says.

You say the husband of this fox spirit hadn't been dead for a full seven—

Full seven what?

In the past when the husband died a woman would have to stay by his corpse for seven times seven equals forty-nine days.

Is seven an unlucky number?

Seven is an auspicious day for ghosts and spirits.

Don't talk about ghosts.

Then let's talk about the one who didn't die. Before she'd taken off the white mourning strips from the tops of her shoes she was like the prostitutes at the Joy of Spring Hall in Wuyizhen, all the time leaning at the gate with her hands on her hips and one foot slightly raised on her toes. As soon as she saw someone coming she'd posture seductively and pretend she wasn't looking in order to entice men.

She says you are debunking women.

No, you say, even the women couldn't stand it and quickly walked away. It was only the shrewish Sun the Fourth's wife who spat in her face.

But when the men walked past, didn't they all look greedily at her?

It was impossible not to. All of them eagerly looked back, even the hunchback. There were more than fifty of them, all staring with their heads turned to one side. Now don't laugh just yet.

Who's laughing?

Let's talk about Old Lu's wife in the house next door. Right after dinner, she was sitting at the doorway sewing shoe soles and saw all this happening. So she said, Hunchback, your foot's treading in dog shit! This really embarrassed the hunchback. On those very hot days when all the villagers sat out on the streets to eat their evening meals, she would walk by every doorway, wriggling her bottom with two empty water buckets on her carrying pole. Maozi's mother poked her husband with her chopsticks and got such a thrashing during the night that she howled with pain. That sexy fox spirit, the women in the village with husbands all wanted to box her ears. If Maozi's mother could have had her way, she'd have ripped the clothes off her, grabbed her by the hair, and pushed her head into a nightsoil bucket.

That's disgusting, she says.

But that's how things turned out, you say. To begin with, it was discovered by Old Lu's wife that Zhu the Eldest, whom the villagers called Blockhead and who couldn't get himself a wife, was always visiting her melon shed. He said he was helping her to spread around fertilizer. And this certainly was a place for spreading around fertilizer. If things hadn't fallen upon the head of Sun the Fourth's wife, events wouldn't have taken such a tragic turn. Before sunrise Sun the Fourth said he was getting up early to go into the mountains to cut firewood. He shouldered a pointed carrying pole, circled around the village lanes and in a flash climbed over the wall of this woman's courtyard. Sun the Fourth's wife suspected what was happening and without waiting for her husband to come out, began beating on the door with a carrying pole. The woman came and opened the door, still fastening the buttons at the waist of her jacket, as if nothing was wrong. As if Sun the Fourth's wife would let her off. Faster than it would take to say it, she had already charged at the woman and the two of them were brawling, crying and shouting, and everyone had turned up. All the women sided with Sun the Fourth's wife but the men watched the fighting in silence. The woman's clothing was torn and her face was scratched. Sun the Fourth's wife later said it was her intention to ruin the woman's looks, the woman sobbed with her hands over her face, writhing in pain. Of course it was a clear case of immoral behaviour but it was after all women's business and both Sixth Grand Uncle and the village head, stood to one side and could only cough drily. However, as it is said, a woman's mind is indeed most venomous and the women themselves decided to punish her. They talked it over and when the woman was on her way to fetch firewood on the mountain path, a few hefty women accosted her, stripped off her clothes, trussed her up, and carried her off on a pole. She called out again and again for help but even when those who got on with her heard and came running, the very sight of these mean women who would strip the skin off someone, deterred them. They carried her into the mountains to Peach Blossom Flat. In the past, because this peach blossom mountain flatland produced wanton women, it became a lepers' village; they dumped her and the pole on the road, spat and stomped on her, cursed her, then left.

Then what happened?

Then it rained, it rained for several days and several nights on end before stopping. At noon people saw her returning to the village. She was wearing a pair of tattered trousers and her bare upper body was wrapped in a straw cape, her lips were bruised and drained of colour. When the children playing under the eaves saw her they ran away and houses one by one closed their doors. A few days later when she re-emerged from her house, she had recovered and was even more bewitching – her lips were bright red and her cheeks were peach-pink. But she no longer dared to walk around in the village and would only go to the stream to fetch water and wash clothes in the early morning before daybreak or else after nightfall, always hurrying with her head down and walking close to the wall. When children saw her they would shout from a distance, "Leper woman, leper woman, your nose will rot first and then your lips!" as they followed her and then run off. Afterwards people forgot about her. Every household was busy harvesting and threshing, and after that it was ploughing, and then seeding and planting. After the busy period of early harvesting and late planting was over, it was noticed that no work had been done in the woman's fields and that she hadn't been seen for a long time. People thought someone should be sent to have a look but no-one wanted to go. In the end it fell upon Old Lu's wife to go and have a look. She came out and said, "It seems that retribution has been meted out to this seductress, her face is covered in sores so it's no wonder she dares not leave the house!" On hearing this the womenfolk all heaved a sigh of relief, for they didn't need to worry about their husbands anymore.

Then what happened?

Later on, it was time to harvest the late crop. By the time the last field was harvested, frost began to fall. The villagers started to prepare for the New Year and the millstones had to be washed for grinding rice flour. Maozi's mother noticed sores on her husband's bare back when he was pushing the mill but didn't dare tell anyone except her husband's younger sister. Unexpectedly, the day after she told her husband's younger sister, when the younger sister got up in the morning she saw that her husband's chest too had developed sores. The matter only needed to be told to another, once one woman had told another it was impossible for any secret to be kept, even Sun the

Fourth had developed running sores on his legs. Following that, it was naturally a very gloomy New Year. In every household the women were fraught with anxieties, while the menfolk of the women either had their heads or their faces wrapped up. However, it was winter so it didn't look too bad. Then it was again time for the spring ploughing and it was cumbersome to still have one's head and face wrapped up. The men weren't too worried about how they looked because at the time everyone was either losing skin, losing hair or had running sores. Even Sixth Grand Uncle had developed a sore on the end of his nose. It was the same with everyone, so they couldn't say anything about one another and just kept raking the soil. When all the seedlings had been planted and people had a bit of free time, they remembered the seductress and wondered if she was still alive. However, everyone said that if you sat in a chair the leper woman had sat in you'd get boils on your bottom, so no-one would go near the door of the seductress.

They all deserved it, these men, she says.

However the first to go to the fields to weed with a kerchief over her face was Sun the Fourth's wife. The older people all said, "A crime was committed and there is retribution in the present world." But what could be done? Even Old Lu's wife didn't escape — she developed mastitis and her breasts rotted completely. Unmarried girls and children were the only ones to escape this bad fate if they went far away to another village.

Is that the end of the story? she asks.

Yes.

She finds the story disgusting.

Because it's a man's story.

But aren't there men and women in the story? she asks.

You say of course it's a story with men in it but it's a story which men tell women and a man's story which women like to listen to. You ask her which type she likes listening to.

She says your stories are becoming wicked and crude.

You say this is what a man's world is.

Then what is a woman's world like?

Only women can know what a woman's world is like.

So there can't be any communication?

It's because there are two different perspectives.

But love can communicate between the two.

You ask her if she believes in love.

If I don't believe in love why do I go looking for it? she asks instead.

This is because you still want to believe in it.

If there's only lust but no love, what meaning would there be in life?

You say this is women's philosophy.

Don't keep saying women this women that, women are also human beings.

They too were moulded from mud by N wa.

Is this your opinion of women?

You say you are simply making a statement.

A statement is also an opinion.

You say you don't want to debate the matter.

32

You say you've finished telling stories, and that they are all common and vulgar or else like the venom of the Qichun snake. You may as well listen to some women's stories, or rather stories women tell men.

She says she can't tell stories, not like you, you can just make them up as you go along. She wants truth, totally undisguised truth.

Women's truth.

Why women's truth?

Because men's truth is different from women's truth.

You're becoming strange.

Why?

Because you already possess me. When you have something you don't treasure it, this is men for you.

But you acknowledge the existence of a woman's world beyond a man's world, don't you?

Don't talk to me about women.

Then what shall I talk about?

Talk about your childhood, talk about yourself. She doesn't want to hear your stories, she wants to know about your past, your childhood, your mother, your old grandfather. She wants to know even the minute details, your memories from the cradle, she wants to know everything about you, your most secret feelings. You say you've already forgotten them. She says she wants to help you recall these memories, she wants to help you recall the people and events you have forgotten, she wants to go wandering with you through your memories, go deep into your soul, to experience with you the life you have experienced.

You say she wants to possess your soul. She says, yes, not just your body. If she is going to possess you she wants to possess everything, she wants to listen to your voice as she goes into your memories, she wants to imagine with you, curl into the deepest recesses of your soul and, together with you, manipulate your imagination, she says, she also wants to become your soul.

You are really a seductress, you say. She says, yes, she wants to become the ends of your nerves, she wants you to touch with her fingers, to see with her eyes, to create images with her, to climb with her up Lingshan, she wants to look down on the whole of your soul from the peak of Lingshan, including secrets of which you are ashamed, hidden in the darkest corners. She savagely says that even your wrongdoings mustn't be concealed, she wants to see everything with absolute clarity.

You ask if she wants you to confess your wrongdoings to her. Oh, don't make it seem so serious. This is something you want to do, this is love, she asks, isn't it?

You say you can't refuse and ask where she'd like you to start. She says talk about whatever you like, the only condition is that you must talk about yourself.

You say when you were young you saw a fortune teller, but you can't remember whether it was your mother or your maternal grandmother who took you.

That's not important, she says.

What you remember clearly is that this fortune teller had very long fingernails. He worked out your horoscope by positioning little brass flags on an Eight Trigram Chart, and he also spun a compass. You ask if she's heard of Ziwei Constellation fortune telling, an ancient school which can predict a person's life, death and future. You say, as he positioned the brass flags he flicked his fingernails loudly, it was scary, and chanted incantations: *ba-ba ka-ka, ka-ka ba-ba*, this child will throughout his life have many demon problems. His parents in a past life want to take him back, it will be difficult for him to survive, he has too many debts in a past life. Your mother, or maybe it was your grandmother, asked whether there was a way of dispelling this calamity. He said this child must change his features so that when the aggrieved ghosts summon his spirit, they won't recognize him. Your grandmother therefore seized the chance while your mother was out, you remember this quite clearly, to put an earring on you. She rubbed your ear lobe with a green soyabean and a pinch of salt and said it wouldn't hurt, but as she rubbed your ear lobe became swollen and began to hurt more and more. However, before she got to piercing it with a needle your mother came home and had a big row with her – she grumbled but had to give up the idea. As for you, at the time you had no fixed ideas about having your ear pierced.

You ask her what else she'd like to hear. You say your childhood wasn't in fact without happy times. You once used your grandfather's walking stick as a punt-pole and your bathtub as a boat in the waterlogged lane after a storm. You recall lying on a bamboo bed in summer and counting the stars in the square of sky in the courtyard to see which was your own star. You also recall that one year at noon during the Duanwu Festival, your mother got hold of you to daub orpiment mixed in spirits on your ears and to write the character "king" on your head, saying it would stop boils and sores developing in summer. You thought it was ugly and before she finished writing, you broke away and ran off. But now, she has been dead for a long time.

She says her mother is dead too, that she died from illness in the May Seventh Cadre School, when she went to the countryside she was already ill. At the time the whole city had been deployed for war, they said the hairy Russians were about to attack. Yes, she says, she too has been a refugee. The platform at the station was lined with sentries, not just military men with red badges on their collars but also civilian militias dressed in the same army uniforms with red armbands. A group of criminals to be reformed through labour were marched under escort onto the platform. They were wearing tattered clothing and looked like a band of beggars. Old men and old women, each with a bed roll on their back and an enamel mug and a rice bowl in their hands, were singing together loudly, "Sincerely, with heads bowed, we acknowledge our crimes. To resist reform can only bring death." She says at the time she was just eight and started crying stupidly and refused to board the train. She lay on the ground yelling that she wanted to go home. Her mother tried to coax her, saying it was more fun in the countryside, that it was too damp in the air raid shelter and if she went on digging any deeper her back would break. It was better to go to the countryside, the air was better and her mother wouldn't have to get her to thump her back every night anymore. At the cadre school she was with her mother every day. When the grown-ups studied the sayings of Chairman Mao and the numerous newspaper editorials she would sit in her mother's arms and when they went to work in the fields she went along with them and played nearby; when they did the harvesting she even helped by picking up ears of rice. They all liked to make her laugh, that was the happiest time in her life. She actually liked the cadre school, except for the struggle-meeting to criticize Uncle Liang session. They pushed him off the stool he was standing on and his front teeth were knocked out and there was blood all over his mouth. And there were lots of watermelons growing at the cadre school, everyone bought them, and whenever anyone was eating watermelon they'd get her to come, she had never eaten so much watermelon in her life.

You say that you also remember the New Year's party the year you graduated from middle school. You danced with a girl for the first time and kept treading on her feet. You were very embarrassed but she kept saying it didn't matter. Light snow was falling that night and the snowflakes that landed on your face melted. After the party you ran all the way home, trying to catch up with the girl you had danced with ...

Don't talk about other women!

You talk about an old cat you once had which was so lazy that it wouldn't catch rats.

Don't talk about old cats.

Then what shall I talk about?

Talk about whether or not you saw her, that girl.

Which girl?

The girl who drowned.

The young student who was sent to the countryside? The girl who killed herself by jumping into the river?

No.

Then which one?

You all tricked her into going swimming at night and then raped her!

You say you didn't go.

She says you must have gone.

You say you can swear you didn't go!

Then you must have felt her.

When?

Under the bridge, in the dark, you also felt her, you men are all bad!

You say you were too young at the time and didn't dare.

She says you must at least have had a look at her.

Of course you looked at her, she wasn't just pretty in an ordinary way, she was really quite beautiful.

She says you didn't just look in an ordinary way, you had a look at her body.

You say you only wanted to have a look.

No, you must have had a look.

You say impossible.

Of course it was possible! You're capable of any sort of wicked behaviour, you were often at her home.

Do you mean, her home?

In her room! She says you pulled it up, you pulled up her shirt.

How did I pull up her shirt?

She was standing against the wall.

You say she pulled it up herself.

Like this? she asks.

A bit higher, you say.

Wasn't she wearing anything underneath? Not even a bra?

Her breasts were only just developing, you say, her breasts protruded but her nipples were still crinkled.

184

Stop talking about this!

You say it was she who wanted you to talk about this.

She says she doesn't want you to talk about these things, she says she doesn't want to hear another thing about it.

Then what shall I talk about?

Just talk about anything, but don't talk about women again.

You ask her why.

She says it is not her that you love.

Why is she saying this? you ask.

She says when you are making love with her it's other women you are thinking about.

Rubbish! you say, she's making this up.

She says she doesn't want to listen, doesn't want to know any of it.

I'm really sorry, you interrupt her.

Don't talk about anything anymore.

You say in that case you'll listen to her.

She says you never listen to what she's saying.

You ask if she was eating watermelon at the cadre school all the time.

What a real bore you are, she says.

You plead with her to go on talking and promise not to interrupt.

She says she doesn't have anything to talk about.

33

Setting out from Jiangkou county and going upstream on the Taiping River, the source of the Jinjiang, the mountain formations on both sides become more and more bizarre. Then after passing the Panqi stockade settlement with its mixed population of Miao, Tujia and Han nationalities, one enters the nature reserve. Here the densely forested mountains begin to close in and the river becomes narrow and deep. The ranger station at Heiwan River is a two-storey brick building situated at the end of the bend in the river. The ranger is a tall middle-aged man who is dark and thin, he has a crew cut and a dark lean face with stubble. The two live Qichun snakes I saw had been confiscated by him from poachers. He says that Qichun snakes are common among the wild flax plants on both sides of the river.

"This is the kingdom of the Qichun snake," he says.

I think it's thanks to the Qichun snakes that this stretch of primeval subtropical forest and undergrowth of evergreen broadleafs has been preserved.

He was first in the army and then a cadre. He has travelled to many places but he says he doesn't want to go anywhere now. Not long ago he turned down an appointment as sub-station chief in the Public Security Bureau and also refused to head the botanical farm unit of the reserve. He just watches over the mountain on his own and has been captivated by the mountain.

He said five years ago tigers used to come to the village settlement and take off cattle but these days no-one sees any signs of tigers. Last year when the peasants killed a leopard, he confiscated it and had it sent to the reserve administrative office in the county town. The skeleton was first treated with arsenic before being made into a specimen and locked in the specimen room, but still it was stolen. Someone had climbed up the water pipe and got in through the window. If the arsenic-treated bones are passed off as tiger bone and sold for soaking in spirits, then drinking it will *really* bring about longevity.

He says he's not an ecology protection agitator and he can't do research, he's just a ranger. When they built this ranger station on the reserve, he decided to stay. There are several upstairs rooms in the building and he can offer hospitality to specialists and scholars to facilitate their investigations and collecting of specimens.

"Don't you get lonely being on the mountain all year round?" I ask, seeing that he doesn't have a wife or children.

"Women are troublesome."

He then started talking about when he was a soldier. During the Cultural Revolution women also joined in causing havoc. There was this nineteen-year-old girl who had civilian militia training and was one of the top-ranking shooters of the province. During the armed battles, she went with her group up the mountain and, one shot at a time, picked off five soldiers in the company which had surrounded them. The company commander was angry and gave orders to take her alive. Afterwards when she ran out of ammunition, she was caught, stripped, and a soldier fired a magazine of bullets from his submachine gun into her vagina. He also spent some time in a small mine as a personnel cadre. When the miners fought over a woman the knives would go in clean and come out red, and this was on top of the more ordinary complications over women. He had a wife once but they separated and he doesn't intend to get married again.

"You can stay here and write your books, it's good having someone to drink with. I drink every meal, not a lot, but always some."

A peasant carrying a string of small fish is crossing the single-log bridge over the bend of the river in front of the house. The chief ranger calls out to him, says he's got a guest and gets him to bring them over.

"I'll make you sesame and chilli fish, it's just the thing to go with liquor."

He says if he wants fresh meat he can get the peasants to get it for him when they go to the markets. And twenty *li* from here, in the settlement, there's also now a little shop where you can even buy liquor and cigarettes. And he regularly gets to eat bean curd because whenever the peasants make it he always gets a portion. He keeps a few chickens so chicken and eggs are never a problem.

At noon, beneath the dark green mountain he and I drink liquor and feast on sesame and chilli fish and a bowl of salted meat which he has steamed.

"You are really living the life of an immortal," I say.

"I don't know about it being an immortal's life but it's peaceful and I'm not troubled by many anxieties. My work is simple, there's only the one path up the mountain, it's right under my eyes, and I have only to fulfil my duty of keeping watch over this mountain."

Coming through the county town I'd heard that his mountain was the best managed in Heiwan River district. It seems to me this is due to his philosophy of not seeking fame and wealth. In his view it is because he gets on really well with the peasants here. Every New Year an old peasant will always bring him a bag of dried roots as a gift.

"When you go into the mountains, if you're chewing a piece of this root the snakes will keep away from you." Saying this he goes into his room and brings out a straw bag, opens it, and gives me a brown root. I ask what plant it is but he says he doesn't know and he doesn't ask. It's the mountain people's secret remedy handed down from their ancestors and they have their rules about it.

He says a round trip to Gold Top, on the main peak, will take three days. I'll have to take rice, oil, salt, as well as some bean curd, green vegetables and eggs. On the mountain, I'll have to spend the night in a cave. The cotton-wadding beds used by scientific researchers earlier on are still there, they'll keep out the cold. It's windy up there, and it's very cold. He says he'll go to the village to have a look, and if he finds someone I'll be able to go today. He heads off in the direction of the single-log bridge.

Afterwards I go for a walk around the bend of the river. In the shallows the river flows fast and sparkles in the sunlight like crystal, but in shady spots it is dark and there seems to be something menacing about it. There is a thick growth of forest and undergrowth on the banks, so thick that it looks black: it has a frightening dark dampness and must be alive with snakes. I cross the single-log bridge and come to the other side. Behind the forest is a small village settlement of five or six families. There are tall, old wooden buildings with walls and rafters which have gone black, probably because of the over-abundant rain here.

The village is quiet and lonely, devoid of human sounds. The doors are all open and the uncovered rafters are crammed with dry grass, farm tools, wood and bamboo. I almost go in to have a look but suddenly a grey-black mixed-breed Alsatian appears, growling ferociously and coming right at me. I quickly beat a retreat and go straight back over the single-log bridge. Before me is the huge black-grey form of the mountain in the sunlight behind the small ranger station.

Jolly laughter comes from behind and looking around I see a woman coming across the single-log bridge. She is toying with a carrying pole in her hands on which is curled a big five- or six-foot snake with a length of wriggling tail. She is obviously calling me and I go up to the edge of the river before I can make out what she is asking me.

"Hey, want to buy a snake?" Quite unperturbed, she giggles as she comes toward me, one hand holding down seven inches of the snake and the other holding the pole with the writhing serpent coiled around it.

Luckily the ranger appears just in time, and from the other side of the river, scolds her, "Go back! Do you hear? Go back right away!"

The woman has to go back to the other side of the bridge as instructed.

"She's crazy, this woman, as soon as she sees a stranger she always wants to get up to some sort of mischief," he says. He tells me he's found a peasant to act as a porter and guide. He'll fix up a few things in his office and then arrange a few days provisions for me. I can go ahead as far as I like, the guide will follow after, the mountain people are used to travelling on these mountain paths and he'll catch up right away with a basket on a carrying pole. There's only the one path up the mountain so you can't go wrong. Seven or eight *li* up is a copper mine which earlier on was half developed before it fell into disuse, if he doesn't turn up by then I can stop there for a while.

He tells me to leave my backpack, the peasant can bring it for me. He also gives me a stick, saying it will help conserve energy going up the mountain and can be used for chasing off snakes. And he tells me to chew a piece of the dried root he gave me. I bid him farewell. He waves to me, turns, and goes inside.

I still think of him and his practical attitude of rejecting fame and wealth and also the gloomy other side of the single-log bridge in the bend of the river, the village settlement with the wooden houses which have gone black, the savage Alsatian with the grey-black fur, and the crazy woman with the snake on the carrying pole. These all seem to be hinting at something, just like the huge gloomy mountain behind the small building. There is something more to it all which I will never be able to fully understand.

34

You are walking in mud and fine rain is falling, it is quiet on the road except for the squelching of the mud sticking to your shoes. You say she has to walk where the mud is firmer but straightaway you hear a plop. You turn and see that she has fallen and is awkwardly holding herself up with one hand in the mud. You put out your hand to pull her up but her foot slips and the dirty hand which had been holding her up smears mud all over her. You say she really has to take off her high heels. She is crying miserably and plonks herself right into the mud. You say, come on, so you're a bit dirty but that can be fixed up, there's a house up ahead and you can have a good wash. But she refuses to go on.

This is women, you say, they want to go travelling in the mountains but don't want any hardships.

She says she shouldn't have come walking with you on these lousy mountain roads.

You say it's not all scenery in the mountains, there's also wind and rain, she's already here so she should stop regretting having come.

She says you tricked her, there isn't a tourist anywhere on this damn Lingshan.

You say if it's people and not mountains she wants to see, hasn't she seen plenty on the streets in the cities? If she hasn't, she can take a trip to the department stores where there's everything a woman needs, from cakes to cosmetics.

She covers her face with her muddy hands and starts crying like a child. You can't take anymore, pull her to her feet and help her along.

You say she can't just stay in the mud and rain, there's a house up ahead, and if there's a house there'll be a fire, and if there's a fire there will be warmth, and she won't feel so alone and will be more comfortable.

But you know that behind the crumbling wall in the rain, the stove is in ruins and the pots have rusted away long ago. On this hillock, there are no weeping women ghosts among the clumps of bushes behind the graves decked with paper streamers. At this very moment you dearly wish to find a house to change into some clean clothes and, clean and refreshed, to sit by the fire on a bamboo chair, a bowl of hot tea in your hands, looking at the fine rain drizzling under the eaves outside, telling her a children's tale which has nothing to do with her, you, or the chaotic human world. She would be like the good little girl of a family on this lonely mountain, sitting on your knee and snuggled in your arms.

You say the god of fire is a prankish naked red boy who appears in forests where trees have been chopped down, stomping loudly on heaps of dry leaves and climbing bare-bottom over fallen branches.

She then starts telling you about her first love, the romance of a young girl, or one could say before she knew about anything: it was a sort of yearning for love. She says he had just returned to the city from the reform-through-labour farm, and was dark and gaunt and looked older than his years with the deep lines on his face. Nevertheless, she had a crush on him and would listen entranced as he told about the hardships he had suffered.

You say this is a very old story you'd heard about your great-grandfather. They said he saw the red boy crawling from under the oak tree he'd cut the previous year and jumping onto a camellia tree. He shook his head, thinking that his old eyes were playing tricks on him. He was on his way down the mountain, hauling a hawthorn log for a boat worker from Loud Water Beach. Hawthorn wood is light, stands up to soaking in water and is good timber for boats.

She says at the time she was just sixteen and he was already forty-seven or forty-eight and could have been her father. He was at university with her father and had been a friend for many years. After the decision on his case had been corrected and he returned to the city, he didn't have many friends and was always at her house drinking with her father and talking about his experiences during those years in the labour camp when he'd been declared a rightist. As she listened tears would come to her eyes. At the time he was very thin and hadn't fully recovered, not like after he had been appointed chief engineer and looked quite dashing wearing a patterned wool suit and a white shirt with a starched and ironed collar which was always unbuttoned. But at the time she was totally besotted with him, she wanted to weep for him and wanted desperately to comfort him so that he would be happy the rest of his life. If at that time he had accepted the love of this young girl, she says, she really wouldn't have worried about anything.

You say your great-grandfather was coming down the mountain shouldering a hawthorn log that was two arm-spans around the girth when he saw the fire god climbing up the trunk of the camellia tree. He couldn't stop abruptly and was afraid to keep looking. He got home, put the log by the door, and before going into the house was saying that bad fortune was upon them! Everyone at home questioned him. You say that at the time your grandfather was still alive and he asked your great-grandfather what was wrong. Your great-grandfather said he'd seen the red boy, the fire god Zhurong and that the good days were over!

But he was totally oblivious to it, he was a simpleton, she says. She only told him after she had been at university for a few years. He said he had a wife and a son and that while he was in the labour camp his wife had waited twenty whole years for him; his son was even older than her. And her father has been a friend for many years, what would he think of him? You cowardly creep! You cowardly creep! She says at the time she wept as she swore at him. She says, even the date was her idea. She was with her father at the door saying goodbye to him when she made up an excuse and said she had to see a girl who used to live in the same building when she was little, and so they left together. She

193

normally addressed him as Uncle Cai and she still called him this. She said, Uncle Cai, she had something to talk to him about. He said fine, we can talk now, we can talk as we walk along. She said no, she couldn't on the street. He thought for a while and said they could talk in the park. He said there was a restaurant at the gate of the park and he invited her to have dinner with him.

You say that afterwards disasters really came one after another. You say at the time you were too small to carry a blunderbuss and couldn't go hunting with your father but could only take a hoe into the bamboo grove with him to dig up winter shoots. Your father said that by that time your great-grandfather's back was already bent and he had a big fleshy tumour on his neck, caused by hauling logs since he was small. When your great-grandfather was young, your father said, he was a great hunter without peer, but within two days of seeing the red boy, he was dead – the bullet went through the back of his head and exploded in his left eye. He lay at the door of the house in a pool of blood, if he'd reached out he would have touched the doorsill. The root of the old camphor tree in the yard was splashed with purple-black lumps of blood. He had pulled himself up by the root of the tree, he didn't have time to go around the bend to come up by the stone steps. He had crawled until he was almost in reach of the doorsill when he stopped breathing. Your great-grandmother discovered him when she got up early the next morning to feed the pigs, she hadn't heard him call out during the night.

She says that at dinner she only talked about inconsequential university things and didn't raise the matter at all. Afterwards, he suggested going for a stroll in the park. In the darkness of the trees, he was happy from the alcohol and, just like any other man, wanted to kiss her. But she wouldn't let him. She said, still calling him Uncle Cai, that she only wanted to let him know how she had once loved him and how she had punished herself: she had given herself to a man she didn't love. It was a moment of confusion, she had let someone toy with her, yes, she says, she had used the words *toy with* on impulse. He said nothing and wanted to embrace her but she pushed him away.

You say it was still before light that your grandmother, at that time pregnant with your father, stumbled, screamed and fainted. It was your grandfather who dragged your great-grandfather into the house and he said your great-grandfather had been murdered and that the cruel shot to the back of the head contained iron pellets for shooting wild pigs. Your father said soon after your great-grandfather died a forest fire broke out on the mountain and burnt for more than ten days on several fronts so that there was no way of stopping it. The flames leapt high into the sky, lighting up Huri Peak like a volcano. But your grandfather said it was right when the fire broke out that your great-grandfather was murdered. Later on your father said your great-grandfather's death had nothing to do with the red boy who lit the fire. He had been murdered and right up until his death your grandfather wanted to find his father's assassin. However, when your father told you about it, it was already a story, and you just heaved a sigh.

She says, he also said he loved her and she said, you're lying! He said in the past he really wanted her, she said it's too late. He said why? She said need you ask! He asked why couldn't he even kiss her? She said she can casually sleep with any man but not him. And she said, Go away! You'll never understand. And she said she hated him and never wanted to see him again, pushed him away and ran off.

You say she isn't in fact some little nurse, and that she has been making up lies all along – she hasn't been talking about a woman friend of hers, but about herself, her own experiences. She says you haven't been talking about your great-grandfather, grandfather, father and yourself, you're just making up a story to frighten her. You say you said it was a children's story. She says she's not a child and doesn't want to listen to some children's story, she just wants to live an honest life, she won't believe in love anymore, she's sick of it, all men are the same and just want sex. What about women, you ask. They are just as immoral, she says, she says she's seen enough of everything, life is sickening, she doesn't want so much suffering, she just wants a moment's happiness. She says do I want her?

Right here in the rain and mud?

Won't it be more exciting?

You say she's a slut. She says don't men like it like that? It's simple, no stress, and exciting. When it's finished, you walk off and that's it, there's nothing to worry about and there are no complications. You ask how many men she has slept with. She says at least a hundred. You don't believe her.

What's there to believe or not to believe? It's really quite simple, sometimes it only takes a few minutes.

In a lift?

Why in a lift? You've been watching Western movies. Under trees, against walls, anywhere.

With total strangers?

That's even better, then you don't feel awkward when you bump into one another again.

You ask if she does this regularly.

Whenever the urge comes.

What if you can't find a man?

They're not hard to find, you only have to signal with your eyes and they come.

You say if she signals with her eyes, you wouldn't necessarily come.

She says you might not necessarily dare, but there are plenty who do. Isn't this all men want?

Then you are toying with men.

Why are only men allowed to toy with women? What's so strange about this?

You say she may as well say she is toying with herself.

And why not?

In this mud!

She starts giggling and says she likes you but it is not love. And she says you should be careful, if she were to really fall in love with you . . .

It would be a disaster.

She asks, a disaster for you or for her?

You say, a disaster for you and for her.

You're clever, she says, what she really likes is your clever mind.

You say unfortunately it's not your body.

She says everyone's got a body, and says she doesn't want to get worn out by living and gives a long sigh. How about telling a happy story, she says.

Shall I keep talking about the fire? The red boy with the bare bottom?

If you like.

You go on to say that this red boy, this fire god Zhurong, is the spirit of these nine mountains. The old fire god temple at the bottom of Huri Peak had long fallen into disrepair, people forgot to make offerings and were only concerned with enjoying the meat and liquor themselves. The neglected fire god became enraged and wreaked havoc. On your great-grandfather . . .

Why don't you go on?

The night he died, when everyone was sound asleep, a line of fire emerged in the forest, burning brightly and slowly travelling through the black mountain shadows. The wind carried the smell of burning and people who were fast asleep felt they were suffocating and hurriedly got up. They saw the forest on fire but just looked on in a daze. By daylight, the dense smoke had descended upon them and it was too late to stop it or even to escape. Pursued by scorching flames, wild animals were also terrified and tigers, leopards, wild pigs and jackals all scurried to the river. Only the deep turbulent stream stopped the spread of the fire. The crowds on the opposite bank watching the fire saw a huge red bird with nine heads spitting out tongues of fire rise from its midst. It soared into the sky trailing a long golden tail and wailing like a baby girl. Giant thousand-year trees shot up into the air like so many feathers, exploding loudly, then lightly falling into the sea of fire . . .

35

I dream that the rock wall behind me creaks open and that within the crack is the fish-belly white sky. Beneath the sky is a small lane, lonely and deserted. To one side is the door of a temple, I know it is the side door of the big temple, that it never opens, and at the doorway is a length of nylon rope with children's clothing hanging on it. I recognize it as somewhere I have been. It is the outside of the Two King Temple at Guanxian in Sichuan province and I am walking along a weir dividing the river which churns below my feet. On the other side there is also a temple which has been commandeered, I have tried to get inside but couldn't ever work out how and could only look at the fish and snakes crawling on the high black curled eaves protruding over the wall. I am holding onto a cable and inching forward over foaming rapids. People are actually fishing there and I want to go up to them to have a look but the tide swells and I have to retreat. All around is the surging torrent, the me in the middle is just a child. The me of the present is standing at a back door overgrown with weeds looking at the me of my childhood years. I am wearing a pair of cloth shoes and am in a predicament – my shoes have cloth knot-buttons and those primary school classmates who use dirty language say I've got girls' shoes and make me feel embarrassed. It is from the mouths of these wild street boys that I first learn the meaning of those words used for swearing at people. They say all women are sluts and that the fat woman on the corner who sells griddle-cakes griddle-cakes with men. I know all this is bad talk and has something to do with the bodies of men and women but only have a vague and hazy idea of just how. They say I like the dark skinny girl classmate who gave me a piece of scented paper and I blush, this is when I run into them at a special summer school cinema program after I have finished primary school and am in junior secondary school. They say she isn't as dark as she used to be and is very sexy. She has asked them about me and they ask why I haven't dated her. Afterwards, I am cast upon the flesh of women, struggling, I reach out and touch a woman's moist lower body, before that I hadn't dared be so bold, I know I have degenerated but am secretly happy, probably I know this is a woman I want but can't have, I can't see her beautiful face, I go to kiss her but the lips of another woman are kissing me. I know in my heart that I don't love her but I derive pleasure from her nonetheless. I then see the worried eyes of my father, he is silent, I know he is dead and so know this is not true, in a dream I can be as wanton as I like. I then hear the banging of the door in the wind and remember that I am sleeping in the cave on the mountain, the wrinkled folds of the strange ceiling over my head is the rock wall lit by the hurricane lamp, I am sleeping in soggy bedding, fully clad, and the clothing which clings to me is also damp, my feet are still icy and haven't warmed, the fierce mountain wind is howling on the other side of the banging wooden door like a blood-spattered wild animal crouching at the mouth of the cave blocked by the door. I listen carefully to the wind coming from the top of the cliff and tearing through the grassy marshland.

No longer able to hold back the urge to urinate, I crawl out of the bed, turn up the hurricane lamp, take it down and pull on my shoes. As I remove the branch against the door made from lengths of tree trunk nailed together, the wind blows the door wide open with a bang. Outside the cave is the pitch-black curtain of night and the hurricane lamp only casts a circle of light at my feet. I take a couple of steps, undo the fly of my trousers, and looking up suddenly see before me a monstrous black shadow. I yell out in alarm and almost drop the lamp. The huge form sways along with me and I immediately realize that this is the "demon shadow" I have read about in *Record of Fanjing*

Mountain. I swing the lamp and it also moves: it is in fact my own shadow in the night.

My peasant guide who came into the mountain with me hears my yells and comes running out with his hacking knife in his hand. Traumatized, I can't talk but just keep yelping, swaying the hurricane lamp and pointing. He also immediately begins yelping and takes the hurricane lamp from my hand. In the pitch-black thick curtain of night, two huge black forms prance wildly along with the jumping and yelping of two people. It is really strange to be terrified and then to discover that one has in fact been terrified by one's own shadow! The two of us piss as we prance about like children making the black demon shadows prance with us, and also to steady our nerves and comfort our spirits which have been scared out of our bodies.

Going back into the cave, I am so agitated that I can't get back to sleep, and he is tossing and turning too. So I ask him to tell me some stories about the mountains. He starts to burble away but now speaks in the local dialect and eight in ten sentences are incomprehensible. He seems to be saying that a cousin from a distant branch of the clan had been mauled by a bear and lost an eye because he had failed to pay homage to the mountain god. I can't tell if he's saying this to chastize me for having come on this trip.

We get up early to go to Nine Dragon Ponds. There is a heavy mist. He is walking in front. Beyond three paces he is only a faint shape and five paces away he can barely hear if I shout. If the mountain mist is thick like this, it is not at all strange that last night the lamp cast shadows overhead. For me this is a new experience and if I breathe out, a white vapour curls up to fill the gap I have made in the mist. However, before we go a hundred paces from the cave, he stops and turns back to say we can't go any further.

"Why?" I ask.

"Last year it was also foul weather like this. A group of six went up the mountain to steal medicinal herbs and only three came back."

"Stop trying to frighten me," I say.

"You go if you like, but there's no way I'm going."

"But you're here to accompany me!"

"I was sent by the ranger."

"He sent you because of me." I don't tell him I'm the one paying for his porter fee.

"If anything happens, it'll be hard explaining it to the ranger."

"You don't have to explain to the ranger, he's not my ranger and he doesn't have to be responsible for me. I'm the only person responsible for me. And I want to see Nine Dragon Lake!"

He says it's not a lake, it's just a few ponds.

I say, lake or ponds, I want to look at the gold hair moss there, I've come to this mountain to look at the one-foot-high gold hair moss, I want to somersault on the thick gold hair moss.

He says you can't sleep there, it is all waterweeds.

I go to say that it was the ranger who told me it was softer than tumbling on carpet, but it is pointless for me to try to explain what carpet is.

He stops talking and head bowed walks on ahead. I am therefore on the road again, this is a victory for me, I am capable of unnecessarily forcing my will upon a guide whose legs I am paying a fee for. I simply want to prove I have my own will which is precisely why I have come to this place where even ghosts wouldn't come.

As soon as I relax and fall a few steps behind, he vanishes in this white miasmic mist. I must hurry after his shadowy form but drawing near I discover it is a mountain oak. I don't know where I'll end up if I try finding my way back through this grassy marshland, I've completely lost my bearings and I start yelling out to him as loudly as I can.

He finally emerges in the mist, gesticulating wildly at me, and it is only after I come right up to him that I hear he is shouting. It's this damn mist.

"Are you angry with me?" I ask, thinking I should be apologetic.

"I'm not angry, even if I were I'm not angry with you, it's you who are angry with me!" He is still gesticulating wildly and yelling but the sound is muffled by the dense mist. I am aware that I am in the wrong.

I'd best follow close behind, virtually treading on his heels. It's impossible to go very far and it's very uncomfortable walking like this, and I certainly haven't come up this mountain to look at his heels. Then why have I come? It seems to have something to do with the dream, the demon shadow, my soaking wet clothing, my not having slept all night and this frustration, that I have a foreboding premonition. I reach into the pocket of my shirt which is clinging to my skin for the medicinal root to fend off snakes. I can't find it.

"Let's turn back."

He doesn't hear and I have to shout out, "Let's go back!"

This is all quite ridiculous but he doesn't laugh and just mumbles, "Should've turned back long ago."

So I end up obeying him. Turning around, I follow after him. He lights a fire as soon as he gets into the cave. The air pressure is so low that the smoke can't escape and soon the cave fills with smoke and we can barely open our eyes. He sits down in front of the fire and begins chanting, *nan-nan na-na*.

"What are you saying to the fire?" I ask.

"I'm saying that humans can't overcome fate."

He then climbs onto the plank bed to sleep and before long I hear him snoring loudly. He is a spontaneous creature with an untrammelled mind I think to myself. My predicament lies in my always seeking to be self-activated and wanting to search for my soul. However, the problem is if my soul manifested itself, would I be able to comprehend it? And even if I were able to comprehend it, what would it lead to?

I am utterly foolish and helpless in this damp cave and my wet underwear clings cold and clammy to me. Right now I realize that all I want is a window, a window with a light, where it is warm inside and someone I love who also loves me is there. This would be enough and anything else would be an invention. But that window too is only an illusion.

I recall it is not just once that I have had this dream: I am looking for the house where I once lived as a child, looking for those warm memories. Courtyards, one after the other, go deeper and deeper like a maze with their narrow and winding dark corridors, but I can never find a path which is the same so that I can come out by the way I came in. Every time I enter the courtyard in this dream, it is always by a different path. Sometimes my family's courtyard is a passageway for families living at the front and at the back and I can't do anything for myself that others won't know about, I am never able to experience the warm intimacy of just being myself. Even in my own room the partitions either do not go to the ceiling, or the papered walls have holes, or one of the walls has collapsed. I climb up a ladder against an upstairs room and look inside the house – it is all rubble. There used to be a pumpkin patch outside and once when I was climbing among the vines to catch crickets, my neck and arms rubbed on the hairy vines and I itched all over. That was in the sunshine and this is in the cold and rain. The empty lot which used to be all rubble is now full of houses belonging to different families. I have no idea when they were put up but the windows are all shut. Below this half of an upstairs room without any walls, my maternal grandmother is emptying clothes from a red wooden chest which is as old as herself, and she has been dead many years. I should look for warm memories such as my childhood dreams, or more precisely dreams about my childhood. I want to look for the friends I had when I was small, the little playmates whose names I have forgotten. There was a boy with a scar from a fall on his lower lip, he was kind and generous and had a purple earthenware pot for his crickets which he said had been left to him by his grandfather. I also liked his older sister, she was a very gentle person but I didn't ever speak to her. I know she later married and even if I went to her home I'd certainly come away empty-handed and wouldn't even be able to meet with that playmate with the scar on his lower lip.

I walk past small streets with houses all huddled closely together, the eaves of the roofs all hang low and stretch almost to the middle of the road. I have to hurry home, my maternal grandmother is waiting for me. When it's time for dinner she yells out to me, she always sounds

203

like she's arguing with someone. She often had rows with my mother, she had a quick temper and it got worse as she got older. She couldn't get on with her own daughter, and went off in a huff to look for some of my maternal relatives. Afterwards they said she died in an old people's home. I must find out what happened to her to do the right thing by my dead mother. My thinking all the time of people who are dead on this occasion is probably because usually I don't ever think about them, yet in fact they are closest to me. In this cave in the mountains, by the fire, the dancing sparks induce reminiscences. I rub my eyes which are stinging from the smoke and won't open.

I get up and go outside, the mist is a little lighter and it is possible to see ten paces away. Fine rain is drifting in the air. I discover some ends of burnt incense sticks poked into the cracks of the cliff, there is also a branch tied with pieces of red cloth poked into a crack. I think to myself this must be the place where women pray for sons which the mountain people call Lingyan.

The huge heaven-propping pillars on the peak completely vanish in the mist. I walk along the mountain ridge and suddenly in the mist a dead city appears.

36

Can't you talk about anything else?

You say these ruins overgrown with weeds are assailed by mountain winds, moss and lichen cover broken slabs of rock and there's a gecko running on one of them.

It is said that in those times, the sound of bells at dawn, the boom of drums at dusk and the smoke of incense filled the air and there were a thousand monk dormitories and nine hundred and ninety-nine monks sworn to solitary existence. The monastery was ruled by a venerable monk and on the day he died there was a grand Buddhist gathering.

It is said that incense burned in each of the censers of the monastery, filling a circumference of several hundred *li* with its aroma, so that devotees smelling it in the wind fought to witness the old monk transform as he sat there and rose to heaven. The tracks and paths through this wooded Buddhist territory were crammed with devout men and women hastening to worship.

It is said that the chanting of sutras filled the air and drifted beyond the mountain pass. There were no vacant cushions in the halls and latecomers knelt on the floor to pray. Those who came even later waited outside the halls. An endless stream kept coming up behind the crowds who couldn't get inside the monastery gates. It was a gathering such as had never been seen before.

It is said that the devout all wanted to receive the grace of the old monk and the multitude of disciples all wanted to receive his rendition of the dharma truth. Before the Venerable Master died he would give an exposition of the dharma from the Sutra Hall which was on the floor below the Sutra Library, to the left of the Hall of Magnificent Treasures.

It is said that in the courtyard in front of the Sutra Hall two cassia trees were in bloom, one a golden red and the other a moonlight white, each exuding a subtle fragrance. Rush cushions were spread from the Sutra Hall into the courtyard and monks sitting with legs folded, hearts immaculate, in the warm rays of the autumn sun calmly waited for the old monk's last exposition of the dharma.

It is said that he had bathed and fasted, neither eating nor drinking, for seven days and seven nights. Eyes closed, he sat with legs folded on the lotus-shaped altar of carved black sandalwood, a voluminous cassock covered in patches draped over his shoulders. Sandalwood chips burned in the bronze upright censer before the altar, spreading their pure fragrance throughout the Sutra Hall. His two senior disciples stood on either side of him and a score of monks he had personally tonsured waited with absolute reverence below the altar. His left hand held a string of Buddha beads and his right hand a Buddha bell. As he gently struck the bell with the steel pin in his hand a magnificent note rippled among the Buddha pennants hanging above the hall.

It is said that the multitude of monks thereupon heard the sound of his mellifluous voice: Buddha tells those awaiting enlightenment that Buddha cannot be perceived by manifestations of the physical body. Buddha says all existing phenomena are illusions, manifestations of the physical body. If manifestations are erroneous manifestations then they are also not erroneous manifestations. All that I teach is what the Buddha ancestor has said and what Buddha has said cannot be grasped and cannot not be grasped, and also cannot be verbally transmitted. This which cannot be verbally transmitted and which cannot be grasped is what I transmit to all of you, and is the Great Dharma transmitted by Buddha. Are there any questions?

It is said that among this multitude of Buddhist disciples not one understood and not one dared ask. Most troubled were the two disciples on either side who had attended him for seven days and seven nights, not daring to relax even a little, just waiting for him to give instructions for the funeral and to pass on his cassock and alms bowl. However, he said nothing about these, and in the censer the last stick of incense for calculating the time had burnt down to the wood. Finally it was the more senior disciple who plucked up the courage, took a step forward, kneeled with his palms pressed together, then prostrated himself and said: This disciple has a question but doesn't know whether or not he should ask.

It is said that the old monk opened his eyes a little and asked what it was that he wanted to ask. This senior disciple raised his head, looked around and asked whether the cassock and bowl would be handed over before he ended his life. Everyone understood what was implied — someone had to receive the cassock and bowl to govern this huge monastery with its multitude of monks and wealth of incense. How could there not be a successor in a whole generation of monks?

It is said that the old monk nodded and took out the bowl from his cassock. As soon as he uttered the words "Take the bowl", the slender stick of incense burnt right down. The smoke slowly rose, trembled, formed an incomplete circle, then vanished. In the Hall of Magnificent Treasures, the 1200-catty iron bell made under supervision of the monks during the Zhengyuan reign of the Tang Dynasty sounded. Immediately drums began to boom and the multitude of monks in the Sutra Hall hastened to beat their wooden clappers and bronze chimes. When the monks saw that the old monk had already handed over his cassock and bowl the sutra chant Namo Amitofu rose into the air from every mouth.

It is said that the two senior disciples were dull-witted and neither had heard the old monk say "and go begging" after the words "Take the bowl". When they saw the old monk's lips tremble neither was interested in obtaining the true teaching but grabbed the alms bowl and wouldn't let go. Consequently, it quietly disintegrated. The two were alarmed and realized that the old monk had willed it and didn't dare to say anything. Only the venerable old monk knew the monastery would be destroyed that day. He couldn't bear to watch, closed his eyes and stopped breathing as he sat there sedately on the lotus seat, one hand resting in the other, staring at the gate of life on his abdomen, and silently willing the end of his life.

It is said that inside and outside the Sutra Hall bells and drums loudly sounded and the chanting of the sutras by the monks in the hall reached the courtyard, whereupon the masses of monks in the courtyard began chanting which spread out all around to the three great halls and to the two side halls and then drifted out to the front of the monastery to the square which was crammed with sedan chairs, donkeys, horses and worshippers. The devout men and women who couldn't get through the mountain pass refused to be left out and, chanting Namo Amitofu as loudly as they could, made a mighty charge through the pass!

It is said that the monks carrying the altar on which the old monk in the sitting position had transformed himself were escorted under a canopy of embroidered satin banners. Two monks flourishing dusters and sprinkling mind-and-body cleansing Buddha water cleared the path before them. The devout men and women charging through the mountain pass fought desperately to catch a lucky glimpse of the old monk. Those who saw him praised his kindly visage so that those who hadn't caught a glimpse became even more desperate. There was a chaotic surging mass of people standing on tiptoe and craning their necks, all crowding against one another. Hats were knocked off, shoes were trodden on and lost, incense burners were pushed over, and sacred precincts were violated.

It is said that the altar was covered and placed on the brushwood pyre in front of the Hall of Magnificent Treasures. Before the lighting of the pyre there was still to be a session of fervent sutra chanting. None of the rituals could be missed, the smallest oversight was intolerable under Buddha's law. However even a larger monastery could not have withstood the pushing and shoving of ten thousand people, even stronger men could not have stemmed the surging throng of people. Those who fell and were injured couldn't help screaming and shouting and in this commotion emerged the tragic event!

No-one could say for sure how the conflagration started, nor how many were burnt or trampled to death, so that whether more burnt to death or more had been trampled to death was never established. In any case for three days and three nights the vast inferno raged until the Lord of Heaven was filled with compassion and sent forth timely rains which left an expanse of ashes. Remaining after the catastrophe were only these ruins and part of a stone tablet for later generations of busybodies to carry out investigations.

37

Behind this broken wall my dead father, mother and maternal grandmother are seated at the dinner table waiting for me to come and eat. I have been wandering endlessly and haven't joined in a family gathering for a long time. I want to sit with them at the table to chat about ordinary family matters in the way that, when diagnosed with lung cancer, I would sit at my younger brother's table talking about things one can't talk about with strangers and can only discuss within the family. In those days, when it was time to eat, my niece would always want to watch television. She was too little to know that the programs were attacks on spiritual pollution, propaganda targeting all sections of society. Cultural celebrities would appear one after another to declare their position and to repeat the set slogans. They weren't programs for children and certainly didn't go well with eating. I'd had enough of television news and newspapers, I just wanted to return to my own life, to chat about forgotten family matters, like my crazy great-grandfather who, determined to satisfy his craving to be an official, gave away a whole street of houses. He couldn't manage to get even half an official position and, realizing he'd been cheated, went berserk and torched all the houses, even the one he was living in. He was much younger than I am now when he died after just turning thirty. Confucius talked about establishing oneself at the age of thirty, but this is a young and brittle age and if one doesn't succeed one can have a nervous breakdown. Neither I nor my younger brother have ever seen photos of this great-grandfather. At the time probably the art of photography hadn't yet come to China or else it was only the nobility who could have their photos taken. However, both I and my younger brother have eaten the wonderful meals grandmother prepared. What I remember most vividly are the drunken prawns: the flesh of the prawns was still twitching and it took a long time to pluck up the courage to eat just one of them. I also remember my grandfather who had a stroke and was paralysed. To escape the bombs of the Japanese planes we rented an old house in the countryside from a peasant and all day long he lay on a reclining rattan chair in the hall. The door was left open and a breeze went straight through the main room so that his white hair was moving all the time. When the air raid sirens went off he became distraught and my mother could only crouch next to his ear and say over and over that the Japanese don't have many bombs and if they are dropping them they will only be dropping them on the cities. At the time I was smaller than this little niece of mine and was just learning to walk. I remember that to get to the back courtyard I had to cross a high sill and after crossing, there was also a step. I couldn't crawl over it on my own so the back courtyard remained a mysterious place for me. Beyond the front door was a big threshing square and I recall tumbling in the hay with the children of peasant families. A small dog drowned in the quiet and beautiful river right next to it. Some nasty person had thrown it in or else it had fallen in by itself. In any case the carcass lay on the shore for a long time. My mother sternly forbade me to play near the river, it was only when the grown-ups went to the river-bank to fetch water that I could go and dig in the sand. They would dig holes in the sand and scoop up clear filtered water.

I am aware that at this moment I am surrounded by a world of dead people and that behind this wall are my dead relatives. I want to be with them again, to sit at the table with them and to listen to them chatting about trifling things. I want to hear their voices, to see their eyes, to actually sit at the same table with them, even if we don't have a meal. I know that eating and drinking in the world of ghosts is symbolic, a ritual, and that living people cannot partake of it, but it suddenly occurs to me that just to be able to sit at the table and to listen would be a blessing. I creep up to them but as I cross the ruins of the wall, they get up and quietly vanish behind another wall. I hear their departing footsteps, rustling, even see the empty table they leave behind. Instantly the table is covered in velvety moss, breaks, cracks, then collapses into a heap of rubble and bushes sprout all over it. I know right now they're discussing me in another room in these ruins. They don't approve of how I am living my life and are worried about me. There's really no need but they insist on worrying, I think maybe the dead just like worrying about the living. They're talking in whispers but as soon as I put my ear to the damp mossy wall they stop and communicate with their eyes. They say I can't go on like this, I need a normal family. They should find me a good intelligent wife, a woman who can tend to what I eat and drink and manage the home for me – they think my prolonged illness is from improper eating and drinking. They're plotting how to arrange my life. I should tell them there's no need for them to worry, I'm already middle-aged and have my own way of life, it's what I have chosen and I'm not likely to go back to what they have in mind for me. I can't live the lives they lived, and in any case their lives weren't particularly wonderful. Still, I can't help thinking about them and wanting to see them, hear their voices, talk with them about past events in my memories. I want to ask my mother if she had taken me on a boat on the Xiang River. I recall being in a narrow wooden boat with a woven bamboo canopy. There were people closely packed on the wooden planks on either side, their knees touching those of the people opposite. The water could be seen coming up to the top of the sides and the boat lurched continuously, but no-one commented. Everyone pretended not to notice but they were clearly aware of it. The overloaded boat could sink at any moment but nobody gave this away. I also pretended not to know. I didn't cry or make a fuss and fought not to think of the disaster which could happen at any time, I want to ask her if this was when we were refugees. If I can find a boat like this on the Xiang River it will confirm this memory. I also want to ask her whether or not we hid in a pig's pen from bandits. That day the weather was like the weather today, fine rain was falling, and going up a mountain road the truck broke down on a sharp corner. The driver blamed himself and said if he'd turned the steering wheel a fraction harder the front and rear wheels on one side wouldn't have got bogged in the soft mud at the edge of the road. I remember they were the wheels on the right because afterwards everyone got out and off-loaded all the baggage onto the left of the highway next to the side of the mountain and then went to push the truck. However, the wheels simply spun in the mud without moving out of it. The truck was fitted with a charcoal combustion stove, it was during the war and it was impossible to get petrol except for military vehicles. To start, each time the truck had to be cranked furiously until it could be heard farting before it would go. Motor vehicles in those days were like people and wouldn't go unless they got rid of gas. However, the truck farted but the wheels only spun and splashed mud into the faces of the people pushing it. The driver kept trying to flag a passing vehicle but none would stop to help. In weather like this and as it was getting dark they were all in a hurry to escape. The last vehicle with yellowish headlights like the eyes of a wild beast sped past. Afterwards, we groped in the dark in the rain up the mountain, each holding onto the clothing of the person in front and slipping time and again on the muddy mountain path. We were old people, women and children and it was with much difficulty that we made it to a farmhouse. They didn't have a lamp inside and refused to open the door so we had to squeeze into the pig pen to get out of the rain. From the ink-black mountain shadows at the back, in the middle of the night, came bursts of rifle shots and a string of burning torches could be seen. Everyone said bandits were going past and, terrified, no-one dared make a sound.

I step over a crumbling wall. On the other side is a little-leaf box sapling with a trunk as skinny as a little finger shivering in the wind in the middle of these ruins of a roofless house. Opposite, part of a window remains, and leaning there I can look out. Among the azaleas and clumps of bamboo are some mossy black stone slabs which from a distance look soft, like human bodies lying there, bent knees sticking up and arms outstretched. In those times, Gold Top, with its one thousand rooms of temples, halls and monk dormitories, had iron roof-tiles to protect it from the onslaught of the mountain winds. In the Ming Dynasty, a multitude of monks and nuns practised the faith alongside the ninth concubine of the father of the Wanli Emperor. There must be some remnants of the grandeur of the morning bells and evening drums. I search for some relic of those times but only turn up the corner of a broken stone tablet. Could it be that within the space of five hundred years even the iron tiles have completely rusted away?

38

Now what will I talk about?

I'll talk about what happened five hundred years later when this monastery, which had been reduced to ruins, was turned into a hideout for bandits. They slept in the caves during the daytime and at night came with flaming torches down the mountain to pillage and loot. It so happened that living at the nunnery at the foot of the mountain was an official's daughter who, without shaving her hair, had devoted herself to Buddhist cultivation and was keeping watch over the ancient black Buddha lamp to atone for a sin in a previous life. However, she was seen by the bandit chief, taken up the mountain, and forced to be housekeeper for the camp. The girl refused, even under the threat of death, so she was first raped and then killed.

What else will I talk about?

I'll go back fifteen hundred years, to a time before the ancient monastery existed when there was only a grass hut. A famous scholar had hung up his cap of office and retired here to live as a recluse. Every morning just before dawn he would face the east and practise Daoist life-prolonging breathing exercises, inhaling the essence of the purple profoundness. Then, head high, he would produce a sustained whistle. The pure sound would reverberate in the empty valley and monkeys climbing on the sheer cliffs would respond with their cries. Occasionally friends would come and they would drink toasts with tea instead of liquor, play chess or engage in pure talk debate in the light of the moon. Although old age was upon him he thought nothing of it, and passing woodcutters in the distance would point at him in wonder. That is why this place is called Immortal's Cliff.

And what else can I talk about?

I'll talk about one thousand five hundred and forty-seven years later, when beyond this mountain a warlord lived. After spending most of his life in the army he eventually became a commander and returned to his village to offer sacrifices to his ancestors. There he fell in love with the servant girl who looked after his mother and in due course an auspicious day and hour were chosen for him to take her as his concubine ... in order of succession she was the seventh. One hundred and one tables of food and liquor were laid out to make an ostentatious show for the villagers. Friends and relatives filled the tables and of course couldn't avoid sending vast amounts of gifts, for how could this feast not come at a cost? While everyone was celebrating, a beggar came to the door. His clothes were tattered rags and his head was covered with ringworms. The gatekeepers gave him a bowl of rice but when they tried to send him away he refused to go and insisted on entering the hall and going up to the main table to congratulate the groom. The commander was enraged and ordered his aide to hit the man with his rifle and chase him off. Late that night when everyone was asleep and the groom was lost in happy dreams, fires broke out everywhere, destroying the larger part of the old ancestral home. Some said it was the Living Buddha Jigong using his magic to punish the wicked on behalf of Heaven. Others, however, said that the beggar was none other than the infamous Mottle Head who was cruel and mean. Beggars great or small a hundred *li* around all gave their allegiance to him, so how could he tolerate such an insult? Brigade commander or army commander made no difference at all. If they didn't show respect, he'd get his ruffians to tie fuses on bundles of incense sticks and, in the middle of the night, shoot them over the high wall into the dry grass and piles of firewood. Even a general with a thousand troops and ten thousand horses wouldn't be able to defend himself against this insignificant person. It's as the old saying goes – the powerful dragon is no match for the snake crawling on the ground.

Now what else can I talk about?

It was more than half of a century afterwards, also on this mountain. This big mountain may look grand and majestic but because of the turmoil in the human world, it too has never known peace. The ugly daughter of the newly-appointed director of the revolutionary committee of a certain county fell in love with the grandson of a former landlord and, against her father's orders, was determined to marry him. The couple eloped after stealing ration coupons for thirty-eight catties of grain and a hundred and seven *yuan* in cash from a drawer. They hid in the mountains confident that they would be able to survive by farming the land. The father, who spent every day preaching about class struggle, had had his own daughter abducted by the offspring of a landlord, so understandably he was righteously indignant. He immediately gave orders for the public security bureau to circulate the man's photo and the entire county was alerted to arrest him. It was impossible for the young couple to escape the armed people's militias scouring the mountains and when the cave they were hiding in was surrounded, the terrified youth used the axe he had stolen to first kill his lover and then himself.

She says she also wants to see blood. She wants to stab her middle finger with a needle. The fingers are connected to the heart and the pain will go straight there. She wants to watch the blood ooze out, swell, spread, soak the whole finger red, run right to the base of the finger, flow between the fingers, along the lines of the palm to the centre. The back of the hand will also be dripping with blood . . .

You ask her why.

She says because you're oppressive.

You say the oppression comes from herself.

She says you are also causing it.

You say you are only telling stories, you aren't doing anything.

She says everything you talk about is stifling, suffocating.

You ask whether she has some pathological illness.

She says it was induced by you!

You say you can't understand what it is you have done.

She says you're a hypocrite! And saying this she starts laughing crazily.

The sight of her frightens you, you admit you wanted to arouse her lust, but you find a woman's blood repugnant.

She says she wants to make you see blood. She wants her blood to run down to her wrist, along her arm, to her armpit, onto her chest. She wants blood to flow all over her white breasts, bright red tinged with purple and black. She will be soaked in the purple-black blood so you will be forced to look ...

Stark naked?

Stark naked, sitting in a pool of blood, the lower part of her body, between her legs and her thighs, all covered in blood, blood, blood! She says she wants to sink, become utterly depraved, she can't understand why it is that she lusts, lusts for the tide to soak her. She sees herself lying on the sandy shore, the tide surging, the sandy shore rustling but unable to suck it all up before another tide irrepressibly surges in. She wants you to come into her body, to thrust and to pull relentlessly. She says she no longer has shame, nor fear. She used to be afraid, then when she wasn't she still said she was, even though she really wasn't. But she's afraid of falling into the black abyss and endlessly drifting down. She wants to sink but is afraid of sinking, she says she sees the black tide slowly swelling, swelling up from some unknown source. The black tide is swallowing her, she says she comes slowly but when she does, she can't stop. She can't understand why she has become so wanton, oh, she wants you to say she is wanton and she wants you to say she is not. From you, only from you does she have this need. She says she loves you. She wants you to say you love her but you never say this, you are so cruel. What you want is a woman but what she wants is love, and she needs to feel it with her whole body and heart, even if it means following you to hell. She begs you not to leave her, not to abandon her, she is afraid of loneliness, afraid of only being afraid of the emptiness. She knows all this is temporary but wants to deceive herself. Can't you say something to make her happy? Tell a story to make her happy?

Oh! It's rowdy as they quaff the liquor from the big bowl passed from hand to hand. They are sitting cross-legged opposite one another before woven bamboo mats laid with a long line of black pig's blood, white bean curd, red chillies, tender green soya beans, soya sauce pig trotters, stewed pork ribs and broiled fatty pork. The stockade village is celebrating – nine pigs and three oxen have been slaughtered and ten big vats of aged liquor have been opened. Everybody's face is flushed and shiny, noses drip with greasy sweat. The crippled chief stands up and starts to shout in his raspy drake's voice. Hemp Flower Peak has been theirs for many generations, how can they let outsiders burn down the forests to plant corn? He has lost all his front teeth and splutters. Don't get the idea that this decrepit old man who is like a piece of straw is all they have in head stockade, don't get the idea that the head stockade can be easily duped. He can't handle a spiked carrying pole or a blunderbuss anymore but the young men of the head stockade are no cowards! Mother of Big Treasure, you wouldn't keep back your son, would you? The silver bangles on the woman fly up with her arms. Venerable old chief, don't say that, the whole stockade has watched my son Big Treasure grow up, he is not respected by outsiders and he's also the butt of the village. Don't just pick on my Big Treasure. Mine isn't the only family in the head stockade. Which of the families produce only daughters and no sons? Suddenly all the women sulk off. Mother of Big Treasure, why are you changing the subject? If the head stockade doesn't stand up to the outsiders how can we not lose face? Flushed with alcohol, the young men open their jackets and beat their chests: Old chief, the blunderbusses we have aren't vegetarian! Venerable elder, just give the order, but don't listen to your daughters-in-law and keep your eldest son and second son locked up in the house, leaving us young people to fight in the vanguard. The daughters-in-law panic at hearing this, and retort: You spoke barbed words even before you started getting hair on your face, your parents don't mind parting with you, so why should we? A young man suddenly stands up, his eyes bulging. Little Two, you're being rash, it's not your turn to interrupt in the head stockade! Are you still listening?

Keep talking, she says, she just wants to hear your voice.

So you muster the energy and go on. Everyone starts clamouring. With a toss of the head he braces himself into a straddle stance, seizes a rooster and snaps its neck, and with its wings still flapping, he sprinkles the hot blood into the bowl of liquor and shouts in a loud voice: Whoever doesn't drink is a son of a bitch! Only a son of a bitch won't drink this! The men roll up their sleeves, tread on the saliva they spit in the dirt, make oaths to Heaven and fiery-eyed turn to their weapons – knives are sharpened and firearms cleaned. The aged parents of each household light lanterns and go to the ancestral burial grounds to dig graves. The women stay at home and with the scissors they had used to cut their hair after marriage and to cut the umbilical cord when they gave birth, they cut streamers for the graves. At dawn when the morning mists are about to rise the chief limps out and pounds on the big drum. The women, wiping away tears, emerge from the houses to keep guard at the gates of the stockade and to watch their menfolk, armed with knives and blunderbusses and striking gongs and shouting, charge down the mountain. For their ancestors, the stockade, the earth, the forests, their sons and grandsons, they go into battle then silently return with the corpses. The women weep and wail to Heaven and Earth, then silence returns. Then there is ploughing, seeding, replanting, harvesting and threshing. Spring passes and autumn comes, then after many winters when the graves are covered in grass and the widows have stolen men and the orphans have grown up, the grief is forgotten and only the glory of the ancestors is remembered. Until one evening, before the annual feast and sacrifice to the ancestors, the old people start talking about the sworn enemies of many generations and the young people have been drinking, and hot blood again boils up . . .

All night the rain continues and you watch the flame shrink to the size of a bean flower. At the base of the bright bean flower is a blue-white shoot which expands as the bean flower contracts and deepens from light yellow to orange and suddenly starts jumping on the wick. The darkness thickens, solidifies like grease, and extinguishes the trembling pale light. You break away from the woman clinging tightly to you, she is bathed in hot sweat and is fast asleep. You listen to the rain beating noisily on the leaves of the trees and the mountain wind groaning in the valley from the tops of the fir forest. The thatched roof, from which the oil lamp is hanging, starts to leak and the water drips onto your face. Huddled in the mountain-viewing shack put together with some thatch, you smell rotting grass and at the same time something sweet and fragrant.

39

I must get out of this cave. The main peak of the Wuling Range, at the borders of the provinces of Guizhou, Sichuan, Hubei and Hunan, is 3200 metres above sea level. The annual rainfall is more than 3400 points and in one year there are barely one or two days of fine weather. When the wild winds start howling they often reach velocities of more than three hundred kilometres per hour. This is a cold, damp and evil place. I must return to the smoke and fire of the human world to search for sunlight, warmth, happiness, and to search for human society to rekindle the noisiness, even if anxiety is regenerated, for that is in fact life in the human world.

I pass through Tongren. On its congested ancient little streets with overhanging eaves reaching to the middle of the road pedestrians and people with baskets on carrying poles collide. I don't stay long, get on a bus right away, and at dusk arrive at a stop called Yubing. A number of privately-operated inns have recently sprung up by the railway station so I take a room which is just big enough for a single bed. The mosquitos unrelentingly harass me but when I let down the mosquito net it is hot and stuffy. The noisy honking of trucks and cars outside the window accompanies the drone of a teary conversation which gives me goose bumps – it seems to be coming from a movie which is showing on the basketball court. It's the same old story of melodramatic separation and reunion, only the time has changed.

At two o'clock in the morning I board the train for Kaili and after some hours reach the capital of the Miao Autonomous District.

I hear there is a dragon boat festival at the Shidong Miao stockade.

This is confirmed by a cadre of the prefectural committee. He says it's a big event which hasn't been held for several decades and he estimates there will be a gathering of some ten thousand Miao from the stockades far and near, as well as senior provincial and autonomous district officials. I ask how I can get there and he says it is about two hundred kilometres away and I wouldn't be able to get there in time without a car. I ask if I can go with them in a prefectural committee car. He winces, but after much pleading on my part, says to come at seven o'clock in the morning to see if there's room.

In the morning I get to the committee office ten minutes early but there is no sign of the big cars which were in front of the building the day before. The only person I find on duty in the empty building says that the cars set out long ago. I realize I've been tricked. However, anxiety breeds genius. I take out my Writers' Association card, which has never been of any use and has only given me trouble, and put on a bit of a bluff. I make a fuss about having come expressly from Beijing to write about this event and ask him to immediately contact the prefectural authorities. He knows nothing about me, makes a series of phone calls, and eventually finds out that the prefectural head's car hasn't left. I run all the way to his office and am in luck. The prefectural head had been informed and without asking questions allows me to squeeze into his small van.

After leaving the city we travel down a potholed highway obscured by a dust haze thrown up by the stream of trucks and cars crammed with people – there are cadres and workers from the prefectural offices, as well as people from enterprises, schools and factories, all hurrying to join in the fun. This former Miao king who is now the prefectural head is probably in charge of some ceremony. The cadre next to the driver has the window down and is shouting out to cars to make way. We keep overtaking and pass through many stockades as well as two county towns but finally come to a stop because a large number of vehicles is jamming the road in front of the ferry crossing. A big car has failed to negotiate the ferry and its front wheels have slipped into the water. Also stuck in the morass of cars is a splendid black Volga which they tell me is the car of the party secretary of the prefectural committee and which appears to be carrying senior provincial officials. Large numbers of police bark orders and directions endlessly and after an agonizing hour or so the big car is partially pushed into the water to clear enough space to put down the plank. Our little van follows close behind the Volga and immediately after the police stop all the cars. The ferry winds up the cables and leaves the shore.

At noon this mighty contingent arrives at the Miao stockade on the broad banks of the Qingshui River. In the blazing sun the clear water sparkles with a dazzling brilliance. Both sides of the highway are awash in colour, teaming with the floral parasols and high silver head ornaments of the Miao women. Alongside the highway is a new two-storey brick building which houses the government offices, then all the way down to the river are the wooden houses on high pylons of the Miao people. Below the veranda of the government building a seething mass of heads, inlaid with round floral parasols and bamboo hats shiny with tung oil, slowly moves between the rows of white canopied stalls on the river-bank. A large number of dragon boats, heads rearing and decked with red streamers, glide about on the clear, green, flat surface of the river.

Following close behind the prefectural head, I slip into the building past the saluting police on guard and receive the warm reception accorded to the cadres in the group. Young Miao women in full festival attire bring basins of hot water and present each of the guests with a brand new scented hand towel to wash their hands and faces. The women, who all have bright eyes and white teeth, then present us with cups of fragrant new season tea, just as they do to visiting officials on the news. I ask the cadre in charge of reception if they are performers from the prefectural dance troupe brought in for the occasion. He tells me they are exemplary middle school students from the county town with weeks of training by a special group of the county people's committee. Two of them put on a performance of Miao love songs. The senior officials make some encouraging comments and then everyone is escorted to their seats in the dining hall. Food and drink have been laid out, there is beer and soft drinks, and only napkins are missing. I am casually introduced to the party secretary and to the town head, who both speak some Chinese, and they shake hands with me along with all the others. Everyone praises the culinary skills of the chef sent by the county administration, and as he announces each of the dishes he clasps his hands and bows humbly. Afterwards we wash our hands and faces again and drink more tea. It is two o'clock in the afternoon and the dragon boat races should be starting soon.

The town head and the party secretary lead the way down the stone steps through a narrow lane crowded with people. Some Miao women in multi-pleated skirts who have come from elsewhere are doing finishing touches to their dresses in the shade of the pylon houses. At the sight of this group with a police escort they stop looking in their little mirrors and combing their hair to stare curiously. The group filing past also stares at the several kilos of various kinds of silver headdress, silver necklets and silver bracelets they are wearing and for a while it is hard to tell who is more keenly scrutinizing who.

Chairs and benches have been arranged on a platform on pylons by the river. It is surrounded by civilian police. Once seated, everyone is given a small floral parasol similar to the ones the young Miao women carry, but held by these cadres they are decidedly *not* pretty. The blazing sun is slanting but even with a parasol I sweat profusely, so I go down to join the bustling crowds by the river.

The scent of tobacco, pickles, sweat and the acrid smell from the tables of beef, mutton, pork and fish all waft up in the intense heat. The stalls sell things from department store cloth to little snacks like toffee peanuts, bean-paste jellies and melon seeds, and there is a lively din of bargaining, flirtatious laughter and children weaving in and out of the crowds.

I am easily carried in the tide of people down to the river until I am almost treading in the water and am forced to jump into a small boat tied to the shore. Up ahead is a dragon boat made from a hollowed out tree trunk. To preserve the balance a shaved branch is fitted at the waterline on the side. In the boat, facing the same direction, are thirty rowers, all dressed identically in indigo-blue trousers and jackets with pleats shining from the ox bone fat in the cloth and small hats of intricately woven bamboo. Each of them is also wearing sunglasses and a shiny metal belt. At the middle of the boat is a boy dressed up as a girl. He is wearing silver neck rings and a headdress and from time to time he strikes the club-gong hanging in front of him. At the prow of the boat a large, carved wooden dragon rears its head. It is strewn with little flags and red cloth streamers, and hanging on it are also quacking, honking live ducks and geese.

There is a burst of firecrackers and people bearing sacrificial objects arrive. The captain at the prow beats the drum and gets the rowers to stand up. A middle-aged fellow with a vat of liquor in both hands walks straight into the thigh-deep water without rolling up his trouser legs and presents bowls of liquor to the crew. The men in sunglasses quaff down the liquor as they sing their thanks and with a flourish rinse the dregs in the river.

An old man runs into the water along with some men carrying a live pig. The terrified animal is hanging upside down by the legs and its frantic squealing heightens the drama and excitement. The vat of liquor and the pig are then put into the small boat containing sacrificial objects tailing the dragon boat.

It is almost five o'clock when I return to the viewing platform. The river resounds with drums which start up in one place and subside in another, at times intense and at others slow. The dragon boats are playing with one another and don't look as if they are about to race, a few boats will bunch together and then suddenly separate. The people on the viewing platform start getting impatient. First they summon the prefectural committee, then they send word to the cadres of the sports committee to say there is advice from above that each participating dragon boat is to be awarded one hundred *yuan* in cash as well as coupons for two hundred catties of grain. Some time later the sun is about to set, the heat has abated, and there is no need for the parasols. However, the dragon boats still haven't started to assemble and there is no sign of a race starting. At this point word arrives that there will be no race today and people would have to go thirty *li* downstream to another Miao stockade tomorrow. There is immediately a stir on the viewing platform and the decision is made to go back.

The procession of vehicles head to tail on the highway starts to move off. Ten minutes later it has vanished in a cloud of yellow dust and on the road there remain only the crowds of young Miao tourists who continue to flock in. It seems that many of the highlights of the festival take place at night.

When I decided to stay, a cadre who had come in the prefectural car warned that there wouldn't be a car if I left tomorrow. I said if I couldn't stop a passing car I'd walk. However, he was very kind and fetched a couple of cadres from the Miao village, entrusting me to their care, and telling them, "If anything happens you'll be responsible!" The secretary and the town head nodded profusely and said, "You can relax, everything will be fine."

When I return to the small building of the town administration office, no-one is there and it is locked up. The party secretary and town head I expect will wake up somewhere from a drunken stupor tonight. Afterwards I don't see anyone wearing a four-pocket cadre jacket and who can speak Chinese and I feel suddenly liberated and freely wander about the stockade.

On the old streets and lanes running along the river, every household is entertaining relatives. Where there are large numbers of guests, tables are laid out onto the street and buckets of rice, bowls and chopsticks are by the door. Lots of people are helping themselves and no-one is keeping watch. I'm hungry and can't worry about standing on ceremony, and in any case I can't communicate, so I also help myself to a bowl and chopsticks and end up with people continually urging me to eat. This is probably an ancient Miao tradition and I have seldom enjoyed such freedom.

The love songs start at dusk, at first drifting across from the other side of the river. The bamboo groves on the mountain opposite are bathed in the gold of the lingering rays of the sun while this side of the river is already cloaked in night. Young women in groups of five or six come to the river-bank, some standing in a circle and others holding hands, and begin calling their lovers. Melodious singing rapidly fills the vast night. Young women are everywhere, still with their parasols up and also holding a handkerchief or a fan. There are also some thirteen- or fourteen-year-old girls who are just becoming aware of boys.

In each group, one girl leads the singing and the other girls harmonize. I observe that the lead singer is invariably the prettiest of the group, I suppose choice by beauty is a fairly natural principle.

The voice of the lead singer rises in the air and I can't help noticing her utter sincerity. The correct word is perhaps not "sing", for the clear shrill sounds come from deep within so that body and heart respond. The sounds seem to travel from the soles of the feet then shoot up between the eyes and the forehead before they are produced – no wonder they're called "flying songs". It is totally instinctive, uncontrived, unrestrained and unembellished, and certainly devoid of what might be called embarrassment. Each woman exerts herself, body and heart, to draw her young man to her.

The young men are even less inhibited and come right up to the women to choose the one they like best, as if they are choosing a piece of fruit. At this point the women move their handkerchiefs and fans, and the more they are examined the more feeling they put into their singing. When a conversation starts, the young man takes the woman's hand and they walk off together. The marketplace with its stalls thronging with ten thousand heads during the daytime is now a vast singing stadium. I am suddenly surrounded by an expanse of passions and think that the human search for love must originally have been like this. So-called civilization in later ages separated sexual impulse from love and created the concepts of status, wealth, religion, ethics and cultural responsibility. Such is the stupidity of human beings.

Night grows palpably thick, the sound of the drums ceases and the black surface of the river is dotted with the lights of the boats. I suddenly hear someone call out in Chinese, "older brother", and the voice seems to be right near me. I turn and see four or five girls on the slope all singing to me. One again calls out in a clear voice "older brother". At this point, I realize this is probably all the Chinese she knows but it would be enough to seek love. I see her expectant eyes in the darkness, unblinking and fixed on me. My heart starts pounding and I seem to return to the long-lost trembling of my passionate youth. I am drawn to her, perhaps affected by the actions of the young men here, perhaps because of the darkness. I see her lips moving slightly although she doesn't speak again and just waits, and the singing of her companions grows soft. She is still a child, her face hasn't lost that childish look – the high forehead, upturned nose, small mouth. If I give the slightest sign I know she will come away with me, snuggle up and, all excited, put up her parasol. But this tension is unbearable. I quickly smile, no doubt very awkwardly, resolutely shake my head, then turn and walk away, not daring to look back.

I've never encountered this style of love. It's what I dream about but when it actually happens I can't cope.

I should confess that the low bridge and upturned nose, high forehead, small mouth and expectant bright eyes of the Miao girl revived painful, tender feelings which had long since become forgotten memories. But I am instantly aware that I can no longer return to those pure passions. I must face the fact that I have become old. It is not just age and various other intangible differences even if she is right here and I can just reach out and take her with me. It amounts to the fact that my heart is old and I can no longer ignore all else and fall in love, body and heart, with a young woman. My relationships with women changed long ago and lost this instinctive youthful love ... only lust remains. I'm afraid of shouldering the responsibility of even pursuing momentary happiness. I'm not a wolf but I would like to be a wolf, to return to nature, to go on the prowl. However, I can't rid myself of this human mind. I am a monster with a human mind and can find no refuge.

Reed pipes sound. On the river-bank by clumps of bushes, lovers embrace under parasols, no longer as couples between heaven and earth but immersed in worlds of their own. But their worlds are remote from me, just like an ancient legend. Sadly, I walk away.

At the reed pipe venue by the highway, a bright kerosene lamp hangs on top of a bamboo pole. Her head is covered with a black cotton scarf and her hair held in a silver ring on top. The silver crown with a dragon and phoenix centre-piece she wears is flanked by five phoenix feathers of beaten silver-leaf which tremble as she moves. The feathers on the left are threaded with a coloured ribbon which hangs to her waist and accentuates her graceful body in dance. Her black gown is drawn in at the waist and the wide sleeves show her silver bracelets. In her black headscarf and black gown only the neck with its pair of big heavy silver rings shows, and over her slightly raised breasts is a spread of delicate longevity chains made of interlocking silver rings.

She knows what she is wearing is more striking than the colourful embroideries of other women and the abundance of silver indicates her high status. Her bare feet are also beautiful and the two silver bracelets on her ankle clink like crystal as she dances to the pipes.

She is from the Black Miao mountain stockade, a beautiful white orchid produced there. Her bright red lips are like the camellias of early spring and her teeth are like small pearls. Her flat childlike nose and round face make her eyes look far apart, always smiling, and the flashing black pupils of her eyes add to her extraordinary radiance.

She doesn't need to go to the river-bank to seek a lover. The toughest young men of every stockade come to bow to her, shouldering reed pipes twice their height tied with flowing ribbons. They puff out their cheeks, sway, step back and forth stamping their feet to get the women in their multi-pleat skirts swaying with them, but she has only to lightly lift a graceful foot to get all of them bowing, and blowing so hard that they wreck their pipes and develop blood blisters on their lips! It is the vitality she exudes that gives her this arrogance.

She doesn't understand what it is to be jealous, doesn't understand the malice of other women, doesn't understand why they make a potion of centipedes, wasps, venomous snakes, ants and cuttings of their hair mixed in menstrual blood and spittle, put it into an urn with their husband's shirt and a pair of his trousers cut into shreds, seal it and then bury the urn in a hole three feet in the ground.

She only knows that there is a man on the other side of the river and a woman on this side, that in their spring years they become restless, meet on the reed pipe clearing, are attracted to one another, and seeds of passion take root.

She only knows that at night after the fire is covered, the old ones are snoring and the young ones are talking in their sleep, she will get up, open the back door and go barefoot into the garden. The young man wearing a hat with silver horns who had followed her will come across from the fence, whistling softly. Her father will be up early and call her many times. Her mother, cross from calling, will open the door to use the stick on her but the bed will be empty.

In the middle of the night, on the river-bank, I am lying on floorboards under overhanging eaves. I don't know when the lights on the river disappeared and there is no starlight. The river and the mountain shadows of the opposite bank stretch into a single expanse. The night breeze has a chill edge and the howling of a wolf can be heard. I wake from a dream startled and listening carefully hear that it is a forlorn call for a mate, something like singing, intermittent, and miserable.

40

She says she doesn't know what happiness is and that she already has everything she should have – a husband, a son, what people think is a perfect little family. Her husband is a computer engineer and you know how highly regarded that profession is at the moment. He is young and capable and people say he'll make lots of money as soon as he patents something. But she isn't happy. She has been married for three years and the thrill of love and marriage has gone. The son, at times, is a hindrance. When she first thought this it gave her a rude shock but she slowly got used to it. However, she loves her son, and it is only this little creature who gives her some consolation. To preserve her figure, she didn't breast feed so when she takes off her white gown to shower at her research institute, the women colleagues who have had babies are filled with envy.

Another white gown, you say.

It's a woman friend of hers, she says, she always comes to tell her about her problems. She says she can't be like those women who talk all day about their children and knit clothes for them and their husbands whenever there is spare time at work. A woman isn't the slave of her husband and child. She has, of course, knitted for her child and it all started with this, she says, her troubles all started from having knitted this pullover.

So what's with this pullover?

She wants you to listen to her, don't interrupt, she also asks what was she saying just now.

You were talking about the pullover and the troubles it started.

No, she says she only feels at peace listening to the organ and singing Mass at church. Sometimes on Sundays she goes to Mass and lets her husband look after the child for a while. He should also do something for the child, it shouldn't all be left to her. She's not a Christian but once she walked past a church and now that churches are open to the public and you can go in and out freely, she went inside to listen. Since then she goes when she has time. She's fond of Bach, yes, and listens to Bach's requiems. She can't stand popular music, it upsets her, she can't even cope with her own anxieties. She asks if she's making any sense.

She says she started taking medications and takes sleeping tablets regularly. She saw a doctor who told her she had some form of neurasthenia. She feels tired and can never get enough sleep but can't sleep unless she takes sleeping tablets. She isn't sexually frustrated, make no mistake, and she does have orgasms with her husband. It's not that he doesn't satisfy her, don't think along those lines, he's a lot younger than you. However, he has his work, he's very career-oriented and ambitious. There's nothing wrong with a man being ambitious but he shuts himself up in the laboratory and often works overtime because he thinks the child is too noisy at home. She shouldn't have had a child so soon but he wanted it, he loved her and wanted her to have a child for him. Problems arose because of the child.

It happened like this, she says, she knitted a pullover with an appliqu which she had designed herself and it looked better than the children's pullovers entered in competitions, at least that's what she thought. She had gone to an export fashion exhibition with a colleague who had just been transferred to the institute. Their testing equipment had broken down and they had been waiting several days for repairs. There was no work so they went to the exhibition during work time to see if there was anything worth buying. He went with her, saying maybe he could buy his wife something. They ended up buying nothing. However, he said the pullover she had knitted for her son was better than the children's clothing on display and that she'd do well at designing clothes. After that she began thinking about it and

233

bought a fashion pattern book, then, using a length of textured dark blue cotton she'd bought but hadn't got around to making up and a scarf she didn't really wear, she made a sleeveless dress to wear into work. He saw her before she changed to go into the machine room and, after praising it, said she should only wear clothes she had designed herself. A couple of days later he got two tickets for a fashion show and invited her to go with him.

The affair started with the fashion show models.

She wants you to listen to her, no, she says he said if she went onto the catwalk wearing the dark blue cotton dress she'd outdo these models. She said she knew she wasn't voluptuous. However he said models didn't need to have big breasts, only long legs and curves, and that she had a slender figure, especially when she was wearing that dark blue dress. She says she really liked wearing the dress to work as she had made it herself, but whenever she wore it he would always eye her up and down. One day when she came out after changing, he looked at her in that way and invited her to have dinner with him.

So she went.

No, she says, she declined, she had to go to the nursery to pick up her child and she couldn't leave the child unattended at night. He asked her if her husband minded if she went out alone at night. She said no, but if she went out she usually took the child with her and she couldn't stay out late as the child had to go to bed early. Of course she'd been out at night and had got her husband to look after the child, but she couldn't go out with him for dinner. One day during the midday break he invited her to his place the following day for lunch to try his four delights meat balls which he said were his specialty.

She declined again.

No, she agreed at first but then he said he wanted her to wear her dark blue dress.

She agreed?

No, she didn't agree and said she probably wouldn't go. But the next day she wore the dark blue dress to work and during the midday break went to his place with him. She didn't know what was so special about the dark blue dress. She had simply added two pieces of silk. The floral silk scarf itself was quite ordinary, she cut out whole flowers from it and sewed them onto the bodice and waist, perhaps that was a bit special. She didn't think her figure was particularly good and her husband had laughed at her for being too flat and not sexy enough. Did she really look that good when she was wearing this dress?

You say it's not the dress.

Then what is it? She says she knows what you're going to say.

You say you haven't said anything but it's not the dress.

It's because her husband doesn't care what she wears, it's his attitude of not caring! She says she hadn't wanted to seduce anyone.

You hasten to deny that you've said anything.

She says she's not going to say anything more.

You say didn't she want someone to talk to? To talk about what was troubling her? You ask her to go on talking about what was worrying this woman friend of hers.

She doesn't know what to go on talking about.

Talk about his specialty, the four delights meat balls.

She says he had it all planned, his wife was away on a job.

You remind her she wasn't there to see his wife but to have lunch. She should have guessed his wife wouldn't have been there and she shouldn't have been defensive.

She concedes that was how it was, and the more defensive she was the greater the pressure.

The harder it was to control herself?

She couldn't resist.

When he was looking at her dress?

She shut her eyes.

Not wanting to see herself acting irrationally like this?

Yes.

Not wanting to see that she was just as wild?

She says she was confused and hadn't thought it would come to this, at the time she knew she didn't love him, in any way at all. Her husband was better than him.

You say actually she doesn't love anyone.

She says she only loves her son.

You say she only loves herself.

Maybe, maybe not. She says afterwards she left and wouldn't see him on her own again.

But she still did?

Yes.

And again at his place?

She says she wanted to talk to him to clarify things—

You say it's hard clarifying this by talking about it.

Yes, no. She says she hated him and hated herself.

And once again there was a bout of wantonness?

Stop talking! She was angry, she didn't know why she wanted to talk about it, she just wanted it all to end quickly.

You ask how could it end?

She says she doesn't know.

chant water but finally spurts from up (feebu??th of coughing with
only some after he has sprinkled sacrificial wine

41

His death takes place two years before I come here. At the time he is the last surviving Master of Sacrifice among the hundred Miao stockades, but for several decades there has not been an ancestor sacrifice on such a grand scale. He knows it will not be long before he will return to Heaven and his living to this venerable age is because he has carried out the ancestor sacrifices and the demon multitudes do not dare to harm him. He is afraid he will not be able to get up one morning and that he will not make it through the winter.

On New Year's eve, while his legs can still move, he hoists the square table from the hall onto his back, carries it down the stone steps of his pylon house, and sets it down. There is no-one else in sight on the desolate river-bank, the doors of the houses are all shut and people are eating New Year's dinner. Nowadays, even if people do have an ancestor sacrifice it's just like a New Year's dinner. It's been shortened and simplified. People simply grow weaker every generation, nothing can stop this.

On the table he puts a bowl of watery liquor, a bowl of bean curd, a bowl of steamed glutinous rice cake and the bowl of ox intestines from his neighbour, and under the table he puts a bundle of glutinous rice stalks. He then heaps wood and charcoal in front of the table. Tired by these exertions, he stops for a while to catch his breath, goes up the stone steps back inside the house to fetch a piece of burning charcoal from the stove and, going slowly down on his hands and knees, begins to blow. The smoke stings his dry old eyes and makes them water but finally sparks leap up. He has a fit of coughing which only stops after he has a sip of the sacrificial wine.

A ray of lingering light on the green mountain tops on the opposite bank vanishes and the night wind begins to blow over the river. Panting, he seats himself on the high stool at the table, steadying himself only when his feet tread onto the bundle of glutinous rice stalks. As he looks up at the mountain range, he is aware of the chill in the mucous in his runny nose and his tears.

In those days when he carried out ancestral sacrifices, he had twenty-four people at his disposal — two trainee masters, two supervisors, two men to handle the props, two overseers of the ritual, two persons in charge of the swords, two persons to pour the libation, two persons to make the food offerings, two dragon girls, two messengers, and several people to make pressed rice cakes. What a splendid event it was! Three oxen were slaughtered and at times even up to nine.

Just to show his appreciation, the head of the family making the sacrifice had to present him with glutinous rice seven times — the first time, seven pots for going into the mountains to chop trees for the drums; the second time, eight pots for carrying the drums into the cave; the third time, nine pots for inviting the drums into the stockade; the fourth time, ten pots for tying the drums; the fifth time, eleven pots for slaughtering the ox for the drums; the sixth time, twelve pots for dancing to the drums; the seventh time, thirteen pots for escorting the drums. From the time of the ancestors these were the rules.

The last time he performed an ancestral sacrifice, the head of the family sent twenty-five people to carry the rice, liquor, and food. What a magnificent time that was! The good days are over now. He recalls those times. Before the ox was slaughtered, just to smooth out the hair whorls on its hide, a decorated pillar had first to be erected on the grounds. All members of the family changed into new clothing and there was a fanfare of pipes and the beating of gongs and drums. He wore a long purple robe and a red felt hat and the head feathers of the great roc stood up from his collar. He waved a bronze bell in his right hand and held an arrowhead fan of plantain leaves in his left hand, ahh—

Ox oh ox,
Born in still waters,
Growing up on sandy banks,
You cross rivers with your mother,
You climb mountains with your father,
Fight the locusts for the sacrificial drum,
Fight the praying mantis for the sacrificial pipes,
Go to battle at Three Slopes,
Charge to attack at Seven Flats Bay,
Defeat the locusts,
Slay the praying mantis,
Snatch the long pipe,
Steal the big drum,
The long pipe is a sacrifice to your mother,
The big drum is a sacrifice to your father,
Ox oh ox,
Bearing on your back four platters of silver,
Bearing on your back four platters of gold,
You follow your mother,
You follow your father,
To enter the black cave,
To tread the drum door,
You guard mountain passes with your mother,
You guard village gates with your father,
To stop fierce demons harming people,
To stop evil spirits entering ancestral tombs,
So your mother will have peace for a thousand years,
So your father will have warmth for a hundred generations.

People tied a rope to the ox's nose, wrapped its horns in bamboo wreaths and brought it out. Members of the family, all in new clothes, performed the three bows and nine prostrations to the ox. As he loudly sang this eulogy the male head of the family took up a spear and stabbed the ox. Thereafter, all the able-bodied male relatives, midst the

239

pounding of the drum, in turn took up the spear and stabbed the ox. Spurting blood, the beast wildly charged in circles around the decorated pillar until it collapsed and died. They then cut off its head and divided up the meat: as Master of Sacrifice the chest was his. The good days are over!

Now his teeth have fallen out and he can only eat a little thin gruel. He has indeed gone through good days but no-one comes to attend to him anymore. The young people all have money. They've learnt to smoke filter-tip cigarettes, carry a screaming electric box and also to wear those evil black glasses. How can they still think about their ancestors? The more he sings the more wretched he feels.

He remembers he has forgotten to set up the incense burner, but to get it from the hall would mean going up and down the stone steps. Instead, he lights the incense sticks on the fire and places them in the ground in front of the table. In the past he would spread out a six-foot length of black cloth and cover it with glutinous rice stalks.

Treading on the glutinous rice stalks, he closes his eyes and sees in front of him the pair of sixteen-year-old dragon girls. They are the prettiest girls in the stockade, their bright intelligent eyes are clear like the river waters but of course not the river in flood. Nowadays the river is very dirty when it rains, and within ten *li* on both sides of the river it's impossible to find big trees suitable for the sacrifices. For these one needs the timber of twelve pairs of different trees, all of the same height and girth. The white wood must be white spruce and the red wood must be maple. When chopped, the wood of the white spruce is silver and the wood of the maple is gold.

> Go! Maple drum father,
> Go! White spruce drum mother,
> Along with the maple,
> Along with the white spruce,
> To the place awaiting kings,
> To the place of the ancestors,
> When the drums have been escorted, the pledge is fulfilled,

Ho! the Master of Sacrifice unsheathes his sword,
Raises his sword to chop the wood,
He has pledged to escort the drums,
Dong-ka-dong-dong-dong-weng,
Dong-ka-ka-dong-weng,
Ka-dong-ka-weng-weng,
Weng-ka-dong-dong-ka,
… … … … …

Many knives and axes chop continuously through the night. After a fixed number of blows, the two dragon girls with their exquisite features and beautiful figures appear.

Wives need husbands,
Men need women,
Go into houses to give birth,
Quietly create people,
Don't let roots snap,
Don't let seeds be wiped out,
Bear seven lively, beautiful girls,
Bear nine spirited, handsome boys.

The pair of dragon girls, two pairs of unmoving eyes, bright black eyes. He sees right into his own heart, lust resurfacing, generating energy. His singing resounds to Heaven: roosters crow, the God of Thunder in Heaven sends down lightning, and crazed demons and monsters wildly dance on the drum skins, leaping like scattered beans. Ahh, high silver headdress, heavy silver earrings, hot steam rising from bronze cauldrons on charcoals. Hands scrubbed, faces washed, hearts full of joy. God in Heaven is happy and lets down the Heavenly Ladder. Father and mother descend, sound the drums and granaries open, spilling forth so much good grain that nine vats and nine urns cannot contain it all. The kitchen stoves burn with hot charcoal and the family is wealthy and noble. As soon as the spirits of the mother's ancestors descend, everything swells up – nine wooden buckets of steaming hot dazzling white rice, and everyone gathers around to make rice balls. Start the drums, start the drums, the drum owner goes first, the men follow after, follow close one behind the other. Then the drum master comes last.

> Go bathe in the waters of wealth and nobility!
> Go drench in the liquids of great riches!
> Waters of wealth and nobility give birth to children,
> Flower-drenching rains give birth to sons,
> Sons and grandsons like palm shoots,
> Progeny like fish fry,
> All come to the drum owner's family,
> Drink nine piculs of watery liquor,
> Take rice as offerings,
> Take liquor for libations,
> Invite the gods of heaven to come and receive it,
> Invite the demons of earth to come and eat it,
> The drum owner swings his axe,
> The ancestors unsheathe their swords,
> To surpass their older ancestors,
> In thinking of the mother who bore them,
> Come chisel a pair of pipes,
> Come make a pair of drums . . .

He exhausts himself loudly singing the eulogy and his old voice, like a broken bamboo pipe, sobs in the wind. His throat is parched and he drinks another mouthful of watery liquor, knowing that this is the last time. His spirit seeps out of his body as his singing disperses in the air.

How would anyone hear him on that dark desolate river-bank? Luckily when an old woman opens the door to throw out some dirty water, she seems to hear someone sobbing and sees the campfire on the bank. She thinks it must be Han Chinese who have come to poach fish: the Han Chinese are everywhere nowadays if there is money to be made. She shuts the door but then thinks, on the night before the New Year the Han celebrate just like the Miao unless they are destitute. Perhaps it is a wandering beggar. So she fills a bowl with leftovers from the New Year meal to take to the person. It isn't until she gets to the campfire that she recognizes the old Master of Sacrifice at the square table. She stops there stupefied.

When her husband sees the door wide open with the cold wind coming in, he gets up to close the door but remembers that his wife said she was taking a bowl of food to a beggar. She hadn't returned so he goes out to look for her. When he gets to the campfire he too is stupefied. Afterwards the daughters and then the sons all come out, but none of them know what to do. A youth who had a couple of years schooling at the village primary school goes up and urges him, "It's a cold night. An old man like you must be careful not to catch a chill. We'll help you inside the house."

The old man's nose is running but he is oblivious to it and, eyes shut, he goes on chanting and singing, his rasping voice trembling in his throat, muffled and indistinct.

Afterwards, the doors of one house after the other open. Old women, old men, as well as young people and children all come and gradually the whole stockade is assembled on the river-bank. Some think to go home for some glutinous rice balls, some bring a duck, some bring bowls of watery liquor and leftover bowls of beef, someone even brought a portion of a pig's head, and all of these are put before him.

"To forget one's ancestors is a crime . . ." the old man mumbles.

A young boat girl is so overcome that she runs home and brings back in her arms a blended wool blanket from her trousseau. She puts it over the old man's shoulders, wipes his nose with a floral handkerchief, and says, "Old uncle, come back into the house!"

The young people all say, "What a sad old man!"

Mother of the maple tree, father of the white spruce, forgetting one's ancestors will bring retribution! The old man's voice rolls about in his throat as tears and mucous stream down his face.

"Old uncle, come quickly, don't say anything more."

"Come quickly back inside the house."

The young people went up to help him.

"I want to die right here..." The old man exerts himself and finally manages to shout out like a spoilt child.

An old woman says, "Let him sing, he won't get through the spring."

This copy of *Drum Sacrifice Songs* I am holding in my hands was written down and transcribed into Chinese by a Miao acquaintance. My writing this story is to thank him.

42

It is a fine day with not a trace of cloud in the sky and the vault of heaven is amazingly remote and clear. Beneath the sky is a solitary stockade with layers of pylon houses built on the edge of a precipitous cliff. In the distance it looks quite beautiful, like a hornet's nest hanging on a rock wall. The dream is like this. You are at the bottom of the cliff, walking one way and the other, but can't find the road up. You can see yourself getting closer and then suddenly you are moving further away. After going in circles for quite some time you finally give up and just let your legs carry you along the mountain road. When it disappears behind the cliff, you can't help feeling disappointed. You have no idea where the mountain road beneath your feet leads but in any case you don't actually have a destination.

You walk straight ahead and the road goes around in circles. Actually, there has never been a definite goal in your life. All your goals keep changing as time passes and as locations change, and in the end the goals no longer exist. When you think about it, life in fact doesn't have what may be called ultimate goals. It's just like this hornet's nest. It's a pity to abandon it, yet if one tries to remove it one will encounter a stinging attack. Best to leave it just hanging there so that it can be admired. At this point in your thinking, your feet become lighter, it is fine wherever your feet take you, as long as there are sights to see.

On both sides are red bayberry forests but it is not the season for picking the berries and by the time the berries ripen you don't know where you will be. Whether berries wait for people or people wait for berries is a metaphysical problem. There are many ways of dealing with the problem, and it has been dealt with in endless ways, but the berries are still berries and the person is still me. One could also say this year's berries are not next year's berries and the person existing today did not exist yesterday. The problem is whether or not the present really exists and how the criteria are established. Best leave it to the philosophers to talk about metaphysics, just keep your mind on walking along your road.

It is uphill all the way and you begin to sweat profusely. However, suddenly you are at the foot of the stockade and, looking at the shadows in the stockade, a chill rises in your heart.

You did not expect to find crowds sitting on the long stone steps under the wooden pylons of the houses and you can only walk in the spaces between their crossed legs. Nobody looks at you, their eyes look down as they softly chant sutras, *nan-nan-na-na*. They seem to be in mourning. You go up the stone steps and follow the lane around a corner. On both sides the wooden houses lean and slant, propping up one another and stopping one another from collapsing. However, if there is an earthquake or a landslide, the collapse of one will cause a total collapse.

The old people sitting next to one another are also like this. Only one needs to be pushed and all of them would topple like the dominoes children have lined up. You don't dare bump any of them for fear of creating a disaster. You carefully plant your feet between the bony ankles of their folded legs. Their feet, which are like chicken feet, are wrapped in cloth socks. While they chant the wooden houses creak and you wonder if it is the houses or their bones which are creaking. They all suffer from palsy and as they sway and chant their heads keep shaking.

The winding lane is endless and people sit crammed on the stone steps at the sides of the lane. The charcoal coloured clothing they all wear is covered in patches, it is local cloth and being very old disintegrates on washing. The sheets and coarse grass-cloth mosquito nets which hang from the railings of the tall buildings add to the intensity of the all-pervasive sadness of these old people.

In the midst of the chanting a shrill sound claws at you like a cat, clutching you and forcing you to walk on. You can't make out where the sound comes from but see strings of paper money hanging outside a doorway and incense smoke wafting out through the door curtains. It seems that someone has died.

It gets harder and harder to walk. They are squashed even more tightly together and there is just nowhere to put down your foot. You are afraid if you tread on an ankle you will break it. You have to be even more careful, and picking somewhere to put down your toes between legs and feet which are like the gnarled roots of old trees, you hold your breath and take one step, then another.

You walk among them but not one of them looks up. They are either wearing turbans or cloth scarves and you can't see their faces. At this point they all start singing. Listening intently, you gradually make out the words.

> Come all of you,
> One day make six rounds,
> One round run six times,
> In the netherland,
> Scatter rice,
> You must all come to help.

The shrill lead is an old woman sitting on a stone doorsill right next to you. There is something special about her. A black cloth is draped over her shoulders, her head is completely covered, and a trembling hand hits on a knee as her body slowly sways backwards and forwards in time with her singing. On the ground alongside her is a bowl of water, a bamboo tube filled with rice, and a stack of square coarse paper with rows of holes in it. She wets a finger in the bowl, takes a square of paper money and tosses it into the air.

> When will you all come,
> When will you all go,

> To the end of the earth,
> To the eastern slope,
> A disaster, a calamity,
> To kill a person doesn't take half a grain of rice,
> To save a person doesn't take half a strand of hair,
> All come to help for there is trouble and distress
> Please all of you come!

You want to get past. You are afraid if you bump her shoulder her frail body will topple so you go to move her foot, but suddenly she screeches:

> All red, all red clothes,
> Feet small like chopsticks,
> Head big as a duck's cage,
> When he comes it will be all right,
> What he says counts,
> Get him to come quickly,
> Tell him not to be late!

Singing shrilly, she slowly gets to her feet then starts gesticulating at you. Chicken feet fingers stretch out at you, menacingly, you don't know where the courage comes from but you block her arms and lift her cloth head cover. Inside is a small wizened face, a pair of sunken lustreless eyes, and a gaping mouth with one tooth. She seems to be smiling, but clearly is not, and while shouting starts to dance.

> Red snakes slither everywhere,
> Tigers and leopards on the prowl,
> The mountain gate creaks open,
> They come in by the stone gate,
> Shouts arise all around,
> One by one everyone shouts together,
> Quickly go to help the person in distress!

You try to get out of her clutches but they are all slowly getting to their feet. One by one these old people, like dessicated timber, surround you and a sea of trembling voices starts shouting:

> All red clothing, all red,
> Quickly open the gate to ask,
> Ask one moment and the next they'll be here,
> Ask Lord Thunder and ask Mother Lightning,
> If there are horses everyone will ride,
> If there is food everyone will eat!

The crowd charges at you, attacking you with sounds muffled in their throats. You are forced to push them aside and one by one they instantly fall, as if made of paper, soundlessly. A deathly loneliness prevails. You suddenly realize that behind the curtained doorway, the person lying on the planks is you. You refuse to die just like this, you must quickly, and right away, return to the world of human beings.

43

Leaving the Miao stockade, I walk from morning to afternoon along this desolate mountain road. Buses and truck convoys hauling bamboo and timber occasionally pass and though I signal none will stop.

The sun is already beginning to descend behind the mountain ridge opposite and chilly mountain winds start blowing all around. On the winding highway, up ahead and below, there are no village stockades in sight and there is no longer anyone walking on the road. The further I go the more desolate it becomes. I don't know how much further it is to the county town or whether I will be able to get there before dark. If I don't flag down a vehicle soon, I'll have trouble finding somewhere to spend the night. I remember the camera in my backpack. What's to stop me from pretending I'm a reporter? Maybe it will work.

At last I hear a vehicle coming from behind so I stand in the middle of the road and start waving my camera. A truck with a canopy is bumping along the road, charging ahead without slowing down. It is only when it is almost upon me that it screeches to a halt.

"Fuck you, think you can get someone to stop like that? Don't you want to go on living?" The driver pokes his head out of the window to swear at me. He is a Han Chinese and I can communicate with him.

I quickly run up to the cabin door to explain. "Driver, I'm a reporter from Beijing doing interviews in the Miao stockade. I'm on an urgent job and have to get back to the county town to send a telegram!"

He has a wide face, a square jaw and a big mouth. This sort of person is usually easy to get on with. He looks me over and frowns.

"The truck's got a load of pigs and doesn't take people. And my truck isn't going to the county town."

I can hear the squealing of pigs coming from under the canopy.

"As long as it's not to the abattoirs, anywhere will do." I put on a smile.

He looks reluctant but finally opens the door. I hasten to thank him and jump into the cabin.

I offer him a cigarette but he declines. We travel some distance without a word. Safely seated, I don't need to explain any further. However from time to time he glances at the camera hanging from my neck. For the locals around here Beijing means the central government and reporters sent by the central government authorities have a certain style. But I have neither a county interpreter nor a special jeep to take me around. Nothing I can say will allay his suspicions.

I suppose he thinks I'm a fraud. I've heard about pranksters going into the mountains with empty cameras and putting on a big act. They say their rates are cheap and go from place to place mobilizing families to have their photos taken, then after a bit of free fun in the mountains, the money they trick out of the locals is just perfect for a night out in a city restaurant. Maybe he thinks I'm in this racket. I start laughing to myself, I have to find something to amuse myself otherwise this long trip will really be boring.

He suddenly looks at me and asks with undisguised coldness, "Where in fact are you going?"

"Back to the county town!"

"Which county town?"

When I came in the Miao king's car I wasn't paying attention and can't come up with an answer. "Anyway, I'll have to go to the nearest county committee reception office!" I say.

"Then get out of the truck." A fork in the road appears up ahead, it is just as desolate and there are no houses in sight. I can't work out if he's trying to frighten me or trying to be funny.

The truck slows down and stops. "I'm turning off here," he adds.

"Where are you taking the truck?"

"The pig buying company." He leans across and opens the door inviting me to get out.

I see that he is not joking and it is inadvisable for me to stay sitting there. As I get out I ask, "Are we already out of Miao territory?"

"We left long ago. It's only ten *li* into town, you'll make it there before dark," he says coldly.

The door bangs shut and the truck goes onto the side road and, in a cloud of dust, disappears into the distance.

If I were a woman on her own this driver wouldn't have been so cold. I know women have been kidnapped and raped by drivers on mountain roads such as these, but then, women wouldn't lightly get in one of these long-distance freight trucks. People are always on guard against one another.

The sun has gone behind the mountain and only a stretch of dusky sky with clouds like fish scales, remains. Up ahead is a long dirt slope. My calves ache, sweat is pouring down my back and I've given up hope that a vehicle will come along. I resign myself to going up to the top of the ridge for a bit of a rest and to prepare myself for walking all night.

I didn't expect to encounter someone like myself on top of the ridge. He arrives about the same time as me. His hair is like a tangle of weeds and he hasn't had a shave for days. He also has a bag, the only difference is that I've got mine hanging on my shoulders and he is clumsily carrying his in his hands. He is wearing dusty work trousers, the sort coal miners or cement factory workers wear. As for me, I have been wearing these jeans since I set out on this trip and they haven't been washed for several months.

The moment our eyes meet, I sense he is a bad person. He looks me over from head to toe, then his eyes immediately return to my backpack. It is like running into a wolf, the difference being that for a wolf the other party is food to be hunted, whereas for people it is the other party's money. Instinctively, I too can't help looking him over. I cast my eyes over the bag he is carrying, does it contain some

252

dangerous weapon? If I walk past him, will he attack me from behind? I stop in my tracks.

This bag of mine isn't light, especially with the camera in it, but it's heavy enough to swing at him. I take the bag off my shoulders, hold it in my hand, and sit down on the dirt slope by the road. I take a deep breath and get ready to deal with him. He also takes a deep breath and sits on a rock on the other side. The two of us are not more than ten paces apart.

He is clearly more powerful than me and if there's a real fight I'll be no match. However I remember the electrician's knife which I always take travelling, it is handy and can also serve as a weapon to defend myself. I don't think he'll be able to produce a decisive weapon and if he pulls out a small knife he won't necessarily come out the winner. If I can't beat him I can turn and run, but this will only encourage him and indicate that I do in fact have money on me. From his eyes I can tell there's no-one behind me, that no vehicles are approaching and that it's as desolate as behind him. I must signal that I am on the alert, that I am on guard, and at the same time that I am not panicking.

I light a cigarette and pretend to be resting. He also takes out a cigarette from the back pocket of his trousers and lights it. Neither of us looks directly at the other but we each watch from the corners of our eyes.

Unless he is sure I have something valuable on me he won't risk his life, but still a fight is inevitable. The old cassette player in my bag is like a brick and the sound is distorted, if I had the money I would have got rid of it long ago. Only my imported Japanese camera is in good working condition but it's not worth risking one's life for. I only have a hundred *yuan* in cash and it certainly isn't worth getting hurt for such a small amount of money. I look at my dusty shoes and blow smoke at them. Sitting still, I feel my cold sweat-soaked singlet sticking to my back and hear the howling of the mountain wind.

He sneers contemptuously, revealing his front teeth. I think that I also have a contemptuous look and probably some of my teeth are showing, and my face is undoubtedly as mean as his. If I open my mouth I can also spew out a barrage of foul language. I can go on the attack and I can stab a person with a knife, and at the same time I am ready to flee for my life. That look of insolence as he holds his cigarette in his fingers, is it because of a similar line of thinking? Is he also protecting himself?

These shoes which I bought for this long trip have been in rain and mud and fully immersed in rivers. They are out of shape, black and dirty, and no-one could imagine that once they had been offered at a high price as fashionable travel shoes. There is nothing about me to make me the target of robbery. I drag hard on what's left of my cigarette, toss down the butt and tread on it. He also flicks his cigarette butt onto the ground, as if in response, of course contemptuously, but at the same time guarded.

After that both of us get up. Neither makes way for the other and both walk in the middle of the road, brushing past one another. People, in the final analysis, aren't wolves but more like feral dogs. They sniff, look one another over, and then walk away.

In that direction it is a long downhill slope. Once I start walking I can't stop and keep going until the road levels. Looking back, the dusty highway crawling on the desolate mountain range under the dusky sky looks even more lonely.

44

She says she's getting old. When she combs her hair and washes her face in front of the mirror in the morning there are deep wrinkles at the corners of her eyes make-up can't hide. The mirror tells her the best years of her life have been wasted. Each morning when she gets up she feels miserable and lethargic. If she doesn't have to go to work she doesn't want to get up, doesn't want to see anyone. It's only after she goes on duty and has to interact with people that she starts talking and laughing, forgets herself, and gets some relief.

You say you understand.

No, you can't possibly understand, she says you can't possibly understand the despair a woman feels when she finds no-one loves her. It is only as night approaches that she starts feeling lively. She likes to have a packed schedule every night and has to go out or have people visit – she can't stand the loneliness. She's anxious to live, do you understand this feeling of urgency? No, you don't.

She says it's only on the dance floor when she closes her eyes and senses the touch of her partner that she feels alive. She knows no-one really loves her, she can't bear someone looking at her close up, she's afraid of the wrinkles at the corners of her eyes, this gradual aging. She knows men, when you need women your words are sweet like honey, then after you have satisfied yourselves, you tire of the woman and just go off looking for new thrills. When you see pretty young women you start talking and laughing again. But how many years are there in a woman's youth? Such is the fate of women. It is only at night, in your bed, when you can't see her wrinkles and she gives you pleasure, that you say words of thanks to her. Just listen to what she has to say! She says she knows you want to get rid of her, that you're making excuses just to make it easier to get away from her. Don't say anything!

You can relax, she says she's not the sort of woman who clings to a man and won't let go. She can find other men, she can console herself. She knows what you want to say. Don't talk to her about a job. When she can't find a man, then she can go and find a job. But she won't bother herself with other people's private affairs, pull strings or act as a go-between for them, or listen to them complaining about their sufferings. She won't become a nun. You don't need to pretend to laugh, the temples today only accept very young women: it's all a put-on show for foreigners. The nuns who enlist nowadays get married and have a family life. She can look after herself and have a child out of marriage: a bastard. Listen to what she's saying!

Surely you can give her a child? Will you let her give birth to it? She wants one of your seeds, will you give it? You don't dare, you're afraid. You don't need to worry, she won't say it's your child, he won't have a father and will be the result of his mother's wantonness. He'd never know his father. She's seen through you, you're only capable of seducing young women. But do they understand love? Will they really care for you? Love you like a wife? A woman's body doesn't have sexuality alone, it's not just for you men to release your lust into. A healthy woman of course needs sexual love but sexual love alone isn't enough, a woman's instinct is also to be a wife and to have a regular life. Whoever you find will inevitably want to become attached to you, a woman wants to attach herself to a man, so what can you do? But another woman will not necessarily care for you like she does, like a mother loving her child: in her arms you are just a pitiful child. You're insatiably greedy. Don't have illusions that you're young and robust, you'll soon be old too, then you'll be nothing. Go ahead and play with young girls, in the end you'll still be hers, in the end you'll still have to come back to her, only she can put up with you, excuse your weaknesses. Where else could you find a woman like her?

She's empty, she says, she has no feelings. She has been drained by pleasure and only the empty shell of her body remains. It's as if she's fallen into a bottomless abyss and she is a piece of torn netting, slowly drifting down. She has no regrets, she has lived and that's all there is to it. She has loved and may count as having been loved. What's left is like a bowl of insipid and tasteless tea, so what if it's thrown out? It's the same loneliness. She doesn't get excited, and if she does, it's like performing a duty. She is a piece of bleeding snake you have chopped off. You're cruel but she has no regrets and only blames herself. Who asked her to be born a woman? She won't run crazily onto the streets in the middle of the night and sit under a streetlight weeping stupidly by herself, and she won't run about in the rain shouting hysterically making cars brake suddenly and swerve to avoid her. She's no longer afraid of high cliffs, she no longer controls her own body, it is already decaying. Her remaining days are lifeless, this piece of torn netting no-one will pick up just drifts on the wind and reaching the bottom will quietly die. She is not like you, so afraid of death, so cowardly. Her heart was dead before this. Women are hurt much more than you men, from the very day they are possessed their flesh and hearts are trampled, what else do you want?

Go ahead if you want to get rid of her! Stop saying nice things to her! It gives her no consolation, she's not the one breaking off with you. Women can be far more vicious than men if they want to because they have been hurt far more by men! She can only put up with it, how else can she get revenge? If women were to seek revenge – she says she's not thinking of taking revenge, she will put up with everything, unlike you men who cry out at the slightest pain. Women are more sensitive than men. She doesn't regret being a woman, a woman has her womanly pride but it's not arrogance. In any case she doesn't regret being a woman and when she is reincarnated in the next world she wants to be born a woman again and to experience the sufferings of being a woman again. She wants again to experience the agony of giving birth, the joy of being a mother for the first time, the sweetness following parturition. And again to enjoy a virgin's first tremors, the unbearable suspense, the unsteady gaze, the confusion at meeting a man's eyes, the unstoppable tears at the pain of invasion. She wants to go through it all again, if there is a next world. Just remember her, remember the love she has given you, she knows you no longer love her, so it is best that she leaves.

She says she wants to go into the wilderness on her own, to where black clouds meet the road, the end of the road. She will head towards the end while clearly knowing that in fact it is an end without an end. The road stretches endlessly and there is always a point where the sky and earth meet, but the road just crawls over it. She will simply follow the desolate road under the shadow of the clouds and go wherever her legs take her. When, after great hardships, she gets to the end of the long road, it will stretch further still and she will keep walking endlessly like this, her body and heart empty. She has thought about death, thought about ending it all just like that. To commit suicide requires the urge but even this urge has completely vanished. Suicide has to be for someone or for something but she no longer exists for any person or any thing, and she no longer has the energy to kill herself. Her heart has been numbed by all the humiliation and pain she has experienced.

45

"Are you leaving?" she asks.

"Doesn't the bus go at seven?" I ask instead.

"Yes, but there's still quite some time." She seems to be talking to herself.

I am getting my backpack ready, bundling up dirty clothes and stuffing them in. I had intended to stay a couple more days in this county town to do my laundry and to get over my fatigue. I know she is standing right behind me, watching me, but I don't look up, afraid I will succumb to the look in her eyes, not be able to leave, and be filled with even greater remorse.

The small guest room is sparse, with only a single bed and a small table by the window, and my things are spread out on the bed. I have just come from her room, having spent last night there, and lying on her bed had watched dawn break with her through the window.

I came down in a bus from the mountains to this small county town and it was at dusk, on the only long street in town, just outside the window, that I met her. The shops all had their shutters up and there were few people on the street. She was walking ahead of me and I caught up and asked her where the cultural office was. I wanted to find lodgings but this seemed a better opening gambit. She turned around. You couldn't say she was pretty but she had a pleasant face, a fair complexion and thick red lips with well-defined corners.

She said I could go with her and asked who I wanted to see there. I said anyone would do but of course it would be best if I could see the head. She asked why I wanted to see the head and I said I was

259

collecting material. What sort of material was I collecting? She also asked me what I did and where I was from. I said I had documents to verify my identity.

"May I see your documents?" She raises her eyebrows and seems to want to interrogate me.

I take the Writers' Association membership card in the blue plastic cover from my shirt pocket and show it to her. I know my name is already on documents circulated to various echelons of the central government down to the provincial cities and county towns, and could be seen by the heads of party committees and cultural offices. I also know there are people who like making reports and can use what I say and do to write up reports along the lines of the government documents. Friends who have had such experiences have warned me to avoid such people and so avoid getting into trouble. However, my experience in the Miao stockade has shown that sometimes showing this card comes in handy. Especially when the other party is such a young woman. I'm sure to be looked after.

She actually stares at me to see if I match the photograph on the card.

"You're a writer?" she asks, her face relaxing.

"I look more like someone hunting for Wild Men," I say, trying to joke with her.

"I'm from the cultural office," she explains.

This is lucky. "May I know your name?" I ask her.

She says her name isn't important. She also says she has read my work and really likes it. Her office has a guest room for cultural cadres from the villages, it's cheaper than the inns and fairly clean. By now there's no-one on duty but she can take me straight to the head's house.

"The head lacks culture." She's already starting to look after me. "But he's a good man," she adds.

The head, who is short and fat, and getting on in years, first asks for my credentials. He carefully examines my card. The embossed seal on the photograph is virtually impossible to fake and after slowly thinking for a while, he breaks into a smile and hands it back, saying, "Writers and journalists sent by the higher authorities are usually received by the county committee office and the county propaganda department, otherwise, the director of the county cultural bureau receives them."

I know that to be head of a cultural office is a sinecure. Cadres appointed to this position are like old people with no-one to look after them being sent to a home for the aged. Even if he has seen the classified documents, his memory isn't necessarily very good. It is my good fortune to encounter such a kindly old man, even if he does lack culture, so I hasten to say, "I am a minor writer, there's no need to trouble so many people."

"Our cultural office here only has some local amateur activities for spreading popular culture," he explains, "for example, going to the villages to collect folk songs ... "

I interrupt him to say, "Folk songs are what interest me most, that's the sort of material I am collecting."

"Isn't the upstairs guest room at the office vacant right now?" she reminds him at precisely the right moment, glancing at me with her intelligent eyes.

"It's very basic. There's no dining room and you'll have to go out to eat," he says.

"That actually suits me better, I also want to travel to surrounding villages," I say.

"Well, if you are prepared to make the best of it," he concludes politely.

So I take up lodgings at the cultural office building, and she takes me upstairs and opens the door of the guest room by the side of the stairs. After I put down my bags she says her room is at the end of the corridor and invites me in.

It is a small room smelling of powder and lipstick. On the bookshelf by the window is a round mirror and a large number of bottles and jars, the toiletries which these days are necessities even for county town girls. The walls are covered with posters of, I presume, her favourite movie stars. One is a stage photo cut from a pictorial of a barefoot actress clad in transparent silk performing an Indian dance. A panda with black and white silk fur is sitting on the neatly folded bedding inside the mosquito net: this is very fashionable at present. Only the delicate wooden bucket in the corner of the room, shiny red with the original lacquer, retains anything of the unique character of the town. I have been travelling around in the mountains for several months with village cadres and peasants, sleeping on straw mats, using coarse language and drinking vitriolic liquor, and on entering this bright room smelling of powder and lipstick, I immediately feel lightheaded.

"I've probably got lice," I say apologetically.

She doesn't believe me, laughs, and says, "Have a wash. I filled the thermos flasks during the day so there's still hot water, you can wash in this room, you'll find everything here."

"That's putting you to too much trouble," I say. "I'll go back to my room, but can I borrow a tub?"

"What does it matter? There's cold water in the bucket." As she says this, she pulls a red lacquered tub from under the bed and fetches some soap and towels. "It's all right, I'll go to the office and read for a while. The archive room is next door, further on is the office, and your room is at the very end."

"What archives do you have here?" I have to find something to say.

"I don't really know. Do you want to have a look? I've got a key."

"Of course, that'd be great!"

She says a reading room with books and periodicals is downstairs and there's a recreational room which she can show me later on.

After a wash I feel much better, although the scent of her soap clings to me. She comes back and makes me a cup of tea. Sitting ensconced in her room I no longer want to look at any archives.

I ask what sort of work she does here. She says she's a graduate of the local teachers' college and studied music and dance. The old woman in charge of the library fell ill so she has to look after the reading room and deal with lending out books. She's been working here for almost a year and, she says, she is almost twenty-one.

"Can you sing the local folk songs?" I ask.

"It would be too embarrassing," she says.

"Are there any of the old singers of folk songs here?" I ask, changing the topic.

"Of course. There's an old man in a small town forty *li* from here who can sing lots of them."

"Would I be able to see him?"

"If you take the morning bus you can get back the same day. He lives in Liupu, a town famous for its songs in this county."

However, she says, unfortunately she can't take me. She doesn't think the head of the cultural office will let her go because there's no-one to go on duty for her, too bad it's not a Sunday. Still, she can make a phone call, her home is in the town; she can call the village authorities, she knows them all well, and get them to tell the old singer to wait at home for me. The bus back is at four o'clock, she wants me to come back to her place for dinner. She says she has to cook for herself, anyway.

Afterwards she goes on to talk about a dressmaker in the town, the older sister of a girl in her class at primary school. She is really good looking, exceptionally beautiful and with such fair skin, like a jade carving. If you see her, for sure—

"For sure?"

She says she's joking, she says the woman has a dressmaker's shop in a small street in Liupu, she works there herself and if you go along the street you're sure to see her. But everyone says she has leprosy. "It's a terrible tragedy and as a result no-one dares to marry her," she says.

"If she really has leprosy she has to be isolated," I say.

"People are deliberately maligning her," she says. "Anyway, I don't believe it's true."

"But that doesn't stop her from going to a hospital for tests and getting a medical certificate," I suggest.

"Nothing in her favour will work, people are bent on vilifying her, they're really mean. What good would a certificate do?"

She also says there's a cousin she gets on well with. She was married off to someone in the tax office and got beaten black and blue all over.

"Why?" I ask.

"Because on the wedding night her husband discovered she wasn't a virgin! People here are rough and mean, not like you people in the big cities."

"Have you ever been in love?" I venture to ask.

"There was a student at the teachers' college, we got on really well and after graduating we continued on corresponding. But not long ago he quite unexpectedly got married. Of course he and I didn't have a relationship, we were very fond of one another but didn't ever get around to talking about it. However when I got his letter saying he had married I cried. Don't you want to listen?"

"Of course I do," I say, "but it'll be hard writing it into the novel."

"I didn't give you permission to write about it. But you novelists can make up anything."

"Only if one wants to."

"It's really sad about her," she sighs. But it's not clear whether she's sighing about the dressmaker in the town or about her young cousin.

"Yes." I must show I'm sympathetic.

"How many days do you plan to stay?" she asks.

"One or two, just to have a bit of a rest before going on."

"Do you still have lots of places to go to?"

"There are lots of places I haven't been to."

"I wouldn't be able to visit the places you've been to in a lifetime."

"Don't you get opportunities to travel on official business? You can also take leave and go travelling on your own."

"I want to go to Shanghai and Beijing to have a look around. If I look you up, will you still know me?"

"Why wouldn't I?"

"By that time you will have long forgotten me."

"From what you say, you don't think much of me."

"I'm being realistic, you must know lots of people."

"I come in contact with lots of people in my work, but there aren't many who are nice."

"You writers are really good at talking. Can't you stay a few days more? Liupu isn't the only place in the county with folk songs."

"Of course," I say.

I am besieged by her naïve warmth, and I sense that she is spreading a net over me. That I am thinking about her like this instantly makes me feel unkind.

"Are you feeling tired?"

"A little." I think I should leave her room and try to find out what time the bus departs for Liupu in the morning.

I didn't think I would let things happen just as she had arranged. Without having a nap and without washing my dirty clothes, I get up early, go to Liupu, rush about all day, and can't wait to get back to see her again. When I return at dusk, she has food arranged on the table. The kerosene stove is on and a small pot of soup is gently simmering. Seeing she has prepared so many dishes I say I'll go and buy some liquor.

"I've got some here," she says.

"Do you also drink?" I ask.

"I can only drink a little."

I open the parcel of salted pork and roast goose wrapped in lotus leaves I bought in the shop opposite the bus stop. Here in this town they still wrap salted meat in lotus leaves. I remember when I was a child, food stalls always wrapped meat in this manner which gives it a unique and clean aroma. The creaking floorboards, the sense of seclusion created by the mosquito net and the charming little red wooden bucket shiny with the original lacquer in the corner all make me feel as if I have returned to my childhood.

"Did you see the old man?" she asks, pouring what turns out to be very fine unblended liquor.

"Yes," I reply, lying.

"Did he sing?"

"Yes," I say, lying again.

"Did he also sing those songs?"

"What songs?"

"He didn't sing them for you? Oh, he won't sing them for strangers."

"Are you talking about ribald love songs?"

She gives an embarrassed laugh. "If there are women there, he won't sing them either," she explains.

"It depends on who it is, if it's amongst old friends, when women are there he sings with greater gusto but he won't have young girls present, this I know," I say.

"Did you get some useful material?" She changes the topic. "After you left I phoned the town and asked the county authorities to tell the singer that a writer from Beijing was coming especially to interview him. What? Didn't they notify him?"

"He was away on business, I saw his wife."

"Then you wasted your time making the trip!"

"It wasn't a waste of time, I spent most of the day sitting in a tea house and actually learnt a lot, I didn't know these tea houses still existed, the upstairs and downstairs were crowded with peasants there for the market."

"I seldom go to such places."

"It was really interesting, people were doing business deals or just chatting, it was very lively. I talked with them about all sorts of things. This is life, too."

"You writers are odd."

"I met all sorts of people, people in all lines of work. Someone even asked if I could buy him a motor vehicle. I asked what sort he wanted, a Liberation sedan or a two-and-a-half ton truck."

At this she breaks into laughter.

"Some people are really making fortunes, one peasant was doing deals starting off with ten thousand. I also saw a man who kept insects, he had a large number of jars of them. The price for one centipede was at least five cents, so if he sold ten thousand centipedes –"

"Stop talking about centipedes, I'm scared of them!"

"All right, I won't talk about insects, I'll talk about something else."

I say that I stayed in the tea house all day. There was a bus back at noon and I should have come back early to wash my dirty clothes, but I didn't want to disappoint her. I felt I should come back at dusk as she had planned so I also went all around the village for most of the day. But naturally I don't tell her this.

"I discussed several business deals." I say, saying whatever came into my mind.

"Did you clinch them all?"

"None of them." I was just carrying on, I don't have any connections for business deals, nor that sort of expertise.

"Drink up, it'll get rid of your fatigue."

"Do you usually drink liquor?" I ask.

"No, I got this when a classmate was passing through and called in, it was some months ago. When there are visitors people here have to treat them to a drink."

"In that case, *ganbei*!"

She cheerfully clinks her cup with mine and drinks it in one gulp.

There's a rustling sound outside the window.

"Is it raining?" I ask.

She gets up, takes a look out the window and says, "Just as well you're back, if you'd got caught in the rain it would have been a problem."

"This is wonderful, in this little room with rain falling outside."

She smiles, her face is slightly flushed. The rain outside the window is quite noisy as it beats down on the roof-tiles of the building and the neighbouring houses.

"Why have you stopped talking?" I ask.

"I'm listening to the rain," she says.

After a while she asks, "Should I shut the window?"

"Of course, it'll be even better, it'll be more cosy," I say straightaway.

She gets up to shut the window and suddenly I feel closer to her. Because of this miraculous rain what follows is quite incredible. She shuts the window and in turning to go back to her desk knocks against my arm. I take her by the waist and pull her to me. She is yielding, warm and soft.

"Do you really like me?" she asks softly.

"I've been thinking of you all day." It is the truth.

She turns her face to me. I find her lips which are suddenly relaxed and parted. I push her onto the bed. She tries to wriggle free, charged with energy like a fish just cast ashore. I can't control myself yet she keeps begging me to pull the cord of the lamp and to let down the mosquito net.

"Don't look at me, don't look..." she whispers into my ear.

"I can't see a thing!" I am urgently clutching her writhing body.

She becomes tense, takes my hand, gently guides it into the shirt I have pulled open, and places it over her heaving breast. Her body goes limp and she falls silent. She and I have lusted for this physical intimacy. The alcohol, the rain, the darkness and the mosquito net have given her a feeling of security. She is no longer shy, lets go of my hand, and allows me to completely undress her. I kiss her from her neck to her nipples, her moist legs readily part and I murmur to her, "I want to possess you ..."

"No ... don't..." But she seems to be sighing.

I immediately mount her.

"I want to possess you now!" I don't know why I keep declaring this, is it to get myself worked up or is it to lessen my responsibility?

"I'm still a virgin..." I hear her weeping.

"Will you have regrets?" I instantly hesitate.

"You wouldn't marry me." She fully understands this, so she's crying.

Unfortunately, I can't lie to her and I know it is only a woman that I want. It's because I am bored and want to have some fun and that's all. I can't accept any further responsibility for her. I get down, disappointed, and kissing her, ask, "Is this precious to you?"

She silently shakes her head.

"Are you afraid when you marry your husband will find out and also beat you?"

She is trembling.

"Yet you're willing to give up so much for me?"

I touch the lip she is biting on, she is nodding. I am filled with compassion for her and holding her head, I kiss her wet face, cheeks and neck. She is weeping silently.

I can't be so cruel as to enjoy myself on her because of my momentary lust and let her pay such a high price for me. I can't help liking her and I know it's not love, but then what is love? Her body is fresh and sensitive and, again and again, I am filled with lust and do everything except for the last boundary. But she waits, alert, does whatever I ask of her and nothing excites me more than this. I want to remember every little tremor of her body and I want to be etched indelibly, body and soul, into her memory. She is trembling all this time, weeping, and both the upper and lower parts of her body are drenched. I don't know whether or not this is more cruel. It is not until dawn breaks on the window, outside the partially drawn mosquito net, that she calms down.

I lean on the bed looking at her pale, unclad body lying in the faint light.

"Don't you like me?"

I don't reply, I can't.

She gets up, gets out of the bed and leans by the window. The shadow of her body and the silhouette of her face is heart-rending.

"Why didn't you take me?" The hurt in her voice shows that she is tormenting herself.

What can I say?

"Of course you've had lots of experiences."

"Not at all!" I sit up.

"Don't come near!" She indignantly stops me and puts on her clothes.

Out on the street, there are already hurried footsteps and the sound of peasants on their way to the morning market.

"I won't cling onto you," she says as she combs her hair in the mirror.

I want to say I'm afraid of her getting a beating, afraid of bringing misfortune upon her afterwards, afraid of her becoming pregnant. I know the implications for an unmarried woman having an abortion in a small county town, I want to say, "I–"

"Don't say anything, you listen to me. I know what you're afraid of, I could quickly find someone to marry me, I wouldn't blame you."

She heaves a big sigh.

"I want to ..."

"No! Don't move! It's too late."

"I think I should go today," I say.

"I know I'm not good enough for you, but you're a good man."

Is this necessarily so?

"Your mind isn't on a woman's body."

I want to say this is not at all so.

"No! Don't say anything."

I should have spoken then but don't say anything.

After combing her hair and getting properly dressed, she fetches water for me to wash my face, sits on the chair and quietly waits for me to finish washing and combing my hair. It is already full light.

I go back to my room and start putting my things together. After a while she comes in. I know she is right behind me but don't dare turn around. It is only when I have stuffed everything into the bag and pulled the zipper that I turn to her.

Before going out the door I embrace her. She turns her head, closes her eyes, and presses her face to my chest. I try to kiss her but she breaks away.

It is a long way to the bus stop. In the early morning there are large numbers of people coming and going on the street and it's very noisy. She is some distance from me and walking very quickly. It is as if we are two people who don't know each other.

She walks with me all the way to the bus stop. There she sees quite a few people she knows and she greets and chats with each of them. She appears comfortable and relaxed but avoids looking at me. I too do not dare to make eye contact with her. I hear her introducing me, saying I am a writer who has come to collect folk songs. It is only in the instant when the bus starts that I see her eyes. Their brightness is shattering.

46

She says she hates you!

Why? Your eyes stare at the knife she is toying with.

She says you have taken her life to the grave.

You say she is still young.

But you have ruined the best years of her life, she says you, yes you!

You say she can start life anew.

You can, she says, but for her it's too late.

You can't see why it's too late.

It's because she's a woman.

Women are the same as men.

You make it all sound very nice. She laughs sarcastically.

You see her raise the knife and instantly sit up.

She can't let you off so lightly, she says she's going to kill you!

There's a death penalty for murder, you say, moving away and watching her anxiously.

My life's no longer worth living, she says.

You ask if she's been living for you, you want to placate her.

It's not worth living for anyone! She points the knife at you.

Put down the knife! You warn her.

Are you afraid of death? She laughs sarcastically again.

Everyone's afraid of death. You admit you're afraid of death and try to persuade her to put down the knife.

She's not afraid, she says, having gone this far, she's not afraid of anything!

You don't dare enrage her but must keep an aggressive edge to what you say and not let her see you're terrified.

There's no need to go to all this trouble to die, you say, there's a better way of dying. Old age.

You won't live that long, she says, the knife in her hand glinting.

You edge away and turn to watch her from the side.

She suddenly starts laughing loudly.

You ask if she's gone mad.

If she has it's because you made her, she says.

Made you do what? You say you can no longer live with her, that it's best to separate. Staying together is voluntary, and so is separating. You try hard to stay calm.

It's not so simple.

Then let's go to court.

No.

Then let both parties separate.

She says she can't let you off so lightly, holds up the knife and comes up to you.

You get out of bed and sit down facing her.

She also gets up, exposing her bare upper body, her drooping breasts. Her eyes are dilated and she's very agitated.

You can't stand her hysteria, can't stand her tantrums. You've made up your mind to leave. To avoid provoking her further, you say let's talk about something else.

Are you trying to get away?

Get away from what?

Get away from death. She mocks you and flourishes the knife, unsteadily, like an inexperienced butcher. Her nipples are shaking.

You say you hate her! Finally, this comes through your clenched teeth.

You've hated her for a long time but why didn't you say so a long time ago? She starts screaming, you've wounded her. Her whole body starts shaking.

It wasn't as bad then, you say you didn't think she would become so disgusting, you say you thoroughly detest her and blurt out cruel harsh words.

You should have said so earlier, you should have said so earlier, she starts weeping and the blade of the knife turns down.

You say everything about her thoroughly disgusts you! You are determined to wound her to the core.

She throws down the knife, shouting, you should have said earlier, it's too late, too late for everything, why didn't you say so earlier? She wails hysterically, pounding the floor with her fists.

You want to comfort her but then all this effort, what you have at last resolved, will have been wasted, everything will start all over again and it will be even harder to get away.

She starts bawling and is rolling naked on the floor with the knife lying next to her.

You bend to take away the knife but she grabs the blade. You try to prise off her fingers but she holds onto it tighter.

You'll cut your hand! Shouting at her, you twist her arm until she drops it. Red blood drips from her palm. You take her wrist and press hard on the artery. She grabs the knife with her other hand. You slap her across the face, stunning her, and she drops the knife.

She looks dumbly at you and suddenly, like a child, eyes full of despair, begins to weep soundlessly. You can't help feeling sorry for her and, taking her injured hand, suck away the blood with your lips. At this she locks her arms around you tightly, weeping. You try to break free but her arms lock around you even more tightly, pulling you to her breasts.

What are you doing? You are furious.

She wants you to make love, right away! She says she wants to make love now!

With great difficulty you pull yourself away and say, panting, you're not an animal!

You are! You are an animal! She screams wildly, her eyes glinting strangely.

You try to comfort her and, at the same time, you beg her not to be like this, beg her to calm down.

She blubbers, crying and saying she loves you. Her outburst is because she loves you, she's frightened that you're leaving.

You say you can't yield to a woman's will, can't live under this sort of shadow. She is suffocating you, you can't be anyone's slave, you won't submit to any authority whatever tactics are used. And you refuse to submit to a woman, to be a woman's slave.

She says she will give you freedom as long as you love her and don't leave, as long as you stay with her, as long as you satisfy her, as long as you want her. She wraps herself around you, kisses you wildly, wet kisses on your face, your body, and rolls around with you. She has won, you can't resist and again sink into carnal lust, unable to free yourself.

47

Walking along a road on the shady side of a mountain, no-one ahead or behind me, I get caught in a downpour. At first it's light rain and feels good falling on my face, then it gets heavier and heavier and I have to run. My hair and clothes are drenched, and seeing a cave on the slope, I hurry to it. Just inside is a big pile of chopped firewood. The ceiling is quite high and one corner of the cave goes further inside. Light is coming from over there. A stove built of rocks with an iron pot on it stands at the top of a few roughly-hewn steps and light is streaming in through a crack in the rock running at an angle above the stove.

I turn around. Behind me is a roughly nailed together wooden bed with the bedding rolled up. A Daoist priest is sitting there reading a book. I get a surprise but don't dare disturb him and just look at the grey-white line of rain shivering in the crack. It is raining so heavily that I don't want to venture back out.

"It's all right, you can stay awhile." It is he who speaks first as he puts down his book.

He has shoulder length hair and is wearing a loose grey top and grey trousers. He looks to be around thirty.

"Are you one of the Daoists of this mountain?" I ask.

"Not yet. I chop firewood for the Daoist temple," he replies.

On his bed, cover up, is a copy of *Fiction Monthly*.

"Are you also interested in this?" I ask.

"I read it to pass time," he says frankly. "You're all wet, dry yourself first." Saying this he brings a basin of hot water from the pot on the stove and gives me a towel.

I thank him, then stripping to the waist, have a wash and instantly feel much better.

"This is really a good place to shelter!" I say as I sit down on a block of wood opposite. "Do you live in this cave?"

He says he is from the village at the foot of the mountain but that he hates the whole lot of them, his older brother and his wife, the neighbours, and the village cadres.

"They all put money first and only think about profit," he says, "I no longer have anything to do with them."

"So you chop firewood for a living?"

"I renounced society almost a year ago but they haven't formally accepted me yet."

"Why?"

"The old head Daoist wants to see whether I am sincere, whether my heart is constant."

"Will he accept you then?"

"Yes."

This shows he firmly believes he is sincere of heart.

"Don't you feel bored living in this cave on your own all the time?" I go on to ask, casting a glance at the magazine.

"It's more peaceful and relaxed than in the village," he calmly replies, unaware that I'm trying to provoke him. "I also study every day," he adds.

"May I ask what you are studying?"

He pulls out a stone-block–print copy of *Daily Lessons for Daoists* from under his bedding.

"I was reading some fiction because on rainy days like this I can't work," he explains when he sees me looking at the magazine on his bed.

"Do these stories affect your study?" I am curious to find out.

"Ha, they're all about common occurrences between men and women," he replies with a dismissive laugh. He says he went to senior high school and studied some literature and when there's nothing to do he reads a bit. "In fact human life just amounts to this."

I can't go on to ask him whether he ever had a wife and I can't question him about the private concerns of one who has renounced the world. The pelting rain is monotonous but soothing.

I shouldn't disturb him any further. I sit with him for a long time in meditation, sitting in forgetfulness in the sound of the rain.

I don't notice the rain has stopped. But when I do, I get up, thank him, and bid him farewell.

He says, "No need to thank me, it is fate."

This is on Qingcheng Mountain.

Afterwards, at the old stone pagoda on the island in the middle of the Ou River, I encounter a monk with a shaven head wearing a crimson cassock. He presses his palms together then kneels and prostrates himself in front of the pagoda. Sightseers crowd around to watch. He unhurriedly completes his worship, removes his cassock, puts it into a black artificial leather case, picks up his umbrella, which has a curved handle and doubles as a walking stick then turns and leaves. I follow him, then, some distance from the crowd of sightseers who were watching him pray, I go up and ask, "Venerable Master, can I invite you to drink tea with me? I would like to ask your advice about some Buddhist teachings."

He thinks about it, then agrees.

He has a gaunt face, is alert, and looks to be around fifty. His trouser legs are tied at the calves and he walks briskly so that I have to half run to keep up.

"The Venerable Master seems to be leaving for a distant journey," I say.

"I'm going to Jiangxi first to visit a few old monks, then I have to go to a number of other places."

"I too am a lone traveller. However, I am not like the Venerable Master who is steadfastly sincere and has a sacred goal in his heart." I have to find something to talk about.

"The true traveller is without goal, it is the absence of goals which creates the ultimate traveller."

"Venerable Master, are you from this locality? Is this journey to farewell your native village? Don't you intend coming back?"

"For one who has renounced society all within the four seas is home, for him what is called native village does not exist."

This leaves me speechless. I invite him into a tea stall in the park and choose a quiet corner to sit down. I ask his Buddhist name, tell him my name and then hesitate.

It is he who speaks first. "Just ask what you wish to know, there is nothing one who has renounced society cannot talk about."

I then blurt out, "If you don't mind, I wish to ask, Venerable Master, why you renounced society."

He smiles, blows at the tea leaves floating in his cup and takes a sip. Then, looking at me he says, "It seems that you are not on an ordinary trip, are you on a special mission?"

"I'm not carrying out any sort of investigation but when I saw the Venerable Master's serene person, I was filled with admiration. I don't have a specific goal but I still can't abandon it."

"Abandon what?" A smile lingers on his face.

"Abandon the human world." After I say this, he and I both laugh.

"The human world can be abandoned just by saying it." His response is straightforward.

"That's indeed so," I say nodding, "but I would like to know how the Venerable Master was able to abandon it."

Without holding anything back, he then tells me about his experience.

He says that when he was sixteen, and still at junior high school, he ran away from home to join the revolution and fought for a year as a guerilla in the mountains. At seventeen he went with the army into the city and was put in charge of a bank. He could have become a party leader but he had his mind set on studying medicine. After graduating he was allocated work as a cadre in the city health bureau although he really wanted to continue to work as a doctor. One day he offended the branch party secretary of the hospital and was expelled from the party, branded a rightist element and sent to work in the fields in the country. It was only when the village built a commune hospital that he got to work as a doctor for several years. During this time he married a village girl and three children in succession were born. However for some reason he wanted to convert to Catholicism and when he heard that a Vatican cardinal had arrived in Guangzhou, he travelled there to ask the cardinal about the faith. He ended up not seeing the cardinal and instead came under suspicion for illicit dealings with foreigners. For this crime he was expelled from the commune hospital and he had no option but to spend his time studying traditional medicine on his own and mixing with vagrants in order to eat. One day he came to a sudden realization – the Pope was far away in the West and inaccessible, so he might as well rely on Buddha. From that time he renounced society and became a monk. When he finishes telling this he gives a loud laugh.

"Do you still think of your family?" I ask.

"They can all feed themselves."

"Don't you have some lingering fondness for them?"

"Those who have renounced society have neither fondness nor hatred."

"Then do they hate you?"

He says he never felt inclined to ask about them but some years after he entered the monastery, his eldest son came to tell him he had been exonerated from the charge of being a rightist element and having illicit dealings with foreigners. If he returned he would be treated as a senior cadre and veteran revolutionary, reinstated in his former position and also receive a large sum of unpaid salary due to him. He said he didn't want any of the money and they could divide it up. The fact that his wife and children had not been unjustly treated could be considered recompense for his devotion to the Buddhist faith and thereafter they should not come again. After that he started wandering and they had no means of knowing his whereabouts.

"Do you now seek alms along the way to support yourself?"

He says people are mean-spirited nowadays. Seeking alms is worse than begging, if you seek alms you don't get anything. He mainly supports himself by practising as an itinerant doctor. When practising he wears ordinary clothes, he doesn't want to damage the image of the Buddhist order.

"Does Buddhism allow this flexibility?" I ask.

"Buddha is in your heart." His face is serene and I believe he has achieved liberation from the worries of the inner heart. He is setting out on a distant journey and he is very happy.

I ask him how he finds lodgings on the way. He says wherever there are temples and monasteries he only needs to show his monk's certificate to be accorded hospitality. However the situation at present is bad everywhere. There are not many monks and all of them have to work in order to feed and clothe themselves: generally long stays aren't possible because no-one is providing support. Only the big temples and monasteries get any government subsidies but these are only minuscule amounts and, naturally, he doesn't want to add to people's burdens. He says he's a traveller and has already been to many famous mountains. He thinks he is in good health and that he can still walk a ten-thousand *li* journey.

"Would it be possible for me to see your monk's certificate?" It seems that this is more useful than the credentials I have.

"It's not a secret document, the Buddhist order doesn't have secrets and is open to all."

He takes from a breast pocket a big piece of folded silk paper with an ink-print Buddha sitting with legs folded on the lotus throne in the top section. It is stamped with a large vermilion square seal. His Buddhist name at initiation, academic achievements and rank are all written on it. He has reached the rank of abbot and is permitted to lecture on the sutras and to deal with Buddhist matters.

"Maybe one day I'll follow in your footsteps." I don't know whether I am joking or not.

"In that case we are linked in destiny." He, however, is quite earnest. Saying this he gets up, presses his palms together, and bids me farewell.

He walks very quickly and I follow him for a while but in an instant he vanishes among the thronging sightseers. I am clearly aware that I am still rooted in the mundane world.

Later, while reading an inscriptions in the Abandon Profit Pagoda, built in the Sui Dynasty, which stands in front of the Guoqing Monastery at the foot of Tiantai Mountain, I suddenly overhear a conversation.

"You'd best return with me," says a man's voice from the other side of the brick wall.

"No, you should leave now." It is also a man's voice, but it is louder.

"It's not for my sake, think of your mother."

"Just tell her I'm doing very well."

"Your mother asked me to come, she's ill."

"What illness is it?"

"She keeps saying she has pains in the chest."

The son makes no response.

"Your mother got me to bring you a pair of shoes."

"I've got shoes."

"They're the sports shoes you wanted, they're for basketball."

"They're very expensive, why did you buy them?"

"Try them on."

"I don't play basketball now, I don't have any use for them. You'd best take them back, nobody wears them here."

In the early morning, birds in the forest are singing cheerfully. In the midst of the twittering of many sparrows, a single thrush warbles but it is concealed by the dense leaves of the nearby ginkgo tree so I can't see which branch it's on. Then a few magpies arrive and make a raucous clamour. It is silent for a long time by the brick pagoda and thinking they have gone I go around and see a youth looking up at the singing birds, his gleaming black shaven head does not yet have the initiation burns made with incense sticks. He is wearing a short monk's jacket, and the ruddy complexion of his handsome face is unlike the dark yellowish complexions of monks who have been vegetarian for a long time. His young father, a peasant, is holding the new white-soled basketball shoes with red and blue striped uppers he has taken out of their box. He is breathing heavily. I surmise the father is putting pressure on his son to get married and I wonder if the youth will take his vows.

48

You want to tell her a *biji* tale of the Jin Dynasty. It's about a powerful and overbearing Grand Marshall and a mendicant nun who comes to his mansion seeking alms. According to procedure, the guards notify the household manager who gives the nun a string of cash, however she declines it and announces that she wishes to see the giver of alms. The household manager notifies the chief overseer who orders a servant to take her a silver ingot and send her on her way once and for all. But the nun refuses this as well and insists on seeing the Grand Marshall, saying he is in trouble and that she has come especially to help him. The chief overseer is left with no choice but to report this to the Grand Marshall who orders that the nun be brought into the front hall.

The Grand Marshall sees that despite the dust and grime, the nun has refined features and doesn't look like the lewd, sham religious, mischief-making type. He asks her why she has come. The nun presses her palms together in greeting then withdraws. She replies: I have long heard of the Grand Marshall's great benevolence so I have come from afar especially to perform the seven times seven equals forty-nine day fast for his deceased mother and at the same time to pray to the bodhisattvas to bring good fortune and to eliminate misfortune. The Grand Marshall then orders the chief overseer to arrange a room in the inner court and to have the servants install an incense table in the hall.

Thereafter, for days in succession, there is the endless sound of wooden clappers from morning till night in the house. The Grand Marshall becomes more relaxed, and with the passing of the days treats the nun with increasing respect. However, before changing the incense each afternoon, the nun insists on having a bath which always takes two hours. The Grand Marshall begins to think to himself, nuns have bald heads and unlike ordinary women, don't need to spend time combing their hair and putting on make-up. The bath is just a ritual for cleansing the heart before changing the incense, why does it take so long? And when she has the bath there is the sound of splashing water, could she be stirring the water without actually bathing? Nagging doubts begin to grow in his mind.

One day while he is strolling in the courtyard, the sound of the wooden clappers suddenly stops. Instantly, he hears the sound of water and knows that the nun will soon be changing the incense sticks, so he goes into the hall to wait. The sound of the water becomes louder and louder, and even after a long time doesn't stop. His suspicion overcomes him and before realizing it, he has descended the stairs and is walking past the door to her room. There is a crack in the door which doesn't close properly, and he goes up and peers inside. He sees the nun facing the door, she has removed all her clothing and is sitting naked with her legs crossed in the tub, scooping water in both hands to wash herself. Her face is totally transformed, it is radiant and she has white teeth, pink cheeks and a jade-white neck, smooth shoulders and plump arms – a veritable beauty. He hurries away and returns to the hall in an attempt to compose himself ...

But the sound of splashing water from her room continues, enticing him to have another look, so going back along the corridor he creeps stealthily to the door. Again, with bated breath, he goes up to the crack in the door and sees her delicate outstretched fingers rubbing her full breasts, which are white like snow and each adorned with a budding cherry flower. Her wet flesh is heaving and the line of life runs down from her navel. The Grand Marshall goes down on his knees and is transfixed. He then sees the white hands in the tub taking a pair of scissors and thrusting them hard into the navel and bright red blood instantly gushing out from it. He is aghast but doesn't dare act hastily. He closes his eyes, unable to look.

Some time passes and the sound of splashing water starts again. He focuses his eyes and sees the bald-headed nun drenched in blood. Her hands are busily moving about as she pulls out her intestines and puts them into the tub!

This Grand Marshall, who comes from a famous family of generals and has been through many battles, doesn't faint. He takes a deep breath and anxiously resolves to get a proper look. By this time the nun's face is drained of colour, her eyelids droop and her eyelashes come together, and her blanched lips quiver as if she is groaning, but when he listens he can only hear the splashing of the water.

She takes length after length of the soft intestines into her bloody hands, washes and untangles them, then winds them around her wrists. This goes on for a long time. When she finally finishes washing, she presses the intestines neatly together and crams them back into her stomach. Then, with a ladle, she washes in turn her arms, chest and abdomen, between her legs, her legs and feet, and even each of her toes. At the end of this, she is whole again. The Grand Marshall quickly gets to his feet, goes up the stairs into the hall, and stands there waiting for her.

Before long the door opens and the nun, holding sutra beads and clad in her nun's robe, arrives in the hall at precisely the moment when the incense sticks in the censer burn right down. As black smoke from each stick vanishes she unhurriedly replaces it.

The Grand Marshall seems to be waking from a dream and, intrigued, is compelled to ask her about it. The nun is unmoved and replies: If you sir are thinking of usurping the state the situation will be like this. On hearing this, the ambitious Grand Marshall, who had indeed been planning to usurp the state, can't help feeling disappointed, but doesn't dare to act improperly and remains a loyal minister.

This story is a political warning.

You say if the ending of the story is changed it could become a morality tale to warn people against lechery and lust.

The story could also be turned into a religious tale to exhort people to convert to Buddhism.

The story can also serve as a philosophy for getting on in society – to teach the morally superior man that each day he should investigate his own personal conduct, or that human life is suffering, or that suffering in life derives from the self. Or the story could be developed into numerous intricate and complex theories. It all depends on how the storyteller tells it.

The Grand Marshall protagonist of the story has a name and surname so a great deal of textual research, examining historical texts and old books, could be carried out. But as you are not a historian, don't have political aspirations, and certainly neither wish to become an expert in Buddhism, nor to preach religion, nor to become a paragon of virtue, what appeals to you is the superb purity of the story. Any explanation is irrelevant, you simply wanted to retell it in the spoken language.

49

In an old street of this county town, he has his calligraphy stall set up on planks laid on two wooden benches outside a general store. Strips of lucky couplets written on red glossy paper hang from the planks. "Dragon and phoenix manifest good fortune. Marriage celebrations arrive at the house", "Going out the door happy events occur. Right on the ground silver is sprouting", "Business flourishing as far as the four seas. Riches in abundance reaching the three rivers" – these are all old sayings which had for many years been replaced by revolutionary slogans and the sayings of Mao Zedong. There are also two strips with the words "Whoever you meet, laugh, and you will be happy. Whatever the problem, shrug it off, and misfortune will vanish", which he could have thought up himself or which could be based on the accumulated experiences of his ancestors for getting along in society. This couplet has been written in a fancy style, the characters are well structured and look like those on Daoist talismans.

He is seated behind the planks, an old man in an old-style jacket fastened down the front who looks quite comical with his faded old army hat perched on the back of his head. I notice the Eight Trigram compass he is using as a paperweight and go up to chat with him.

"Venerable elder, how's business?"

"All right."

"How much does a set of characters cost?"

"Some are two *yuan* and some are three *yuan*, it costs more for more characters."

"What about the single character for good fortune?"

"That would cost one *yuan*."

"But wouldn't that be only one character?"

"I'd have to write it for you on the spot."

"What about drawing a talisman to dispel disaster and ward off evil?"

He looks up at me and says, "Can't be done."

"Why?"

"You're a cadre, surely you know."

"I'm not a cadre," I say.

"But the state feeds you," he says emphatically.

"Venerable elder," I begin, I need to win him over, "are you a Daoist priest?"

"I gave it up a long time ago."

"Of course," I say. "Venerable elder, I'm asking if you know how to perform Daoist rituals."

"Yes. But the government doesn't allow the performance of superstitious practices."

"Nobody's asking you to. I'm collecting the music of scriptural texts which are sung, can you sing them? The Qingcheng Mountain Daoist Association has been re-registered and is open again, what are you afraid of?"

"That's a big temple, we torchlight Daoists aren't allowed to practise."

"Folk Daoists like you are just the people I'm looking for." My interest has been further aroused. "Would you sing a couple of pieces for me? For example, scriptures for the Daoist funeral rites or for exorcising demons and spirits?"

He sings a couple of sentences but suddenly stops, and says, "Ghosts and spirits shouldn't be disturbed without good reason and incense has to be burnt to invite them."

While he was singing a crowd had gathered and someone shouts out, "Hey, old man, sing us a bawdy ditty!" The crowd laughs.

"I'll sing you a mountain love song instead," the old man says good-naturedly, declaring his boldness.

The crowd shouts, "Good for you! Good for you!"

The old man suddenly bursts into loud song.

> Young girl on the mountain picking tea,
> Your young man is down cutting brushwood,
> In both places startled mandarin ducks fly up,
> Young girl quickly marry your young man.

The crowd shouts bravo, then someone insists, "Give us a bawdy song!"

"Come on, give us one, old man!"

The old man shrugs his shoulders and shakes his hands to the crowd. "No, no. It's against the regulations."

"It's all right, old man, come on, sing us one." The crowd clamours and the little street becomes jammed with people and bicycles can't get through and are ringing their bells.

"But it's you who have put me up to it!" Egged on by the crowd the old man stands up.

"Sing 'Horse-Monkey Wearing a Skullcap Steals Into the Maiden's Bedroom!'" Someone has picked a title. The crowd yells bravo and starts clapping.

The old man wipes his mouth and is about to sing when suddenly he says in a low voice, "The police are here!"

People turn to look – a big hat with a white brim edged with red is moving about not far behind the heads of the crowd.

"What does it matter?" the crowd says.

"What's wrong with having a bit of fun?"

"As if the police can look after so many things?"

"It's all very well for you to talk, you'll be able to go off but will I be able to stay in business?" The old man sits down, refusing to give in to the crowd.

The policeman comes up and the grumbling crowd scatters. After the policeman leaves, I say, "Venerable elder, could I invite you to my lodgings to sing some songs? When you've closed up the stall, how about I treat you to some food and liquor?"

The old man is still excited and hasn't calmed down, he immediately agrees, "Good! I'm closing right now, I'll pack up my things, just wait while I return the planks."

"I'm stopping you from making money." I want to let him know I feel bad about it.

"It's all right, I'm making a friend. I don't depend on this to eat. If I come into town I sell a few pieces while I'm here to get a bit of extra cash. If I relied on selling calligraphy to eat wouldn't I starve to death?"

I go into a restaurant diagonally opposite and order some liquor and food. Before long the old man turns up with a set of baskets on a carrying pole.

Hot food is brought and we talk and eat. He says when he was ten his father sent him to a Daoist monastery to help attend to the stove and the cooking, as promised by his father when he was ill. He can still recite the textbook *Daily Lessons for Daoists* which the old Daoist priest had used to enlighten him. When the old priest died he managed the monastery so he knows the procedures for all the Daoist rituals. Later on during the land reforms when the land was divided up and he could no longer practise as a Daoist priest, the government ordered him to return to his village and he worked in the fields again. I ask him about Yin-Yang and geomancy, the Five Thunder Finger Techniques, the Constellation Dances, physiognomy and massage. He explains each of these with such eloquence that I am positively elated. However the restaurant is full of peasants who are making a lot of noise. They have finished trading for the day, made a bit of money, and are drinking, playing drinking games and shouting loudly. I tell him I have a tape recorder in my bag. What he is telling me is valuable material, after eating I would like him to come to my lodgings to make some recordings, it will be quieter when he sings.

"Bring some liquor," he says, "we can drink at my house, I have a Daoist robe and all the regalia there."

"Do you have the sword of office to drive away demons?"

"That's essential."

"And do you also have the command tablet for deploying spirits and despatching generals?"

"There are also gongs, drums and other things, these are all vital for Daoist rituals. I'll put on a performance for you."

"Excellent!" I strike the table, get up and go out the door with him. "Is your house in town?" I ask.

"It's not far, it's not far, I'll just leave my pole with someone, you go on ahead and wait for me at the bus stop."

In less than ten minutes he comes hurrying along, pointing to a bus that is about to leave and telling me to quickly get on. I hadn't expected the bus to keep going without any stops along the way and watch through the bus window as the lingering rays of the sun pale and vanish behind the mountains. The bus arrives at the small town destination twenty kilometres from the county town, immediately turns around, and departs. It is the last bus.

This town has only the one little street, at most it is fifty metres long, and I have no idea whether or not there is an inn. He tells me to wait for a while and goes into one of the houses. I think to myself, since I am here I might as well just relax, and that bumping into such a character who turns out to be so enthusiastic is a stroke of good luck. He comes out of the house holding in both hands a washbasin half filled with bean curd and tells me to follow him.

Outside the small town, the road is a dirt road. It is already dark.

"Is your home in a village near this small town?" I ask.

"It's not far, it's not far," he says.

Gradually the farm houses by the road can no longer be seen, the darkness of night has descended and in the paddy fields all around is the croaking of frogs. I am anxious, but feel awkward asking so many questions. Suddenly from behind comes the chugging of a motor, a bulldozer is upon us. He immediately calls out to it and chases it, half-running and half-jumping, and I clamber after him onto the shovel. On the dirt road, we are tossed about in this shovel like dried beans in a sieve for a distance of almost ten *li*. It is completely dark with just the bulldozer's single beam of yellow light, like a one-eyed dragon, illuminating ten or twenty paces of bumpy dirt road, there is no-one else around. He talks non-stop in a loud voice with the driver in the local dialect. I can't make out a single sentence and can only hear the deafening noise of the motor. If they are talking about butchering me, I can only let fate take its course.

Eventually we get to the end of the road and a house without a light appears – it is the house of the driver of the bulldozer. The old man opens the door of the house and gives the man a few big pieces of bean curd. Following him I feel my way in the dark along a small winding track between the paddy fields.

"Is it still a long way off?" I ask.

"It's not far, it's not far." He still says the same old thing.

Luckily, he is walking in front and has to put down the washbasin of bean curd to do breathing exercises. I know that all the old Daoists know martial arts and if I were to turn and run I'd probably fall into the paddy fields and get covered in mud. The croaking of frogs becomes less frequent and the reflected light on the terraced fields behind shows that we are on a mountain. I try to think of things to say to engage him in conversation, and I ask him about the harvest and about the hard life of working in the paddy fields. He says truly, if one relies on working in the fields one needn't think of becoming rich. This year he spent three thousand *yuan* converting two *mu* of paddy fields into fish ponds. I ask if he raises soft-shell turtles and say it's trendy to eat them in the cities at present: some say they prevent cancer and others say they're a tonic for men. They fetch a high price. He says he's only put in small fingerlings, if he puts in soft-shell turtles won't they eat all the fish? He says he's got the cash but it's hard to get timber – he has seven sons and only the eldest is married, the other six are all waiting to build houses so that they can have separate households. Then he'll be able to relax, lie down, look at the stars in the sky, and enjoy the night scenery.

In the grey gloomy shadows of the mountain is a cluster of flickering lights. He says that's where we are headed.

"I told you it wasn't far, didn't I?"

I think village people have their own concepts of distance.

At ten o'clock at night we finally reach a little mountain village. Incense is burning in the hall of his house, offerings to the large number of wooden and stone carvings. They are all broken and damaged, he probably rescued them from the Daoist temple some years ago when the "four olds" were destroyed and temples and monasteries were smashed. He now has them on display and there are Daoist talismans hanging on the rafters. Six sons come out, the eldest of these is eighteen and the youngest just eleven, and only the eldest married son isn't present. His wife is a small woman, and his mother, who is eighty, is still quite agile. His wife and sons busy themselves for a while and suddenly I am an honoured guest. They fetch hot water for me to wash my face, get me to wash my feet and put on a pair of the old man's cloth shoes, then bring me a cup of strong tea.

Before long the six sons bring out gongs, drums, small cymbals and also two gong-chimes, a large one and a small one, hanging on wooden frames. Suddenly all the drums sound and the old man comes down the stairs. He is wearing a tattered old purple Daoist robe adorned with the insignia of the Yin-Yang fish and the Eight Trigrams, and is carrying the command tablet, the sword of office and an ox horn. He looks totally different, majestic, and walks with slow measured steps. He lights a stick of incense and bows with it to the altar in the hall. Men, women and children from the village, startled by the drums and gongs, crowd at the doorway. Immediately, a bustling Daoist ritual commences. He hasn't been leading me on.

First he takes a bowl of clear liquid and, chanting, flicks the watery liquor into the four corners of the house. When he flicks it onto the feet of the crowd at the door, everyone roars with laughter. He is expressionless – his eyes partly close, his mouth slackens and his face takes on a serious look, as if he is communicating with the spirits. At this the crowd laughs even more. Suddenly he shakes the sleeve of his Daoist robe and slams the command tablet on the table. The laughter instantly stops. He turns and says to me, "These texts are all sung: 'Year of the Big Journey Song', 'Nine Stars of Good Fortune and Bad Fortune Song', 'Sons and Grandsons Song', 'Transformations Song',

'Arithmetic Chants for Negating the Four Inauspicious Stars', 'Deity Names of the Door Gods', 'Salutary Texts for the Sacrifices to the God of the Earth', 'Invoking the Spirit of the Northern Dipper'. Which would you like to hear?"

"Please sing 'Invoking the Spirit of the Northern Dipper' first," I say.

"This is to protect small children and to expel illness and calamity. Which of you children will give your name and the time of your birth?"

"Get Little Doggie to come out," someone interjects.

"No."

A small boy sitting on the doorstep gets to his feet and quickly worms his way through to the back. Everyone breaks out laughing again.

"What are you frightened of? After old grandpa does it you won't get sick anymore," a middle-aged woman outside the door says.

The boy hides behind the crowd and adamantly refuses to come out.

The old man waves his sleeve and says, "It doesn't matter." He turns to say to me, "Generally one has to prepare a bowl of rice and stand a cooked egg upright in it and then burn incense to invoke the spirits. The child kneels, prostrates himself, then prays to invite the spirits to accept the offerings: the True Ruler of the Four Directions, the Great Emperor Ziwei, the Star Ruler of the North Who in Nine Shakes Dispels Evil, the Star Ruler of Longevity of the Southern Dipper Temple, the two Guardian Deities of the Village, the deceased generations of clan ancestors, the sons and grandsons of the Kitchen God—"

Saying this he takes up his sword of office, flourishes it, and begins to sing loudly, "Spirit-soul, spirit-soul, you've had your play now quickly go home! In the east is a boy in blue, in the south is a boy in red, in the west is a boy in white, all on guard, and in the north a boy in black will bring you home. Lost and wandering spirit-soul cease your play, the road is long and it's hard to get home. I will measure the road for you with a jade ruler, should you come to dark places. If you fall into the net of Heaven and the mesh of Earth my scissors will cut them. If you are hungry, thirsty, and weary, I have grain for you. Don't stay in the forest listening to the birds singing, don't stay by deep ponds looking at the fish swimming. If someone calls you a thousand times don't reply, spirit-soul, spirit-soul, hurry back home! May the gods and deities protect you, may past virtues not be forgotten! From now on the spirit will protect the body and the soul will protect the house, wind and chill will not enter, water and the earth will find it hard to transgress. Sturdiness in childhood brings greater strength in old age, so that you will enjoy a long life to a hundred years and be of healthy spirit!"

He flourishes his sword of office and draws a big circle in the air, then puffing out his cheeks starts blowing on the ox horn. Afterwards he turns and says to me, "I then draw a talisman which carried on the person brings good fortune!"

I can't decide whether or not he believes his own techniques but he dances and waves his arms and legs about, walks with a swagger, and looks very pleased with himself. Arranging a Daoist ritual in the hall of his own house with the help of his six sons wins him the respect of the villagers and, in addition, with such an appreciative outsider as his guest, he can't contain his delight.

Next he makes a string of incantations to invoke the spirits of Heaven and Earth. His words become incomprehensible and his movements wilder as he circles the table and demonstrates a whole range of martial arts sword techniques. Following the pitch of his singing and the movements of his dance the six sons beat the gongs and drums with increasing gusto and produce endless variations. This is especially so with the young man on the drums. He throws off his jacket, exposing his dark skin and the rippling muscles on his shoulders and ribs. The crowd of onlookers outside the door grows so that the people at the front are pushed over the threshold and then along the walls, some even sit down on the floor. As each piece finishes everyone claps and cheers with me which pleases the old man even more and he doesn't hesitate in performing every movement he knows to summon forth, one after the other, every spirit and demon in his heart. He starts to go into an intoxicated, crazed state. It is only when my tape gets to the end and I stop the recorder to change the tape that, panting, that he too comes to a stop. The men and women inside and outside the house are all excited and are chatting, laughing and joking. The village meetings are definitely never this much fun.

As he wipes the sweat off himself with a towel, the old man points to a group of girls close by and says, "Now how about all of you sing a song for this teacher."

The girls start to giggle and after pushing and shoving one another for a while they shove Maomei forward. This wisp of a girl is only fourteen or fifteen but she doesn't lack confidence, and flashing her big round eyes asks, "What shall I sing?"

"Sing a mountain love song."

"Sing 'Two Sisters Marry'."

"Sing 'Flowers of the Four Seasons'."

"Sing about the two sisters weeping as they go off to marry."

"This song is really good," a middle-aged woman by the door says, recommending it to me.

The girl glances at me, turns away, and a very high pitched soprano voice cuts through the noise of the crowd and spirals upwards, instantly transporting me from the shadows into the mountain wilds. The sadness of a murmuring stream and the mountain wind are remote but clear. I recall the pine torch of night travellers flickering in the dark mountain shadows and that picture floats before my eyes again: an old man holding a pine torch and a girl, about the singer's age, who is emaciated and wearing trousers and a floral jacket. They are going past the front of the house of the primary school teacher in a mountain village. At the time I was sitting idly in the main hall of the house and didn't know where they'd come from nor where they were going, but I did know that up ahead was a big black mountain. They looked inside the main hall at me but didn't stop and headed straight toward the black mountain shadows, leaving behind bright sparks in front of the house which glowed for quite a while. My gaze returned to follow the torch. When it re-emerged from behind the shadows of the trees and cliffs it had become a small unsteady flickering flame moving in the black mountain shadows, leaving intermittent sparks to mark their trail. Afterwards there was nothing, the sparks and dark red embers vanished, like a song, a song of loud and pure grief flickering in a flame the size of a bean seed on a candle in the shadows of a room. In those years I was just like them and worked barefoot in the paddy fields. As soon as it was dark there was nowhere to go, and the house of the primary school teacher was the only place I could go for a chat, to drink tea, and just sit, to idle away the loneliness.

The grief moves everyone inside and outside the house and no-one is talking. Some time after she stops singing, a girl a little older than her, probably a girl waiting to be married, heaves a sigh as she leans on the doorway, "It's so sad!"

Only then do people start clamouring. "Sing a bawdy song!"

"Old Uncle sing us 'The Sky at the Fifth Watch'!"

"Sing us 'The Eighteen Strokes'!"

It is mostly young men shouting.

After a break the old man takes off his Daoist robe, gets up from the bench and begins to chase off the young singer and the children sitting on the doorsill. "All the children go home to sleep! Go home to sleep, there's no more singing, there's no more singing."

No-one wants to leave. The middle-aged woman standing outside the door calls the children by their names one by one, and chases them off.

The old man stamps his feet, pretends to lose his temper and shouts loudly, "Everyone get out! Shut the door, shut the door, I want to go to sleep!"

The middle-aged woman comes through the door, drags out the girls and shouts to the youths, "All of you get out as well!"

The youths grumble and make rude noises.

"Ye—"

Finally two older girls catch on, and leave. Then with everyone pushing and yelling at them, the other girls and children are all chased out. The woman goes to close the door and the adults who were outside take the opportunity to squeeze inside. The door is bolted and the inside of the house is hot and filled with the smell of sweat. The old man clears his throat, spits, and winks at the crowd. He has transformed again and looks crafty, rakish and wicked. He slinks around to look over the crowd and then starts singing in a rasping voice.

> Men cultivate, what do they cultivate?
> They cultivate a rod.
> Women cultivate, what do they cultivate?
> They cultivate a ditch.

There is a round of cheers and the old man wipes his mouth with his hand.

> When the rod is thrown into the ditch,
> It becomes a leaping, lively eel – Ah!

The crowd roars with laughter, some doubling over and others stamping their feet.

Someone calls out, "Let's have 'The Old Idiot Takes a Wife'!"

The young men all cheer.

The old man is invigorated and drags the table back to make a space in the middle of the hall. He gets down on his haunches but at that very moment there is pounding on the door. He balefully yells, "Who is it?"

"Me," the person on the other side of the door replies. The door is immediately opened and a young man with a coat over his shoulders and wearing a part in his hair, enters.

"The village head is here, the village head is here, the village head is here, the village head is here," the crowd murmurs.

The old man gets up. The person who arrives is smiling but as his eyes fall upon the tape recorder on the table and he scans the audience and sees me, his smile instantly retracts.

"My guest," says the old man. He turns to me and makes an introduction. "This is my eldest son."

I stretch out my hand to him. He tugs the coat draped over his shoulders but doesn't shake my hand. Instead, he asks, "Where are you from?"

The old man hastens to explain. "He's a teacher from Beijing."

His son frowns and asks, "Do you have an official letter?"

"I have identification," I say, taking out my Writers' Association membership card.

He looks it over back and front several times before returning it to me, saying, "It's no good without an official letter."

"What sort of official letter do you want?"

"One with the official seal of the village or county authorities."

"There's an embossed seal on my membership card!" I say.

He half believes me and takes it back, scrutinizes it under the light, but again returns it to me, saying, "It's not clear."

"I've come especially from Beijing to collect folk songs!" I won't give in, and I am not worried about being polite. Seeing that I am inflexible, he turns to his father and severely rebukes him, "Father, you know quite well this is against regulations!"

"He's a friend I've just made," the old man argues but in front of his son who is village head he is clearly deflated.

"Everyone go home to bed! This is against regulations." Some have already slipped away and his younger brothers have quietly put away all the gongs, drums and other props. I am not the only one who is disappointed, the old man is even more so. It is as if a bucket of cold water has been poured on his head and he is devastated. His eyes have lost their sparkle and he is so miserable that I feel quite bad on his behalf. I feel I have to explain, and say, "Your father is a unique folk artist, I've come especially to learn from him. There's nothing wrong with your regulations but there are other things governing these regulations, even greater regulations—" However I flounder in clarifying these even greater regulations on the spot.

"Go to the village authorities tomorrow morning, if they approve get them to stamp their seal before coming back." The tone of his voice moderates and he takes his father aside, quietly says something to him, then pulls his coat up onto his shoulders and leaves.

Everyone has left, the old man bolts the main door and goes off to the kitchen. Before long his tiny, thin wife brings in a big bowl of braised salted meat with bean curd and a variety of pickled vegetables. I say that I can't eat but the old man insists that I have a little. There is nothing to say at the table. Afterwards he arranges for me to sleep with him in a room next to the kitchen which opens onto the pig pen. It is after one o'clock in the morning.

After the lamp is blown out the mosquitos take turns to make air raid attacks. My hands don't stop slapping my face, head and ears. The room is hot and stuffy and there is a terrible stench. The family dog is excited because there is a stranger and paces about, disturbing the pigs so they grunt endlessly, rubbing their snouts in the dirt. Under the bed the few chickens which they'd forgotten to lock into the chicken yard can't get to sleep because of the dog and from time to time flap their wings. Although I am wretchedly tired it is impossible for me to fall asleep. Before long the rooster under the bed is crowing while the old man is producing heaven-shaking snores. I wonder if it's because the mosquitos don't bite him and only suck the blood of strangers or whether once he's asleep he loses consciousness. Utterly exhausted, I get up, open the door of the hall, and sit down on the doorstep.

A cool wind starts up and I stop sweating. The hazy, starless, grey sky appears between the dim outlines of the trees of the forest. Before dawn the people under the overlapping grey-black tiles of the houses of this small mountain village are still fast asleep. I hadn't imagined I would come here, nor that in this small mountain village of only ten or so households that I would have such an exciting night. Gusts of cool air dispel my feelings of regret that it was interrupted. This is usually called the ineffability of life.

50

She says she's had enough, stop talking!

You are walking with her along a precipice, and the turbulent waters of the river below are churning into whirlpools. Up ahead is a bend in the river, and there it swirls into a dark green abyss where the surface is so smooth the ripples vanish. The road becomes more and more narrow. She refuses to go any further with you, says she wants to go back, that she's afraid you will push her into the river.

You can't stop yourself, lose your temper and ask if she's gone mad.

She says being with a monster like you has turned her into a void, her heart is totally desolate and she can't stop herself going mad. She says you brought her to this river-bank in order to push her in, so that she would drown without a trace.

Go to Hell!

She says, you see, you see, that's exactly what you have in mind, that's how wicked you are. You are incapable of love, so be it if you can't love, but why did you seduce her? Why did you trick her into coming to this deep abyss?

You see the terror in her eyes and want to reassure her.

No! She won't let you come a step closer. She begs you to go away and allow her to go on living. She says when she looks at the bottomless abyss she is gripped with terror. She must hurry back, back to her old life. It was because she had wrongly blamed him that she let a monster like you bring her to this desolate wilderness. She wants to go back to him, back to his little room, it doesn't matter that he was impatient and rough with her, she can forgive him. She says only now does she realize it was because he loved her that he was so driven by passion. His naked lust was somehow exciting, but she can't endure your cold indifference any longer. He is a hundred times more sincere than you. You are a hundred times more hypocritical than he, you tired of her long ago, only you didn't say so. You have tormented her soul more cruelly than he had ravaged her body.

She says she longs for him and that with him she was uninhibited. She needs the security of a home, she wants to be a housewife, he said he wants to marry her and she believes him, but you have never mentioned these words. When he is making love to her, it doesn't matter if he talks about other women, it's only to arouse her passion, but everything you say makes her more and more cold. She realizes she really loves him, that it was because of her love for him that she suffered from anxiety and nervous imbalance. She ran away to make him suffer but now she's had enough of it. She's had her revenge and has taken it too far. If he finds out he'll definitely go mad, but he'll still want her and will forgive her.

She says she also misses her family, even her stepmother. Her father must be frantic and is certain to be looking for her everywhere. He's getting old and if he's not careful anxiety will affect his health.

She also misses her workmates in the laboratory. They're petty, narrow-minded and jealous, but if anyone buys a fashionable dress they always take it off so everyone can try it on.

She also misses those troublesome dance parties but wearing new shoes and putting on perfume, the music and the lights still tug at her heart.

So what if the smell of antiseptic in the operating theatre was even stronger, still it is clean and orderly, and each medicine has a specified pigeonhole so that you can just reach out for it – all these are familiar and dear to her. She has to get away from this hellish place, all this talk about Lingshan is just to trick her!

She says it was you who said love is an illusion which people conjure up to delude themselves. You don't believe in the existence of something called love – it's either the man possessing the woman or else the woman possessing the man. And you just go on making up all sorts of beautiful children's stories to provide a refuge for her weak and fragile soul. You say all this then straightaway forget that you've said it! You can deny you said any of this but the shadow you have left on her heart is indelible. She shouts out that she can't go any further with you! The water at the bend looks calm but it's bottomless, she can't go any further with you towards that deep abyss. If you make a move she'll cling onto you and drag you down with her so that you will go together to visit the King of Hell!

She says she can't cling onto anything, it's best that you give her a way to go on living. She won't implicate you so you won't be culpable, you'll be able to travel comfortably, whether it's to Lingshan or to Hell. There's no need to push her, she'll go away, far away from you, never see you again and never want to see you again. There's no need for you to worry about her, it is she who is leaving so you will not have wronged her, there'll be no remorse, no responsibility. Just treat it as if she hadn't ever existed and your conscience won't trouble you. You notice that you can't utter a single sentence, this is because she has spoken about your sore spot, spoken about how you think. She has said for you exactly what you don't dare say yourself.

She says she'll go back, go back to him, back to that small room, back to her operating theatre, and back to her own home to restore her relationship with her stepmother. She was born an ordinary person and will return to being ordinary, and like an ordinary person marry an ordinary man. In any case she can't go a step further with you, you monster, on your way down to Hell!

She says she's afraid of you, you torment her, then of course she has also tormented you. Don't say anything more, she doesn't want to know anything, she knows everything, she already knows too much. It's better to know nothing, she wants to completely forget all this, sooner or later she'll have to forget it all. If finally there's something she should say it would be that she's grateful to you, grateful to you for the part of the journey you have taken her on and grateful for saving her from loneliness. However, she is even more lonely and it keeps getting worse and she can't cope.

Eventually, she turns and walks off. You deliberately don't look, you know she is waiting for you to turn your head. If you turn to look, she won't leave, she will look at you, holding back her tears until they begin streaming down her cheeks. You will give in, beg her to stay. Then there will be embraces and kisses, she will again go limp in your arms, tearfully utter a jumble of endearing words, passionate and full of sadness. And with her arms like willow branches, her body will encircle you and drag you back down the same old road.

You resolutely refuse to look at her and go off on your own, straight along the precipitous river-bank. When you get to a bend you can't help looking back, but she has vanished. Your heart is suddenly desolate, it's as if you've lost something yet at the same time it's as if you've attained some sort of release.

You sit on a rock as if waiting for her to come yet knowing she will not come back to you.

It is you who are cruel and not she and you simply think of her curses to convince yourself she is mean like this, so that she will totally vanish from your heart, so that you will not be left with any lingering remorse.

You drifted together like floating waterweeds, in that place Wuyizhen, because you were lonely and because she was depressed.

You don't really know her at all, whether what she told you was truth or only half truth. Her inventions and your fabrications merge and are indistinguishable.

She also knows nothing about you. It was because she was a woman and you a man, because in the flickering light of the solitary lamp the dark upstairs room had the clean fragrance of paddy-rice straw, because it was a dream-like night in a strange place, because in the early chill of the autumn night she stirred your memories and your fantasies, your fantasies about her and your lust.

For her you were exactly the same.

Yes, you seduced her but she also seduced you. Is there need to attribute proportions of responsibility to a woman's intrigue and a man's lust?

But where will I find this Lingshan? There's only that dumb rock where the mountain women go to pray for a son. Was she a *zhuhuapo*? Or was she the young girl those boys took swimming at night? Anyway, she is not a young girl and you are certainly not a youth. While recalling your relationship with her you suddenly discover you can't say what she looks like or how her voice sounded. It seems to be something you have experienced but even more so it seems to be wishful thinking. But where is the boundary between memory and wishful thinking? How can the two be separated? Which of the two is more real and how can this be determined?

Wasn't it in some small town, a bus stop, a ferry crossing, a crossroad, on a roadside, that you encountered a young woman who aroused in you many daydreams? But by the time you return how will you be able to find any traces of her in that town, that bus stop, that ferry crossing, that crossroad or that roadside?

51

The Temple of the White Emperor, on a sheer cliff of the Yangtze River, is bathed in the rays of the setting sun. Whirlpools in the river below can be heard in the distance, and right ahead loom the two cliff walls of Kuimen, as straight as if chopped with a cleaver. Looking down from the iron railing the rippling crystal clear water of the smaller river divides the swift flowing muddy waters of the Yangtze.

On the far side of a little stream a woman with a mauve parasol is making her way through the shrubs and bushes on the mountain slope. She is on a track leading to the barren top of the rocky cliff, but it is hidden from view, and after a while she disappears.

I watch the brilliant gold of the setting sun disappear along the cliff tops and both sides of the gorge are suddenly plunged into darkness. Red navigation lights set on rocks close to the sides of the river appear, one after the other. An upstream steamboat heading east is crammed with passengers on all three decks as it enters the gorge, and the dull blast of its whistle reverberates long after it has gone.

It is said that at the fork in the river beyond Kuimen, Zhuge Liang heaped rocks for his Eight Trigram battle strategy. I have travelled by boat several times past Kuimen and people on board always eagerly point out the spot for me, but even now that I am in this ancient city of the White Emperor, I am still not sure of the location. It was in this ancient city that Liu Bei entrusted to Zhuge Liang his soon-to-be orphaned son who had been brought up to inherit the throne. But who can attest to the truth of storytellers' tales?

In the Temple of the White Emperor, the smashed altars have been replaced with brightly painted clay figures modelled on new versions of the historical opera so that the place looks like an opera, theatre instead of a temple.

I go around the front of this ancient temple and discover a fairly new hostel. The landscape here is rough and barren with just a few bushes, but halfway up the mountain are the ruins of a large semi-circular Han Dynasty city wall. It can only be seen here and there but it stretches for several kilometres. The director of the local cultural office points it out to me, he's an archaeologist and is passionate about his work. He tells me he submitted a report asking the relevant government department to allocate funds for preserving the wall. I think it's better in its present state – if funds are allocated, they're sure to put up a gaudy building, then a restaurant, and the scenic beauty of the place will be utterly destroyed.

He shows me a four-thousand-year-old stone dagger, ground and polished to a jade-like sheen, which was unearthed in the area. The hole drilled through the handle suggests it probably hung from a belt. Along both banks of the Yangtze they have excavated many beautifully crafted stone implements as well as red pottery from the latter period of the Neolithic Age. In a cave at one site on the bank, a cache of bronze weapons has been found. He tells me that straight ahead, just a little way into Kuimen, in the cliff caves where legend says that Zhuge Liang had hidden his books on military strategy, the last hanging coffin was pulled down on ropes and smashed up by a deaf-mute and a hunchback a few months ago. They sold the wind-dried bones as dragon bones to a Chinese medicine shop and when the shop owner was asked for authentication, the matter was reported to the public security office. The police tracked down the deaf-mute but after spending a long time interrogating him, they were none the wiser. It was only after they slapped him a few times that he took them there. He rowed out in a small boat to the bottom of the cliff and demonstrated his skill in scaling cliffs. Wind-dried slivers of wood were found at the site which was ascertained to be a tomb of the Warring

States period. The coffin must also have contained bronze relics which hadn't been smashed but it was impossible to find out from the deaf-mute what had happened to these.

There are a large number of earthenware spinning wheels in the display room of the cultural office. They are painted with red and black swirling patterns and are probably from the same period as the four-thousand-year-old earthenware spinning wheels unearthed at Qujialing in the lower reaches of the Yangtze in Hubei province. In both cases there is a close resemblance to the Yin-Yang fish design. When the wheel turns emptiness and fullness diminish and grow in the one rotation then return to the beginning again. It has the same source as the Daoist Taiji Chart. My guess is that these are the earliest origins of the Taiji Chart, and also the origins of the complementarity of the Yin and the Yang, the alternation of good fortune and bad fortune, and the concepts of natural philosophy dating from the *The Book of Changes* to the Daoists. Mankind's earliest concepts are derived from totems, afterwards these came to be linked with sounds to form speech and meanings.

Initially, the kiln stokers firing the spinning wheels had inadvertently added some extraneous material to the clay, but it was the women using the spindles who discovered that after one rotation there was a return to the beginning. The man who gave this meaning was called Fuxi. However the bestowal of life and intelligence to Fuxi must be attributed to a woman. The general name for the woman who created man's intelligence is N wa. The first named woman, N wa, and the first named man, Fuxi, constitute the collective consciousness of men and women.

The depiction on Han Dynasty tiles of the mythical union of Fuxi and N wa, both with the bodies of snakes but human heads, is derived from the sexual impulses of primitive humans. The animals subsequently became spiritual beings, and then ancestral divinities. Surely these all embody the basic instincts to sexual lust and lust for life?

At that time the individual did not exist. There was not an awareness of a distinction between "I" and "you". The birth of I derived from fear of death, and only afterwards an entity which was not I came to constitute you. At that time people did not have an awareness of fearing oneself, knowledge of the self came from an other and was affirmed by possessing and being possessed, and by conquering and being conquered. He, the third person who is not directly relevant to I and you, was gradually differentiated. After this the I also discovered that he was to be found in large numbers everywhere and was a separate existence from oneself, and it was only then that the consciousness of you and I became secondary. In the individual's struggle for survival amongst others, the self was gradually forgotten and gradually churned like a grain of sand into the chaos of the boundless universe.

In the quiet of night, listening to the faint lapping of the waves of the Yangtze, I ponder what I might do in the remaining years of my life. Should I continue along the banks of the Yangtze collecting stone fishing net weights used by the Daqi people? I've already got one of these rocks with the middle chipped out by a stone hammer – it was given to me the day before yesterday by a friend upstream in Wanxian. He told me you can pick these up all along the riverbed when the river dries up. The silt accumulates and the riverbed gets higher each year and this is why they want to build a dam at the end of the Three Gorges. When this ridiculous dam is built, even this ancient Han Dynasty wall will be submerged so what meaning would there be in collecting the memories of people of remote antiquity?

I am perpetually searching for meaning, but what in fact *is* meaning? Can I stop people from constructing this big dam as an epitaph for the annihilation of their selves? I can only search for the self of the I who is small and insignificant like a grain of sand. I may as well write a book on the human self without worrying whether it will be published. But then of what consequence is it whether one book more, or one book less, is written? Hasn't enough culture been destroyed? Does humankind need so much culture? And moreover, what *is* culture?

I get up early to catch a small steamboat. This sort of boat, with the waterline reaching almost to the top of the sides, is swift in the water. At noon I reach Wu Mountain where King Huai of the state of Chu one night dreamt he and a goddess made love. The Wu women filling the streets of the county town however, are not at all attractive. On the boat are seven or eight jean-clad young women and men with Beijing accents. Carefree and uninhibited, they talk, laugh, romance and squabble over money. It is they, with their kettle drum and electric guitar and a few pop songs and disco (rock'n'roll is banned), who in their own words win hearts on both sides of the Yangtze.

A volume of the county gazette, with the tattered pages mounted onto brown paper, contains the following entries:

> During the time of Emperor Yao of the Tang Dynasty, Wu Mountain was so named after Wu Xian who through his knowledge of the occult became physician to Emperor Yao. In life he was an aristocrat and after death a noble spirit. This mountain was his fief, hence its name (See Guo Pu, "Wu Xian Mountain, a *Fu* Poem").
>
> Yu Dynasty. The *Shundian* says: "Wu Mountain is a part of Jingliang."
>
> Xia Dynasty. The *Yugong* says: "Nine prefectures were established. Wu Mountain remains within the boundaries of the three prefectures of Jingliang."
>
> Shang Dynasty. In "Jiu you jiu wei" of the *Shang Songs* is the annotation: "Wu Mountain continued to be administered as during the Xia Dynasty."
>
> Zhou Dynasty. Wu was Yong Kingdom, then in the Spring and Autumn period became the territory of Kuizi Kingdom. In autumn of the thirty-sixth year of Duke Xi, the Chu people subjugated Kui and absorbed it into Chu. Wu thereupon belonged to Chu.

Warring States period. There was a Wu Commandery in Chu. The *Zhanguo ce* says: "Su Qin told King Wei of Chu: 'In the south there is Wu Commandery.'" The *Kuodi zhi* says: "The commandery lies one hundred *li* east of Kui, later it became Southern Commandery."

Qin Dynasty. The "Record of Qin" in the *Shiji* says: "In the thirtieth year of King Zhaorang, Wu Commandery of Chu Kingdom was changed to Wu County under the administration of Southern Commandery."

Han Dynasty. As in the Qin Dynasty, it continued to be called Wu County and was administered by Southern Commandery.

Later Han Dynasty. During the Jian'an period, the early rulers placed it under the administration of Yidu Commandery. In the twenty-fifth year, Sun Quan placed it under Guling Commandery, then Wu Sunxiu placed it under Jianping Commandery.

Jin Dynasty. First, as Wu County lay at the border of Wu and Shu it was administered by the Jianping Commandery Military Command, and established as Beijing County. In the fourth year of Xianhe, the military command changed to Jianping Commandery, and it was established as Nanling County.

The dynasties of Sung, Qi and Liang continued this.

Later Zhou. In the first year of Tianhe, Wu County was administered by Jianping Commandery, and established as Jiangyin County.

Sui Dynasty. At the beginning of the Kaihuang period, Jianping Commandery was abolished, re-named Wu Mountain County, and administered by Badong Commandery.

Tang and Five Dynasties. Administered by Kuizhou Prefecture.

Song Dynasty. Administered by Kuizhou Prefecture.

Yuan Dynasty. As before.

Ming Dynasty. Administered by Kuizhou Prefecture.

Qing Dynasty. In the ninth year of Kangxi, Dachang was incorporated into Wu Mountain County ...

The ruins are located 50 *li* to the south.

The Wheat Bran Monk's name was Wenkong and his style name Yuanyuan. A native of Ji'an Prefecture in Jiangxi Province, he built a temple on the northern cliff of Jidong Mountain where he sat in meditation. After forty years he attained enlightenment. He ate only bran and hence his name. Many years later when the monk died and there was no-one in the temple, for three years people living on the opposite mountain saw lamps burning there at night.

Legend says that the Red Emperor's daughter Yaoji drowned when travelling on the river. She was buried on the south side of this mountain and a temple erected. Shamans dance to summon her spirit.

Anping town is ninety *li* southeast of the county ...

... (text missing) the above towns are now wasteland. After the ravages of troops in the late-Ming period, the villages and towns became deserted. Most of the people have settled here from other provinces and the name is constantly changing ...

Do these villages and towns still exist?

52

You know that I am just talking to myself to alleviate my loneliness. You know that this loneliness of mine is incurable, that no-one can save me and that I can only talk with myself as the partner of my conversation.

In this lengthy soliloquy you are the object of what I relate, a myself who listens intently to me – you are simply my shadow.

As I listen to myself and you, I let you create a she, because you are like me and also cannot bear the loneliness and have to find a partner for your conversation.

So you talk with her, just like I talk with you.

She was born of you, yet is an affirmation of myself.

You who are the partner of my conversation transform my experiences and imagination into your relationship with her, and it is impossible to disentangle imagination from experience.

Even I can't distinguish how much is experience and how much is dream within my memories and impressions, so how can you distinguish between what I have experienced and what are figments of my imagination? And in the end is it necessary to make such distinctions? In any case, they aren't of any significance whatsoever.

She who is the creation of experience and imagination transforms into various images which beckon and seduce you, because you who are my creation also want to seduce her. Neither of you want the loneliness of your selves.

I am on a journey – life. Life, good or bad, is a journey and wallowing in my imagination I travel into my inner mind with you who are my reflection. The perennial and perplexing question of what is most important can be changed to a discussion of what is most authentic and at times can constitute what is known as debate. But let others discuss or debate such matters, they are of no consequence for I who am engrossed in my journey or you who are on your spiritual journey.

Like me, you wander wherever you like. As the distance increases there is a converging of the two until unavoidably you and I merge and are inseparable. At this point there is a need to step back and to create space. That space is he. He is the back of you after you have turned around and left me.

Neither I nor my image can see his face, it is enough to know that he is someone's back.

You who are my creation, created her and her face naturally would have to be imagined, but why must one insist on describing the face? She is a hazy image of associations induced by memories and is therefore indefinite, so let her remain indistinct. Moreover, her image is forever changing.

For you and me, the women who constitute they are simply a composite image of her.

And the men who constitute they are also a composite image of him. In the boundless world, there are all sorts of mysteries external to you and me. In other words, they are all projections of my back which I can't get rid of. If I can't get rid of them, why try?

I don't know whether or not you've noticed but when I speak of me and you, and she, him, feminine they and masculine they, I never speak of we or us. I believe that this is much more concrete than the sham we which is totally meaningless.

Even if you and she and he and masculine they and feminine they are images of the imagination, for me they are all more substantial than what is known as we. As soon as I refer to we I am immediately uncertain, how many of me are in fact implicated? Or how many of you who are the image of me, or he who is the back of you and me, or the illusion of she who was borne of you and me, or the composite image they of she or he? There is nothing more false than this we.

However I can use a plural you when I confront many people. Whether I am trying to please or criticize, am angry with, happy with, or scornful of, I am occupying a definite position and I am more substantial at such times than at any other time. What does we imply except for that incurable affectation? So I always avoid this bloated sham affectation of we. Should at any time I use the word we it is when I am being extremely hypocritical and cowardly.

I have established for myself this way of sequencing which can be thought of as a sort of logic or karma. Ways of sequencing, logic or karma, have been established by people in this vast unordered world in order to affirm oneself, so why shouldn't I invent my own sequencing, logic or karma? I can then take refuge in this way of sequencing, logic or karma, and be secure in my own actions and have peace of mind.

However the totality of my misfortunes also exist within you, the unlucky demon I have invoked. Actually, you are not unlucky for all your misfortunes have been conferred upon you by me, they are all derived from my self love – this damned I loves only himself!

I don't know if God and the Devil in fact exist but both were invoked by you who are the embodiment of both my good fortune and my misfortune. When you vanish, God and the Devil will in the same instant disappear.

It is only by getting rid of you that I can get rid of myself. However having invoked you, it is impossible to get rid of you. I've thought of an idea. What would happen if you and I were to change places? In other words I would be your image and you instead would be the concrete form of me – this would be an interesting game. If you listen carefully to me from my position I would then become the concrete expression of your desires, it would be a lot of fun. It would also be yet another school of philosophy and the writing would have to start from the beginning again.

Philosophy in the end is an intellectual game. At limits unattainable by mathematics and the empirical sciences, it constructs all sorts of intricate structures. And as a structure is completed, the game ends.

Fiction is different from philosophy because it is the product of sensory perceptions. If a futile self-made signifier is saturated in a solution of lust and at a particular time transforms into a living cell capable of multiplying and growing, it is much more interesting than games of the intellect. Furthermore, it is the same as life and does not have an ultimate goal.

53

I am riding a hired bicycle. At noon in the height of summer the temperature is over forty degrees and the freshly repaired bitumen road to the ancient city in Jiangling has begun to go soft. The wind passing through the city gate archway of the ancient Three Kingdoms city of Jingzhou is also hot. An old woman is stretched out dozing on a cane chair behind a tea and drinks stall. Unabashed, her hemp jacket, thin and frayed from washing, is unbuttoned, and exposes the sagging skin of her sunken breasts. I drink a bottle of soft drink which gives off heat in my hand. She doesn't even bother to look if I've paid enough. At the end of the archway a dog is sprawled with its tongue hanging out, panting and dribbling.

Beyond the city wall are paddy fields with patches of unharvested rice which are bright yellow and heavy with ripe grain. In the harvested fields the new seedlings of late crop are lush green. The road and the fields are empty, everyone is at home resting and cooling off.

I am cycling down the middle of the highway and the surface of the road is steaming with waves of air like transparent flames. Sweat is running down my back so I strip off my polo-neck sweater and tie it around my head to block off some of the sun. As I cycle faster my T-shirt flaps up so there is a bit of a damp breeze around my ears.

In these dry areas the cotton plants have big red and yellow flowers, and the plants with strings of white flowers are sesame. Beneath the brilliant sun is an eerie loneliness and, strangely, no cicadas or frogs are to be heard.

As I cycle on my shorts become soaked through and cling to my thighs, it would be good to cycle with them off. I can't help recalling the peasants I saw as a child working naked on the waterwheels, plying the big poles with their sun-tanned arms. When women passed by in the fields they would start singing ribald ditties but without bad intent, and when the women heard them they would just smile. The men sang simply to relieve themselves of their weariness, isn't this precisely the origin of such folk songs? This entire area is the home of work songs known as "gongs and drums in the reeds". However waterwheels aren't used today and the irrigation machines are driven by electricity, so such sights are no longer to be seen.

Although I know there is nothing to see at the site of the ancient capital of the Chu Kingdom, and that it will be a waste of time going, it is just a twenty kilometre return trip and I would regret not making a visit before leaving Jiangling. I disturb the afternoon nap of the young couple in charge of the archaeological station. They graduated just a year ago from university and have come here as wardens to keep watch over the expanse of ruins sleeping underground. It is not known when the excavation work is to commence. Perhaps it is because they have recently married and have never experienced such loneliness that they are so hospitable. The young wife pours me two bowls of a slightly bitter herbal infusion to dissipate the effects of the heat and the young man takes me onto a hill and points to a paddy field which has already been harvested and a high stretch of land at the side of the hill covered with cotton and sesame.

"After Qin conquered the Kingdom of Chu," the young man says, "no-one lived in the city of Ji'nan. No artefacts from after the Warring States period have been found, although tombs from the Warring States have been excavated in the city. The city would have been built in the middle period of the Warring States. Historical documents record that the capital had moved to Ying prior to the time of King Huai of Chu, so calculating from the time of King Huai of Chu, Ying was the capital of Chu for four hundred years. Of course some historians have a different view and argue that Ying was not located here. Whatever the case, our starting point is archaeological – while ploughing here peasants time and again have found numerous relics of pottery and bronze vessels dating from the Warring States period. If the site is excavated, it will really be quite spectacular." He points in one direction. "When the great generals of Qin left Ying without any booty, they released the river waters into the capital. The capital had dams on three sides and the Zhu River flowed eastwards from the South Gate to the North Gate. On the east, this hill right underfoot was a lake extending to the Yangtze River. The Yangtze at the time was in the vicinity of Jingzhou city but now it has moved south almost two kilometres. On Ji Mountain up ahead are the graves of the Chu aristocracy. The Baling Mountains on the south contain the graves of successive generations of Chu kings but they have all been looted."

In the distance are some small undulating mounds, they are referred to as mountains in documents, so probably they once were.

"This was originally the tower of the city gate," he says pointing again to the stretch of paddy field by our feet. "When the river floods, there is a build up of at least ten millimetres of silt."

Quite right, because judging by the lie of the land, to borrow the archaeological term, the area underfoot is slightly higher than the fields stretching into the distance, if one doesn't count the earthen dykes in between them.

"The south-east section had the palaces, the north was the market district, and the remains of smelting furnaces have been discovered in the south-west district. The positioning of the aqueducts in the south was high but these haven't been preserved as well as the ones in the north."

I nod in agreement and can roughly make out the outer city walls. If there was not this harsh glare of the noon sun and all the ghosts had crawled out, the night markets would no doubt be very lively.

As we come down the slope he says we have just left the city. The lake of those times is now a small pond but lotus is growing in it and their pink flowers have emerged from the water in full bloom. When the Officer of the Three Wards, Qu Yuan, was driven from the palace gates he probably passed along the bottom of this slope and certainly would have plucked a lotus to wear in his belt. Before the lake shrank to this small pond the banks were covered with fragrant plants which he would have used to weave a hat. It was here, in this fertile water-rich land, that he gave vent to loud singing and left to posterity his peerless songs. Had he not been driven from the palace gates perhaps he might not have become the great poet.

Similarly, if Li Bai had not been driven from the court of Emperor Xuanzong of the Tang Dynasty, he would probably not have become the immortal poet and there would not be the legend of his setting out in a boat while drunk and trying to scoop up the moon from the water. It is said that the spot where he drowned was at Coloured Rock Crag in the lower reaches of the Yangtze. The water has receded far from there and it is now a heavily silted-up sandbar. Even this ancient city of Jingzhou is now below the riverbed and if it were not for the big ten-metre-high dykes, it would long ago have become a palace of the Dragon King.

I go on to Hunan Province, passing along the Miluo River in which Qu Yuan drowned himself. However, I do not go to the shores of Dongting Lake to retrace his footsteps because several ecologists I saw told me that of this eight-hundred-*li* stretch of water, only a third of what is on the maps now remains. They also predict with clinical coldness that at the present rate of silt accumulation and land reclamation, within twenty years the biggest freshwater lake in the country will vanish despite how it is drawn on maps.

I wonder if little dogs still drown in the river in front of the peasant home in Lingling where my mother took me as a child to get away from the Japanese planes. Even to this day I can still see the dripping wet fur of the dog's corpse on the sandy shore. My mother also drowned. At the time she responded to the call and bravely volunteered to work on the farms to reform her thinking. She finished the night shift and went to the river to have a wash and at dawn her body was discovered. She was only thirty-nine. I have seen the commemorative volume, from when she was seventeen, with poems by her and a group of zealous youths who had taken part in the national salvation movement. Of course, their poems were not as great as Qu Yuan's.

Her younger brother also drowned. I'm not sure whether it was because of youthful heroism or patriotic fervour that he took the examination for the airforce academy, but on the day his enrolment was accepted he was wild with joy and went swimming with a group of lads in the Gan River. When he dived off the plank which stretched out to the middle of the river into the rapid current, his so-called friends were busy dividing up the change he had left in his trouser pockets. Then, when they saw something was wrong, they all ran off. Perhaps it was a case of having brought disaster upon himself. He was just fifteen when he died and my maternal grandmother was devastated with grief.

Her eldest son, my eldest maternal uncle, was not so patriotic. Although the scion of an old scholar gentry family, he did not go in for prostitutes or dog fighting and instead was keen on being *modeng*, at the time anything from overseas was *modeng*: the current translation for the word is "modern". He used to wear a suit and tie and looked really fashionable for his time. His hobby was photography and back then the price for a camera was *really* "modern". He took snapshots everywhere and developed them himself; he wasn't interested in being a journalist but photographed crickets. The photos he took of fighting crickets have been preserved to this day and were never burnt. However he died quite young from a chill. From what my mother told me, he was starting to get better then after greedily eating a bowl of fried rice with eggs, his illness flared up and he died. His fondness for the modern was useless for he didn't know about modern medicine.

My maternal grandmother died after my mother. Compared with the early deaths of her children, she may be considered as having lived a long life, having outlived all her children. She died in an institution for the solitary aged. Not being a Miao descendant of the Chu people, undeterred by the heat, I have paid homage to the ancient capital of the Chu kings, so there is no reason for me not to look for the resting place of my maternal grandmother who took me by the hand to buy a spinning top at the Palace Facing Heaven Temple market. I heard of her death from my paternal aunt. This aunt did not live a full lifespan and is also dead. How is it that my relatives are all dead people? I really don't know whether it is I who have grown old or it is the world which is too old.

When I think about it now, my maternal grandmother was like a person from another world. She believed in ghosts and spirits and was terrified of going to Hell so she always tried to accumulate virtue in her life in the hope that she would be rewarded in the next world. She was widowed young, then when my maternal grandfather died and left some property there was always a crowd of spirit mediums milling around her like flies. They colluded to urge her to give up her wealth so that her wishes would be granted and got her to throw silver coins into the well at night. In fact they had put a wire sieve into the bottom of the well and the silver she threw in was scooped into their purses. When they all got drunk they let out what they'd done and it became a big joke. Finally she was reduced to selling off all the houses and was left with only a bag of deeds to fields which had been leased out many years before and she and her daughter lived off these. Afterwards, when they heard about the land reforms, my mother remembered the deeds and got grandmother to immediately rummage through her trunk. They found the bundle wrapped in wrinkled yellow backing-paper and the cotton-paper used for pasting on windows. Mortified, they hastily stuffed these into the stove and burnt them.

This maternal grandmother of mine had a violent temper and when she spoke with people it sounded as if she were arguing with them. She didn't get on with my mother. When she was about to leave for her old home she said she would wait for this grandson of hers, me, to grow up into the best scholar in the country and bring her back in a car so that he could care for her in her old age. However, she was not to know that this grandson of hers did not have what it required to be an official and, without even having sat in any office in the capital, was sent to undergo thought reform by working in the fields in the countryside. It was during this period that she died in an institution for the solitary aged. In those chaotic years, no-one knew whether she was alive or dead. By pretending to have revolutionary contacts my younger brother was able to travel free on the trains and he made a special trip to search for her. He asked at several old peoples' institutions, but they said they didn't have such a person. They then asked him instead: Is she in an institution for the venerable aged or one for the solitary aged? My brother then asked how these were different. They said harshly: Institutions for the venerable aged are for the aged without class origin problems and who have unblemished personal histories. People with class origin or personal history problems, or who can't be properly classified, are sent to institutions for the solitary aged. He then telephoned an institution for the solitary aged. An even harsher voice asked: What relationship do you have with her? Why are you making enquiries about her? At the time my younger brother was fresh out of college and wasn't yet drawing a wage to feed himself; he was afraid of having his city residence permit cancelled so he quickly put down the phone. A few years later, the academic institutions implemented military instruction. Organizations and colleges came under military supervision and people discontented with their lot all became contented. My paternal aunt had just come back to work in the city after undergoing reform in the countryside and wrote that she heard my grandmother had died two years earlier.

I eventually find out that there is in fact this institution for the solitary aged ten kilometres away at a place in the suburbs called Peach Blossom Village. After cycling in the blazing sun for an hour or so, I come across a courtyard complex with a sign saying "home for the aged". It is next to a timber factory and there is not a single peach tree in sight. The complex consists of several two-storey buildings, but I don't see any old people. Perhaps they are more sensitive to the heat and have all gone back to their rooms to rest where it is cooler.

I find an office with the door open. The cadre, in a singlet with his feet crossed on the table and leaning back in a cane chair, is engrossed reading the news. I ask if this was the institution for the solitary aged during the years my grandmother was in such a place.

He puts down his newspaper and says, "It's all changed again, today there are no institutions for the solitary aged, they are all called homes for the aged."

I don't question if there are still institutions for the venerable aged but simply ask him to check if such and such an old person who was already dead had once lived here. He is easy to talk to and without asking me for identification papers takes out the register of the deceased, looks up the years, stops at a page, and asks me the name of the deceased again.

"Female?"

"Yes," I confirm.

He pushes the register over so that I can have a look. It is clearly my maternal grandmother's name, and the age tallies.

"She has been dead for ten years," he says with a sigh.

"Yes," I reply. "Have you been working here all this time?"

He nods to affirm that he has and I then ask if he remembers what the deceased looked like.

"Let me think." He leans back to rest his head on the back of the chair. "Was she a short thin old woman?"

I nod, but then I recall from the old photograph hanging at home that she was a very plump old woman. It was a photograph taken some decades earlier and it showed me by her side playing with a top. After that she probably didn't have any photos taken. With the passing of a few decades people can change completely in appearance even though their bone structure does not change. My mother was quite short so my grandmother couldn't have been very tall.

"When she spoke did she always shout?"

There are few old women of her age who don't shout when they talk but what is important is that the name is correct.

"Did she ever mention she had two maternal grandchildren?" I ask.

"You are her maternal grandson?"

"Yes."

He nods and says, "I think she mentioned that she had grandchildren."

"Did she ever say they would come and fetch her?"

"Yes, she did."

"But at the time I was in the countryside."

"It was the Cultural Revolution," he explains on my behalf. "She died of natural causes."

I do not ask how those who did not die of natural causes died but simply ask where she is buried.

"She was cremated. Everyone is cremated. It's not just the old people in homes for the aged, even when we die we will be cremated."

"The cities are over-populated, there's no room for the dead," I bring the conversation to an end for him, then ask, "Have you kept her ashes?"

"It's been dealt with. The people here are all old people without relatives, their ashes are dealt with together."

"Is there a common grave?"

"Er..." he thinks about how he can reply.

It is this unfilial grandson who is to blame, and not him, the only thing I can do is to thank him.

I come out of the home for the aged, get on my bicycle, and think to myself that even if there is a communal grave it will in future not be of archaeological significance. Nevertheless, I have finally visited my deceased maternal grandmother who once bought me a spinning top.

54

You are always searching for your childhood and it's becoming an obsession. You want to visit each of the places you stayed during your childhood, the houses, courtyards, streets and lanes of your memory.

Your home was once upstairs in a small solitary building on a vacant lot with a big pile of rubble at the front: the building that once stood there had been destroyed by a bomb or a fire and had never been rebuilt. Green bristlegrass grew in the rubble and broken walls, and crickets could often be found when the broken tiles and bricks were turned over. There was a very clever type of cricket called Black Satin Cream and when their shiny ink-black wings vibrated they made a clear, resonating sound. There was also another kind called Locust which had a big body and a big mouth and was good at fighting. As a child you had a wonderful time on that rubble heap.

You also recall that you once lived in a courtyard compound which went a long way inside. It had a big heavy black door at the entrance and you had to stand on your toes to get to the metal ring-latch. When the door was opened you had to go around a carved screen. The horns and the heads of the stone unicorns on each side of the screen were shiny because children would touch them whenever they came in or out. Behind the carved screen was a damp and mossy courtyard onto which water was regularly thrown out, so if you were not careful you would slip and fall. You had a pair of albino rabbits at the time. One was savaged in the wire cage by a yellow weasel and later on the other one also disappeared. Days later, when you went to play in the back courtyard, you discovered it had drowned in the urine pot and its once white fur was now stained and dirty. You looked at it for a long time but from then on, as far as you can remember, you did not go into the back courtyard again.

You also recall that you once lived in a courtyard complex with a round gateway. Yellow chrysanthemums and crimson cockscombs grew in the courtyard and perhaps because of these flowers it was always bright and sunny. There was a little gate at the back of the courtyard and behind it, at the bottom of the stone steps, was the lake. On the night of the Mid-Autumn Festival the grown-ups opened the gate and laid out a table with moon cakes and melon seeds and, with the lake before them, they admired the moon as they ate and drank. A bright full moon hung in the sky over the deep, serene, far side of the lake while in the lake its elongated reflection wobbled. One night you passed by there on your own and pulled open the bolt: you were terrified by the lonely deep waters of the lake, its beauty was too deep, more than a child could bear, and you ran away as fast as you could. Thereafter, whenever you passed by the gate at night you were always very careful and did not again ever dare to touch the bolt.

You also recall that you once lived in a house with a garden but you can only remember the patterned brick floor of your big downstairs room on which you used to play marbles. Your mother wouldn't let you play in the garden. You were sick and spent much of your time in bed and could only play in your room with your box of marbles. When your mother wasn't home you would stand on the bed and, holding onto the windowsill, look at the colourful flags on the steamers and on the wharf. There were always strong winds blowing along the Yangtze.

You revisit these old places but find nothing. The rubble heap in front of the small two-storey building is not there, nor is the heavy black door with the metal ring-latch, nor even the quiet little lane in front of the house, and certainly not the courtyard compound with the carved screen. Probably that place has already been turned into a bitumen road heavy with traffic – trucks with full loads honking their horns and sending up dust and ice-block wrappers, and long distance buses with missing windows carrying on the roof an assortment of bags of local products, clothing and foodstuffs to be resold elsewhere – and itself covered in melon seed husks and chewed up sugar cane spat from bus windows. There is no moss, no round gateway, no yellow chrysanthemums or crimson cockscombs, no elongated moon in the lake, nor terrifying stillness and loneliness. Instead, there are only the same standard red brick buildings with economy-coke stoves lining narrow corridors like sentries at the door of each apartment. Along the banks of the Yangtze the noisy flapping of flags in the wind can no longer be heard. Instead there are only warehouses, warehouses, warehouses, silos, warehouses, silos, cement in tough paper bags, chemical fertilizer in thick plastic bags and loud shouting or singing blaring from speakers.

You wander in a daze like this from city to city, county town to district capital then to provincial capital, then from another provincial capital to another district capital, then one county town after another. Afterwards you pass through a certain district capital then return to a particular provincial capital. Sometimes, in some small lane which city planners had missed, or couldn't be bothered with, or had no intention of doing anything about, or which they couldn't do anything about even if they wanted to, you suddenly see an old house with the door open, and you stop there and to look into the courtyard where clothes are drying on bamboo poles. It is as if you have only to enter and you will return to your childhood and those dim memories will be resurrected.

When you go in you discover that wherever you go it is possible to find remnants of your childhood. Ponds with floating duckweed, small town wineshops, windows of upstairs rooms overhanging the street, arched stone bridges, canopied boats passing under arched bridges, stone steps at back doors of houses leading to a river, and a dried up old well are all linked to your childhood memories and evoke irrepressible sadness, and it doesn't matter whether or not you had actually stayed in these places as a child. The old slate-roof houses in a small seaside town and the little square tables outside where people sit

327

drinking cold tea arouses this homesickness of yours. The tomb of Lu Guimeng of the Tang Dynasty, probably containing nothing but his clothes and headwear, is a grave covered with creepers and wild hemp in the back courtyard of some anonymous old school next to fields and a few old trees, yet the slanting rays of the afternoon sun are stained with your inexplicable grief. The lonely compounds in the Yi districts and the wooden houses on pylons of the remote Miao stockades halfway up mountains, which you had never dreamed about, are telling you something. You can't help wondering whether you have another life, that you have retained some memories of a previous existence, or that these places will be your refuge in a future existence. Could it be that these memories are like liquor and after fermentation will produce a pure and fragrant concoction which will intoxicate you again?

What in fact are childhood memories? How can they be verified? Just keep them in your heart, why do you insist on verifying them?

You realize that the childhood you have been searching for doesn't necessarily have a definite location. And isn't it the same with one's so-called hometown? It's no wonder that blue chimney smoke drifting over roof-tiles of houses in little towns, bellows groaning in front of wood stoves, those translucent rice-coloured little insects with short forelegs and long hind-legs, the campfires and the mud-sealed wood-pail beehives hanging on the walls of the houses of mountain people, all evoke this homesickness of yours and have become the hometown of your dreams.

Although you were born in the city, grew up in cities and spent the larger part of your life in some huge urban metropolis, you can't make that huge urban metropolis the hometown of your heart. Perhaps, because it is so huge that within it at most you can only find in a particular place, in a particular corner, in a particular room, in a particular instant, some memories which belong purely to yourself, and it is only in such memories that you can preserve yourself fully. In the end, in this vast ocean of humanity you are at most only a spoonful of green seawater, insignificant and fragile.

You should know that there is little you can seek in this world, that there is no need for you to be so greedy, in the end all you can achieve are memories, hazy, intangible, dreamlike memories which are impossible to articulate. When you try to relate them, there are only sentences, the dregs left from the filter of linguistic structures.

55

I arrive in this bustling city ablaze with lights, streets full of pedestrians and an endless stream of traffic. At the change of traffic signals, like sluice gates opening, there is a surging tide of bicycles. And there are also the T-shirts, neon lights, and advertisements sporting beautiful women.

I had planned to find myself a reasonable hotel near the train station so that I could have a hot bath, eat a decent meal, spoil myself a bit and then have a good sleep to recover from the accumulated weariness of the past ten days. I go from street to street but all the single rooms of the hotels are taken: it seems people are better off and are intent on having a room to themselves. As I have made up my mind to be extravagant tonight and refuse to sleep in a big shared room stinking of sweat or in a corridor with an added bed which must be vacated and dismantled at daybreak, I have no choice but to wait in a hotel lobby for people catching the night train to vacate their rooms. It is all very annoying. I suddenly remember I've got a phone number of a good friend of an old friend in Beijing who said that if I passed through I should feel free to contact this person.

I decide to give it a try. The person who answers is curt and tells me to wait. I never like making phone calls, first I don't have my own private phone and second I know that some people in positions which entitle them to have a phone installed at home often use this tactic on strangers who phone up, then when the other party gets impatient they say the person's not in or just hang up. Only a few of my friends have their own telephones, so this friend of my friend must be an official. I'm not prejudiced against all officials, I haven't got to the stage of giving up on human society but for me the phone lacks human feeling and I wouldn't use it except under exceptional circumstances. I'm still waiting. Even if I hang up I'll still have to go on waiting in the hotel lobby so I may as well keep listening. Whatever the outcome it's one way of passing time.

A unfriendly voice eventually answers, questions me, then calls out in surprise and asks where I am. He says he will come right away to fetch me. He is indeed the good friend of my old friend who didn't know me before but indeed acknowledges this friendship anyway. I instantly give up the idea of staying at the hotel, ask him what number bus to take, pick up my bag and leave.

As I knock on the door I feel a bit anxious. The owner of the house opens the door, relieves me of my bags and, without shaking my hand or showing any formality, leads me in with his arm around my shoulders.

What a comfortable house it is. The hallway leads on to two rooms which are arranged elegantly with cane chairs, glass-block coffee tables and a display cabinet with antiques and foreign ornaments. Painted porcelain plates hang on the walls and the brown-lacquered floors are so clean and shiny that I don't know where to put my feet. I first become aware of my filthy shoes then in the mirror I see my messy hair and dirty face. I haven't had a haircut for months and it is hard even for me to recognize myself.

"I've come out of the mountains and look like a Wild Man," I say, embarrassed about my grubby appearance.

"If it wasn't for this chance, it would be hard getting you to come," my host says.

His wife shakes my hand and busies herself getting cups of tea. His daughter, who is not yet ten, greets me with "hello uncle" from the door and looks at me with a hesitant smile.

My host says his friend in Beijing had written so he knew I was wandering everywhere and he has been looking forward to seeing me for some time. He tells me all the news about the political and literary world – this person has reappeared and that person has fallen from power, who has given such and such a speech and who has put forward such and such a theory. There has also been an article referring to me by name and saying that this writer's works are problematical but that it is wrong to beat him to death. I say that I am no longer interested in these things, what I need is life, for example, at this moment what I need is to be able to have a hot bath. His wife bursts out laughing and says she will heat some water right away.

After I have a wash, my host takes me to his daughter's room, which also serves as his study, and says if I am tired I can sleep for a while and then he'll wake me to have something to eat. I can hear his wife frying something in the kitchen.

I lie on his daughter's small clean wire bed, my head resting on a pillow with a tabby cat embroidery and I think that it was lucky I made the phone call and that the phone is not such a bad gadget after all. I ask if he is an official and has joined the telephone-owning class. He says the phone is for public use in the office downstairs and someone is on duty to let people know when there is a call. He tells me he has some young friends who are keen to meet me. On these hot summer days everyone sleeps late, some just live in nearby buildings and some can be phoned, that's if you'd like to see them. I am keen on the idea and soon hear him opening the door and footsteps on the stairs, I also hear talking in the lounge room through the closed bedroom door. They are discussing your writings and the disasters which have befallen you. You seem to have become a champion for social justice. You say you are not up to championing social justice, you say that absurdity does not apply only to those in official positions, the world and humanity itself is becoming more and more grotesque. You did not think there would still be some friends worried about you and it makes you feel that it is worth living after all. They then talk about getting the women to come the next day so you can all go dancing. Why not? it is you who say this and the women turn out to be a jolly crowd, either young performers or recent university graduates, they egg one another on and you all go to the pine forest to pick mushrooms, this is a brilliant idea but aren't any of you afraid of getting poisoned? you try first, we'll eat after you've tried them, who asked you to be a hero? heroes must sacrifice themselves for women! they won't let you off, you say it is most fitting to die for women, they say that they are not so cruel, they are not Empress Wu Zetian or Jiang Qing, or Empress Dowager Cixi, they don't care whether those old sirens are alive or dead, they want to keep you so you can light a fire to cook the mushrooms, and saying this they bring a big washbasin and firewood, you sprawl on the ground to blow at the dry pine needles and leaves, the smoke makes your eyes smart as flames suddenly start, they all shout for joy and begin to dance around the fire, someone starts playing a guitar and you are so happy you do a somersault on the grass, they all clap and shout bravo, a young man does a no-hands headstand then harasses one of the women to do somersaults in the air, she says she can do any dance anyone else can, what they want to see is her specialty, she says she is wearing a skirt, so what's the problem with wearing a skirt, people aren't interested in looking at the skirt, they want to see free-flying acrobatics, the young men won't let her off, it's her fault for winning the championship! the women also laugh and torment her so that she does a series of somersaults until she is out of breath, you say you learnt shaman magic in the mountains and can make the living die and the dead come back to life, they all say you are bullshitting, if you don't believe then who's game enough to try? they all point at her, this woman lying on the ground with her eyes closed and pretending to be dead, you break off a willow frond and flourish it and rolling up the whites of your eyes and chanting you circle around her, using the willow branch to chase off the demons on all sides, the young men all kneel around her, their palms pressed together in prayer, the women get jealous and all start shouting, quick open your eyes to see how many are here wanting to be your lover! you give a yell, strip to the waist and go into battle, sticking out your tongue and shouting and dancing, everyone dances around her in a frenzy, they lift her up, sacrifice her to the spirits! cast her into the river to be the wife of the Lord of the River! she keeps screaming, spare me! spare me! she says she will dance, she will dance anything as long as she is not thrown into the river, the young men announce the penalty, she must do the splits and hold up her arms without swaying, sadists! sadists! the women protest, only then does it all stop, everyone rolls about on the grass laughing until their stomachs hurt, all right, all right, tell us about it then, what about? tell us about things that happened on your travels? you say you went looking for the Wild Man? oh, did you really see the Wild Man? you say you saw a panda? what's special about a panda? there are plenty in the zoo, you say the one you saw came into the tent looking for food and poked its head into your bedding, you're lying! you say you really want to get to Shennongjia, people say there are Wild Men there, you want to capture one, take it home and teach it to talk, don't treat us like children, you say you tried to be a child and failed, you really wanted to return to your childhood and travelled everywhere looking for traces of your childhood, the women agree that childhood is better, that everyone has happy memories, not me a voice says, my childhood was totally boring, I only want to live in the present, to look at the stars above just like this, tell us about your writing, another woman's voice says, everything written has been published and what hasn't been published hasn't been written, you're never serious, you say you are too serious all the time and just want not to be serious for a while, you poor poor thing another voice sighs pityingly! lalalalala, hey listen, I'm going to sing! as if you're the only one who's beautiful, as if you're the only who's spiteful, you two fight it out, whoever wins is beautiful, I don't want you to judge, you say people always want to judge you, your fault for wanting to be famous, you admit wanting a bit to be famous but didn't think it would cause so much trouble, everyone laughs, someone says let's all go to the other side of the river, everyone holds hands to go into a cave, the leader gives a yelp, he's bumped his head, this sets everyone off in fits of laughter again, it's pitch-black inside the cave, afraid of bumping our heads we have to bend down then bump into the backside of the person in front, this cave is great for kissing! we can't see one another, if you're game enough you can kiss whoever you like, this is no fun at all, let's go for a swim instead, everyone jumps into the little stream, careful don't let him do anything bad! who? whoever is bad knows who it is! how about singing a song together? let's have a palm tree, not palm trees all the time, let's have a dragon's messenger, who's sending a message to whom? it's you who is patriotic, it's you who gets on people's nerves, it's you who is getting on my nerves, why don't the lot of you stop bickering? father and brothers—I'm drowning! who's being such a pest? picking mushrooms in the murky river of the nether world—what? what? there's nothing here, you won't be able to pick anything here except sadness, let's play bridge, no it takes too much concentration, then let's play a game of turtle with cards, who's drawn ... I've drawn a king! what luck, people who don't think about being lucky are always lucky, that's fate, hey, do you believe in fate? fate just plays games with people, to the Devil with fate! don't talk about demons, it's scary when people talk about demons at night, you're walking along the murky river of the nether world, didn't you go to Fengdu, the City of Ghosts? was it good fun? at the city gates there's now a couplet exhorting the destruction of superstitions: "If you believe in them they exist, if you don't believe in them they do not exist." what sort of couplet is that? do lines have to be parallel and matching in length to be called a couplet? can't there be couplets with uneven lines? you want to destroy everything, can you destroy truth? don't threaten others with such a big hat, aren't you an atheist who's not afraid of anything? you say that you are afraid, what of? loneliness? a big man like you and a hero! hero or not, I'm afraid of beautiful women, what's there to be afraid of in beautiful women? I'm afraid of being bewitched, what a useless idiot! hey, compatriots! what are you up to? do you want to save the nation? just save yourself, an unredeemable individualist! you get such a shock that you break out in a cold sweat all over, you want, you want, you want to return to the group but can no longer find anyone ...

56

She wants you to read her palm. She has small, soft hands, very delicate, and very feminine. You open her palm and place it in your hand. You say she has an easygoing nature, that she is a very gentle person. She nods, agreeing.

You say this is a passionate palm and at this she smiles sweetly.

But this easygoing nature is superficial for within her heart is a raging fire, a burning anxiety. At this she frowns.

Her burning anxiety lies in her longing for love and the difficulty of finding a person to whom she can entrust herself, body and soul. She is too fussy and hard to please, you are saying what is in her palm. She pouts and makes a face.

She has loved more than once ...

How many times? She asks you to guess.

You say she began when she was small.

At what age? she asks.

You say she's a romantic and that from a very young age she longed for love. She laughs.

You warn her that in life there is not a prince on a white charger and that she will be disappointed time and again. She avoids your eyes.

You say time and again she has been deceived and that time and again she will deceive others ... She tells you to go on with the reading.

You say the lines of her palm are complicated and that she is invariably involved with quite a few people at the same time.

Wrong, she says.

You interrupt her protest and say while involved with one person she is thinking of another, that she has a new lover before breaking off with the previous one.

You're exaggerating, she says.

You say sometimes it's conscious and at other times not. You are not saying this is not good, you are simply saying this is in the lines of her palm. Is there something you shouldn't talk about? You look into her eyes.

She hesitates then resolutely says you can talk about anything.

You say she is destined not to be devoted in her love. You feel the bones of her hand and say that you don't just examine the lines of the palm but also the bone structure. You say that any man can lead her away just by holding this small soft hand.

Try leading me! She pulls back her hand but you hold on and won't let go.

She is destined to suffer, you are talking about what is in her hand.

Why?

You will have to ask yourself this.

She says she only wants to single-heartedly love one person.

You acknowledge that this is what she wants but the problem is it's impossible.

Why?

You say she must ask her own hand, the hand belongs to her, you can't answer for her.

You're really cunning, she says.

You say it isn't you who is cunning, it's this hand of hers which is too delicate, too soft, too unfathomable.

She sighs and asks you to go on with the reading.

You say if you go on she'll get cross.

She won't.

You say she is already angry.

She insists she isn't.

You say she doesn't know what to love.

337

She doesn't understand, she says she doesn't understand what you're saying.

You ask her to think about it.

She says she has but she still doesn't understand.

This means she doesn't know what to love.

To love someone, someone really special!

What do you mean by really special?

Someone who can make her fall in love so that she can give her heart to him and follow him anywhere, even to the end of the world.

You say this is momentary romantic excitement . . .

What she wants is excitement!

After calming down it's impossible.

She says it is possible.

But after calming down there will be other concerns.

She says if she falls in love there will be no calming down.

That means she has never been in love. You stare into her eyes, she looks away and says she really doesn't know.

She doesn't know whether she has been in love because she loves herself too much.

Don't be so wicked, she cautions you.

You say it's because she is too beautiful and is always concerned about what impression she gives.

Keep talking!

She's annoyed. You say her not knowing is instinctive.

What do you mean? She frowns.

What you are saying is simply that this instinct is particularly obvious in her case, this is because she is too lovely and so many people love her. This is her misfortune.

She shakes her head and says you're incorrigible.

You say it was she who wanted her hand read and furthermore wanted you to be frank.

But you're a bit excessive, she quietly protests.

The truth can't be quite as you'd like it or all sound good, it's bound to be a bit bleak, otherwise how can one confront one's fate? You ask if she wants you to go on with the reading.

Hurry up and finish.

You say she must spread her fingers and you separate them, saying you must see if it is she who controls her fate or fate which controls her.

Then who do you think is in control?

You get her to clench her fists tight, grab them and pull up her arms then yell out for everyone to look!

They all start laughing and she pulls herself free.

You say what bad luck, you're referring to yourself and not her. At this she too bursts out laughing.

You ask if anyone else wants a reading. The women are all silent. Then a hand with long fingers stretches out and a timid voice says, look at me.

You say you only read hands, not faces.

I'm asking you to look at my fate! she corrects you.

This is a hand with strength, you say feeling it.

Don't talk about anything else, just tell me if I will have a career.

You say you are saying that this hand shows a strong character.

Just tell me whether or not I'll be successful in my career.

You can only say she will have a career but having a career is not necessarily the the same as being successful.

Without being successful how can it count as a career? she retorts.

A career can be something to support oneself.

What are you implying?

I'm saying there's a lack of ambition.

She sighs and her fingers go slack. There is a lack of ambition, she admits.

You say she is strong but she lacks ambition and doesn't want to control others.

That's how it is, she bites her lip.

Often career and ambition are inseparable. To say a man has ambition is to say he has a career. Ambition is the basis of a career, with ambition one invariably wants to be outstanding.

Yes, she says, she doesn't want to be outstanding.

You say she wants only to affirm herself, she isn't pretty but she is kind hearted. Success in a career always requires struggle but because she is too kind hearted she can't beat her opponents and so naturally she will never succeed in the sense of being outstanding.

She quietly says she knows this.

Having a career but not necessarily being a success can be lucky, you say.

But she says it can't count as good fortune.

Not being a success in one's career is not the same as being unlucky, you reiterate.

What sort of good fortune are you talking about?

Emotional.

She sighs softly.

You say someone secretly loves her but she doesn't take him seriously, she hasn't even noticed him.

Then who is it?

You let go of her hand and say she'll have to think about it.

Her eyes open wide and everyone listening intently bursts out laughing, she is embarrassed but puts down her head and also starts laughing.

This is a happy night, the women surround you and all put out their hands clamouring for a reading. You say you aren't a fortune-teller, that you're just a shaman.

A shaman, that's too scary! the women all call out.

Not me, I like shamans, I just love shamans! A woman puts her arms around you and sticks out a plump hand. Have a look for me, will I have money? Pushing away the other hands, she says, I don't care about love and a career, I just want a husband, a wealthy husband.

Won't you just have to find yourself an old man? another woman says caustically.

Why do I have to find an old man? the woman with the plump hand retorts.

When the old man dies won't all the money belong to you? Then you can go and find the young man you love. The woman is pretty harsh.

What if he doesn't die? Won't that be tragic? Don't be so mean! the woman with the plump hands retaliates.

This voluptuous, plump hand is very sexy, you say.

Everyone claps, whistles and shouts.

Read my palm! she commands, nobody interrupt!

When you say this hand is sexy, you are serious. This means that this hand brings many suitors so it's hard to choose and hard to know what to do.

There are plenty of people who love me and this is fine, but what about money? she mumbles.

At this everyone laughs.

People who don't seek money but seek love don't have love and people who pursue money don't have money but have many who love them. That's fate, you sternly declare.

This fate is pretty good! one woman calls out.

The woman with the plump hand turns up her nose, if I don't have money how will I be able to dress up? As long as I can dress up and make myself pretty I won't need to worry about nobody wanting me, will I?

Well spoken! the women all chime in.

And you, you just want women milling around you, you're really greedy! a woman behind you says, will you be able to love them all?

But you've yearned for such a happy night and you say you love every hand and you want every hand.

No, no, you only love yourself! Each hand is shaking, protesting, shouting.

57

I enter Shennongjia through Fangxian in the north. Even now rumours are rife that there are Wild Men around these parts. It is recorded in the late Qing Dynasty work *Annals of Yunyangfu* that in this forest running 800 *li* from north to south, "all day long is the roaring of tigers and the screeching of apes". I am not here to carry out an investigation into Wild Men, but have come to see if this primitive forest still exists. I am not mercilessly driven by some burning missionary zeal, it is simply because I have come down all the way from the high plateau and the huge mountains of the upper reaches of the Yangtze and it would be a pity to miss out seeing this mountain region of the middle reaches. So not having a goal is a goal, the act of searching itself turns into a sort of goal, and the object of the search is irrelevant. Moreover, life itself is without goals, and is simply travelling along like this.

The rain falls heavily during the night and although by morning it has lessened somewhat, it is still fine and continuous. There is nothing resembling forest along the two sides of the highway and the mountains are covered only with creepers and actinidia vines. The rivers and creeks are all brown and muddy. I arrive in the county town at eleven in the morning and go to the forestry bureau hostel hoping to get a ride into the forest proper. I run into a meeting of three grades of cadres, and although I can't work out which three grades, it seems the meeting is about timber.

At noon the cadres assemble for lunch and it becomes known that I am a writer from Beijing. The section chief in charge gets me to join them and arranges for a driver who is setting out in the afternoon to sit next to me while urging me to drink up.

"All writers are good drinkers!" he says. The section chief has a solid build and is very direct.

Big bowls of hot rice wine go down easily and faces are flushed bright red with alcohol. I can't disappoint them and quaff down the wine. After the food and drink, I have a fuzzy head and the driver isn't in any condition to drive.

The meeting reconvenes in the afternoon but the driver takes me to one of the guest rooms where we find beds and sleep right into the night.

At dinner there is leftover food and drink so all of us get drunk all over again. The only thing I can do is to stay the night at the hostel. The driver comes and tells me the mountain waters have washed away some of the road and it is hard to say whether or not it will be possible to set out the next day. It is a chance for a good rest and he is quite pleased.

At night the section chief comes to chat and wants to find out what they eat at banquets in the capital. What dishes are served first? What dishes are served last? He says people who have visited the Imperial Palace in Beijing tell him that when a meal was prepared for the Empress Dowager a hundred ducks had to be killed, is this really true? Is the residence of Chairman Mao in Zhongnanhai still open for public inspection? Have I seen the Chairman's old patched pyjamas they show on TV? I take the opportunity to ask what stories he can tell me about the place.

He says that before Liberation there were only a few inhabitants in the area, a family in Nanhe and another at Douhe; they cut the timber and set the logs in the river before strapping them. The annual timber export was less than 150 cubic metres. From here all the way to Shennongjia there were only three households. Right up to 1960 the forest hadn't been damaged but after that the highway went through and everything changed – today every year 50,000 cubic metres of timber have to be delivered. As production developed the population increased. In earlier times, every year at the first clap of spring thunder the fish would emerge from the mountain caverns and if we blocked the mouths of the caves with large bamboo trays we would haul in a basketful. Nowadays we can't eat fish.

I also ask about the history of the county town. He takes off his shoes, sits cross-legged on the bed, and says, "It's very old. In mountain caves not too far from here, archaeologists have found the teeth of the Ancient Ape Man!"

He sees that I am not very interested in the Ancient Ape Man and starts talking about the Wild Man instead.

"If you run into one of these creatures, he will grab you by the shoulders and shake you until your head starts spinning, roar with laughter, then turn and run off."

I get the impression this is what he's read in some old books.

"Have you ever seen a Wild Man?" I ask.

"It's better not to see one. This creature is bigger than humans, generally it's more than two metres in height. The body is covered with red fur and it has long hair. It's fine talking about it like this but to really see one is quite frightening. However, it doesn't set out to hurt people, as long as people don't hurt it. It goes *yiyiyaya* trying to speak, and when it sees a woman it smiles."

He's heard all this and probably it's been going around for several thousand years. There's nothing new in what he's saying so it's best that I interrupt him.

"Have any of your staff seen it? Not the peasants or villagers but cadres and workers of the reserve, have any of them seen it?"

"Sure. The head of the revolutionary committee of Songbaizhen was with several others travelling in a small jeep along the highway when they were stopped by a Wild Man. They were all terrified and just watched it amble off. These are all cadres on our reserve, we all know them and we get along well with them."

"That incident with the revolutionary committee happened some years ago, has anyone seen it recently?"

"Lots of people come to carry out investigations on the Wild Man, several hundred every year. They come from all over the country, the Central Academy of Social Sciences, university teachers from Shanghai, and even someone from the political committee of the armed forces. Last year a pair came from Hong Kong, a merchant and a fire fighter, but we didn't let them go in."

"Did any of these people see the Wild Man?"

"Of course! The political committee person in the Wild Man investigation squad I mentioned is a military man and he had two guards in the car with him. Heavy rain had fallen all night and the road had washed away. The following day, there was a heavy fog. That was when they came face to face with the Wild Man!"

"They didn't capture it?"

"Their headlights only had a range of two or three metres and by the time they got out of the car with their rifles the creature had run off."

I shake my head to indicate that it was a pity.

"They've recently established a Wild Man Study Association and a former propaganda department chief of the party committee of the area is personally leading it. They have photographs of the Wild Man's footprints as well as hair from the Wild Man's body and head."

"I've seen all of this," I say. "I saw an exhibition which was probably organized by the Wild Man Study Association and I have seen enlarged photographs of the footprints of the Wild Man. They have also published a book of Wild Man material ranging from records of the Wild Man in ancient texts to foreign accounts of the Yeti and Big Foot, including a number of eyewitness reports." I indicate that I approve of all this. "In a local newspaper, I've even seen the photograph of a Wild Man's foot which had been cut off."

"What was it like?" He leans forward to interrogate me.

"It was like a dried bear's paw."

"That's not right," he says, shaking his head. "A bear's paw is a bear's paw, the Wild Man's foot is longer than a bear's paw and is similar to a human foot. Why did I first tell you about the teeth of Ancient Ape Man? In my opinion, the Wild Man is an Ape Man which did not evolve into man. What do you think?"

"It's hard to be certain," I say, yawning from the effects of the alcohol.

He starts to weary and also yawns, he is quite tired from a whole day of meetings and eating.

The following day the cadres resume their meetings. The driver comes to tell me that the road hasn't been repaired and that I'll have to stay put for another day. I seek out the section chief and say, "You're all very busy with meetings and I don't want to disturb you. Are there any retired cadres here who know about the history of the county? I can go and chat with them."

He thinks of someone, an acting county magistrate of the former Guomindang period who has returned after being released from a labour camp. "This old man knows everything, he's an intellectual. When the county committee established the county record compilation group they always got him to check and verify materials."

In a damp muddy lane, I call at various homes and eventually come to his.

This gaunt old man with piercing eyes invites me to sit in the main room. He coughs incessantly and keeps offering me tea one moment and melon seeds the next. I can tell he is agitated because he can't work out why I am here.

I tell him I want to write a historical novel which has nothing to do with the present and that I have come especially to seek his advice. At this point he relaxes, stops coughing, and his hands stop moving things about. He lights a cigarette, sits up straight with his back against the wooden chair and finally begins to talk confidently.

"This was part of the state of Peng during the Western Zhou period, then during the Spring and Autumn period it belonged to the state of Chu. By the Warring States period it was territory contested by the states of Qin and Chu. The population was decimated during the wars and although that history is now remote the area remains sparsely populated, for when the Manchus came through the Pass the county's total population of 3000 was cut down to one-tenth by the slaughter. In addition, from the time of the Red Turban Uprising in the Mongol Yuan Dynasty, local bandits have been rife."

It is not clear if he thinks the Red Turbans are local bandits.

"It was in the second year of the Kangxi Emperor's reign in the Qing Dynasty that Li Zicheng's Ming Dynasty forces were finally crushed. But later on, in the first year of the reign of the Jiaqing Emperor, this area was overrun by the White Lotus Sect; and later still it was attacked and occupied by Zhang Xianzhong and the Nian Army. There was also the Taiping Army and then in the Republican period there were hordes of bureaucrat bandits, local bandits and soldier bandits."

"So this place has always been a bandit hide-out?" I ask.

He smiles but doesn't respond.

"In times of peace, people came from other places, or were born here and grew up here and the population multiplied and even prospered. It is recorded in historical texts that King Ping of Zhou came here to collect folk songs which means that in 700 BC folk songs were in abundance."

"That's too long ago," I say. "May I ask you to talk about your personal experiences? For example, what sort of havoc was wreaked by the bureaucrat bandits, local bandits and soldier bandits during the Guomindang period?"

"With bureaucrat bandits, I can give an example, one of these, who was in charge of two thousand men, rebelled. They raped several hundred women and abducted two hundred adults and children for 'leaves': leaves is bandit jargon for flesh vouchers or ransom notes. Rifles, ammunition, cloth and electric torches were required to redeem someone – one person was usually worth one or two thousand silver *yuan*, and there was a deadline. People had to be hired to take the ransom in baskets to a designated spot and if the families were as much as half a day late, even the vouchers for kidnapped children were torn up and only an ear would be redeemed. As for local petty bandits, they just carried out murder and robbery and then absconded."

"What about times of peace and prosperity, have you seen any of these?" I ask.

"Peace and prosperity..." He thinks for a while then nods. "Yes, there were such times and for the temple festivals on the third day of the third month this county had nine opera stages with painted rafters and carved pillars and there would be ten or so opera troupes performing non-stop day and night. After the revolution of 1911, during the fifth year of the Republic, this county had boys and girls in the same school and even large-scale sporting competitions where girls competed wearing shorts. By the twenty-sixth year of the Republic customs changed radically and from New Year's Day to the sixteenth day of the New Year, scores of gambling tables were set up at every intersection. In one night one big landlord lost one hundred and eight local temples, so you can calculate the area of the fields and forests involved! There were more than twenty brothels. Signs were not put up but this was the business they carried out and people from far and near within a radius of several hundred *li* all came, and guests were received day and night. Thereafter came the battles between the warlords Jiang, Feng and Guan, and then the War of Resistance when the Japanese carried out further mass destruction.

After that the gangsters took over and they were rampant just before the People's Government was established. At the time, the town of Chengguan's population of 800 had 400 members belonging to the Green Gang. They infiltrated every stratum of society from the secretaries of the county government down to the destitute. And they would stop at nothing – kidnapping brides, robbery, and selling widows. Even petty thieves had to pay homage to the gangster boss. At the weddings and funerals of big families there would be hundreds of beggars at the gate and if the beggar boss wasn't located and bought off there would be no holding them at bay. Most of the Green Gang were youths in their twenties, whereas the members of the Red Gang were a bit older. The bosses of the local bandits were mainly members of the Red Gang.

"What secret signs did gang members use to communicate with one another?" My interest has been aroused.

"The Green Gang used the surname Li inside the home but outside they used the surname Pan. If they met they addressed one another as 'brother' and this was known as the mouth keeps to Pan, the hand keeps to three." He makes a circle with his thumb and index finger and spreads out the other three fingers. "This was the secret sign and in addressing one another, the men were called Elder Brother Five or Elder Brother Nine and the women were called Elder Sister Four or Elder Sister Seven. Where they were of different generations, they would refer to one another as father or son or teacher and teacher's wife. The Red Gang addressed one another as master and the Green Gang addressed one another as older brother. If one of them went into a tea house and put down his hat with the brim upturned, his tea and cigarette bill would be paid."

"Were you a gang member?" I ask cautiously.

He smiles and has a sip of tea. "In those times if I didn't have connections, I wouldn't have been an acting county magistrate." He shakes his head. "It's all in the past."

"Do you think the factions in the Cultural Revolution were something like this?"

"That was between revolutionary comrades and can't be compared." He decisively rejects this suggestion.

For a while there is an awkward silence. He gets up and again starts offering me melon seeds and tea. "The government treated me well by locking me away in prison, a criminal like me encountering those mass movements might not be alive today."

"Times of peace and prosperity are rare indeed," I say.

"Surely it is at present! Surely at present the country is prosperous and the people enjoy security of life?" he asks me guardedly.

"There's food and even liquor."

"What else does one want?" he asks.

"Indeed," I reply.

"I'm happy being able to read books. Seeing people is troublesome and I appreciate my leisure," he says looking up at the ceiling.

Fine rain has started falling.

58

When N wa created humans she also created their sufferings. Humans are created from the entrails of N wa and born in the bloody fluids of women and so they can never be washed clean.

Don't go searching for spirits and ghosts, don't go searching for cause and retribution, don't go searching for meaning, all is embodied in the chaos.

It is only when people refuse to accept that they shout out, even while not comprehending what they are shouting. Humans are simply such creatures, fettered by perplexities and inflicting anxiety upon themselves.

The self within you is merely a mirror image, the reflection of flowers in water. You can neither enter the mirror nor can you scoop up anything, but looking at the image and becoming enamoured of it you no longer pity yourself.

You may as well resign yourself to being infatuated with that physical form and drown in a sea of lust, spiritual need is only self profanity. You grimace.

Knowledge is an extravagance, a costly expense.

You have only the desire to narrate, to use a language transcending cause and effect, or logic. People have spoken so much nonsense, so why shouldn't you say more.

You create out of nothingness, playing with words like a child playing with blocks. But blocks can only construct fixed patterns, the possibilities of structures are inherent in the blocks and no matter how they are moved you will not be able to make anything new.

Language is like a blob of paste which can only be broken up by sentences. If you abandon sentences, it will be like falling into a quagmire and you will flounder about helplessly.

To flounder helplessly is like suffering and the whole of humanity is made up of individual selves. When you fall in, you must crawl out yourself because saviours aren't concerned with such trifling matters.

Dragging weighty thoughts you crawl about in language, trying all the time to grab a thread to pull yourself up, becoming more and more weary, entangled in floating strands of language, like a silkworm spitting out silk, weaving a net for yourself, wrapping yourself in thicker and thicker darkness, the faint glimmer of light in your heart becoming weaker and weaker until finally the net is a totality of chaos.

To lose images is to lose space and to lose sound is to lose language. When moving the lips can't produce sounds what is being expressed is incomprehensible, although at the core of consciousness the fragment of the desire to express will remain. If this fragment of desire cannot be retained there will be a return to silence.

How is it possible to find a clear pure language with an indestructible sound which is larger than a melody, transcends limitations of phrases and sentences, does not distinguish between subject and object, transcends pronouns, discards logic, simply sprawls, and is not bound by images, metaphors, associations or symbols? Will it be able to give expression to the sufferings of life and the fear of death, distress and joy, loneliness and consolation, perplexity and expectation, hesitation and resolve, weakness and courage, jealousy and remorse, calm and impatience and self-confidence, generosity and constraint, kindness and hatred, pity and despair, as well as lack of ambition and placidity, humility and wickedness, nobility and viciousness, cruelty and benevolence, fervour and indifference, and aloofness, and admiration, and promiscuousness, and vanity, and greed, as well as scorn and respect, certainty and uncertainty, modesty and arrogance, obstinacy and chagrin, resentment and shame, surprise and amazement, lethargy, muddle-headedness, sudden enlightenment, never comprehending, failing to comprehend, as well as just allowing whatever will happen to happen.

59

I am lying on a spring bed made with clean sheets in a room with pale yellow print-patterned wallpaper, white crocheted curtains and dark red carpet. There are two lounge chairs with towelling covers and the bathroom has a bathtub. If I were not holding a stencilled manuscript of farm-work songs, *Gongs and Drums to Accompany Weeding*, I would find it hard to believe that I am in the forest of Shennongjia. This new two-storey building built for a team of American researchers who for some reason didn't arrive has become a hostel for cadres to carry out investigations. Through the good auspices of the section chief, when I arrive I am again given special treatment and charged the cheapest rates for food and lodgings. Beer even comes with the meals, although I would would have preferred liquor. To be able to enjoy such cleanliness and comfort completely relaxes me and I could stay for a few extra days without any problem. After all, there is no real need for me to hurry on my journey.

There's a sort of a buzzing in the room. At first I think it's an insect but looking around there's nowhere for an insect to hide as the ceiling is painted white and the light shade is a cream colour. The sound continues and hangs elusively in the air. When I listen carefully it is like a woman's singing and it hovers around me. As soon as I put down the book it vanishes and when I pick up the book the sound is again in my ears. I think my ears must be ringing so I get up, walk around for a bit, and open the window.

The sun produces a glare on the gravel square in front of the building. It is almost noon and no-one is in sight, could all this be in my mind? It is an elusive tune without words but it seems to be familiar, a bit like the sad wailing of women I have heard in the mountain regions.

I decide to go outside to have a look, leave the room, and go through the main door and out to the square in front of the building. The small fast-flowing river at the bottom of the slope is green and clear in the sunlight and the green mountain peaks, although devoid of vast stretches of forest, are nevertheless covered in lush vegetation. A dirt road for motor vehicles stretches for a couple of kilometres down the slope to the little town in the middle of the reserve. On the left, at the bottom of a towering green mountain, there's a school and an empty football field. The students are probably all in the classrooms: and the teachers in this mountain village wouldn't be teaching their students dirges. It is quiet and there is only the sound of the wind on the mountain and the lapping of the river. There is a makeshift workers' hut by the river but there is no-one outside the hut. The sound of the singing has vanished.

I return to my room and sit at the desk by the window, thinking to select and copy some of this folk song material, but again I hear the singing. It seems to be the slow outpouring of irrepressible grief after the pain of excruciating agony has settled. Something odd is happening and I must get to the bottom of it. Is there someone singing or is there something psychologically wrong with me? I look up and hear it behind me, I turn around and it is suspended in the air like a strand of floating silk. A spider web blowing in the wind has form but this is without form, intangible. Tracking the sound, I stand on the armrest of the sofa and at this point discover that it is coming through an air vent above the door. I get a chair and stand on it. The glass vent is spotlessly clean and when I open it the sound goes out into the corridor. I get off the chair and open the door and the sound goes out under the eaves of the balcony. I move the chair out onto the balcony, stand on it, but can't reach high enough. Below the balcony is the small sunlit cement courtyard where the clothes I washed in the morning hang on a wire. Of course *they* can't be singing. I can't see any tracks in the distance but there seems to be a fence along the mountain which cuts off a stretch of thick tangled undergrowth and brambles on the slope. As I come down from the balcony into the sunlight the sound becomes clearer and seems to be coming from the sun. I squint and look up and in the bright light hear the sharp, heavy thud of metal on stone. I can't see a thing at first, then when the blinding sun becomes a blue-black image and I shade my eyes with my hand, I see small figures moving about halfway up the mountain on a bare cliff face. The metallic sound is coming from far away over there. I walk towards them and make out that they are quarry workers – one seems to be wearing a red singlet and the others are stripped to the waist and are hardly distinguishable from the brown dynamited cliff face. The sound of their singing flies up into the sunlight with the wind and is sometimes loud and sometimes indistinct.

It occurs to me that I can bring them in for a closer look through the zoom lens of my camera so I go back to my room for it. It is in fact the person in the red singlet who is singing in a voice that sounds like a woman's high-pitched wailing as he swings a big sledge hammer and keeps time to the sound of a rock drill. The bare-chested man wielding the rock drill seems to be harmonizing with him.

Suddenly the singing stops, they must have seen the sun glinting off my camera. They stop work and look in my direction. There is an absence of any sound and the silence is searing, but I am pleased that I don't have some psychological disorder and that my hearing is normal.

I return to my room and want to write something, but what can I write about? What about something on the singing of the quarry workers? When I pick up my pen I can't write a thing.

I think, I'll try and get them to come for a drink and a chat in the evening – it'd be a way of passing time. I put down my pen and head for the small town.

When I emerge from a little shop with a bottle of brown rice wine and a bag of peanuts, I bump into the friend who lent me the stencilled material. He tells me he has also collected many hand-written copies of mountain folk songs. This is just what I want so I ask him to come for a chat. He's busy at the moment but promises to come after dinner.

I wait for him until ten o'clock. I am the only guest in the hostel and it is frustratingly quiet. I start regretting not having asked the quarry workers when I suddenly hear knocking on the window. It is my friend. He says he couldn't get anyone to open the main door, the girls in charge must have locked up and gone to sleep. I take the torch and a paper parcel from him and he climbs in. Nervous with excitement I immediately open the rice wine right away and pour out half a teacup each.

I can't recall his face but I recall that he was thin and not too tall, that he looked timid but once he started talking there was an enthusiasm which hadn't been crushed by life. His looks are irrelevant, what delights me is this treasure of his which he opens before me. He unwraps the newspaper parcel. Apart from a few notebooks, these are all badly tattered hand-written texts which used to be circulated among the people. I read through them one by one and when he sees my utter delight, he says magnanimously, "Go ahead and copy any that you like. There used to be lots of folk songs in these mountains. If you found an old master singer, he wouldn't be able to get through them all if he sang for several days and several nights."

At this I start asking him about the songs of the quarry workers on the mountain.

"Oh, they're falsetto singers from Badong," he says. "The forests on the mountains there have been stripped bare so they've had to leave to work in the quarries."

"Are there also different sets of music and words?"

"There are some books of music but the words are largely improvised, they just sing whatever comes to mind, much of it is quite crude."

"With lots of coarse swear words?"

"These quarry workers are away all year round and don't have any women, they take out their frustration on the rocks," he says with a smile.

"Why is the music so haunting and sad?"

"It's that sort of music. If you don't listen to the words it's like resentful wailing and sounds great, but the words aren't particularly interesting. Take a look at this." He takes a notebook from the paper parcel, leafs through to a particular page and hands it to me. Under the heading *Record of Darkness* is written:

On a good day at a good hour, Heaven and Earth open.
The filial family has asked us, a drummer and a singer,
To lead the singing at the song square.
One two three four five, metal wood water fire earth.
It is not easy to lead the singing,
And we sweat even before we start.

Deep at night when all is quiet a bright moon and stars,
And we get ready to start the singing.
It is late at night to start a long one,
If we start a short one it won't last till dawn,
We must start one not too long and not too short,
So you the assembled singers will not waste time.

One calling heaven, earth and waters
Two calling the sun, moon and the stars,
Three calling the five directions and the land,
Four calling the goddess of lightning,
Five calling Pan Gu who separated Heaven and Earth,
Six calling the Three Emperors and Five Kings, and all the
    kings of past ages,
Seven calling the Black Lion and the White Elephant, the
    Yellow Dragon and the Phoenix,
Eight calling the fierce dogs guarding the gates,
Nine calling sprites of marshes and mountains,
Ten calling tigers, leopards, jackals and wolves,
We ask all of you to stand aside, to give passage,
To the singers entering the song square!

"This is wonderful!" I gasp in praise. "How did you get hold of it?"

"I got this a couple of years ago when I was a primary school teacher in the mountains. I asked an old master singer to sing it while I wrote it down."

"The language is really beautiful and flows straight from the heart, it isn't at all constrained by the five-word and seven-word prosody of the so-called folk song genre."

"Quite right. This is a genuine folk song." As he drinks, his façade of timidity totally vanishes.

"This is a folk song which hasn't been vandalized by the literati! It is song gushing straight out of the soul! Do you realize this? You've saved a culture! It's not unique to the smaller nationalities, the Han nationality also has a genuine folk culture which hasn't been contaminated by Confucian ethical teachings!" I can't contain my excitement.

"You're right again, but take it easy and read on!"

He is beaming and that superficial modesty put on by grass-root cadres disappears. He takes the notebook from me and, imitating the singing pose of a master singer, chants in a high-pitch voice:

> I clasp my hands high in greeting,
> Whence do you come singer? Whence do you come?
> What province what prefecture? What brings you here?
> We respond to your greeting:
> I am a drum singer from Yangzhou,
> And I a singer from Liuzhou,
> We travel to song squares and call on friends,
> Here in your honourable territory,
> We beg hospitality.
>
> What do you carry on your shoulder pole?
> What do you carry in the basket you hold?
> The weight bends your back and shoulders,
> Yet you seek the advice of the master singer.

My pole carries song books,
My hand carries a rare book,
We do not know if the master singer has seen these?
But we have come to your home for instruction.

I can see the people, hear their voices, the sound of a gong and the beat of a drum. However outside the window is only the sound of the mountain wind and the lapping of water.

There are three hundred and sixty pole loads of songs,
Which load do you carry on your pole?
There are thirty-six thousand books of songs,
Which book do you carry in your hand?
Address me as master singer for I know,
The first book is the book born within us,
The first book is the script born within us.
I understand when I hear,
The master singer is an expert.
To know the things born within us,
Is to know the principles of Earth and Heaven.
I venture to ask him,
In which month of which year was song born?
On which day of which month was song born?

A tragic ancient sound in the darkness accompanies the sound of the wind and the beat of the drum and I seem to hear it all.

Fuxi made the strings of the *qin*,
N wa made the pipes of the *sheng*,
With Yin there is language,
With Yang there is sound.
With the matching of Yin and Yang there is man,
With man there is sound,
With sound there is song,

The songs grew many, and song books came into being.
These books were rejected by Confucius,
And dumped in the wilderness.
One was blown up into the sky,
So there came to be the Cowherd and the Weaving Maid.
Another was blown into the sea,
Fishermen picked it up and sing for wronged ghosts.
A third was blown into a temple,
So Buddhist monks and Daoist priests sing their scriptures
A fourth landed in a village lane,
So girls sing of their longings.
A fifth landed in a paddy field
So farmers sing them as mountain songs
The sixth book is the *Record of Darkness*
When the master singer holds it, he loses his soul in song.

"But this is just the prelude. What about the *Record of Darkness*?" I have been pacing about the room but I stop to ask him this.

He says this is the filial song they used to sing in early times at mountain funerals before the interment of the coffin. It was sung on the song ground in front of the spirit hall for up to three days and three nights, however it can't be sung frivolously and when it is sung all other songs must be suppressed. He had only taken down a small part when the master singer suddenly fell ill and died.

"Why didn't you write it down at the time?" I say looking at him.

"At the time the old man was ill and sat with his bedding wrapped around him in a small wooden chair," he explains. It is as if he is to blame and he resumes his timid appearance.

"Isn't there anyone else in the mountains who knows how to sing it?"

"Some can sing the prelude but no-one can sing all of it."

He says that he knew an old master singer who had a brass chest full of song books, amongst which was a complete set of the *Record of Darkness*. At the time they were confiscating old books and the *Record of Darkness* had been targeted in the search for reactionary and superstitious works. The old man buried the brass chest. A few months later he dug out the chest and found the books had gone mouldy so he spread them out in the courtyard to dry. He was seen and reported. The head of the forest district had the public security officials come and the old man was forced to hand over the whole set. It wasn't long afterwards that he died.

"Where else can reverence of the soul be found? Where else can we find these songs which one should listen to while seated in quiet reverence or even while prostrated be found? What should be revered isn't revered and instead only all sorts of things are worshipped! A race with empty, desolate souls! A race of people who have lost their souls!" I angrily declare.

He watches me with a worried look without saying so much as a word. I realize that I must have drunk the rice wine too quickly and that I am consumed by my rage.

In the morning a jeep stops in front of the building and someone comes to tell me that several of the leaders and cadres of the forest reserve have called a special meeting on my behalf and have invited me to hear a report on their work. This makes me feel ashamed. I think it must be because I had been bragging and boasting while addle-brained during that drinking orgy in the county town. As a result they think I've come from Beijing to make an investigation and they want me to let their superiors know about the situation here. The car is waiting at the main door and it is impossible for me to make up an excuse.

The cadres are already seated with their cups of tea in front of them in the conference room of the administrative office and as soon as I take my place, a cup of tea is brought out for me. It is just like the "experience-life" group visits organized by the Writers' Association to factories, military units, farms, mines, folk craft research centres and revolutionary memorial halls. In those times, the leaders of the writers would speak at the main table, but minor writers like me who were there to make up numbers were free to find some inconspicuous corner in which to drink tea and be silent. However, as they have convened this meeting especially for me I have to think about some things to talk about.

A cadre in charge first presents a review of the history and construction work of the reserve. In 1907 an Englishman called Wilson came here and collected specimens. At the time it was inaccessible, so he could only get to the fringe areas, indeed before 1960 you still couldn't see the sun and could only hear the sound of the water, it was still a vast expanse of virgin forest. During the 1930s the Guomindang Government made plans for logging the trees but there were no roads and they couldn't get in.

"In 1960 the Forestry Ministry made aerial maps. There was a total area of 3,250 square kilometres of mountain forest. Development started in 1962, proceeding from both the northern and southern extremities at the same time. In 1966 the road was put through. In 1970 an administrative district was formed, containing 50,000 peasants and about 10,000 cadres, forestry workers and their families. At present 900,000 cubic metres of timber is supplied to the state.

"In 1976 scientists petitioned for the protection of Shennongjia.

"In 1980 a proposal was made for a reserve.

"In 1982 the provincial government approved the setting aside of 80,040 hectares for the reserve.

"In 1983 the reserve was established and the timber industry units within the protected area were withdrawn, four sign-posted gates were erected and a surveillance unit was established. It was possible to stop vehicles but not people. Last year, in one month, three to four hundred people came in for traditional medicines. They dug up the rhizomes of goldthread and stripped off the bark of winter jasmine and eucommia. People also come in to illegally cut trees and to hunt. There are also those who come to look for the Wild Man.

"As for scientific research, a research unit has artificially cultivated seven hectares of dove trees, and spice bush has also been successfully propagated by cloning. Wild medicinal herbs have also been cultivated – pearl on top, a bowl of water at the river-bank, one of King Wen's writing brushes, seven leaves to one flower, and the dying and returning to life plant (none of which seem to have scientific names).

"There is also a wildlife unit which carries out investigations into the Wild Man, the golden monkey, the leopard, the white bear, the civet, the muntjac, the masked civet, the serow, the golden pheasant, the giant salamander, as well as yet unnamed animals such as the pig-bear, and the donkey-headed wolf which peasants have reported to be eating their piglets.

"After 1980, animals started returning, and last year a fight between a grey wolf and a golden monkey was discovered. The screams of a golden monkey were heard and a king golden monkey was seen blocking the path of a grey wolf ... in March they caught a small golden monkey but it refused food and died. The sunbird, which eats the honey of azaleas and has a red body, an orchid tail and a small pointed beak, has also been sighted.

"Problematical issues: There are conflicting views on environmental protection. If the workers protest they don't get bonuses. If the lumber supply decreases the higher authorities complain and the finance organization refuses to allocate funds. There are 4000 peasants in the reserve and it's hard to manage them. There are twenty cadres and workers in the reserve still living in rough worksheds; they are extremely unhappy about it as they don't have any facilities. The crux of the matter is inadequate funding, we have appealed many times ... "

The cadres all start talking in earnest and it is as if I can appeal for funds on their behalf. I stop taking notes. I am neither one who leads writers nor one of those writers who leads other writers, who can speak with assurance, talk off-the-cuff about anything and then make a whole lot of empty promises such as: I'll talk about the matter with this bureau chief and report on it to the leadership of relevant departments, I'll make a lot of fuss and stir up public discussion, mobilize the whole population to come forth to protect the ecology which sustains our people! I can't even manage to protect myself, so what can I say? I can only say that protecting the environment is important work and has implications for later generations of our children and grandchildren. The Yangtze has already become a brown river bringing down mud and silt, and yet a big dam is to be built on the Three Gorges! Of course I can't say this and so the best thing is for me to change the topic to the Wild Man.

"The Wild Man is really creating a stir throughout the country …" I begin, and in an instant everyone is talking about the Wild Man.

"That's right, the Academy of Social Sciences in Beijing has organized a number of investigations. The first was in 1967, then in 1977 and 1980, people were sent here especially. The one in 1977 was the biggest, with the most people, the research team alone numbered one hundred and ten and that's not counting the cadres and workmen sent by our reserve. Most of the research team were army personnel and there was also a commanding officer …"

They start giving reports again.

What sort of language can I use so that I can chat freely with them? Should I ask what it's like living here? They will certainly want to talk about the availability of commodities, prices and wages. But then my own financial resources are sorely deficient. However, this isn't a venue for idle conversation and I can't say, when the world is becoming increasingly incomprehensible, where man and mankind's behaviour is so strange that humans don't know how humans should behave, why are they looking for the Wild Man. So apart from the Wild Man what else is there to talk about?

They say that last year a primary school teacher saw the creature. It was in June or July, round about this time of the year, but he didn't dare publicize it. He just mentioned it to a close friend and told him to keep it to himself. That's right, not so long ago someone published an article called "Tragic History of the Wild Man of Shennongjia" in the *Dongting Magazine* of Hunan Province. Someone got hold of it, circulated it and everyone read it. The search for the Wild Man started here and has spread to the provinces of Hunan, Jiangxi, Zhejiang, Fujian, Sichuan, Guizhou, Anhui … It's been reported everywhere (except Shanghai!). In Guangxi they actually captured a small Wild Man, it's called a Mountain Devil there. The peasants thought it was unlucky and set it free (unfortunately). Also there have been reports of Wild Man flesh being eaten. It's all right to talk about it. When the research team came this was investigated and confirmed and books have been published on it. It was in 1972 that Zhang Renguan, Wang Liangcan and about twenty others who were mostly workers from our reserve, ate the foot and calf of a Wild Man in the dining hall of Sunshine Bay Farm! The foot was about forty centimetres long, the big toe five centimetres in circumference and ten centimetres long. The documentation they put together has all been stamped. The calf was twenty centimetres in circumference and weighed fifteen kilograms and they all had a big bowl of it. The Wild Man was killed by a peasant in Panshui with a rifle fitted with a silencer and he sold a leg to the Sunshine Bay Farm dining hall. Also, in 1975, on the mountain road from Qiaoshang Commune to Yusai Number One Work Brigade, Zeng Xianguo was struck on the face by a two-metre-high Wild Man with red hair. He blacked out for some time and when he regained consciousness ran home but couldn't talk for three or four days afterwards. This is all from a comparative anatomy statistical analysis carried out on a documentation of his oral account. Didn't Zhao Kuidian see a Wild Man eating coriaria fruit when he was on the road back to his home village? What year was that? 1977 or 1978? It was a few days before the investigation team came for the second time from the Academy of Social Sciences. Of course, you can believe or not believe all this, the people of the investigation team are also divided about it. But if you listen to the peasants in the mountains talking about them it is quite sordid. The Wild Man chases women, looks for young girls to play with and for sex, some even say that the Wild Men can talk and makes different sounds when happy and sad.

"Are there any here who have seen one with his own eyes?" I ask.

They all laugh and stare at me but I can't tell if it means they've seen one or not.

Afterwards, I go with a cadre guide into the cleared central section of the reserve. In 1971 an army truck convoy came and logged the main peak for two years for national defence material, or so they said, and left it denuded. At an altitude of only 2,900 metres I can see an expanse of beautiful low sub-alpine marshland, young green grassy waves undulating endlessly in the mist and rain, dotted with tangled clumps of Cold Arrow Bamboo. I stand for a long time in the icy wind, thinking to myself that this stretch of natural wilderness is probably one of the last bits of primitive ecology.

Zhuangzi, who lived more than two thousand years ago, said that useful timber dies prematurely by the axe and only useless timber enjoys good fortune. People today are greedier than the ancients and this casts doubt on Thomas Huxley's theory of evolution.

In a mountain homestead, I come across a bear cub in the shed. It has a rope collar around its neck and looks like a little brown dog as it clambers up and down a pile of wood. It keeps growling and still doesn't know to bite to defend itself. The owner says he picked it up in the mountains and there is no point asking if he had killed the mother, but the little dog-like bear is very cute. Seeing how much I like it, he says for twenty *yuan*, I can take it with me. I don't have plans to learn a circus act and if I take it with me how can I go on wandering? It's best for me to leave the cub where it is.

Outside someone's house, I also see a wormholed piece of leopard skin bedding airing in the sun. Tigers have been extinct for more than ten years. I also see a stuffed golden monkey. I guess it's the one they caught in the tree, the one which refused food and died. When animals are captured and refuse to be domesticated, this is all they can do. But this requires considerable resolve, and not all humans can do this.

It is also in front of the administrative office of the reserve that I see a large sign newly posted on the wall: "Congratulations on the establisment of the Old People's Sports Committee!" I think that a new political campaign is to be launched and hasten to ask the cadre who has put up the sign. He says a telephone instruction came from higher up – they wanted it up so he put it up. It's got nothing to do with you or me, it's only for revolutionary cadres who are over sixty and who are receiving at least a hundred-*yuan* sports subsidy. The oldest cadre here is only fifty-five and just old enough to receive the consolation prize of a commemorative booklet. Later on I meet a young reporter who says the chairman of the Old People's Sports Committee is the retired former district party secretary, and had insisted on the reserve contributing a hundred *yuan* towards celebrating the establishment of the committee. The reporter says he is writing an internal reference document which he wants to go direct to the Central Discipline Investigation Committee and asks if I have any connections. I sympathize with his righteous indignation but suggest that posting it would be much more reliable than giving it to me.

I see a pretty young woman with a light sprinkling of freckles on her nose. She is dressed differently from the people on this mountain and is wearing an open-neck short-sleeved cotton-knit top. When I ask, it turns out that she comes from Zigui, on the south bank of the Yangtze, the birthplace of Qu Yuan. She has finished middle school and has come here to look for her maternal cousin and to see if she can find work on the reserve. She says the county government in Zigui has announced that the construction work of the big dam on the Three Gorges is about to start and that the county will be totally inundated. All households have filled in population evacuation registration cards and residents have been mobilized to make plans for their own livelihood. Afterwards, I travel south along the Xiang Stream which produces beautiful women, and before arriving in Yichang pass the home of the famous beauty of ancient time, Wang Zhaojun, with its black tiles and flying eaves on the mountain slope. An amateur writer tells me that the city is set to become the provincial capital of the future Three Gorges Province and that even the chair-elect of the future Writers' Association has been internally decided. To my surprise the chair-elect is an award-winning poet of whom I've heard but who I can't say I like.

I lost my poetic sensibility a long time ago and can't write poetry. In any event I doubt that the present is an age for poetry. It seems that everything to be sung or shouted has already been sung or shouted. What remains is simply typeset, printed, and called impressions. If this is the case, then the artist's drawings I have seen of the Wild Man with gangling arms, stooped back, thick legs and long hair, who giggles at people, and are based on scientifically-assessed eyewitness accounts appearing in Wild Man Research Association publications, are also impressions. Can, therefore, the strange sight I saw on my last night at Wooden Fish Flat in this primitive forest called Shennongjia also count as a poem?

A bright moon is in the sky. On the square in the shadow of the towering mountain, two high bamboo poles have been put up and kerosene lamps hung on them: a stage curtain stretches across the bottom section. An acrobatic troupe starts the show on the square to the sound of a battered, slightly out of tune trumpet and the muffled beat of a moisture-affected big drum. About two hundred people have turned up — grown-ups and children from the homes of this small village, including the cadres and workers of the reserve administrative office and their families and the pretty freckle-faced young woman wearing an open-neck, short-sleeved cotton-knit top who comes from the birthplace of Qu Yuan. There are three rows, packed tightly into a large semi-circle. Those in the front row are sitting on wooden stools brought from home, those in the middle row are standing, and those who come last are poking their heads in between the heads of the people in the middle row.

The program is the usual thing — *qigong* brick-chopping, one brick, two bricks, three bricks halved with a single chop of the hand; pulling in the belt and swallowing iron pellets and then spewing them up in a spray of spittle; a fat woman climbing up a bamboo pole and hanging upside down from a golden hook; and flame throwing. It's all fake, it's all fake. At first the women say this quietly then the young men start yelling it. The bald leader of the troupe shouts out, "All right, now for the real stuff!"

He hands a javelin to the iron pellet swallower and gets him to push the metal tip at his chest and throat until the bamboo javelin curves like a bow and the blue veins stand out on his bald head. People start to clap and it appears the audience has been won over.

368

The tension on the square relaxes, the trumpet reverberates through the shadows of the mountain, the drum ceases to be muffled, and everyone is in good spirits. The bright moon moves into the shadows of the clouds and the kerosene lamps become brighter. The sturdy fat woman balances a bowl of water on her head as she spins porcelain plates on bamboo sticks. At the end of the act she wriggles her rotund hips in imitation of the singers and dancers on TV as she skips and prances around to thank the audience. A few people clap. The troupe leader is glib of tongue and starts saying more and more audacious things as the skill content of the acts decreases, but everyone is in a good mood and is happy with whatever is put on.

The last item is a contortionist act. The girl dressed in red silk trousers and top, who up to this point has been picking up props, now leaps onto a square table. Two wooden benches are put onto the table, then another table put onto the benches. Her figure stands silhouetted high up against the black shape of the mountain, a brilliant red in the bright glow of the lamps, and instantly the full moon in the sky darkens and turns an orange-yellow.

First she does The Golden Pheasant Standing Alone, gently clasping her legs and lifting them right over her head. The audience loudly applauds. Then she does front-on splits, sitting perfectly still, flush on the bench. The audience cheers. Next with legs apart she bends backwards until the mound under her belly protrudes between her thin legs. The audience holds its breath. Her head slowly emerges between her legs and then, even more strangely, she puts her legs tightly together to hold in pincers this young girl's head with long plaits. Her big black eyes look sad, as if they are staring at an alien world. Then her hands clutch this child-like face, and she is like a grotesque humanoid spider scrutinizing the audience. Some go to clap but stop. She props up her body on her hands then raises her hanging legs and proceeds to spin on one hand, her nipples showing clearly through her red silk top. The breathing of the audience is audible and the smell of hair and sweat permeates the air. A child wants to say something but the woman holding it silences it with a quiet slap.

369

The girl in red, her teeth clenched, her abdomen gently heaving and her face shining with a rich glow in the clear pure moonlight with the black shape of the mountain behind, is contorted beyond human semblance. Only her thin lips and black eyes reveal her pain and it is this pain which inflames the human lust for cruelty.

Tonight, everyone is wildly excited, it's as if they've been injected with the blood of chickens. It is deep into the night but most houses far and near are still lit up and there is talking and the clattering of things for a long time. I also find it impossible to sleep and wander back to the empty square. The kerosene lamps on the bamboo poles have been taken down and only the limpid moonlight remains. I find it hard to believe that just now, below this majestic, austere, deep mountain, people have just enacted these scenes of grossly unnatural human distortion and I wonder if it has all been a dream.

60

"Don't think about anything else while you're dancing." You have just met her, and are dancing together for the first time when she says this to you.

"What do you mean?" you ask.

"When you're dancing just dance, don't put on an act of being lost in thought."

You laugh.

"Be a bit more earnest, put your arms around me."

"All right," you say.

She giggles.

"Why are you laughing?"

"Can't you hold me tighter?"

"Of course."

You hold her tight and become aware of the springiness of her breasts and the fragrant warmth of her neck from her open-neck top. The room is dark, the table lamp in the corner has been covered with an open black umbrella and the faces of the couples dancing are indistinct. The tape recorder is playing soft music.

"This is good," she says quietly.

Your breathing blows the soft strands of hair brushing against your cheek.

"You're lovely," you say.

"What are you saying?"

"I like you but this is not love."

"It's better that way, love is stressful and wearisome."

You say you feel the same way.

"We're two of a kind," she says with feeling and with a smile.

"A perfect match."

"But I wouldn't marry you."

"Why would you want to?"

"But I really want to get married."

"When?"

"Maybe next year."

"That's a long way off."

"It wouldn't be with you next year either."

"That goes without saying, but who will you marry?"

"Sooner or later I'll have to marry someone."

"Just anyone?"

"Not necessarily. Anyway, sooner or later I'll have to get married."

"And then get divorced?"

"Maybe."

"Then we'll dance together again."

"But I still wouldn't marry you."

"Why would you want to?"

"There's something nice about you." She really seems to mean it.

You thank her.

Through the glass window the lights from countless homes can be seen. These lights, some on and some off, go up in a regular manner and belong to building after building of the same rectangular box-style high-rise residences. A couple suddenly starts to whirl around in the small room and crashes into your back. You quickly come to a stop and hug her.

"Don't think I'm praising how you dance," she seizes the chance to start up again.

"I'm not a professional dancer."

"Then why do you dance? To get close to women?"

"There are ways of getting even closer."

"You've got a sharp tongue."

"That's because your tongue never stops."

"All right, I'll keep quiet."

She snuggles against you and you close your eyes. Dancing with her is sheer bliss.

You meet again one night in the middle of autumn, when a chilly north-west wind is blowing. You are riding your bicycle into the wind and from time to time, chased by the wind, leaves and scraps of paper on the road fly up into the air. You decide to drop in on an artist friend to wait for the weather to calm down a bit before going on and turn off into a small lane lit by a dim yellow street light. Only one solitary person can be seen walking ahead with his head huddled down into his coat. You feel wretched.

In this dark little courtyard, there is a faint, flickering light coming from his window. You knock on the door and a deep voice answers. He opens the door and warns you to watch out for the step because it is dark. The room is lit by a small candle which flickers from a sawn coconut shell.

"This is great," you say, really appreciating the warmth. "What are you doing?"

"Nothing in particular," he replies.

It is very warm in the room. He is only wearing a bulky woollen pullover and his hair is a mess. The chimney has already been fitted on the heater-stove for the winter.

"Are you sick?" you ask.

"No."

Something moves by the candle, you hear the springs creak on his dilapidated old sofa and realize that a woman is sitting at one end of it.

"You've got a guest?" you say apologetically.

"It's all right." Pointing to the sofa he says, "Sit down."

It is then that you see it is her, she lethargically puts out a limp and soft hand to shake. She is wearing her hair long and she blows away a loose strand hanging over the corner of her eye. You joke with her.

"If I remember rightly, your hair wasn't as long before."

"Sometimes I wear it up, sometimes I have it down, you simply didn't notice." She smiles petulantly.

"Do you know one another?" your artist friend asks.

"We danced together at a friend's place."

"You still remember." There is a tinge of sarcasm in her voice.

"Is it possible to forget having danced with someone?" you say, sniping back.

As he pokes the stove, the dark red fire lights up the paper canopy on the ceiling.

"Do you want a drink?"

You say you're just passing by and can only stay for a short time.

"I'm not doing anything in particular either," he says.

"It's all right..." she adds, quietly.

Afterwards, they both fall silent.

"You two go on with what you were talking about," I say. "I came in to warm up, there's been a cold snap. When the wind dies down a bit, I'll be on my way."

"No, you've come just at the right time," she says. Again there is a silence.

"It would be more accurate to say I've come at the wrong time." You think you really should make a move to go but your friend doesn't wait for you to start getting to your feet. He presses you down by the shoulders and says, "As you're here, it will be possible to talk about something else. We've already finished saying what we were saying."

"You two go ahead, I'll just listen." She curls up on the sofa and only the outline of her pale face is visible, her lovely nose and mouth.

After quite some time, she turns up on your doorstep at noon one day.

"How did you know where I live?"

"Aren't I welcome?"

"Quite the opposite. Come in, come in." Your get her to come inside and ask if your artist friend had given her your address. In the past you had only seen her in dim lighting and didn't dare say it was her for sure.

374

"Maybe, maybe it was someone else, is your address a secret?" she answers with a question.

You say you hadn't thought she would honour you with a visit and that you are indeed greatly honoured.

"You've forgotten it was you who invited me."

"That's also quite possible."

"And it was you who gave me the address, had you forgotten that too?"

"I must have," you say. "Anyway, I'm really pleased you've come."

"How can you not be pleased with a model coming?"

"You're a model?" You're even more surprised.

"I've done modelling, moreover nude modelling."

You say, unfortunately, you're not an artist but that you do do some amateur photography.

"Do people who come always have to stand?" she asks.

You hasten to point around the room. "Make yourself at home, feel free to do whatever you like. By looking at this room you can tell that the owner doesn't have rules and regulations."

She sits herself down by the desk, glances around and says, "The place looks like it needs a woman owner."

"If you'd like to be, but it would only be owning the owner of the room, because the property rights to the room don't belong to the owner of the room."

Each time you meet you engage in verbal sparring, but you mustn't lose to her.

"Thanks." She takes the tea you have made and smiles. "Let's talk about something serious."

She's ahead again. You only have time to say, "All right."

After you fill your own cup and sit on the chair at the desk, you relax and turn to her.

"We can start by discussing what to talk about. By the way, are you really a model?"

"I was an artist's model but I'm not anymore." She blows away some strands of hair hanging on her face.

"May I ask why?"

"He got sick of painting me and found someone else."

"Painters are like that, I know. They can't spend a whole lifetime painting the one model." You have to defend your artist friend.

"Models are the same, they can't live just for the one painter."

She's right, of course. You must get off the topic.

"But are you actually a model? I'm asking about your occupation, is that job?"

"Is that so very important?" She laughs again, she's quite ingenious, always one step ahead of you.

"It's not all that important. I'm just asking so that I'll know what to talk about, so that I can talk about something which might be of interest to both you and me."

"I'm a doctor," she says with a nod. And before you get a chance to follow up, she asks, "Can I smoke?"

"Of course, I smoke too."

You move the cigarettes and ashtray across the table to her.

She lights a cigarette and inhales the smoke.

"You don't look like one," you say, starting to catch onto her game.

"That's why I said what I do is unimportant. When I said I was a model, did you think I really was?" She tilts her head back and slowly exhales the smoke.

And when you say you're a doctor are you really a doctor? But you don't articulate this.

"Do you think all models are frivolous?" she asks.

"Not necessarily, modelling is serious work, and there's nothing bad in exposing one's body, I'm talking about nude modelling. If nature endows one with beauty, then to present nature's beauty can only be considered magnanimous, it has nothing at all to do with frivolity. Furthermore a beautiful human body is superior to any artwork. Art is invariably pale and insipid compared to nature and only a lunatic would think that art is superior to nature."

You prattle away with passion and conviction.

"Then why are you involved in art?" she asks.

You say you haven't got the expertise for art and are just a writer, saying what you want to say and whenever you want to.

"But writing is also a form of art."

You insist that writing is a technical skill.

"It just requires learning the technique, like you for example, you've learnt how to operate with a scalpel. I don't know if you're a surgeon or a physician but that's not important. As long as you acquire the technique anyone can write just like anyone can learn how to use a scalpel."

She laughs.

You go on to say you don't believe that art is sacrosanct, art is just a way of life. People have different ways of life, art can't represent everything.

"You're very intelligent," she says.

"You're not exactly stupid yourself," you say.

"But some people are stupid."

"Who?"

"Artists. They only perceive with their eyes."

"Artists have artists' modes of perception, they rely more on visual perception than writers."

"Can visual perception allow one to understand a person's intrinsic value?"

"I don't think so, but the crux of the matter is what is value? This differs according to the individual, people have their own ways of looking at this. It is only for those with similar values that different values have any meaning. I won't be ingratiating and say that you are beautiful and I don't know whether you are all beautiful inside, but I can say that it is enjoyable talking with you. Don't people exist in order to have some pleasure? Only fools go out looking for unhappiness."

"I also feel happy when I am with you."

While saying this she unthinkingly picks up your key from the table and starts toying with it. You can see she is unhappy, so you start talking about the key with her.

"What key?" she asks.

"The key in your hand."

"What about the key?"

You say you lost it.

"Isn't it here?" She shows you the key in her hand.

You say you thought you had lost it but right now it is in her hand.

She puts the key back on the table suddenly stands up and says she is leaving.

"Is there something urgent?"

"Yes," she says, then adds, "I'm married."

"Congratulations," you say with a tinge of bitterness.

"I'll come again."

That's a relief. "When?"

"When I'm feeling happy. I won't come when I'm unhappy and make you unhappy. Nor when I am particularly happy—"

"That's obvious, suit yourself."

You also say you'd like to believe she will come again.

"I'll come and talk to you about the key you lost!"

She tosses her head and her hair falls about her shoulders, then with an enigmatic smile she walks out the door and goes down the stairs.

61

This old schoolmate of mine whom I haven't seen for more than ten years takes out a photo from a drawer. It's of him and another person in front of a broken-down temple with a vegetable patch next to it. The person could be middle-aged, elderly, or in between, and could be a man or a woman. He says it's a woman. He asks if I know the Woman Warrior of the Desolate Plains.

I do. When I had just started junior high school a classmate used to bring from home old righteous warrior novels, which were banned at school, like *Seven Swords and Thirteen Righteous Warriors*, *Biography of the Swordsman of Emei* and *Thirteenth Younger Sister*. If you were a friend you could take the book home for the night and if you weren't a friend you had to put it in the drawer of your desk and surreptitiously read it during class.

I also remember when I was even younger, I had a picture-book set of *Woman Warrior of the Desolate Plains* and lost some of the pages at a game of marbles. The set was broken and I was really upset.

And I recall it was this Woman Warrior of the Desolate Plains or Thirteenth Younger Sister or some other woman warrior who had something to do with my awakening from youthful ignorance about sex. It was probably an illustrated book in a second-hand bookshop. Early in the book a picture showed a branch of peach blossoms scattered by a storm with a caption below, something like "Untold misery after a night of wind and rain", implying that the woman warrior had been raped by some rogue who was also an exponent of the martial arts. On a later page the woman warrior has sought out an expert from the highest ranks of the martial arts world and she has learnt the secret art of the flying knives. Her mind set on revenge, she eventually tracks down her enemy. Her flying knives pin him by the head but for some reason she is sad and simply cuts off one of his arms and leaves him with a means to go on living.

"Do you believe that women warriors still exist?" my old schoolmate asks.

"The woman in the photo?" I can't tell if he's joking.

This tall, bespectacled, old schoolmate of mine in the photo is wearing a geological fieldwork outfit. He has a rustic look and reminds me a little of Pierre in Tolstoy's *War and Peace*. When I first read the novel he was quite thin although at the time he was already wearing glasses on his kindly round face. His glasses as always are sitting on his nose and he looks very much like that bookish character in the illustrations of Tolstoy's works by a Russian artist. However the woman warrior by his side, who comes just to his shoulders, is dressed like a peasant in a big coat with buttons down the front, baggy trousers and a pair of shovel-nose army galoshes. She has a genderless face with small eyes and the only indication of her being female is her ear-length hair cropped in the style for women cadres in the villages. She in no way resembles the women warriors of my novels, paintings, and picture-books, poised for battle in their belted fighting clothes in breathtakingly heroic stances and with beautiful phoenix-like eyes.

"Don't underestimate her. She's every bit an expert in the martial arts and has killed lots of people," he says seriously.

On my way east from Zhuzhou, the train is running behind schedule and stops at a small station, probably to let through the special express coming from the other direction. When I see the name of the station, I suddenly remember that this old classmate of mine works here with a mining exploration team. We hadn't been in touch for over ten years, then last year the editor of a publishing house forwarded the manuscript of a novel this old classmate had sent me. The name of this place was written on the envelope. I don't have his address on me but there couldn't be that many exploration teams in a small place like this and it shouldn't be hard to track him down. I get off the train right away. He is a good friend from childhood days. There aren't many happy things in life and it is wonderful to meet old friends by chance.

When I set out from Changsha with a change of trains at Zhuzhou I had not intended to make a stopover. I had neither relatives nor anyone I knew in Zhuzhou, and there were no folk customs or archaeological artefacts to investigate. Nevertheless, I spent a whole day wandering along the Xiang River and in the city. It was only afterwards that I realized it was to track down yet another, it would seem, futile image from the past.

It was twelve or thirteen years since I was hounded out of Beijing carrying a bedroll like a refugee to undertake "re-education" at what was known as the May Seventh Cadre School located in this mountainous region. As a child, I had once fled as a refugee through this very region. Personal relationships within organizations were tense because of the constantly changing political movements and people were shouting slogans and clinging tenaciously to their own factions for fear of being labelled the enemy by their opponents. Then suddenly a new "highest instruction" arrived and army representatives were stationed in all cultural organizations and everyone was moved en masse to this mountain region to work in the fields.

I have been a refugee from birth. When my mother was alive she said she gave birth to me while planes were dropping bombs. The windows of the delivery room in the hospital had strips of paper pasted on them to stop them shattering when there were explosions. Luckily she escaped the bombs and I was born safely. However, I couldn't cry and it was only with the doctor slapping my bottom that I could cry. My birth probably predetermined my habit of being perpetually on the run in life and I have grown accustomed to upheavals and learnt to find a little pleasure in the intervals between. So while the others of our group of evacuees at the time were sitting in a daze on their bedrolls and waiting on the platform, I left my bedroll with someone and, like a stray dog, wandered around the streets and alleys of the city. I ran into a diehard from an opposition faction in a little restaurant. At the time pork was rationed and each person was allotted one meat coupon per month which could be used to buy one *jin* of meat. I guessed that he, like me, must have wanted to eat meat. The restaurant turned out to have dog meat with chilli. I and he each ordered a plate. I and he had both been reduced to living away from home and so shared a table and began to squabble over buying the liquor. The two of us drank liquor and ate dog meat as if this life and death class struggle did not exist, neither was an enemy and of course neither mentioned politics. There was in fact quite a lot to talk about – in this old street without coupons you could buy toilet paper smelling like hay, local cloth and tea. You could also buy five-spice peanuts which you couldn't even get in Beijing. He and I had bought some and took them from our bags to put on the table to eat with the liquor. It was this scrap of inconsequential memory led me to spend an entire day at Zhuzhou when changing trains during the journey from Changsha. So there is every reason for me to bring some unexpected happiness to a good friend from the days of my youth.

I book a bed at a hostel and deposit my backpack. If I can't find him, at least I'll be able to have a sleep at the hostel then catch the early morning train.

I eat a bowl of green soya bean porridge at the stall selling late night snacks and my fatigue vanishes. I ask the public office cadre who is slouched in a chair and cooling off outside the entrance to the tax office if there is a mining exploration team in the area. He sits up and immediately confirms that there is – first he says it is two *li* off, then three, and at most five. At the end of the street where there are no streetlights, I go into the small lane, through the paddy fields, across the small river over the wooden bridge, and on the other side not far off are some isolated new-style buildings. That's the exploration team.

It is a summer night and the sky is filled with stars and everywhere I can hear the din of croaking frogs. I step into a puddle but this doesn't worry me, I am determined to find my friend and about midnight I have groped my way through the dark and am knocking on his door.

"You devil!" he calls out, excited and surprised. Big and fat and clad in nothing but a pair of shorts, he wildly hits at me with his big reed fan and stirs up a breeze. It is that old habit from childhood when everyone used to slap one another on the shoulders. At the time I was the youngest and everyone in the class called me Little Devil. Now I suppose I am an old devil.

"How did you get here?"

"I crawled up out of the ground," I say. I too am really happy.

"Bring out some liquor, no, bring some watermelon, it's too hot," he calls out to his wife, a solid, sturdy woman who seems to be a local. She smiles but says very little. He has obviously settled here but has lost nothing of his earlier bravado.

He asks if I received the manuscript he sent. He says he saw some of the things I had published over the past few years, thought it had to be me, so he sent the manuscript to the editorial department of one of the publishers and asked them to forward it. It worked and we have actually made contact. He says he also has an urge to write, an irrepressible urge, so he wrote this to see how it would go.

What can I say? This novel of his was about a country boy scorned by his classmates because his grandfather was an old landlord and every day he listened to his teacher saying that the lines between class enemies had to be clearly demarcated. He felt that the source of all his miseries stemmed from this ailing old man who simply wouldn't die, so he put into the old man's medicinal brew some medical cherry flower, a noxious weed which even has to be picked out of greenfeed for pigs. The next morning, when the village public broadcast system started singing "The East is Red" to summon the villagers to the fields to work, the boy woke and saw the old man sprawled on the ground. His mouth was covered in black blood and he was dead. It was a novel about the psychology of a child, and examined this senseless world through the eyes of a peasant boy. I showed the manuscript to an editor I knew. He didn't give the usual spiel for rejecting manuscripts by spouting off a whole lot of official literary jargon like the episodes lack refinement, it is poorly conceived, the characters are not convincing or it lacks typicality in presentation.

Instead, he said bluntly that he thought it was well written but that the author had gone too far – the leadership would certainly not approve so the work was therefore unpublishable. I could only say that the author was doing exploration work in the countryside and was used to how it was in the mountains. He couldn't be expected to understand the criteria of the present literary world. This is exactly what I tell him.

"But where is the criteria?" he says with incomprehension showing in his eyes just like the bookworm Pierre. "Didn't the newspapers announce some days ago that creative freedom has to be considered and that literature has to portray the truth?"

"It's because of this damn portraying the truth that misfortune has befallen me and I have fled here," I say.

He laughs heartily and says, "Then forget the story about this Woman Warrior of the Desolate Plains."

He throws the photo into the drawer, then says, "I stayed for a few days in that broken-down temple while I was doing exploratory work and got to know her. While chatting I hit on something that was troubling her and she ended up talking to me for a whole day. I filled half a notebook with her personal experiences."

He takes out a notebook from the drawer and, waving it in front of me, says, "There's enough here to write a book. I've even thought of a title: *Jottings from the Broken-down Temple*."

"This doesn't sound like the title for a woman warrior novel."

"Of course not. If you're interested, take it with you to use as material for a novel." Saying this he tosses the notebook back into the drawer and says to his wife, "Bring out the liquor after all."

"It's not just fiction," I say, "I can't even publish those prose pieces I used to write. As soon as they see my name on a manuscript they reject it."

"You'd best stick to doing your geology and not fool around with writing," his wife says when she brings the liquor.

"Now tell me the situation with you now!" He's very concerned.

"I'm wandering everywhere to avoid being investigated. I've been gone for several months. I'll go back when it's safe, after the trouble blows over. If things get worse, I'll look over a few places and if necessary slip away. In any case I'm not going to be the way I was during those years I was labelled a rightist, obediently allowing myself to be led like a sheep to be reformed through labour."

The two of us laugh heartily.

"How about I tell you a happy story? When I was part of a small team sent to look for gold, we captured a Wild Man in the mountains," he says.

"Stop joking, did you see it with your own eyes?" I ask.

"So what if I saw it, we captured it! We were going along a mountain ridge to cut down on the distance so that we could get to the campsite before dark. A patch of the forest under the ridge had been burnt off and planted with corn. Something was moving in the yellow cornfield and looking down we could clearly see it was some sort of wild animal. At that time we all carried rifles for safety into mountains like these. The team said it's either a black bear or a wild pig, if we can't find gold but can get hold of some meat, at least it'll be lucky for our mouths. We split up and started closing in. This thing heard us moving and charged away towards the forest. It was past three in the afternoon and the sun had moved to the west but it was still quite light. When the thing started running its head popped out from amongst the ears of corn. It was a long-haired Wild Man. We all saw it and, wild with excitement, started yelling Wild Man! Wild Man! Don't let it get away! Then there were gunshots. We had been going through the mountains and gullies all day and hadn't had a chance to fire a shot, so we were letting off steam. We had all livened up and were running, yelling and shooting. When we closed in we managed to force it out. It was stark naked and its balls were shining. It raised its hands to surrender then crashed to its knees onto the ground. It had a pair of glasses tied to its head with a piece of string, the lens were so worn they were like frosted glass."

"You're making this up, aren't you?" I say.

"Did all this really happen?" his wife isn't asleep and calls out from the bedroom.

"If I were making it up I wouldn't be able to make it up better than you, you're a novelist."

"He's the real storyteller," I call out to his wife, looking in the direction of the bedroom. "He's a brilliant storyteller, in the old days no-one could outdo him at storytelling. Whenever he started telling a story he had everyone listening. Unfortunately, the only story he has written was executed before it was published." I can't help feeling somewhat sorry for him.

"He's only talking like this because you're here. Usually he never says a sentence more than he has to," his wife says.

"Stick to listening," he says to his wife.

"Go on with the story!" He's really got me interested.

He takes a drink and is refreshed.

"They went up to him, took off his glasses, prodded him with their rifles and questioned him harshly. If you're human, why are you running? He was shaking all over and making incomprehensible noises. One of the fellows pressed a rifle at him and threatened, if you keep putting on this act I'll shoot you! At this he started crying and said he had escaped from a labour camp and was too afraid to go back. We asked, what crime did you commit? He said he was a rightist element. Our man asked, what year was the rightist element campaign? The decision changing all that was long ago, why didn't you go back? He said his family was too afraid to take him back so he hid on this mountain. We asked where his home was and he said Shanghai. The men said, your family are all fucking fools, why didn't they take you in? He said they were afraid of getting implicated. The men said, like hell they'd get implicated, rightist elements have all received compensations plus big salary back payments. Everyone is just wishing for a rightist element in the family. They also asked, are you suffering from some sort of mental illness? He said he didn't have any illness, except for severe shortsightedness. The men in the team thought it was all too hilarious."

We can hear his wife laughing in the bedroom.

"It's you who's a devil, only you could tell this sort of a story." I also can't help laughing. It has been a long time since I've been so happy.

"He was labelled a rightist in 1957 and in 1958 was sent to a labour reform farm in Qinghai. During the famine of 1960 there was nothing to eat and he became bloated with beri-beri and almost died. He escaped to Shanghai and hid at home for two months to recuperate. His family insisted that he return because at the time grain rations weren't enough to feed the family and what was more, how could they possibly hide him at home for such a long time. It was then that he was forced to flee into the mountains, some twenty years ago. We asked him how he had survived all these years. He said in the first year a family in the mountains took him in and he helped them by chopping wood and doing some farm work. Afterwards the commune below heard rumours about him and wanted to investigate his background. He then escaped to this big mountain and relied on the family to secretly bring him some food, matches and a bit of oil and salt. We asked how he came to be branded a rightist. He said he was doing research on the oracle scripts on tortoise shells and animal bones, at the time he was young and hot-blooded and said a few crazy things about the authorities at a meeting. Everyone said come with us and go back to doing research on your oracle scripts. He stubbornly refused and said he had to harvest the corn because it was his grain supply for the year. He was afraid if he went, it would be trampled by wild pigs. We uproariously said, let them shit on it! He said he had to fetch his clothes. We asked him where they were. He said in a cave under the cliff. If it wasn't too cold he usually begrudged wearing them. Someone gave him a shirt and got him to tie it around his waist, then we took him back with us to camp."

"Is that the end?"

"Yes," he says. "I've thought of another conclusion but I'm not too sure about it."

"Try telling it then."

"A day later, after having plenty to eat and drink, he woke from a deep sleep and suddenly started to bawl loudly. We couldn't work out what was wrong and went to ask him. Tears and mucus were streaming down his face and he blubbered for a long time, before blurting: 'If I'd known there were so many good people in the world I wouldn't have endured so many years of unjust punishment!'"

I feel like laughing but can't.

There is a wily glint behind his glasses.

"The conclusion is superfluous," I say after some thought.

"I deliberately tacked it on," he admits, taking off his glasses and putting them on the table.

I discover that his far-sighted eyes are not so much wily as miserable and that he is completely different from the perpetually jovial good-natured person he is with his glasses on. I have never seen him like this before.

"Do you want to lie down for a while?" he asks.

"It's all right, I wouldn't be able to sleep anyway," I say.

Outside the window, dawn is breaking. The summer heat has completely subsided and a cool, gentle breeze is coming in.

"We can chat lying down," he says.

He sets up a bamboo-slat bed for me, takes a canvas deck chair for himself, puts out the light, and lies back in the deck chair.

"I must tell you that at the time I was investigated by this very group which captured the Wild Man. They almost shot me – their bullets whizzed past my head and it was sheer luck that I wasn't accidentally killed. When things don't concern oneself, everyone is a good fellow."

"This is what is special with your story about the Wild Man, people enjoy listening to it. People are cruel and there's no need for you to try to explain it."

"You're talking about fiction, I'm talking about life. It seems that I wouldn't be able to write fiction."

"As soon as there's talk of lice, everyone starts catching them, afraid that they themselves are lice. So what can you do?"

"What if people don't try to catch them?"

"Then they'll be afraid of being caught."

"Didn't you refuse to catch them?"

"So I was caught."

"And so the wheels roll on like this."

"I guess there must have been some progress, otherwise would I have dared to come to look you up for a drink? I would have gone off long ago to become a Wild Man."

"And I wouldn't have been able to take you in either. Otherwise, maybe we two good friends would have gone off together to be Wild Men." He laughs so much that he has sat up. "It's better without the conclusion," he says on reflection.

62

You say he's lost the key.

She says she understands.

You say he clearly sees the key on the table then when he turns around it is no longer there.

She says, yes, yes.

You say, it is a plain key, a key without a key ring. It used to have a key ring with a curly-haired red plastic Pekinese dog on a chain, but before that it didn't have a key ring. That was a present from a friend of his, of course a girl friend but not a girlfriend.

She says she understands.

You say, afterwards the dog broke. It was quite funny, it broke at the neck so that there was only the little red head of the dog. He thought it was cruel so he took the key off the key ring.

I understand, she says.

You say it is just a plain key. He seems to think he put it on the lamp stand on the table, together with some drawing pins. The drawing pins are there but the key has vanished. He shifts the books from one end of the table to the other. There are a few letters waiting to be answered but he hasn't worked out how to answer them. There is also an envelope over the switch. You say he just can't see the key.

It's often like that she says.

He has to go out for an appointment but can't leave the door unlocked. And if he locks the door and doesn't have the key he won't be able to get back in. He has to find the key. Books, paper, letters, a bit of money, a few coins are on the table. It is easy to see a key amongst coins.

Yes.

But the key isn't there. He crawls under the table and sweeps out quite a bit of dusty fluff with a broom, there's even a bus ticket. If the key had fallen onto the floor it would have made a noise. There are some books on the floor and he goes through them and restacks them. Books and keys are quite different and aren't easily confused.

Of course not.

The key has vanished just like that.

What about the drawer?

He goes through that. He seems to recall opening the drawer. He used to have a habit of putting the key in the right-hand corner of the drawer but stopped doing that a long time ago. The drawer is full of letters, manuscripts, bicycle licence plates, medical cards, gas supply cards, and all sorts of bills. There are also some commemorative badges, a gold pen box, a Mongolian knife and a small cloisonn sword. None of these are worth anything but it's a pity to throw them out because they hold a few memories.

Everyone has memories they treasure.

Not all memories are worth treasuring.

Yes.

Losing them is a form of liberation. There are also buttons which have come off and aren't likely ever to be used again. The shirt this ink-blue perspex button came off was used for a mop a long time ago but the button is still there.

Yes, and then?

Afterwards he pulls out the drawer and takes everything out.

So it can't be there.

He knows quite well it can't be there but he still goes through it.

It's like that. Does he go through his pockets?

He goes through all of them. He goes through his front and back trouser pockets at least five or six times, and also through the pocket of the shirt on the bed. He goes through the pockets of every item of clothing he has out, the only things he doesn't touch are the things in the suitcase.

Then—

Then he moves everything from the table onto the floor, re-stacks the magazines on the bedhead, opens the bookcase, and even shakes the bedding, the mattress, and looks under the bed, oh, and in his shoes! Once a five cent coin dropped into a shoe. He put on the shoes, went out, and only noticed when it started hurting his foot.

Doesn't he have his shoes on?

He had them on to start with but after shifting everything from the table to the floor, there is nowhere to put his feet. He can't tread on the books with his shoes so he takes them off and kneels on the books to search through them.

Poor thing.

This plain key without a key ring is buried somewhere in the room. He can't go out and, looking at the abyssmal mess in the room, is at his wit's end. Ten minutes earlier his life was orderly. This is not to say that the room was particularly clean and neat, the room has never been all that clean and neat but it always looked good. His life had its own order and he knew where everything was, he lived quite comfortably in this room. In any case he was used to it and because he was used to it, it was comfortable.

Right.

It was not all right, everything is in the wrong place, everything is wrong!

Don't panic, now think carefully.

He says he is sick of it all. There is nowhere to sleep, nowhere to sit, nowhere even to stand. His life has turned into a heap of rubbish. He can only squat there on the piles of books. He can't help being angry but can only be angry with himself. He can't blame anyone, it is he who has lost his key and got himself into this predicament. It's impossible for him to escape this mess, his messed up life, he can't go out, but he has to go out!

Right.

He doesn't want to see or even to return to the room again.

Doesn't he have an apppointment?

An appointment, that's right, he does have to go out but he's already an hour late, he's missed the appointment. No-one would foolishly wait for an hour and he can't remember where the appointment is or who it is with.

It's an appointment with a girl friend, she says softly.

Maybe, maybe it is. He says he really can't remember, but he has to go out, he can't put up with the mess any longer.

Without locking the door?

He's got no choice but to go out and leave the door unlocked and he goes down the stairs and out onto the street. People are coming and going as usual and there's an endless stream of traffic, it's always busy like this but he can't work out why. No-one knows he has lost his key, no-one knows he has left his door unlocked so of course no-one will go in and take his things. Anyone who comes would be at least someone he knows if not a friend. When they see there isn't anywhere to put a foot, they will either sit on the books and browse through them while waiting for him or if they can't wait they will leave, and there's really no need for him to worry about it. However he can't help worrying about this room of his which isn't worth robbing. There are only some books and some very ordinary clothes and shoes – his best pair of shoes are on his feet – but other than that there are only those unfinished manuscripts which he already hates. At this point he starts feeling happy, there's no need to worry about his room or the damn key, and he just wanders aimlessly around the streets. Usually he's always busy rushing about either for some matter or for some person or else for himself but right now he's not doing anything for any purpose and he's never been so happy. Normally it's hard for him to slow his pace but this time he manages; he puts out his left leg there's no hurry to lift his right leg, but this is quite hard. He's forgotten how to walk slowly, how to stroll. He begins to stroll, his entire sole coming in contact with the ground and his whole body and mind relaxing.

He feels odd walking like this and people passing by all seem to be looking at him, thinking he's odd. He surreptitiously observes some of them and discovers that those many pairs of eyes looking straight ahead are actually focused upon themselves. Sometimes they look in shop windows but when they do their minds are working out whether these are good prices. He suddenly realizes that on this street full of people it's only he who is looking at people and no-one is taking any notice of him. He also discovers that it's only he who is walking like a bear with the whole of his foot. The others are all walking with their heels striking the ground and, day after day and year in year out, jarring their bodies, and, making themselves tense, anxious and stressed.

Yes.

As he goes along this busy street he feels more and more lonely and begins to sway as if he were sleepwalking. In the interminable noise of the traffic, in the glare of gaudy neon lights, he is squashed in the thronging crowds on the pavement. He wants to slow his pace but can't and is all the time being knocked and jostled by the people behind. If you look at him from an upstairs window over the street, he looks just like a discarded cork swirling helplessly as it floats down the gutter after the rain, together with dry leaves, cigarette packs, ice-cream wrappers, used take-away plastic plates and the paper wrappings from all sorts of snacks.

I can see it.

What?

The cork floating in the thronging crowd of people.

It's him.

It's you.

It isn't me it's a state of being.

I know. Go on with what you were saying.

What about?

About the cork.

It's a discarded cork.

Who threw it away?

He had thrown himself away. He tries to remember but can't. He struggles to remember, he struggles to recall the relationships he has had with other people, why he has come to this street. It's clearly a street he knows well, this big, ugly, grey department store. The building is all the time being extended and all the time being made higher, it's always thought to be too small. It's only the little tea shop across the street that hasn't ever been renovated, it still has an old-style upstairs room. A bit further on is a shoe shop and opposite that is a stationery shop and a bank, he has been into all of these. He seems to have had dealings with the bank, made deposits or withdrawals, but that was a long time ago. He seems also to have had a wife but then they separated, he no longer thinks about her, nor does he want to.

But he once loved her.

It seems that he once loved her but it's all very hazy. In any case he feels there has been a relationship with a woman.

And not just with one woman.

That seems to be the case. There must have been some good things in his life but they seem to be very remote and only a few pale impressions remain. They are like negatives where there wasn't enough light and no matter how long you soak them in fixer, there are still only faint outlines.

But there must also have been a woman who deeply moved him, who left some details worth remembering.

He only remembers she had a small mouth with clearly defined lips and that she blushed when she said no. And when she said no, her body was yielding.

And?

She asked him to turn off the light, she said she was afraid of the light ...

She didn't.

She did.

All right, forget about whether or not she said it, next comes whether or not he finds the key.

He then remembers the appointment he has to go to, in fact he doesn't have to go to it. When they meet they only talk about trivialities, then go on to talk about people they know – who's going through a divorce, who's with who, and what new books, new plays and new movies are on. The next time they meet, these new books, new plays and new movies will be old and be of no interest anyway. They also talk about a speech some important official has given, the content is stale and obsolete and has been recycled many times over the years. He goes simply because he can't bear the loneliness, after that he still has to return to that chaotic room of his.

Isn't the door unlocked?

Yes, he pushes open the door and stops in front of all the books on the floor. There next to the wall at the side of the desk is the key without the key ring. It is blocked from view by a letter waiting to be answered propped against the lamp stand. However when he walks over the piles of books right into the room it can no longer be seen.

63

I had planned to go to Dragon Tiger Mountain to visit Profound Sky, the famous Daoist, but when the train stops at Guiqi I don't get off straightaway. People are sitting on the floor in the passageway of the hot and stuffy carriage and I will have to pick my way through, stepping over legs, and it will take several minutes just to get to the end of the carriage by which time I will be soaked in sweat. Right now I am lucky to be sitting in the middle section, at a window seat on the left, and there is a cup of strong tea on the little table in front of me. While I am procrastinating, the carriage shudders and the train slowly leaves the station.

Then there is the rythmic sound of shaking, and the lid on my cup begins to gently rattle. A breeze blows in my face, so it's quite cool. I want to have a nap but can't fall asleep. This east-west train is always overloaded, day or night. Whichever little station it is, people are always squeezing on or off and there are always large numbers of people in a desperate hurry for some unknown reason. The words of Li Bai's poem could be changed to: "Getting out of doors is hard, harder than ascending the blue sky." It is only in the few carriages with soft sleeping berths that the pleasures of travel are enjoyed, but only by foreigners with their foreign currency and by leadership cadres above a cerain rank with their public expense accounts. I must calculate how much more time I can last on the bit of money I have at my disposal. My savings were used up long ago and I am living off a loan. A kind-hearted editor of a publishing house paid me several hundred *yuan* as advance royalty for the manuscript of a book he might not be able to publish for many years. I don't know yet if I will be able to write the book but I have already spent more than half of the royalty. It is a debt of friendship, but who can tell what will happen in a few years time? In any case, I must try hard not to stay at inns anymore and to seek lodgings which cost nothing or else very little. However, I have already missed the chance of getting off at Guiqi, where a girl promised I could stay in her home.

It is while waiting for a boat on a wharf that I meet her – two little plaits, vivacious, a ruddy complexion, intelligent eyes. I can see she is full of fresh curiosity about this chaotic world. I ask where she is going and she tells me she is going to Yellow Rock. I say that under the dusty sky of that place there is nothing but black smoke belching out of the steelwork chimney stacks. What fun will you have there? She says she is visiting her aunt and asks me the same question. I say wherever I happen to go, I don't have a specific destination. Her eyes open wide and she goes on to ask what work I do. I say I'm a speculator and profiteer. She bursts out laughing and says she doesn't believe me.

"Do I look like a trickster?" I ask her.

She shakes her head to refute this suggestion, "Not even a bit."

"What do you think I look like?"

"I don't know," she says, "but definitely not a trickster."

"In that case, I'm a wanderer."

"Wanderers aren't bad people," she says with conviction.

"Most wanderers are actually good people." I must affirm her conviction. "People who look very proper are often tricksters."

She can't stop laughing, it's as if she's being tickled, she's a very happy girl. She says she also wants to wander everywhere but her parents won't let her, they'll only let her visit her aunt. They also say that as soon as she finishes school she has to start working. This is her last summer vacation and she has to make the most of it. I commiserate with her and she sighs and says, "Actually, I really want to go and have a look at Beijing but I don't know anyone there. My parents won't let me go on my own. Were you born in Beijing?"

"I've got a Beijing accent but that doesn't mean I was born there; I live in Beijing and the people in that city have suffocating existences," I say.

"Why?!" She is startled.

"There are too many people, it's so crowded it drives people to distraction, if you're off guard for a moment, someone will tread on your heels."

She pouts.

"Where do you live?" I ask.

"Guiqi."

"Does it have a Dragon Tiger Mountain?"

"It's just a desolate mountain, the temple was destroyed long ago."

I say I am looking for this sort of desolate mountain, the more people don't want to go to a place, the more I want to go to it.

"Are such places good for cheating people?" She has a cheeky look.

I can't help smiling as I say, "I want to become a Daoist."

"There's no-one to take you in, the Daoists who used to be there have either run off or have died. If you go there you'll have nowhere to stay, but the scenery is quite wonderful. It's just twenty *li* from the county town and you can walk there, I've been there on excursions with my schoolmates. If you really want to go, you can stay at my place, my parents like having guests." She is quite earnest.

"But don't you have to go to Yellow Rock? They don't know me."

"I'll be there in ten days. Aren't you going to be wandering about anyway?" As she says this the boat arrives.

Outside the window of the train, clusters of grey-brown mountain ranges rise straight up from the plains. That's Dragon Tiger Mountain at the back so this range must be Immortal Cliffs. In the course of my travels, through a chain of introductions I visited a museum director who showed me photographs of Immortal Cliffs. Hanging coffins have been found in many of the caves on the cliffs along the river, a burial site for the ancient Yue people of the Warring States period. While they were putting these in order, they also found a black lacquered wooden box-drum as well as a two-metre wooden zither which, from the holes, they ascertained had thirteen strings. If I went there now, I wouldn't be able to hear the beat of the fishing drums nor the pure, intense notes of the zither.

The Immortal Cliffs slowly recedes into the distance, growing smaller and smaller until they finally vanish. When we parted after getting off the boat we gave one another our names and addresses.

I drink some tea and experience a moment of bitter regret. Maybe she will one day look me up, maybe not. However this chance meeting leaves me with a pleasant feeling. I would not pursue such an innocent young girl, perhaps I will also never truly love a woman. Love is too burdensome, I need to live my life unburdened. I want to find happiness but I don't want to take on responsibilities. Marriage always follows and then the tiresome anxieties and resentment. I have become too indifferent and no-one can make my blood surge with passion anymore. I suppose I'm getting old and there's only a bit left of what can barely count as curiosity, and there is a lack of desire to bring about an outcome. The outcome isn't hard to imagine and would end up being burdensome. I would rather drift here and there without leaving traces. There are so many people in this big wide world and so many places to visit but there is nowhere for me to put down roots, to have a small refuge, to live a simple life. I always encounter the same sort of neighbours, say the same sort of things, good morning or hello, and once again am embroiled in endless daily trivia. Even before this becomes solidly entrenched, I will already have tired of it all. I know there is no cure for me.

I meet a young Daoist nun with delicate fair skin and a beautiful face. The graceful person beneath the loose Daoist robe exudes dignity and freshness. She installs me in the guest room in the temple hall in the side courtyard off the main hall. The unvarnished floorboards which clearly show the grain and colour of the timber are spotlessly clean and the bedding smells as if it has just been washed and starched. I am staying in the Palace of Supreme Purity.

Each morning the nun brings hot water in a washbasin for me to wash my face, then makes tea and stays to chat for a while. Her voice rings with a clear purity like the first picking of the green tea that I am drinking and she talks and laughs in an open manner. She says she finished high school and voluntarily took the examinations to become a Daoist nun, but I don't ask why she made this decision.

They enlisted ten other young men and women along with her and all have at least primary school education. The head Daoist is a master. He is over eighty but has a clear voice and walks with a spritely stride. He doesn't shirk hard work and it was only after spending several years liaising with the local government and various levels of the establishment, then convening a meeting with the few old Daoists on the mountain, that he was able to re-establish the Palace of Supreme Purity on Qingcheng Mountain. Both the old and the young chat freely with me and, to use her words, everyone likes you. She says everyone, but doesn't say she herself.

She says you can stay as long as you like, Zhang Daqian the painter lived here for many years. I saw a portrait of Zhang Daqian's father engraved on stone in the temple of the three legendary rulers – Fuxi, Shennong and the Yellow Emperor – situated alongside the Palace of Supreme Purity. Afterwards I also learn that Fan Changsheng of the Jin Dynasty and Du Tingguang of the Tang Dynasty lived here as recluses in order to write. I am not a recluse and still want to eat from the stoves of human society. I can't say that I am staying because of the charming spontaneity of her movements and her unaffected gracefulness, I am simply saying that I like the tranquillity here.

My room leads out onto the temple hall with its ancient colours and ancient smells. Inside is a long table made of nanmu hardwood and some square chairs with armrests and small low tables. Calligraphy is hanging on the walls and the freizes of the horizontal central tablet and the pillars are early wood carvings which have luckily been preserved. She says you can do some reading and writing here and when you get tired you can go for a stroll in the courtyard at the back of the hall. Ancient cypresses and ink-green indigo plants grow in the square courtyard and the artificial stone mountains in the pond are completely covered in thick green moss. Early in the morning and at night the talk and laughter of the nuns can be heard coming through the carved lattice windows. Here, the oppressive and prohibitive harshness of the Buddhist monasteries doesn't exist. Instead there is tranquillity and fragrance.

After dusk when the few tourists have all gone, I like the solitude and austerity of the lower courtyard of the Palace of Three Purities. I sit alone on the stone threshold at the centre of the palace gate and look at the big rooster of inlaid ceramic tiles directly in front of me. The four round pillars in the centre of the palace hall are each inscribed with couplets. The outer couplet is:

> The Way gives birth to one, one gives birth to two, two gives birth to three, three gives birth to the myriad things

> Man follows earth, earth follows heaven, heaven follows the Way, the Way follows Nature

This is the source of what I had heard from the old botanist in the primitive forest. The inner couplet is:

> Invisible and inaudible, mystical indeed is its imperceptibility, joining the trinity of jade purity, superior purity and supreme purity

> Know its workings, observe its profundity, pure indeed is its tranquillity, forming the principle of the Way of heaven, the Way of earth and the Way of man

The old head Daoist tells me about the two couplets. "The Way is both the source and the law of the myriad things, when there is mutual respect of both subject and object there is oneness. This source gives birth to existence from non-existence, and to non-existence from existence. The union of the two is innate and with the union of heaven and man there is the attainment of unity in one's view of the cosmos and of human life. For Daoists, purity is the principle, non-action the essence and spontaneity the application; it is a life of truth and a life requiring absence of self. To put it simply, this is the general meaning of Daoism."

As he is expounding the Way to me, the young disciples, men and women, crowd around to listen and sit all huddled together. One of the young nuns even puts her arm on the shoulders of one of the young men as she listens intently and wholeheartedly. I doubt that I would be able to attain this realm of purity where there is an absence of self and lust.

One evening after dinner the men and women, old and young alike, all come into the lower courtyard to see who can make the porcelain frog in the hall whistle by blowing into it. It is bigger than a dog and some get it to whistle while others don't. They amuse themselves doing this for quite some time and then disband to do their evening studies. I am left on my own and again sit on the stone threshold, looking at the temple rooftop with its intricate decorations of benevolent dragons, snakes, turtles and fish.

The flying eaves curling upwards are lines of pure simplicity and the majestic forests on the mountain behind soundlessly sway in the night breeze. Suddenly the myriad things turn silent and the sound of pure pipes can be heard, serene and flowing, then abruptly vanishing. Then, beyond the gates of the temple complex, the noisy surging of the river under the stone bridge and the soughing of the night wind all seem to be flowing from my heart.

64

The next time she comes, her hair is cropped short, and this time you
see her clearly.

"Why have you cut your hair?" you ask.

"I've cut off the past."

"Is that possible?"

"It had to be cut off even if it's impossible. For me it has been cut."

You laugh.

"What's funny?" She goes on to say softly, "I still feel some regret,
you know, all that wonderful hair."

"It looks good like this and it's less trouble. You don't have to blow
it off your face all the time, it's a nuisance having to blow at it."

It's her turn to laugh.

"Stop going on about my hair. How about talking about something
else?"

"What shall I talk about?"

"Talk about that key of yours. Didn't you lose it?"

"I've found it. Of course you can put it that way, but if it's lost it's
lost, if it's lost why look for it?"

"Once it's been cut off, it's been cut off."

"Are you talking about your hair? I was talking about my key."

"I was talking about memories. You and I are really a natural
couple," she says pursing her lips.

"But there's always that little difference."

"What do you mean 'that little difference'?"

"I wouldn't presume to say that you aren't as good as me, I am saying that we are always just passing by one another."

"Haven't I come?"

"You could suddenly just get up and leave."

"I could also stay and not leave."

"That of course would be wonderful." But, you feel awkward.

"You're all talk but you never do anything."

"Do what?"

"Make love, I know that's what you need."

"Make love?"

"A woman, you need a woman." She's quite blunt.

"Then what about you?" You stare into her eyes.

"It's the same, I need a man." Her eyes flash provocatively.

"I don't think one would be enough." You feel hesitant.

"Then let's say I need men." She is more direct than you.

"That's more like it." You relax.

"When a man and a woman are together—"

"The world no longer exists."

"And there is only lust," she adds.

"I surrender." You really mean this. "Then right now a man and a woman are together here—"

"Then let's do it," she says. "Draw the curtains."

"You still want to be in darkness."

"I can forget myself."

"Haven't you forgotten everything, why are you afraid of yourself?"

"You're such a wimp, you want to but don't dare. I'll have to help you."

She comes up to you and starts stroking your hair. You bury your head in her bosom and say softly, "I'll draw the curtains."

"No need."

She shakes herself, looks down and pulls down the zip of her jeans. You see a vortex in the firm white flesh at the edge of her floral underpants, you put your face to it and kiss her soft belly.

She stays your hand, saying, "Don't be so impatient."

"Will you manage by yourself?"

"Yes, won't it be more exciting?"

She pulls off her sweater and shakes her head from habit even though she doesn't need to with her short hair. She stands before you in a pool of clothing, exposing a mound of tangled black hairs lustrous like the hair on her head. She has removed everything but the bra enclosing her full breasts. She puts her arms behind her and frowning says resentfully, "Why can't you do even this?"

She has you in a state of shock and you don't immediately catch on.

"How about being a bit helpful!"

You get up right away, go behind her and undo it for her.

"Okay, now it's your turn," she says heaving a sigh of relief as she goes and sits in the chair facing you. Her eyes are riveted on you and there is a hint of derision on her lips.

"You're a demon!" You angrily throw down the clothes you take off.

"I am a goddess," she corrects you.

Stark naked she is majestic and unmoving as she waits for you to approach. Afterwards she closes her eyes, lets you kiss her all over. You mumble, trying to say something.

"Don't, don't say anything!"

She holds you in her embrace and you silently merge with her body.

Half an hour, maybe an hour later, she sits up in the bed and asks, "Do you have any coffee?"

"On the bookshelf."

She makes a big cup, and stirring it with a spoon comes and sits on the edge of the bed. She has a mouthful of the hot coffee as she looks at you and says, "Now, wasn't that good?"

You are at a loss for words. She is enjoying her coffee as if nothing has happened.

"You're a strange woman," you say, looking at the veins radiating outwards on her breasts.

"There's nothing strange about me, everything was very natural, you just need a woman's love."

"Don't talk to me about women and love, are you like this with everyone?"

"As long as I like the person and I'm in the mood."

Her diffidence infuriates you and you want to blurt out hurtful things, but only say, "You're wanton!"

"Isn't this what you yourself would like to be able to do? It's just that it's easier for women. If a woman can see through you, why shouldn't she enjoy herself? What else do you have to say?" She puts down the cup and turning her large brown nipples to you, says with a pitying expression, "You're really such a pitiful big child, don't you want to have another go?"

"Why not?"

You welcome her.

"You're satisfied now, aren't you?" she says.

You want to nod instead of replying, aware only of a comfortable weariness.

"Talk about something," she urges by your ear.

"What shall I talk about?"

"Anything."

"Not talk about the key?"

"Talk about anything you want to."

"It could be said that this key—"

"I'm listening."

"If it's lost then so be it."

"You've already said this."

"In any case he went out—"

"What happened when he was out?"

"People on the street were rushing about."

"Go on!"

"He was surprised."

"Why?"

"He couldn't understand why people were rushing about."

"The only thing they can do is to rush about like this."

"Surely there's no need for it?"

"If they were not busy doing something they would be anxious."

"That's right, they all had strange expressions on their faces and they were all preoccupied,"

"And they were all very solemn,"

"They solemnly went into shops and solemnly came out, solemnly carrying a pair of scuffs under their arms, and solemnly taking out some loose coins to solemnly buy an ice cream,"

"And solemnly licking at it,"

"Don't talk about ice cream,"

"It was you who started talking about it,"

"Don't interrupt, where did I get to?"

"You were talking about taking out a handful of loose coins and solemnly bargaining at the stall, solemnly, why still solemnly? What need is there for solemnity?"

"Pissing into a urinal,"

"And then?"

"The shops had all shut,"

"And people were all scurrying home,"

"He wasn't hurrying to go anywhere, he seemed to have somewhere to go, people usually call it home, to procure this room he had even argued with the caretaker,"

"Still he has a room,"

"But he can't find the key,"

"Wasn't the room unlocked?"

"The question is, did he have to go back?"

"Couldn't he have stayed the night just anywhere?"

"Like a drifter? Just drifting wherever he liked in the city at night, like a gust of wind,"

"Just jumped on a train and let it take him anywhere!"

"It had never occurred to him, one journey after another, whatever he felt like, getting off wherever he wanted,"

"To find someone, to passionately make love with!"

"To ravish until he was totally exhausted,"

"Even if it killed him it would have been worth it,"

"It was like that, the night wind was coming from all directions, he was standing in an empty square and he heard a rustling noise, he couldn't make out whether it was the wind or the sound of his heart, he suddenly felt he had discarded all responsibilities, had attained liberation, he was at last free, this freedom in fact came from himself, he could begin everything all over again, like a naked baby, thrown into the washbasin, kicking his little legs, crying without restraint to let the world hear his voice, he wanted to have a good cry to unleash the full extent of his emotions but discovered he only had the one physical body, it was empty inside and couldn't produce shouting, he stared at this physical body of his standing there on the deserted square not knowing where it wanted to go, he should greet it, pat it on the shoulder, joke with it, but he knew that if at this moment he were so much as to touch it, it would die of fright,"

"It's like sleepwalking, when the soul comes out of the orifices of the body,"

"It was then that he understood, his sufferings all came from this physical body,"

"You wanted to awaken him?"

"But you were afraid he wouldn't be able to cope. When you were little you heard the old people say it only took pouring a bucket of cold water on a sleepwalker to kill him, you hesitated and didn't dare to make a move, your hand was raised but you hesitated and in the end you didn't pat him on the shoulder,"

"Why didn't you gently awaken him?"

"You just followed behind that physical body of his, he seemed to want to go somewhere,"

"Did you still go back to that home of his? That room of his?"

"You can't say for sure, you just followed him, passed along a big street, went into a lane and came out at the other end, came back to a big street, went into another lane and emerged from it again,"

"And returned to the street you started off from!"

"Dawn is about to break,"

"Come do it again, once more . . ."

65

I have long tired of the struggles of the human world. In all the fine-sounding discussions, controversies and debates, I have invariably been made the topic, subjected to criticism, made to listen to instructions, made to wait for a verdict, and then waited in vain for some kindly divinity to intervene, to turn Heaven and Earth and get me out of my predicament. This divinity eventually emerged but wasn't sympathetic and just looked somewhere else.

Everyone wants to be my teacher, my leader, my judge, my good doctor, my adviser, my referee, my elder, my minister, my critic, my guide, my acknowledged leader. Whether I need it or not, people want to be my saviour, my hit man (that is to say my hit-my-hand man), my reborn parents (even though both my parents are dead), or else grandly represent my country for me when I myself don't know what is country or whether or not I have a country. Others invariably represent me. And my friends, those who argue for me, that is to say are willing to argue in my defence, have all been reduced to circumstances similar to my own. Such is my fate.

I can't play the tragic role of the defeated hero who fights against fate but I greatly revere those dauntless heroes who charge into danger and when badly injured will still fight on. I can only silently extend my respect and grief to them.

It is also impossible for me to be a recluse. For some reason, I hastily depart from the Palace of Supreme Purity. Is it because I can't endure the purity of non-being? Is it because I lost patience with reading the several thousand extant volumes of the Ming Dynasty edition of *Daoist*

Scriptures which escaped being burned through the pleading of some old Daoists and are stored in the Daoist Scripture Pavilion? Or is it because I can't be bothered with hearing any more of the sufferings of the lives of the old Daoists? And that I am also afraid of prying into the secrets locked in the heart of the young Daoist nun? Or is it because I don't want to destroy my own heart? It seems, in the end, I am just a connoisseur of beauty.

In Haiba, more than 4,000 metres into Tibet, I am warming myself by the fire in a road worker's stone hut blackened from smoke. Up ahead are huge ice-clad snowy mountains. A bus appears on the highway and a crowd of excited people get off, some have backpacks and some have little iron hammers, some also have specimen folders on their backs. They look like university students here to do practical work and, after poking their heads into the smoke-blackened hut with the windows shut tight, they go off. Only a girl with a red cotton umbrella comes in. Light snow is falling outside.

She thinks I'm a local roadworker and asks for a drink of water as soon as she enters. I use the iron ladle to scoop some from the sooty black pot sitting on the stone slabs around the fire and hand it to her. She takes it, starts drinking, and gives a yell. She's scalded herself. I can do nothing but apologize. She comes up to the light of the fire, looks at me, and says, "You're not a local, are you?" Her face, wrapped in a woollen scarf, is red with cold. Since coming onto this mountain I haven't seen a girl with such beautiful skin and I want to tease her.

"Don't you think mountain people know how to apologize?"

Her face goes a brighter red.

"Are you doing practical work here too?" she asks.

I can't say that I could even be her teacher, so I say, "I'm here taking photos."

"Are you a photographer?"

"I suppose so."

"We're here collecting specimens. The scenery is superb!" she exclaims.

"Yes, beyond words."

It does seem that I am just a connoisseur of beauty. On seeing such a pretty girl I can't help being affected and suggest, "May I take your photo?"

"Can I put up my umbrella?" she asks, twirling her red umbrella.

"This is black and white film." I don't tell her the film I'm using was cut and put together from a whole lot of reject movie stock I'd bought.

"It doesn't matter, artistic photographers all use black and white film." She seems to know a bit about it. She follows me outside. A large part of the sky is filled with fine swirling snow and she puts up her bright red umbrella to fend off the wind.

Although it is May and already spring, the snow on the mountain still hasn't completely thawed and in between the patches of white, little purple fritillary flowers are growing everywhere and occasionally there are squat bushes of dark red stonecrop. Beneath the bare cliff, a green velvety artemesia stretches out a furry stalk with a big yellow flower.

"How about here?" I say. The big snow-covered mountain in the background was clearly visible early in the morning but right now the fine snow has turned it into a faint grey shadow.

"Does this look all right?" She poses and tilts her head but the mountain wind is quite strong and she can't hold the umbrella steady.

She looks even better struggling to hold up the umbrella against the wind.

Further ahead is a trickling creek with a thin crust of ice flanked by big yellow alpine buttercups.

"Go over there!" I yell, pointing to the creek.

She struggles with her umbrella in the wind as she runs and I zoom in with my lens. She is panting, the fine snow has turned to misty rain and her scarf and hair sparkle with drops of water. I signal to her.

"Have you finished?" she calls out against the wind. Drops of water sparkle on her eyelashes and she looks even better. Unfortunately, I've already come to the end of my film.

"Can you send me the photo?" she asks hopefully.

"If you leave me an address."

As my bus is about to leave, she runs up and hands me through the window a page torn out of her notebook with her name and a number of some street in Chengdu written on it. She says I am welcome to come, and waves goodbye.

Later, when I return to Chengdu, I pass by this old street. I remember the number of her house and go past the front of it but don't go in. I don't send her the photo afterwards either. After developing my big pile of film, apart from the few I really need, I don't print most of it. I don't know whether or not one day I'll have all this film made into prints, nor do I know whether she will look as stunningly beautiful in the photo.

On Huanggang Mountain, which is the main mountain of the Wuyi Range, I manage to photograph a splendid deciduous pine growing in the belt of conifers in the lower section of the sub-alpine grassy marshland adjoining the peak. Halfway up the trunk it suddenly divides into two almost horizontal branches. It is like a giant falcon flapping its wings ready to take off and the part right between the two wings is exactly like the head and beak looking down.

Nature creates, in this mystical way, not only powerful vitality such as this but also exquisite, ever-changing feminine beauty. It also creates evil. It is also in the Wuyi Mountains, on the south side of the mountain reserve, that I see a huge decaying torreya. The core of the tree is hollow and could be a nest for a python, but on the sparse branches growing out at an angle from the iron-like black bark, small dark green leaves tremble. At sunset, the valley is plunged into shadows and above a sea of fine gentle bamboos burnished green and orange by the setting sun, this ancient tree suddenly looms up, its decaying black branches wilfully outstretched like a malevolent demon. This photo I do develop and print and whenever I look at it, it chills my heart and I can't look at it for long. I realize that it brings to the surface the dark aspect in the depths of my soul, which terrifies even me. I can only recoil when confronted by beauty or evil.

413

It is on Wudang Mountain that I see possibly the last Daoist of the Pure Unity Sect. He is the embodiment of this sort of evil. I heard about him on the way up the mountain at a place I made my camp site. An old Daoist nun has made her home in a ramshackle hut outside the wall of the Courtyard of Steles of the sacked Ming Imperial Palace. I ask her about this famous Daoist mountain in those better times of long ago and she starts to talk about the main school of Daoism. She says there is only one old Daoist of the Pure Unity Sect alive. He is over eighty and has never come down the mountain, preferring to stay all year round keeping guard at the Gold Top. No-one dares to provoke him.

I rush to catch the first bus early in the morning to South Cliff, then make my way on foot up the mountain track to the Gold Top. Already past noon, it is overcast and bleak on the mountain and there are no tourists about. I go right around the cold winding corridors and find that the doors are either bolted from the inside or have iron padlocks hanging on the outside. Only one thick and heavy door fitted with iron bars is slightly ajar. I push hard and finally get it open. An old man with dishevelled hair and bristling whiskers in a long gown, turns and stands up at the side of the brazier. He is large and tall and his dark ruddy face shows a violent streak. He barks ferociously, "What are you up to?"

"May I ask if you are the custodian of the Gold Top?" The tone of my voice is very polite.

"There is no custodian here!"

"I know the Daoist temple here hasn't yet resumed activities, but would you be the former head Daoist?"

"There is no head Daoist here!"

"Then may I ask if you, venerable elder, are a Daoist?"

"What if I am a Daoist?" His black eyebrows which have a sprinkling of white hairs also bristle.

"May I ask if you are a member of the Pure Unity Sect? I heard that it is only at the Gold Top that there is still–"

"I don't belong to any sect!"

Without letting me finish he opens the door and chases me out.

"I'm a journalist," I hasten to say. "The government is now implementing religious policies, I can help you get a report through."

"I don't know what a journalist is!" And with that slams the door shut.

At the time, I saw an old woman and a young woman sitting by the brazier, they were probably his family. I know that the Pure Unity Sect can marry and have children and even join with all sorts of men and women to practise sexual techniques. I can't help imagining the most wicked things about him. His eyes shone like bronze bells under his bushy eyebrows and his voice was gruff and booming. His whole presence was menacing and he was clearly an exponent of the martial arts: it is little wonder that for years no-one has dared to provoke him. Even if I knocked on the door again the outcome would not necessarily be any better, so following the narrow path with the iron hand rail I make my way up to the golden temple cast in yellow bronze.

The mountain wind impregnated with fine rain is howling. I come to the front of the temple where I encounter a middle-aged woman with big hands and feet. She has her hands clasped in prayer before the bronze temple. She is dressed like a peasant but her threatening stance is that of a drifter who has travelled around. I amble away and holding onto the iron railing threaded through stone posts pretend to be looking at the scenery. The wind howls and the dwarf pines growing from crevices in the cliff shake violently. Gusts of clouds and mist brush over the mountain path below, from time to time revealing the sea of dark forest there.

I look around. She is right behind me in the martial arts iron post stance, her eyes narrowed to slits and devoid of expression. They have their own closed world which I will never be able to enter. They have their own methods of survival and self-protection and roam beyond the fringes of what is known as society. However, I can only return to pass my existence in what people are accustomed to calling a normal life, there is no alternative for me, and probably this is my tragedy.

I make my way down the mountain path. A restaurant on a level part of the slope is still open but there are no tourists inside, just a few waiters in white jackets eating dinner around a table. I don't go in.

On the slope, a big iron bell taller than a person is lying in the dirt. I hit it with my hand but it is solidly stuck and doesn't ring. There must have been a temple here once but now as far as the eye can see there are only weeds trembling in the wind. I follow the slope down and before me is a steep rock path.

I can't stop myself and go faster and faster and within ten minutes I am in the secluded valley. On both sides of the rock steps the forest blocks out the sky, the sound of the wind is muffled and I can no longer feel the drizzling rain. Probably the rain is only in the clouds and mist on the mountain top. The forest becomes darker and darker, I don't know if I am in the dark forest I saw looking down through the mist and rain from the Gold Top, nor can I remember if I came along a path like this on my way up. I look back at the many steep rock steps I have come down: to climb back up to look for the way I came would be just too exhausting, so I keep going down.

Here the rock steps have deteriorated, unlike the path up which has had some repairs. I realize I have reached the dark side of the mountain and just let my legs carry me down: when people are about to die their souls probably rush unstoppably to Hell like this.

At first I hesitate and from time to time look back, but afterwards, beguiled by the sight of Hell, I no longer bother. The round tops of the stone posts along the gloomy mountain path look more and more like bald heads. Further down in the valley it is damper and the stone posts are all askew. They are badly eroded and look more like two rows of skulls on top of the posts. I fear that my impure thoughts about the old Daoist have incurred his curses and that he is using his magic on me to make me lose my way. Terror suddenly rises from the depths of my heart and I become confused.

Swirling mists and vapours spread around me. The forest becomes even darker and the damp stone slabs lying askew and the lurid grey-white stone posts are like skeletons. I make my way through the white bones, my feet disregarding my commands. Unable to stop myself I plunge headlong into the abyss of death, sweat oozing from my spine.

I must stop my feet and quickly get off this mountain path. Ignoring the brambles at a bend, I charge into the forest and by embracing the trunk of a tree, I finally come to a stop. My face and arms sting and hurt and probably it is blood that is running down my face. I look up and see a cow's eye on the trunk observing me. I look around. All around, far and near, the trunks of the trees all have huge eyes and all of them are looking at me, coldly.

I must calm down – this is just a forest of lacquer trees. It is only after the mountain folk tap them for raw lacquer and abandon them that they develop this nether world appearance. I could also say that this is simply hallucination induced by my inner fears, my soul in the darkness is spying on me, this multitude of eyes is simply me scrutinizing myself. I always have the feeling of being spied upon which makes me feel uneasy all over, in fact this is only my fear of myself.

When I return to the mountain path, fine rain is falling. The stone slabs are all wet, I no longer look and just blindly charge down.

66

The initial reactions of panic, terror, struggling and wild thrashing pass, then there is confusion. You are lost in an eerie, primeval forest, standing bewildered under a leafless tree which is dead, withered and waiting to topple. For a long time you loiter about this strange fish skeleton pointing at an angle into the grey misty sky, reluctant to leave the only signpost you recognize, even if it's just something in your hazy memory.

You refuse to be skewered to death on a fishbone like a fish out of water. Instead of wasting energy scouring your memories, why not discard this last thread to the familiar human world? Of course you will be more lost but you do still clearly have in your embrace a thread of life.

You find you are at the edge of the forest and the valley, and confronting you is yet another choice. Should you return to the endless forest or go to the bottom of the valley? On the cold dark mountain is a stretch of alpine grassland with the grey shapes of a few trees here and there, the black towering places would be bare cliffs. Somehow the churning foam of the river in the valley attracts you and without further thought, you stride towards it and run straight down to it.

You realize you will never return to the human world with its anxieties and warmth. Those distant memories are tiresome. You cannot stop yourself from giving a loud shout and charging towards this dark River of Forgetting. Running and yelling, roars of joy emerge from deep in your lungs and bowels like a wild animal. To start with you came fearlessly shouting and yelling into the world, then you were stifled by all sorts of customs, instructions, rituals and teachings. Now finally you have regained the joy of shouting with total freedom. Strangely, however, you can't hear your own voice. You are running with arms outstretched, shouting, panting, shouting again, running again, but still there is no sound.

You see the line of churning white foam but cannot distinguish the upper or lower part of the river which flickers then vanishes in the mist. You are weightless, relaxed, and experience a never before experienced freedom. You feel a slight trepidation but you don't know why you are afraid.

You seem to glide into the air, disintegrate, disperse, lose physical form, then serenely drift into the deep gloomy valley, like a thread of drifting gossamer. This thread of gossamer is you, in an unnamed space. All around is the stench of death, your lungs and bowels are chilled, your body icy cold.

You fall, scramble to your feet, howl, and start running again. The undergrowth gets thicker and it is harder going on. You plunge into bushes, keep pushing away branches and all this takes more energy than just charging down the mountain. You need to calm down.

You are utterly exhausted, come to a halt and pant, listening to the lapping of the water. You know you are close to the river-bank, and in the darkness can hear the greyish-white springs gurgling in the riverbed. The churned up beads of water shine like quicksilver. The sound of the water is not uniform, and listening carefully you hear countless droplets cascading down. You have never listened carefully to river water and as you listen you see its image glowing in the darkness.

You feel you are walking in the river, under your feet are river weeds. You are submerged in the River of Forgetting, in tangled river weeds, and you seem to be anxious. At this moment, however, the despair of not belonging vanishes and your feet simply feel their way along the riverbed. You tread on smooth pebbles and curl your toes tightly around them. It is like sleepwalking in the darkness of the River of Death, it is only where the spray is churned up that there is a dark blue glow tinged with beads of quicksilver. You can't help being amazed, and it is amazement tinged with joy.

Afterwards you hear heavy sighing. You think it is the river but gradually you make out that it is not one but several women who have drowned in the river. They are wretched, groaning, and their hair is bedraggled, and one by one they go past, their faces waxen and devoid of colour. There is a girl who killed herself by jumping into the river where the water gurgles in the holes at the roots of the trees, and her hair drifts with the flow of the current. The river threads through the dark forest which blocks out the sun and not a glimmer of sky is visible. The drowned, sighing women drift by but you do not think to rescue them, do not even think to rescue yourself.

You know you are wandering in the nether world, that life is not within your grasp. You are still breathing because of your bewilderment and life is suspended from one moment to the next of this bewilderment. If your feet slip, if the pebbles under your toes start rolling and in your next step you can't touch the bottom, you too will drown in the River of Death like the floating corpses, and you will sigh with them. It is as simple as that, so there is no need to be especially cautious and you just keep walking. Silent river, black dead water. The leaves of low-hanging branches sweep the surface and there are lines of currents, like bed sheets which were snatched off by the current as they were being washed in the river, or like the pelts of so many dead wolves.

There is not a great deal of difference between you and wolves, you have suffered many disasters and you were bitten to death by other wolves. There is no logic to it all and there is no greater equality than in the River of Forgetting – the resting place for humans and wolves is ultimately death.

This realization brings you joy, you are so happy you want to shout. You shout but there is no sound, the only sound is the gurgling of the water as it strikes the holes at the roots of the trees in the river.

Where do the holes come from? The watery region is vast and boundless but it is not very deep and there are no banks. There is a saying that the sea of suffering is boundless, you are drifting in this sea of suffering.

You see a long string of reflections and hear a choir singing a dirge as if it were a hymn. The dirge isn't sad but is happy. Life is joyous, death is joyous, it is nothing more than your memories. However, there are no choirs singing hymns amongst the images of your remote memories. Listening carefully, you find that the singing is coming from under the moss, thick soft undulating waves of moving moss which cover the earth. You lift it up to have a look and a squirming mass of maggots disperses. This disgusting sight fills you with wonder. You realize that these are maggots feeding off rotting corpses. Your body sooner or later too will be eaten up and this is not a particularly wonderful prospect.

67

I have been travelling for several days on this network of waterways with a couple of friends as my guides. We are doing whatever we feel like, walking several tens of *li*, going some distance by bus, taking a boat ride. It is by chance that we arrive in this town.

This new friend of mine is a lawyer and knows everything about the local conditions, customs, society and politics. He has his woman friend with him who speaks the gentle Suzhou dialect, and with the two of them as guides I am utterly relaxed touring these riverside towns. I, this drifter, am a celebrity in their eyes and they say that taking this trip with me gives them the chance to be carefree and happy. Each of them has family complications but, in the words of my lawyer friend, humans are basically free-flying birds so what harm is there in seeking some happiness?

He has only been a lawyer for two years. When this long-forgotten profession was resumed, he passed the entrance exams and quit his government job. He is determined to open his own legal office one day and claims that being in law is like being a writer. It is a profession with freedom. If one wants to defend someone one accepts the case so there is an element of choice. Unfortunately, at the moment he can't defend me but, he says, when the legal system is stronger and I want to take my case to court I can certainly get him to represent me. I say that my situation doesn't amount to a court case: no money is involved, I have neither damaged a hair on anyone's head nor anyone's reputation, there is no theft or fraud, no drug peddling, and no rape. There is no point going to court and if I did I couldn't win. He throws up his hands, he knows this and is just saying it anyway.

"Don't rashly say you'll do the impossible," his woman friend says.

He looks at her, winks, and turns to ask me, "Don't you think she's beautiful?"

"Don't listen to him, he has lots of girlfriends," she says.

"What's wrong with saying you're beautiful?"

She puts out her hand and pretends to hit him.

They pick a restaurant overlooking the street and treat me to dinner. It is ten o'clock at night when we finish. Four young men turn up, order a big bowl of liquor each and a spread of dishes and it looks as if they intend drinking deep into the night.

When we come downstairs, some of the shops and eateries on the street are still ablaze with lights and haven't closed, the bustle of former times has returned to this town. After a full day, at this moment what is urgent is finding a clean hostel, having a wash, brewing a pot of tea, letting the weariness disssipate, relaxing, and having a bit of a chat either sitting up or lying down.

On the first day we visited a few old communal villages with buildings dating back to the Ming Dynasty, inspecting old opera stages, looking for ancestral temples, taking photos of old memorial archways, reading old inscriptions, visiting old people. We also went inside a number of temples which had been restored or built with funds raised by the villagers and even had our fortunes told while we were there. We spent the night on the outskirts of a small village with a family in a newly-built house. The owner was an old retired soldier who welcomed us as lodgers and even cooked us a meal. He sat and told us about the heroic events which occurred during his participation in the work of bandit extermination, then told us stories about the bandits of earlier times in the area. Afterwards, when he saw that we were tired, he took us upstairs, which wasn't partitioned, spread out some fresh straw, brought in some bedding, and said if we wanted the lamp to be careful not to cause a fire. We didn't need the lamp and let him take it downstairs with him, then lay down in the dark. The two of them went on talking as I drifted off to sleep.

The next night, with the stars overhead, we arrived at a county town. We knocked on the door of a small inn and got them to open up. There was only an old man on duty and no other lodgers. The doors of several rooms were open and the three of us each chose one. This lawyer friend of mine came to my room to chat and his woman friend said she was scared of staying in the empty room by herself. She picked an empty bed and got under the covers to listen to him and me raving on.

He had a lot of astonishing tales and they weren't like the old soldier's tales which had gone stale and lost their bite. As a lawyer he had access to verbal and written testimonies of cases and had even come in contact with some of the criminals. He livened up the stories as he told them, especially the sex crime cases. His woman friend, curled up like a cat under the quilt, kept interrupting to ask whether it was all true.

"I've personally questioned a number of the criminals. The year before, there was a crackdown on hooligan offenders and one county arrested eight hundred of them. Most were sexually frustrated youths who didn't deserve to be sentenced and certainly only a very small minority deserved the death sentence. Nevertheless large numbers were executed each time as stipulated in the directives from higher up. Even some of the clearer-thinking cadres in the public security bureau felt bad about it."

"Did you defend them?" I asked.

He sat up and lit a cigarette.

"Tell the one about them dancing in the nude," his woman friend prompted him.

"There's this granary which used to belong to a production team on the outskirts of town. All the fields have now been divided up and the grain produced is stored in people's homes, so it was empty and unused. Every Saturday, as soon as it got dark, a big group of youths from the cities and towns would come on their bikes and motorbikes. They would bring along a record player and go inside to dance. They had people guarding the door and the local peasants weren't allowed in. The granary ventilators were very high so people couldn't see in from the outside. The villagers were curious and one night some of them brought a ladder and climbed up. It was pitch-black inside. They couldn't see a thing and could only hear music, so they reported it. The public security came out in force, raided the party and arrested over a hundred. They were all about twenty years of age, the sons and younger brothers of local cadres, young workers, petty merchants, shop assistants and unemployed youths. There were also a few adolescent boys and girls who were still at high school. Afterwards some were sentenced to prison and others to labour camps, quite a few were also executed."

"Were they really dancing in the nude?" she asked.

"Some of them were, most were indulging in minor sexual activities. Of course some inside were having sex. One girl barely twenty years old said she had been penetrated more than two hundred times. She was really wild."

"How did she manage to keep count?" It was still her asking.

"She said afterwards she became numb and simply counted. I have seen her and spoken with her."

"Didn't you ask her why she allowed this to happen?" I asked.

"She said at the beginning she was curious. Before going to the dance she had not had any sexual experiences but once the floodgates had opened there was no stopping. Those were her own words."

"That's quite true," she said from under the quilt.

"What did she look like?" I asked.

"To look at her, you wouldn't believe it, she was very ordinary. You would even think her face was rather homely, it was expressionless and had nothing wanton about it. Her head had been shaved and she was dressed in a prison uniform so you couldn't tell what sort of a figure she had. Anyway, she wasn't tall and she had a round face. And she didn't baulk at talking about anything. She talked about whatever you asked her without any emotion."

"Of course . . ." she said softly.

"Afterwards she was executed."

All three of us fell silent.

"What was her crime?" I asked after quite some time.

"Her crime?" he asked himself. "A hooligan who incited others to crime. She didn't go on her own but took other girls with her and of course these girls also ended up indulging in these activities."

"The point is whether she had lured others into engaging in illicit sexual activities or had been an accomplice in rape," I said.

"Strictly speaking, there was no rape. I saw the testimonies. However, as to her enticing others into engaging in illicit sexual activities, that's hard to say."

"Under those circumstances . . . it's all very hard to say for sure," she said.

"What about her motives? Not regarding herself, but for taking other girls along. What made her do this? Had someone asked her to do it or given her money to do it?"

"I asked her about this. She said she had only been intimate with men she knew and with whom she had eaten and had been drinking. She had never taken anyone's money. She had a job, it seems, in a pharmacy or was in charge of drugs in some clinic, she was educated . . ."

"This has nothing to do with education. She wasn't a prostitute, it was just that she had a psychological problem," she cut in.

"What psychological problem?" I turned to ask her.

"Why do you need to ask? You're a writer. She was dissolute and wanted women around her also to be dissolute."

"I still don't understand," I said.

"You understand perfectly well," she retorted. "Everyone has sexual feelings, only she was unlucky. She must have loved some person but couldn't have him. So she wanted revenge, first on herself . . ."

"Do you also want revenge?" the lawyer turned to ask her.

"If I got to that, I'd kill you first!"

"Are you as violent as that?" he asked.

"There's violence in everyone," I said.

426

"The question is whether it is a capital offence," the lawyer said. "In my view, in principle only murder, arson and drug peddling should be treated as capital offences because these cause the deaths of others."

"So you're saying rape is not a criminal offence?" she got up to ask.

"I'm not saying rape is not a criminal offence. However soliciting for illicit sexual activities isn't, because there are two consenting parties."

"So do you think that enticing young girls into illicit sexual activities is not an offence?"

"That depends on how you define a young girl, if it's an adolescent girl under eighteen years of age."

"Do you mean to say that girls under eighteen don't have sexual feelings?"

"Legally, there has to be a cut-off point."

"I'm not concerned with the law."

"But the law is concerned with you."

"Why is it concerned with me? I haven't committed any crimes, it's you men who are the criminals."

The lawyer and I burst out laughing.

"What are you laughing about?" She was targeting him.

"You're worse than the law, are you even concerned about my laughing?" he turned and asked her instead.

She was unfussed about being only in her underwear and, hands on her hips, she glowered as she asked him, "Then tell the truth, have you ever been with prostitutes? Speak up!"

"No."

"Tell the story about the hot soup noodles! Let him be the judge."

"What's there to tell, it was just a bowl of hot soup noodles."

"Heaven only knows!" she yelled.

"What happened?" I was naturally curious.

"Money isn't the only thing prostitutes want, they too are sensitive human beings."

"Say whether or not you treated her to hot soup noodles," she cut in.

"Yes, but I didn't sleep with her."

427

She scrunched up her lips.

He said it was a night when light rain was falling and there were very few people about. He saw a woman standing under a streetlight and went up to tease her. He didn't think she would really follow him to the dumpling and noodle stall under a big oil-cloth umbrella. She said she wanted to have a bowl of hot soup noodles. He kept her company and each of them had a bowl, that was all the money he had on him at the time. He said he didn't sleep with her but he knew she would have gone with him anywhere. He sat with her on some cement pipes for repairing gutters stacked on the side of the road and he put an arm around her as they chatted.

"Was she young and pretty?" she said giving me a wink.

"She was about twenty and had an upturned nose."

"And were you really so virtuous?"

"I was frightened she might have been unclean and had some disease."

"You men are just like that!" She angrily lay down.

He said he really felt sorry for the woman, her clothing was thin and wet through. It was raining and quite cold.

"I can believe all that. Apart from being violent, people also have something compassionate in them," I said. "Otherwise how would they be human?"

"This is all external to the law," he said, "but if according to the law having sexual urges is criminal then all human beings are guilty!"

At this she gave a soft sigh.

We leave the restaurant, walk halfway down the road and come to an arched stone bridge, but do not see any inns. There is only one dim light on the river-bank at one end of the bridge. After our eyes get used to the dark we discover there is a line of black canopy boats moored along the stone embankment.

Two women come across the stone bridge and walk past close to him and me.

"Look, those women are in that sort of work!" the lawyer's woman friend grabs my arm and says quietly.

I hadn't noticed and quickly turn, but only see the back of a head of well-combed shiny hair pinned back with a plastic floral clip of one of them, and the profile of the other who seems to be wearing makeup. Both women are short and fat.

My friend stares at them for a while and watches them slowly walking off into the distance.

"Their customers are mainly boat workers," he says.

"Can you be sure?" What's surprising is that nowadays it's quite open, even in a small town like this. I know they hang around some railway stations and wharves in the big cities.

"You can pick them out straightaway," his woman friend says. Women are born with sharper instincts.

"They've got a secret code, if you give the right signal there's a deal. They're from the nearby villages, out to make a bit of extra money at night," he says.

"They saw me here. If it were just the two of you they would have taken the initiative to come and chat."

"But they've got to have somewhere to go, do they go back with the women to the villages?" I ask.

"There's sure to be a boat nearby or they could go with the men to an inn."

"Do the inns openly engage in this sort of business?"

"They have arrangements. Haven't you come across this on your travels?"

I then remember a woman trying to get to Beijing to file a lawsuit. She said she didn't have the money for her train fare and I gave her one *yuan*, but I couldn't say for sure if she was one of these.

"Hey, you're supposed to be carrying out social surveys. All sorts of things are going on today."

I apologize for not being much good at carrying out social surveys, I'm incompetent. I'm just a stray dog poking around everywhere. They think I'm funny and laugh.

"Come with me, I'll show you a good time!"

He's got an idea again and yells towards the river into the dark, "Hey, are there any takers?"

He jumps off the paved embankment onto a black canopy boat.

"What for?" a muffled voice comes from under the canopy.

"Do you take the boat out at night?"

"Where to?"

"The wharf at Xiaodangyang." He's quick to give the name of a place.

"How much are you offering?" A middle-aged man says, emerging from under the canopy.

"How much do you want?"

They bargain.

"Twenty *yuan*."

"Ten."

"Eighteen."

"Ten."

"Fifteen."

"Ten."

"For ten *yuan*, this boat's not going." The man goes back under the canopy and we hear a woman speaking in a low voice.

We look at one another, shake our heads, and can't stop laughing.

"I can go to the wharf at Xiaodangyang," someone says from quite a few boats away.

My friend motions the two of us to be quiet and shouts out, "We'll go if it's ten *yuan*." He's having a lot of fun.

"Go over there and wait, I'll bring the boat over."

He can really bargain. The outline of someone in a jacket appears, plying a punt-pole.

"What do you think of that? We'll also save the cost of lodgings for the night. This is called drifting on a boat in the moonlight! Unfortunately there's no moon, but we can't be without something to drink."

He gets the boatman to wait. The three of us run back to a little street in town to buy a bottle of Daqu liquor, a bag of brine-soaked broad beans and two candles, and gleefully jump onto the boat.

The boatman is a wizened old man. We open the canopy flap, jump in, feel around in the dark and sit cross-legged on the planks. My friend goes to light the candles with his cigarette lighter.

"You can't light a fire on the boat," the old man says in a wheezing voice.

"Why?" I think maybe it's prohibited.

"You'll set fire to the canopy," the old man grumbles.

"Why would we want to set fire to your canopy?" the lawyer says. The wind keeps blowing out the flame of his lighter so he pulls the canopy flap tighter.

"Venerable elder, if we set fire to the canopy we'll pay you for it." His woman friend is even more cheerful squashed between him and me. We are all suddenly very lively.

"Don't light a fire!" The old man puts down his pole and comes in to stop us.

"Do as he says, it's even more fun going out on a boat in the dark," I say.

The lawyer opens the bottle, stretches out his legs, and puts the big bag of beans on the bamboo mat on the floor of the boat. I am sitting opposite him, feet to feet, and the bottle passes back and forth. She is leaning on him and from time to time takes the bottle from him to have a sip. In the calm bay of the river only the creaking of the punt-pole and the sound of the splashing water can be heard.

"That guy was at it for sure."

"He would have gone for an extra five *yuan*, it isn't very much."

"Just the price of a bowl of hot soup noodles!"

We are becoming mean.

"These rivers and lakes have been infested with opium and prostitution since ancient times, can they be effectively prohibited?" he says in the darkness. "The men and women here are all dissolute, can you slaughter them all? This is how the people spend their lives."

The dark night sky opens fleetingly to expose the brilliance of the stars, then darkens again. At the tail end of the boat is the continual creaking of the punt-pole and, from time to time, the soft lapping of the river. The cold wind seeps in through the tightly closed canopy flap at the front and even the used chemical fertilizer plastic bags which serve as curtains to keep out the wind and rain.

Weariness assails us and the three of us curl up in the middle of the narrow cabin of the boat. The lawyer and I, one at each end, push ourselves to the sides and she squeezes in between the two of us. Women are like this, they always need warmth.

I vaguely know there are cultivated fields up from the embankments on both sides and that in places where there are no embankments there are reed marshes. After passing a series of inlets the boat enters a waterway with such a dense growth of reeds that a person could be killed and the corpse disposed of without leaving a trace. Anyway it is three to one, even if one is a woman, and the other party is an old man. It is all right to completely relax and fall asleep. She has already turned to her side. My heels are touching her spine and her buttocks are pressed against my thighs but I am past caring.

October on the rivers and lakes is the season when things ripen. Everywhere, heaving breasts and bright flashing eyes are to be seen. Her body has an unaffected feminine sensuousness which seductively draws you to her and to want to caress her. Cuddled in his arms she must have sensed the warmth of my body and she puts an arm on my thigh as if to comfort me, though I can't tell if it is out of playfulness or kindness. Then I hear growling but on listening carefully it turns out to be a sort of groaning which is coming from the back of the boat. At first I want to complain but something compels me to listen. It is a mournful wail wafting on the chilly wind over the river into the still night air. It is the old man plying the punt-pole singing, he is totally engrossed and totally uninhibited. The sound isn't coming from his mouth but from deep down in his throat and chest, it is a wail of accumulated sadness being released. At first it is a jumble but afterwards I gradually make out some of the words, but they are fragmented, his Wu dialect has a strong village accent. What I hear seems to be saying, your seventeenth younger sister and eighteenth paternal aunt ... went away with a maternal uncle and had wretched existences ... drifting

... wandering ... with nothing ... became nuns ... good scenery ... I lose the thread and understand even less.

I pat them and ask softly, "Can you hear? What's he singing?"

Both move, they weren't asleep.

"Hey, old man, what are you singing?" The lawyer pulls up his legs to sit up and loudly directs his question outside the canopy.

There is the flapping of wings as a startled bird flies with a screech over the top of the canopy. I open the canopy a little and see the boat is travelling close to shore and the grey tangles growing along the ridges of the furrows on the embankment are probably bristle-pod beans. The old man has stopped singing and a chilly wind is blowing. I am fully awake and ask very politely, "Venerable elder, were you singing a folk song just now?"

The old man doesn't respond and just plies the punt-pole, and the boat moves ahead at an even speed.

"Take a break, come in to have a drink with us and sing something for all of us!" The lawyer also tries to win him over.

The old man remains silent and continues to punt.

"Relax, come on in for a drink and get warm. How about singing something for us and I'll give you another two *yuan*?" The lawyer's words, like rocks cast into water, fail to produce echoes. The old man may be embarrassed or cross, but the boat glides in the water to the accompaniment of the gurgling eddies as the pole enters the water and the lapping of the waves on the boat.

"Let's go to sleep," the lawyer's woman friend says gently.

We are all disappointed but all we can do is lie down. This time the three of us all sleep on our backs and the cabin seems even narrower. Our bodies are pressed closer together and I feel the warmth of her body. Either from lust or kindness, she grasps my hand. This is all that happens, there is a reluctance to further spoil the disturbed and mystical pulsations of this night. No sounds come from her or the lawyer. I sense a quiet tenseness building up in the soft body transmitting the warmth, and as the stifled excitement heightens the night resumes its mystical pulsations.

After a long while I vaguely hear the wailing again, the groans of a distorted soul, unrealizable desires, weary and laboured, in ashes fanned by the wind is a sudden spark then darkness again. There is only the warmth of her body and the rich reverberating sensations, her fingers and mine grip one another tightly at the same instant. Neither of us makes a sound, neither dares to further provoke the other, and with bated breath we listen to the howling tempest raging in our blood. Fragments of that hoary old voice sings of a woman's sweet-smelling breasts and the wonderful feel of a woman's legs but there isn't a complete sentence I can properly hear so I can't grasp the full meaning of the song. The singing is indistinct but it has life and texture, sentence is piled upon sentence, none exactly the same ... stamens of flowers and a blushing face ... don't fondle the stem of the lotus ... dazzling white skirt on a slender waist ... taste of the persimmon is a bitter taste ... waves with a thousand eyes ... roaming dragonflies skimming the water ... don't, oh don't entrust yourself to ...

He is clearly absorbed in his memories and is using all sorts of phrases to give them linguistic expression. The words don't necessarily have specific meanings but transmit direct perceptions to arouse sexual feelings which flow into the song, it seems both like wailing and lamenting. A long piece finally ends and she pinches my hand, then lets go. No-one moves.

The old man is coughing and the boat is heaving. I sit up and open the canopy a fraction. The surface of the river is infused with pale lights, the boat is passing a small town. On the shore the houses are huddled close to one another and under the streetlights the doors are all shut, there are no lights in the windows. The old man is coughing continuously and the boat is rocking badly. I can hear him urinating into the river.

68

You go on climbing mountains. As you near the peak and are feeling exhausted you always think it is the last time but when the exhilaration of reaching the peak subsides you feel the urge again. This feeling grows as your weariness vanishes and looking at the rising and falling lines of the peaks in the hazy distance your desire to climb mountains resurges. But once you climb a mountain you lose interest in it and invariably think the mountain beyond will have things you haven't encountered. When you eventually get to that peak the wonders you hoped for aren't there, and once again there is just the lonely mountain wind.

After some time you get used to this loneliness and climbing peaks becomes an obsession. You know you will find nothing but are driven by this blind thought and keep on climbing. However, while doing this you need to have some distraction and as you fabricate stories for yourself, images are born.

You say you see a cave at the bottom of the limestone cliffs. The entrance is almost completely sealed off by a pile of stone slabs. You think it is the home of Grandpa Stone and that living inside is the legendary figure talked about by the Qiang mountain folk.

You say he is sitting on a plank bed, the wood is rotted and crumbles at your touch and the rotten bits of wood in your hands are soggy. It is very damp inside and there is even water running by the plank bed set on rocks. There is also moss growing everwhere you put your feet.

He is leaning on the rock wall and when you enter he is looking right at you. His eyes have sunken deep into their sockets and he is emaciated like a piece of firewood. His rifle hangs above his head on a branch wedged into a crack and is within his reach. Oiled with bear fat which has turned to black grease, there is no rust on it.

"Why have you come here?" he asks.

"To see you, venerable elder." You assume a respectful demeanour, look frightened even. He doesn't have the childish petulance of senility and it seems that being respectful works. You know that if he were to get upset he could very well grab the rifle and shoot you, so it is important to show that you are afraid of him. Confronted by his cavernous eyes you do not dare to look up even a little lest you give the impression of coveting his rifle.

"Why have you come to visit me?"

You can't say why nor can you say what you want to do.

"No-one has visited me for a very long time," he drones, his voice seeming to come out of the emptiness. "Hasn't the plank road rotted away?"

You say you climbed up from the River of Death down in the gully.

"You've all forgotten me, I suppose."

"Not at all," you hasten to say, "the mountain folk all know about you, Grandpa Stone. They all talk about you when they've had something to drink but they don't have the courage to come and visit you."

It is not courage but curiosity that has brought you here. You came because you had heard about him but it is of course not appropriate to say this. Now that the legend has been verified and you have seen him, you still have to think of something else to say.

"How much further is it to Kunlun Mountain?"

Why do you ask about Kunlun Mountain? Kunlun Mountain is the mountain of our ancestors, the Queen Mother of the West lived there. Bricks with carved pictures of her with a tiger's face, human body, and leopard tail have been excavated from Han Dynasty tombs.

"Oh, go straight ahead and you'll come to Kunlun Mountain." He says this like someone saying go straight ahead and you'll come to the lavatory or to the movie theatre.

"How much further ahead?" You pluck up the courage to ask.

"Go straight ahead–"

While waiting for him to continue, you furtively look into his cavernous eyes. His sunken lips move a couple of times and then close again, but you can't decide whether he has spoken or is about to speak.

You want to flee but are afraid he will suddenly get angry, so you just look at him reverently, as if waiting to receive his instructions. But he gives no instructions or maybe there are no instructions to give. In this predicament you feel that the muscles on your face are very tense so you quietly draw in the corners of your lips, allow your cheeks to relax, then put on a smiling face. He doesn't react, so you move a leg and shift your weight. Your body lurches forward and you see close up into his sunken eye sockets: the eyeballs are blank, as if they are fake. Maybe he's a mummy. You have seen such undecomposed ancient corpses excavated from the Chu tombs at Jiangling and the Western Han tombs at Mawangdui. He must have died in a sitting position.

You move forward a step at a time, not daring to touch him in case he collapses, and reach out for the hunting rifle covered in grime and bear fat on the rock wall behind him. However, as soon as you grasp the barrel it crumbles as if it had been fried to a crisp. You immediately retreat, undecided as to whether you still want to go to see the place of the Queen Mother of the West.

Overhead there is an explosion of thunder, the Heavenly Court is angry! Heavenly soldiers and generals are pounding with the thigh bones of the Thunder Beast on huge drums made from the hides of walrus from the Eastern Ocean.

Nine thousand nine hundred and ninety-nine white bats shriek and fly about the cliff cave. The mountain divinities have all awoken, huge boulders roll from the mountain top in an avalanche and the cliff completely collapses. It is as if a thousand mounted soldiers are galloping up from the earth and the whole mountain turns to smoke and dust.

Oh, oh, suddenly nine suns appear in the sky! The five rib-bones in men and the seventeen nerves in women are struck and pulled and no-one can help screaming and groaning ...

Your soul flees through the orifices of your body and you see countless toads with their big mouths gaping at the sky. They are like a flock of headless tiny people with arms outstretched to the hoary sky, calling out in despair: Give my head back! Give my head back! Give my head back! Give back my head! Give back my head! Give back my head! My head give it back! My head give it back! My head give it back! Give me back my head! Give me back my head! My head give it back to me, my head give it back to me, give back my head to me, give back my head to me, to me give back my head, my head to me give back … give back to me my head, to me give back my head …

69

Startled from a dream by the sound of urgent bells and drums, for a moment I don't know where I am. It is pitch-black and only gradually do I make out a square window which seems to have a grille on it, though I can't be sure. I must find out if I am still dreaming and forcing my heavy eyelids to open, I manage to read the phosphorescent dial on my watch. It is exactly three o'clock in the morning. I realize morning prayers have started, then remember I am lodging in a temple. I quickly roll over and get out of bed.

I open the door and go into the courtyard. The drums have stopped and each peal of the bell is more distinct. The sky is grey against the shadows of the trees and the sound of the bell is coming from the direction of the Palace of Magnificent Treasures behind the high wall. I feel my way along the serpentine corridor to the door of the vegetarian hall but it is bolted on the other side. I turn and go back to the other end of the corridor, and groping about find there is a high brick wall all around and that I am locked like a prisoner in this courtyard. I shout a few times but no-one answers.

During the day I had begged to be allowed to stay in this Temple of National Purity. The monk who accepted my incense donation looked me over but was dubious about the sincerity of my devotion. But, I obstinately refused to leave and when the monastery gates were about to close, after seeking instructions from the old monk in charge, they installed me all on my own in this side room in the back section of the temple.

I refuse to be locked up and am intent on seeing if this big temple, whose incense burners have been burning for over a thousand years, still preserves the rituals and ceremonies of the Tiantai Sect. I do not believe I have transgressed the temple's rules of purity and I go back to the courtyard. I discover in one corner a sliver of weak light coming through a crack. I touch it. It turns out to be a small door which immediately opens. This is after all a Buddhist temple so there are no prohibited areas.

I go around the screen behind the door and enter a medium-sized sutra hall with a few candles burning and incense smoke curling into the air. In front of the incense table hangs a piece of purplish-red brocade embroidered with the four characters "incense burners very hot" which makes my heart jump. It seems foreboding. In order to demonstrate the purity of my heart and that I haven't come to spy on the secrets of the Buddhist world, I take a candle in a holder. There are ancient scrolls of calligraphy and painting on all the walls. I didn't imagine there would be such an elegant and secluded inner room within the temple, probably it is a place reserved for the Buddhist masters. Having come in uninvited, I can't help feeling a bit guilty and do not spend time seeing if they still have the works of the two eminent Tang monks collected by Han Shan. I return the candle and, following the sound of the bell for morning prayer, go out through the main door of the hall.

I enter another courtyard. The side rooms on all four sides are ablaze with candles and are probably the monks' dormitories. A monk in a black cassock brushes past and overtakes me. I give a start then think he is probably leading the way, so I trail behind him and pass through several corridors one after the other. Then in an instant he vanishes. I am a little perplexed and can only look for somewhere with some candlelight. Just as I am about to cross a threshold, I look up and see a four- or five-metre high guardian of the Buddha wielding a demon-subduing cudgel. He is charging right at me, his fierce eyes glaring, and I am bathed in cold sweat from fright.

I flee along the dark corridor and see a dim light. Nearing it I see a round doorway, and going through I realize it is the large courtyard below the Palace of Magnificent Treasures. The palace roof has flying eaves and two green dragons, one on each side, guarding a bright mirror in the centre. The dark blue of the night sky before dawn, showing through the towering old cypresses, looks extraordinary.

Behind the huge incense burner at the top of the stairs the sound of the giant bell pours out of the hall lit with a blaze of candles. The monk in the black cassock is striking this enormous bell with a big wooden pole suspended from the ceiling. It does not so much as quiver but, as if in response, from the ground beneath, the sound of the bell slowly ascends to the rafters and fills the hall – booming reverberations gush through the doorway, engulfing my body and mind in its sound waves.

Some monks light the red candles in front of the eighteen arhats lining the two sides and plant whole bunches of burning incense sticks into each of the burners. The monks surge into the hall, all wearing the same dark grey cassocks, serene figures slowly moving to their positions in front of the individual rush cushions, each of which is embroidered with a different lotus design.

Two resounding booms of the drum follow with tones so deep and penetrating that it makes a person's insides reverberate. The drum is located on the left of the hall and is mounted on a drum stand the height of a person. The round drum skin is a head higher than the monk standing on the platform of the ladder. The drummer, the only person not in a cassock, is wearing a short sleeveless jacket, trousers trussed at the calves and hemp shoes. His hands are raised high above his head.

Da-da

Boom! Boom! Another two times.

Da-da

As the lingering sounds of the bell vanish the drum takes over, shaking the ground underfoot. At first it is possible to make out the individual sounds as they reverberate from the heart of the drum but as the speed increases and the momentum builds up they become one continuous sound which makes the heart palpitate and the blood surge. The overpowering sound of the drum does not slacken, it is simply breathtaking. Then a slightly higher note with a slightly clearer beat drifts from the heart of the drum above the robust, long booming sound, creating interludes of even faster drum beats. Afterwards there emerge countless changing drum beats with high or low notes which mingle or harmonize with both the deafening booms and the faster interludes. All this is produced from the one drum!

The drummer is a thin, middle-aged monk without drum sticks. The back of his shiny head can be seen moving continuously between his bare arms as he slaps, punches, knocks, hits, jabs, pokes and kicks, making use of his palms, fingers, fists, elbows, wrists, knees and even toes. His body seems to be like a lizard sticking to the drum skin, and as if possessed he pounces and jumps at the drum, striking it everywhere from its centre to their sides encrusted with iron nails.

In this unbroken intense booming symphony, suddenly there is the tinkling of a bell so faint that I almost think I am hearing things. It is like the trembling cry of a cicada on a late autumn night. It is so ephemeral, so delicate, so pitiful, yet it is so distinct and clear above the chaotic booming of the drum that it is unmistakable. This bell first activates six or seven big and small wooden fish with gloomy, lonely, melodious and resonant timbres and then a series of vigorous brass chimes all in harmony. These sounds intermingle and dissolve in the booming of the drum.

I search for the source of the bell and find it is an old senior monk wearing a billowing mended and re-mended cassock who is conducting the music. He is holding a small goblet-like bell in his left hand and a thin steel pin in his right hand. At the touch of the pin on the bell, a gossamer-like tinkling slowly drifts up with the smoke of the incense. It is like the threads of a fishing net dragging in a world of sounds so that people cannot stop themselves drowning in it. At this my initial surprise and excitement vanishes.

At the back and the front of the palace are two tablets, one inscribed with the words "Majestic Land" and the other with "Profit and Pleasure is the Existence of Emotion", and from the ceiling hang layers of curtains in the midst of which sits Buddha, with such dignity as to immediately banish vanity and with such kindness as to induce indifference to the point of absence of emotions so that the cares of the world of dust are extinguished in an instant, and time in that instant becomes frozen.

The sound of the drum stops without my noticing. The senior monk with the bell is in front, and as his sunken mouth moves his sunken cheeks and his eyebrows also move. The motley group of monks slowly begins to chant sutras after the last note of the bell. One, two, three, four, five, six, seven, eight, nine, ten ... altogether ninety-nine monks follow in single file after him, circling around Buddha in the centre of the hall, walking as they chant. I too join in, and like them press the palms of my hands together and chant Namo Amitofu, but I clearly hear another sound. As each sentence of the sutra is about to end there is always a voice with a slightly higher pitch than the chanting. So there is therefore still the unextinguished passion of a soul still being tormented.

70

– Facing this snow scene scroll by Gong Xian what more can one say! There is such tranquillity one can almost hear the snow falling. It seems audible and yet is soundless.

– It is a dream scene.

– The wooden bridge on the river overlooks the clear stream and solitary hut. You can feel the signs of human existence but also the pure isolation and serenity.

– This is petrified dream, the intangible darkness at the edges of dream is faintly visible.

– It is all wet ink, his brush uses ink extravagantly but he attains such depths of artistic conception. His brush-work is meticulous and embodied in the charm of the brush-strokes is the clarity of his images. He is a genuine artist and not just a member of the literati who paints.

– The insipid elegance of literati painting often only has ideas but no art, I detest this affectation of pedantry.

– What you are referring to is that contrived lofty purity which manipulates the brush and ink but loses natural sensuousness. Interesting brush-strokes can be acquired but sensuousness comes into existence together with life and also exists with mountains, rivers, plants and trees. The wonder of Gong Xian's landscapes lies in the brilliant flashes of sensuousness in his brush-work. To be boundless to the point of forgetting one's existence cannot be acquired. Zheng Banqiao can be imitated but not Gong Xian.

– Ba Da also can't be imitated. His monster bird with the fierce eyes can be copied but that infinite loneliness of his lotus flowers and ducks cannot.

– Ba Da's best works are his landscapes, his works showing his contempt and rejection of the vulgar are his minor works.

– People think contempt for the vulgar is lofty purity. They don't realize that this lofty purity inevitably sinks to vulgarity. Rather than pitting the vulgar against the vulgar, it is better just to be vulgar.

– Zheng Banqiao was destroyed by people like this. His lofty purity became the decorations of people who failed to achieve their ambitions, those few bits of bamboo of his have been painted to death and have become the most vulgar of painting transactions.

– The worst is his "It is difficult to be muddle-headed". If he really wanted to be muddle-headed he should have just gone ahead with it, what was so difficult about it? He didn't want to be muddle-headed but pretended to be muddle-headed while striving to appear clever.

– He was a cowardly genius and Ba Da was a lunatic.

– At first Ba Da pretended to be mad, then he really went mad. His artistic achievement lies in his real madness and not in his feigned madness.

– Or one could say he viewed the world with a strange pair of eyes and the sight of the world made him go mad.

– Or one could say the world cannot tolerate rationality and it is only with madness that the world becomes rational.

– Xu Wei in old age went mad like this and killed his wife.

– Maybe it would be better to say that his wife killed him.

– It seems cruel to say this but he couldn't bear the world so he had no choice but to go mad.

– However Gong Xian didn't go mad, he transcended the world. Because he did not want to fight against the world he was able to preserve his innate nature.

– He did not want to pit rationality against being muddle-headed, he withdrew far away to a remote corner and immersed himself in a realm of pure dream.

– This was just another form of self-defence when he came to the realization that it was impossible to fight the world which had gone mad.

– He did not fight, he did not rationalize, and hence preserved the totality of his being.

– He was not a recluse, nor did he turn to religion, he was neither Buddhist nor Daoist. He supported himself with a half *mu* vegetable plot and by teaching. He did not think of thrushes as vulgar nor did he despise the vulgar. His painting transcends language.

– His paintings were not for money, painting itself was an expression of feelings in his heart.

– Would you and I be capable of this?

– He achieved it, as in this snow-swept landscape.

– Can you verify that this painting is authentic?

– Surely that's not important? If you think it is then it is.

– What if I think it isn't?

– Then it isn't.

– In other words, you and I think we have seen his work.

– Then it is his work.

71

Leaving Tiantai Mountain, I go on to Shaoxing where rice liquor is produced. This small city is not famous only for its rice liquor, it has also produced numerous famous personalities, including great politicians, writers, artists and heroic women whose old homes have now all been converted into museums. Even the local grain temple where Ah Q, the lowliest of the characters created by the pen of Lu Xun, sheltered from the storm one night, has been restored and painted in bright colours. There is a horizontal tablet with an inscription by a famous contemporary calligrapher. When Ah Q was beheaded as a local bandit he could not have imagined he would be so honoured after his death. I begin to reflect that it was difficult even for minor characters of this small town to escape being killed. So it goes without saying that the heroic revolutionary martyr Qiu Jin who believed it was her duty to save her race was doomed from the outset.

Her photo is hanging in her old residence. This talented daughter of a big family wrote beautiful poetry and prose and has elegant eyebrows, bright eyes and a gentle expression. She was just twenty when she was tied up, paraded through the streets to the market place and beheaded in broad daylight.

That literary giant of the age, Lu Xun, was a fugitive on the run all the time. Afterwards, he luckily moved into the foreign concession, otherwise he would have been killed long before he died of illness. It seems in this country nowhere was safe. There is a line in one of Lu Xun's poems, "I spill my blood for the Yellow Emperor", which I used to recite as a student, but which now I can't help having doubts about.

The Yellow Emperor was, according to legend, the first emperor of this land and can also mean one's homeland, the race, or one's ancestors. But why is it necessary to use blood to promote the spirit of one's ancestors? Can one achieve greatness by spilling one's hot blood? One's head is one's own, why does it have to be chopped off for the Yellow Emperor?

Xu Wei's couplet, "The world is a false illusion created by others, what is original and authentic is what I propose", seems to be more penetrating. However, if it is a false illusion why is it created by others? And whether or not it is false is irrelevant, but is it necessary to allow others to create it? Also, as for what is original and authentic, at issue is not its authenticity but whether or not it can be proposed.

His Green Vine Studio is tucked away deep in a little lane and consists of a smallish courtyard with several old vines and a hall with large spotlessly clean windows, said to be the original structure. These peaceful surroundings nevertheless sent him mad. Maybe the human world is not meant for human habitation, yet human beings continue to survive. In seeking to survive and yet to retain the authenticity existing at parturition one will either be killed or go mad, if not one will constantly be on the run.

I can't stay long in this small town and flee.

Kuaiji Mountain beyond the city is the tomb of Yu the Great, historically, the first dynastic emperor with a documented genealogy. About the twenty-first century BC he unified the empire and at an assembly of all the commanders proclaimed their meritorious achievements and rewarded them.

I pass the stone bridge at Ruoye Stream, below pine-forest-covered hills. Paddy rice is drying on the square in front of the site of Yu the Great's tomb, the late crop has already been harvested. It is still quite warm in the mid-autumn sun and I feel comfortably drowsy.

Within the gates is an enormous deserted courtyard. I can only try to imagine how it was that right here the Miao descendants of the Hemudu people who seven thousand years ago grew paddy rice, raised pigs, fired clay figures with human heads and faces, together with the descendants of the Liangzhu people who five thousand years ago inscribed geometric designs and circular symbols, and the ancestors of the Baiyue who had birds as totems, shaved their heads and tattooed their bodies, had all submitted to a review of the troops by Yu the Great. At the ceremony it happened that the hapless giant Fang Feng came late, wearing a hemp coat with a leather cord around his waist and looking generally slovenly. Yu the Great ordered his retainers to decapitate him.

Two thousand years ago, Sima Qian came here to carry out investigations and wrote that great work the *Historical Records*. He offended the emperor and, although he managed to keep his head, he was castrated.

On the roof of the main hall, between two dark green dragons, is a round mirror reflecting the dazzling sunlight. The new statue of Yu the Great inside the gloomy main hall has a kindly, almost commonplace look. However, the nine battle axes behind the statue, symbolizing his curbing of the floods in the nine kingdoms, succeed in indicating something closer to the truth.

According to the account in the "Records of the State of Shu", Yu was born in Shiniu and was a native of Guangrou County in Wenshan. I have just come down from that area which is the present Qiang nationality district of Wenchuan as well as the home of the giant panda. Yu was born from the womb of a bear and this can be substantiated in an earlier work, the *Classic of the Mountains and Seas*.

His achievement of curbing the floods is generally thought to have been through his dredging of the Yellow River but I have reservations about that. My theory is that he set out from the upper reaches of the Min River (the main source of the Yangtze in ancient times was the Min River and references can be found in the *Classic of the Mountains and Seas*), followed the course of the Yangtze and passed through the Three Gorges. In the north he fought in the mountains of the Jishan people, in the south against the kingdom of Gonggong, and in the east in the mountains of the Yunyu people. He waged war all the way to the shores of the East China Sea. In the kingdom of Qingqiu which at the time produced the nine-tail fox symbolizing good fortune in the verdant place of Tushan, later renamed Kuaiji, he encountered the seductive beauty Yaorao. When on their wedding day he revealed his original bear appearance, the young virgin was panic-stricken. The divine Yu the Great, wild with lust, chased after her and shouted: "Open up!" Hence the first prince was born into the world to inherit the position of emperor. For his wife Yu was a bear, amongst the ordinary folk he was a god, for the historian he was an emperor, for those who write fiction he can be described as the first person to kill another in order to realize his ambitions. As for the legend about the flood, it is possible to search for elements of prenatal memory in the amniotic fluids of the womb. In overseas countries there are people carrying out this type of research.

In Yu's tomb there are now artefacts for reference but the experts still cannot decipher the tadpole-like script on the stone epitaph opposite the main hall. I look at it from various angles, ruminate for a long time, and suddenly it occurs to me that it can be read in this way: history is a riddle,

> it can also be read as: history is lies
> and it can also be read as: history is nonsense
> and yet it can be read as: history is prediction
> and then it can be read as: history is sour fruit
> yet still it can be read as: history clangs like iron
> and it can be read as: history is balls of wheat-flour
>   dumplings
> or it can be read as: history is shrouds for wrapping corpses
> or taking it further it can be read as: history is a drug to
>   induce sweating
> or taking it further it can also be read as: history is ghosts
>   banging on walls
> and in the same way it can be read as: history is antiques
> and even: history is rational thinking

or even: history is experience
and even: history is proof
and even: history is a dish of scattered pearls
and even: history is a sequence of cause and effect
or else: history is analogy
or: history is a state of mind
and furthermore: history is history
and: history is absolutely nothing
even: history is sad sighs
Oh history oh history oh history oh history
Actually history can be read any way and this is a major
    discovery!

72

"This isn't a novel!"

"Then what is it?" he asks.

"A novel must have a complete story."

He says he has told many stories, some with endings and others without.

"They're all fragments without any sequence, the author doesn't know how to organize connected episodes."

"Then may I ask how a novel is supposed to be organized?"

"You must first foreshadow, build to a climax, then have a conclusion. That's basic common knowledge for writing fiction."

He asks if fiction can be written without conforming to the method which is common knowledge. It would just be like a story, with parts told from beginning to end and parts from end to beginning, parts with a beginning and no ending and others which are only conclusions or fragments which aren't followed up, parts which are developed but aren't completed or which can't be completed or which can be left out or which don't need to be told any further or about which there's nothing more to say. And all of these would also be considered stories.

"No matter how you tell a story, there must be a protagonist. In a long work of fiction there must be several important characters, but this work of yours ...?"

"But surely the I, you, she and he in the book are characters?" he asks.

"These are just different pronouns to change the point of view of the narrative. This can't replace the portrayal of characters. These pronouns of yours, even if they are characters, don't have clear images they're hardly described at all."

He says he isn't painting portraits.

"Right, fiction isn't painting, it is art in language. Do you really think the petulant exchanges between these pronouns can replace the creation of the personalities of the characters?"

He says he doesn't want to create the personalities of the characters, and what's more he doesn't know if he himself has a personality.

"Why are you writing fiction if you don't even understand what fiction is?"

He then asks politely for a definition of fiction.

The critic is cowed and snarls, "This is modernist, it's imitating the West but falling short."

He says then it's Eastern.

"Yours is much worse than Eastern! You've slapped together travel notes, moralistic ramblings, feelings, notes, jottings, untheoretical discussions, unfable-like fables, copied out some folk songs, added some legend-like nonsense of your own invention, and are calling it fiction!"

He says the gazetteers of the Warring States period, the records of humans and strange events of the Former and Later Han, the Wei and Jin, and the Southern and Northern Dynasties, the *chuanqi* romances of the Tang Dynasty, the prompt books of the Song Dynasty, the episodic novels and belles-lettres of the Ming and Qing Dynasties, as well as the writings through the ages on geography and the natural sciences, street talk, morality tales, and miscellaneous records of strange events, are all acknowledged as fiction. But none of these have ever had any fixed models.

"Are you from the searching-for-roots school?"

He hastens to say you sir have stuck such labels on him. However, the fiction he writes is simply because he can't bear the loneliness, he writes to amuse himself. He didn't expect to fall into the quagmire of the literary world and at present he is trying to pull himself out. He didn't write these books in order to eat, fiction for him is a luxury beyond earning money and making a livelihood.

"You're a nihilist!"

He says he actually has no ideology but does have a small amount of nihilism in him, however nihilism isn't the equivalent of absolute nothingness. It's just like in the book where you is the reflection of I and he is the back of you, the shadow of a shadow. Although there's no face it still counts as a pronoun.

The critic shrugs his shoulders and departs.

He feels confused and uncertain about what it is that is critical in fiction. Is it the narrative? Or is it the mode of narration? Or is it not the mode of narration but the attitude of the narration? Or is it not the attitude but the affirmation of an attitude? Or is it not the affirmation of an attitude but the affirmation of the starting point of an attitude? Or is it not the starting point but the self which is the starting point? Or is it not the self but perception and awareness of the self? Or is it not the perception and awareness of the self but the process of that perception and awareness? Or is it not the process but the action itself? Or is it not the action itself but the possibility of the action? Or is it not the possibility but the choice of action? Or is it not whether there is a choice but whether there is the necessity of a choice? Or is it not in the necessity but in the language? Or is it not in the language but whether the language is interesting? Nevertheless he is intrigued with using language to talk about women about men about love about sex about life about death about the ecstasy and agony of the soul and flesh about people's solicitousness for people and politics about people evading politics about the inability to evade reality about unreal imagination about what is more real about the denial of utilitarian goals is not the same as an affirmation of it about the illogicality of logic about rational reflection greatly surpassing science in the dispute between content and form about meaningful images and meaningless content about the definition of meaning about everyone wanting to be God about the worship of idols by atheists about self worship being dubbed philosophy about self love about indifference to sex transforming into megalomania about schizophrenia about sitting in Chan contemplation about sitting not in Chan contemplation about meditation about the Way of nurturing the body is not the Way about effability or ineffability but the absolute necessity for the effability of the Way about fashion about revolt against vulgarity is a mighty smash with a racquet about a fatal blow with a club and Buddhist enlightenment about children must not be taught about those who teach first being taught about drinking a bellyful of ink about going black from being close to ink about what is bad about being black about good people about bad people about bad people are not people about humans by nature are more ferocious than wolves about the most wicked are other people and Hell in fact is in one's own mind about bringing anxieties upon oneself about Nirvana about completion about completion is nothing completed about what is right about what is wrong about the creation of grammatical structures about not yet saying something is not the same as not saying anything about talk is useless in functional discourse about no-one is the winner in battles between men and women about moving pieces backwards and forwards in a game of chess curbs the emotions which are the basis of human nature about human beings need to eat about starving to death is a trifling affair whereas loss of integrity is a major event but that it is impossible to arbitrate this as truth about the fallibility of experience which is only a crutch about falling if one has to fall about revolutionary fiction which smashes superstitious belief in literature about a revolution in fiction about revolutionizing fiction.

Reading this chapter is optional but as you've read it you've read it.

73

When I arrive in this small city on the coast of the East China Sea a middle-aged single woman insists that I go to her home for dinner. She comes to my lodgings to invite me and says that before going to work she had gone out and bought all sorts of seafood for me – crab, razor clams and even wonderful fat saltwater eel.

"You've come from far away to this port and must sample some seafood. It's not just difficult to find inland, but you can't always get it in the big coastal cities." She is very earnest.

It is difficult to refuse so I say to the owner of the house, "How about coming with me?"

He knows her well and says, "This is a special invitation for you. She gets bored living on her own and she's got something to discuss with you."

They have evidently worked it out between them so I have no choice but to follow her out the door. She wheels her bicycle over and says, "It's some distance and will take a bit of time to get there, get on and I'll double you."

People are coming and going in the lane, and I am not a cripple.

"What if I double you and you tell me the way?" I say.

She gets on the back seat. We attract a great deal of attention as we weave through the crowds the handlebars swaying and me ringing the bell continuously.

It is great getting an invitation to dinner from a woman but she is past the best years of her life. She has a pale sallow complexion and prominent cheekbones, and the way she talks and how she wheels out the bicycle and gets on is devoid of feminine grace. I glumly pedal away and try to find something to talk about.

She says she is an accountant in a factory. No wonder. She's a woman in charge of money, I've had dealings with such women. You could say that every one of them is bright but they never pay a cent more than they have to for anything. Of course, this is a habit resulting from that line of work, it isn't a basic trait of women.

Her apartment is one of several around an old courtyard and she parks the old bicycle which will barely stand upright under her window. A huge padlock hangs on the door which opens into a small room with a big wooden bed occupying half of the room. At one side is a square table laid out with liquor and food. Two big wooden chests are stacked one on the top of the other onto bricks on the floor and there are some cosmetics on a slab of glass on top of the chests. There is a pile of old magazines at the bed head.

She notices me looking around and hastily says, "I'm so sorry, it's all a terrible mess."

"Life is like that."

"I just muddle through life, I'm not very fussy about anything." She puts on a light and gets me to sit at the table, goes to the stove by the door to put on the pot of soup then pours me a drink and sits down opposite. Propping her elbows on the table, she says, "I don't like men."

I nod.

"I don't mean you," she explains. "I'm talking about men in general. You're a writer."

I don't know whether to nod or not.

"I got divorced long ago and live on my own."

"It's not easy." I am referring to life being hard and that it is like that for everyone.

"I had a girlfriend, we were very good friends from primary school days."

It occurs to me that she is probably a lesbian.

"She's dead now."

I make no response.

"I invited you here to tell you her story. She was very beautiful. If you saw her photo you'd like her, everyone who saw her fell in love with her. She wasn't beautiful in a normal sense, she was extraordinarily beautiful – a melon-seed shaped face, a small cherry mouth, willow frond eyebrows, big crystal-clear almond eyes. Her figure, needless to say, was like that of classical beauties described in the fiction of the past. Why am I telling you all this? Because, unfortunately, I wasn't able to keep a single photo of her. At the time I wasn't prepared, when she died her mother came and took away everything. Drink up."

She has a drink as well and I can immediately tell by the way she drinks that she is experienced. There are no photos or paintings on the walls and certainly none of the flowers and little animals women usually like. She is punishing herself and probably most of her money is converted into something which goes from a cup into her stomach.

"I am asking you to write her life into a work of fiction. I can tell you everything about her, you have a good writing style. Fiction–"

"Is existence produced from nothingness," I say with a smile.

"I don't want you to make it up, you can use her real name. I can't afford a writer, I can't pay the manuscript fee. If I had the money, I would willingly pay. I'm seeking your help, asking you to write about her."

"This is–" I sit up to show that I appreciate her hospitality.

"I'm not bribing you. If you think this girl has been unjustly treated and is worthy of sympathy, then you can write about her. It's a pity you can't see her photo." Her eyes look blank. The dead girl clearly weighs heavily in her heart. "I was born ugly so I always admired pretty girls and wanted to be friends with them. I wasn't at the same school but always ran into her on the way to school or on my way home, but these were always fleeting encounters. Her oval face moved not just men but also women. I wanted to get to know her better. I saw that she was always on her own and one day I waited for her coming back from school, followed her and said I wanted to talk with her and hoped she wouldn't mind. She agreed and I walked with her.

Thereafter on my way to school, I would always wait for her near her house and in this way got to know her. Don't hold back, drink up!"

She serves up the stewed eel, the soup is delicious. As I eat, I listen to her telling how she became a member of the girl's home. The mother treated her like her own daughter and often she didn't go home and just slept with her in the same bed.

"Don't go thinking *that* sort of thing was going on. I only knew about sexual matters after she was sentenced to ten years in prison. She had a big argument with me and didn't want me to visit her. Afterwards I just found some man and got married. She and I had the purest love, that which exists between young girls. You men wouldn't understand, a man's love for a woman is like an animal's. I'm not talking about you, you're a writer. Have some crab!" She breaks up into pieces the strong smelling raw crab marinated in salt and spices and piles some into my bowl. There are also cooked clams with a sauce dip. It is another battle between men and women, a battle between the spirit and the flesh.

Her friend's father was a military officer in the Guomindang and when the Liberation Army came south, her mother was pregnant with her. Her father sent word but when she rushed to the wharf, the troop ship had already left. It is one of those old stories again. I lose interest in her friend and simply apply myself to eating the crab.

"One night when we were in bed together, she threw her arms around me and started crying. I was alarmed and asked her what was wrong. She said she missed her father."

"But she'd never seen him."

"Her mother burnt all the photos of him in military uniform but they still had wedding photos of her mother in a white net gown with her father. Her father was wearing a Western-style suit and was quite dashing. I tried my best to comfort her and I felt really sorry for her. Afterwards I hugged her tight and sobbed with her."

"That's understandable."

"If everyone thought that, it would have been fine. However, people didn't understand, they treated her as an anti-revolutionary and said she was hoping for a reactionary restoration and was planning to flee to Taiwan."

"The policies of those times aren't like they are today. It's changed now and people are being urged to come back to the mainland to visit their relatives." What else can I say?

"She was a young girl and although she was in high school at the time she couldn't understand all this. She wrote about missing her father in her diary!"

"If this was seen and reported she would certainly have been sentenced," I say. I am interested in knowing if there were certain changes when the girl's infatuation with her father got mixed with lesbian love.

She starts talking about how, because of her family background, the girl couldn't go to university but was selected by the Peking Opera Troupe as a trainee performer, how she was instantly a big hit when the lead woman performer was sick and they put her in as a temporary replacement, how the lead woman performer was jealous, how when the girl's opera troupe went on tour the woman secretly read her diary and reported her, how when the opera troupe returned to the city the public security officials got her mother in for questioning, asked her to urge her daughter to confess and to hand over the diary, how the girl was afraid of the public security officials ransacking her home and had transferred the diary to her home. However she too was afraid of the public security officials coming in to search so she took the diary to the home of the girl's maternal uncle. During questioning the mother testified that her daughter only ever went to her home and the home of her maternal uncle. The maternal uncle was summoned and, afraid of being implicated, handed over the diary. The public security officials then turned to the girl, who of course was terrified, and made a full confession. At first she was isolated in the opera troupe and not allowed to go home and then later she was indicted on the criminal charge of writing a reactionary diary and recklessly planning restorationist anti-revolutionary activities. She was put under arrest and imprisoned.

"Are you saying that everyone informed on her and exposed her, even her mother and uncle?" The crab is too strong, I can't eat anymore and put it aside. My fingers are covered in crab meat and there's nothing to wipe my hands on.

"We wrote confessions exposing her and put our thumb print to it. Even her uncle who was much older was so frightened he didn't even dare to see me again. Her mother insisted it was I who had led her daughter astray, that it was I who had fed her those reactionary ideas, and she forbade me to enter her home again!"

"How did she die?" I am anxious to find out the outcome.

"Listen to what I'm saying–" she seems to be defending herself.

I am not judging. If this had happened to me at that time I wouldn't necessarily have been more level-headed. As a child I had seen my mother pulling out the roll of land deeds from the bottom of my grandmother's chest and burning them in the stove, and I saw this as destruction of criminal evidence. Fortunately no-one came to investigate. If at the time investigations had involved me, there is no doubt that I would have denounced my maternal grandmother who had bought me the spinning top and my mother who had raised me. It was the way things were in those times.

It isn't just the strong-smelling crab marinated in brine which is disgusting, it's also me. I can't eat anything else and just kept drinking.

She suddenly starts sobbing and covers her face with her hands, and next she is wailing loudly.

I can't comfort her with my hands covered in crab roe, so I ask, "May I use a towel?"

She points to the basin containing clean water on the rack behind the door. I wash my hands and it is only after I give her a rinsed hand towel that she stops crying. I detest this ugly woman and have no sympathy for her.

She says at the time she was confused. A year later she gradually recovered and made enquiries about the girl's whereabouts, bought a whole lot of foodstuffs and went to visit her at the prison and the girl had been sentenced to ten years and didn't want to see her. The girl accepted the things she had brought only after she said she wouldn't marry and would work to support her after she had served out her sentence.

She says the happiest days in her life were those spent visiting her friend. They swapped diaries, spoke lovingly as if they were sisters, swore never to marry and always to be together. Who would be the husband? Who would be the wife? Of course she would be the wife. Together in bed they would tickle one another until they couldn't stop laughing, she was happy just to hear the sound of her laughter. However I prefer to imagine the worst of her.

"Then why did you get married?" I ask.

"It was she who changed first," she says. "Once when I went to see her, her face was swollen and she was very cold to me. I was puzzled and kept questioning her. Right at the end of visiting time, it was always twenty minutes each time, she told me to get married and not to come again. Only after I pressed her about it did she say she had someone. I asked her who it was and she said another prisoner! I did not see her again after that. I wrote her many letters but never got a reply, it was then that I got married."

I want to say that she had harmed her, that her mother justifiably hated her, otherwise the girl would have loved normally, married normally, had children, and not have ended up like this.

"Do you have children?" I ask.

"I didn't want any."

A mean woman.

"I separated after less than a year, then we squabbled for about a year before going through a divorce. Since then I have lived alone, I hate men."

"How did she die?" I change the subject.

"I heard that she tried to escape and was shot by the guards."

I don't want to hear anymore and just want her to quickly finish the story.

"Shall I reheat the soup?" She looks at me apprehensively.

"Don't bother." She shouldn't have got me here, to give vent to her frustrations, eating this meal disgusts me.

She also tells me how she tried all means to seek out a fellow inmate who had been released after serving out her sentence, and found out that her friend had been caught passing notes to a male prisoner and deprived of going out into the open and of having visitors. She had also tried to escape but by that time she was already deranged and would often laugh and weep for no apparent reason. She says that later she found out the address of the male prisoner who had been released. When she arrived at his place there was a woman there and when she asked him about the girl's circumstances, either because he was afraid of the woman being jealous or because he was quite callous, he said he didn't know. They didn't exchange ten sentences and she departed in a rage.

"Can you write this up?" she asks, her head bowed.

"I'll have to see!" I eventually say.

She wants to take me back or let me ride her bicycle back but I flatly refuse. On the way, gusts of cool wind blow from the sea and it looks like rain. When I get back to my lodgings in the middle of the night I have an attack of vomiting and diarrhoea. I imagine the seafood wasn't fresh.

74

They say along the sea coast that strange music with bells and drums can always be heard at night coming from this mountain – it is the Daoist priests and nuns holding their secret ceremonies. He and she witnessed one of these by accident and reported it as soon as they got back. However, if people go up the mountain during the day to look for the Daoist temple they can't find it. As they recall, it was on a cliff facing the sea. He says it was almost at the peak. She disagrees, it was up a small path on a cliff facing the sea but it would be halfway up the mountain.

Both say it was a beautiful Daoist temple built inside a crack in the cliff and the only access was this narrow mountain path, so in the daytime it couldn't be seen by fishermen on the boats at sea or people climbing the mountain for medicinal herbs. It was while they were travelling at night and following the sound of the music that they stumbled onto a Daoist ceremony. They suddenly saw in a blaze of light the temple with its doors wide open and incense smoke curling up.

He saw a hundred or so men and women, all with painted faces, wearing Daoist robes and holding flying knives and flame torches as they sang and danced with their eyes half closed and wailed with tears streaming down their faces. The men and women intermingled freely as they went into trances of ecstasy and hysteria, throwing back their heads and stamping their feet.

She says the time she went there weren't as many people but they were all dressed in bright colours. There were young girls and old women but no men present. They had rouged faces, lips painted blood red and eyebrows blackened with charcoal. Their hair was combed into buns which were tied with red cloth and decorated with garlands of jasmine. Some wore copper earrings but she can't remember whether they had rings in their noses. They were singing, dancing, and waving their hands. It was a lively scene with some extraordinary chanting.

You ask her whether she could have dreamt it. She says a classmate was with her; they had gone up the mountain for the day, got lost, and couldn't get back before dark. When they heard the music, they moved towards it in the dark and came upon the scene. The Daoists didn't mind and the temple doors were wide open.

He says it was also like that with him, except that at the time he was on his own. He was used to travelling on mountain roads at night and wasn't afraid. He was on guard against bad people but these Daoists were only carrying out their rituals and weren't out to hurt anyone.

Both of them say they had seen it with their own eyes otherwise they wouldn't have believed it. Both have tertiary education, are sound of mind, and don't believe in ghosts and spirits. If they had been hallucinating they would have known.

Neither knew the other before and take turns telling you about it. In both cases they say it was on this mountain by the sea. Although it is the first time you meet with them, it is as if you are old friends and they talk quite candidly with you. There is no struggle for advantage so there is no need to be on guard, there is no blaming or boasting on either side, and they have no motive for getting you to fall into a trap. They have thought a lot about their experience and are puzzled by it, but they are obviously neither disgusted nor think it funny.

They say that as you have come all the way to this coast in search of the bizarre it is worth going there. They would like to accompany you but are afraid if they go there specifically for that purpose, they won't necessarily find it. This sort of thing occurs when you're not looking for it and when you set out expressly to seek it, your efforts will be futile. You can believe it or not but when they saw it with their own eyes in the blazing light of red candles, their weariness instantly vanished. They can swear to it under oath. If it would convince you they could immediately swear to it, but their swearing to it is still no substitute for you yourself going there. It is impossible for you to doubt their sincerity.

You end up going up the mountain and reach the peak before sunset. You sit there watching the fiery red sun withdrawing its rays and sinking into the vast horizon of the sea. It leaps up on striking the surface of the water then with a tremble plummets into the watery regions which have turned grey-blue. Golden lights writhe like water snakes and the lopped off semi-circular bright red crown floats on the black water like an oval hat, bobs up and down a couple of times, and is swallowed by the vast sea leaving only a red haze.

You begin to descend the mountain and very quickly are overtaken by dusk. You pick up a branch to use as a walking stick and a step at a time tap on the steep stone path. Before long you have plunged into a dark valley and can see neither the sea nor the road.

You stick close to the cliff face which is covered in small trees and bushes, terrified of losing your footing and falling into the abyss on the other side of the path. Your legs gradually turn to jelly and you rely on the stick in your hand to feel the way. You do not know whether or not the next step is safe, and it seems that this turbid darkness is growing from the bottom of your heart. You lose confidence in your stick and remember the lighter you have in your pocket. Even if it can't help you get onto the level main path, it will be able to light a part of the way, but the sparks of the lighter can only produce a flame which shakes violently as if in fright and you have to use your hand to block the wind. A step away looms another black wall which makes you suspect it is certainly luring you to make that step into the abyss. The flame goes out in the chilly wind and like a blind person, with nothing to rely on but the branch in your hand, you tap a little at a time near your feet and tremble as you anxiously shuffle along the path.

Somehow you make your way into a hollow in the mountain which seems to be a cave and you see a dim light as if it is a crack in a door. When you get to it, this is what it is, you push but it is bolted.

You press your eye against the crack in the door and see a solitary lamp in an empty hall honouring statues of the Three Supreme Purities – Lord Daode, Lord Yuanshi and Lord Lingbao.

"What are you up to?" a stern voice shouts from behind. You are startled but it is a human voice and you relax.

You say you are a tourist lost in the dark and need somewhere to stay for the night.

Without saying much he leads you up some wooden stairs into a room lit with an oil lamp. It is only then that you see he is wearing a Daoist robe and trousers with the legs tied at the calf. His deep-set eyes glow with energy, he is clearly an old master. You don't dare say you've come to spy on the secrets of the Daoist temple and repeatedly apologize for disturbing him, beg to stay the night, and promise to leave at dawn.

He hesitates for a moment, but then gets a bunch of keys from the timber wall and picks up the lamp. You obediently follow him up another flight of stairs. He opens a room and without a word goes downstairs.

You flick your lighter and see there is a bare wooden bed and nothing else. So you lie down fully clothed, curl into a ball, and don't dare think about trying to do anything else. Afterwards, you hear from the floor above the tinkling of a bell. Accompanying the tinkling there seems to be the faint sound of a woman chanting. You are surprised and start wondering if this is one of the strange ceremonies they had told you about. You think perhaps upstairs some secret ritual is taking place. You want to find out but in the end don't move. It is a relaxing sound which induces sleep and in the darkness weariness unceasingly assails you. You seem to see the back of a young girl wearing her hair tied up in a bun. She is sitting sedately, legs crossed, and is striking a bell. The delicate sound spreads out in waves like light, you cannot stop yourself believing in destiny and fate, and pray that in the nether world your soul will have peace . . .

It is light early in the morning and you get up and go up the stairs to the top floor. The door is wide open. It is an empty hall and there are no incense tables and curtains, nor any statues or tablets. Only a huge mirror hangs in the middle of the wall. The mirror faces the cave entrance which has a wooden railing across it. Walking up to the mirror you see a stretch of blue sky which brings you to a silent halt.

On the way down the mountain you hear sobbing and going around the bend see a naked child sitting in the middle of the road. He is relentlessly sobbing and has become hoarse, evidently he is tired and has been crying for some time.

You walk up to the child and bend down to ask, "Are you all on your own?"

Seeing someone has come, he starts crying even more loudly. You grab his small shoulders, pull him to his feet, and pat off the dirt from his bare bottom.

"Where are the grown-ups of your family?"

The more you question him the more he cries, and there are no villages in sight.

"Where are your parents?"

He just shakes his head and looks at you, his eyes brimming with tears.

"Where do you live?"

Still whimpering, his little mouth pouts.

"Keep crying and I won't take any notice of you!" you threaten.

This works and he instantly stops crying.

"Where are you from?"

He doesn't speak.

"Are you all on your own?"

He just looks dumbly at you.

"Can you talk?" You put on an angry look.

He immediately starts crying again.

"Don't cry!" You stop him.

He opens his little mouth, wanting to cry but not daring to.

"If you cry again I'll smack your bottom!"

He somehow stops himself from crying and you pick him up.

468

"Little fellow, where do you want to go? Speak up!"

He clings instinctively to your neck.

"Surely you can talk?"

He looks dumbly at you, his face streaked with mud from his grubby hands rubbing at his tears. You are at a loss. He probably belongs to a peasant family nearby, his parents should look after him better. This is absurd.

You carry him for some distance but still see no sign of any houses. Your arms are numb and in any case you can't keep going down the mountain with this mute child. You talk it over with him.

"How about getting down and walking for a while?"

He shakes his head and looks miserable.

You force yourself to walk on but still see no sign of any houses nor smoke from chimneys down in the valley. You wonder if he has been abandoned on the mountain road. You must take him back to where you found him, if no-one takes him his parents will come back for him.

"Little one, get down and walk a bit, my arms are numb."

You pat his bottom and he actually falls asleep. He must have been left on the mountain road for a long time, the people who left him must be quite callous. You start cursing the parents who gave birth to him. If they can't manage raising him why did they have him?!

You look at his little tear-stained face, he is fast asleep. He is so trusting, probably he has never been shown this amount of affection. The sun pierces through the thick clouds and shines onto his face. His eyebrows twitch and he moves, his face snuggling against your chest.

A gush of warmth wells up from deep in your heart and you realize you have not experienced such tenderness for a very long time. You discover that you are still fond of children and that you should have had a son a long time ago. As you look at him, you start to think he looks like you. While seeking pleasure did you by chance give him life? And then not care for him and abandon him? Did not even ever think about him? It is yourself that you are cursing!

You are afraid, afraid he will wake up, afraid he can talk, afraid he will understand. Luckily he is mute, luckily he is asleep and is not aware of his misfortune. While he is still asleep you must put him back on the mountain road and make a getaway before anyone discovers.

You return him to the mountain road where you found him. He rolls, huddles his little legs up to himself and puts his arms over his face. He must feel the cold of the ground and will soon wake up. You run off, in broad daylight, like a fugitive criminal. You seem to hear sobbing behind you, but don't dare look back.

75

I pass through Shanghai. In the long queue at the ticket office I manage to get a ticket for the special express to Beijing which someone has returned and within an hour or so I am on the train – it's a stroke of good luck. This huge metropolis with its teaming population of ten million people no longer interests me. The distant uncle I would have liked to have visited died even earlier than my father, neither of them was able to live to a venerable old age.

The black Wusong River which goes through the city gives off a perpetual stench. Fish and turtles are extinct but the inhabitants of the city somehow manage to survive. Even the treated tap water used for everyday consumption is brackish and worse still always smells of chlorine. It would seem that people are hardier than fish and prawns.

I have been to the mouth of the Yangtze. There, apart from the rustproof steel cargo ships floating on vast murky yellow waves, there are only reed-covered muddy shores which are washed by the same murky yellow waves. The silt in the water keeps building up and one day will turn the whole of the East China Sea into sandbars.

I recall that when I was a child the water of the Yangtze was always clear, both on fine and rainy days. Along the banks, from early morning to dusk fish vendors had fish that were the size of a child, and they sold them in sections. I have been to many ports along the Yangtze but there are no longer any fish that size and it's even hard finding any fish stalls. It was only at Wanxian before the end of the Three Gorges, on the steps of the thirty- or forty-metre stone embankment, that I saw a few of them and the fish in the baskets were all a few inches long and in days gone by would only have been used as cat food. In those days, I used to like standing on the wharf on the Yangtze watching people on the pontoons casting their fishing reels. It was exciting when the fish emerged from the water, a real contest between fish and man. Today, there are more than ten thousand people working out strategies to clean up the river. After his superiors had left, an official from some section or department showing me around told me quietly that over one hundred species of the river's freshwater fish were on the verge of extinction.

While the boat was moored for the night at Wanxian, the chief officer smoked and chatted with me on deck as we looked at the lights on the shore. He said that hiding in the cabin he had witnessed a terrible massacre in the period of armed conflicts during the Cultural Revolution and of course it was people and not fish that were killed. People were tied with wire at the wrists in groups of three and forced into the river by spraying them with machine gun fire: if one was hit all three fell. They were like fish on a hook, they splashed and struggled for a while, then floated down the river like dead dogs. Oddly, the more people are killed off the more people there are, whereas with fish the more that are caught the fewer there are. Wouldn't it be better if it were the other way around?

However, people and fish do have something in common. Big fish and big people have all been done away with, clearly the world isn't meant for them.

I think this distant uncle of mine was perhaps the last of the big people. I am not referring to big personalities. There's an abundance of these any time as long as there are celebrations and banquets. By big people, I mean people I admire. This uncle I admire was given the wrong injection. He was in hospital being treated for pneumonia but two hours after an injection he was in the morgue. I've heard about people being killed in hospitals but I refuse to believe he died so wretchedly. It was during those chaotic years that I saw him for the last time. I was young and it was the first time he seriously discussed literature and politics with me. Before that he only joked and played with me. He had a deep voice and could sing l'Internationale in Esperanto. He was slightly asthmatic, a problem he had from when he was young; he said it was because he had smoked too many tobacco substitutes during the war. When he couldn't get hold of tobacco, if he got the urge, he would smoke anything, from cabbage leaves to cotton leaves which he dried over a fire. People in such circumstances will always think of something.

He knew how to make children happy. I was probably cross with my mother and in protest I refused to eat the chicken broth with noodles and let it go cold. It was a contest of wills. I was small but I still had my dignity. However, once bent a bow can't be straightened: my mother was on the verge of losing her temper and an embarrassing scene for me was imminent. This uncle of mine grabbed me and took me onto the street to buy some ice cream. There had just been a storm and the street had turned into a river. He took off his big army boots, rolled up his trouser legs and treading through the water took me into a shop which sold ice cream and cold drinks. I ate two big pieces of ice cream. Since then I have never eaten that amount of anything cold at once. When we got home, my mother saw him carrying his shoes and looking such a sorry sight that she couldn't help laughing and the cold war between my mother and me ended. It was he, this uncle of mine, who truly had the style of a big man.

His father, who died much earlier from opium smoking and prostitutes, was a comprador capitalist and at the time gave him several thousand silver dollars to go to America to study so that he wouldn't get further involved in communist underground activities. However, he refused to take a single cent and ran off to Jiangxi province and joined the New Fourth Army to fight in the patriotic war of resistance against the Japanese.

He said when he was in the army headquarters of the New Fourth Army in the mountain regions of southern Anhui province, he bought a leopard cub from a peasant and secretly kept it in an iron cage under his bed. At night, the animal's instincts would become activated and it would keep growling. When the soldiers discovered it, he couldn't bear to have it killed and gave it away.

He and my father liked to yarn. Whenever he visited he would send away his driver as well as his bodyguard, and take from his leather bag a bottle of good liquor which you wouldn't be able to get in the shops and he would give me a big bag of Shanghai mixed sweets. Once they started talking, they would talk through the whole night until morning. They would talk about their childhood and youth, just like now when I occasionally get together with my old classmates.

He talked about the desolation of their old home, of grass sprouting from the roof-tiles, and he talked about coming home from the primary school outside town in the autumn wind and cold rain with his clothes covered in blood from his bleeding nose. He was in a state of shock, running and crying, but the long street of people he knew and distant relatives just stood under their eaves or sat behind their counters looking on with indifference. Only the old woman who sold bean curd came out, took hold of him and dragged him into the mill. She stuffed bits of toilet paper into his nose and stopped the bleeding.

He also talked about their old village, the old house the family rescued after that lunatic great-grandfather of mine set fire to it, and about the girl next door who suicided because of her betrothal. People saw her coming out of the haberdashery shop with a length of patterned cloth and thought she was going to make clothes for her trousseau. Two days later, dressed in a new jacket and trousers made from the cloth, she killed herself by swallowing needles.

I would wrap myself up in a quilt and listen enraptured, refusing to sleep. I saw this uncle wheezing and chain-smoking one cigarette after another and getting up to pace around the room when he got to an exciting part. He said his only wish was that one day, after retiring, he would find somewhere to write a book.

The last time I went to see him in Shanghai he had some sort of puffer and whenever he had an attack of asthma, he would spray it down his throat. When I asked if he had written his book he said luckily he hadn't otherwise he probably wouldn't be alive. This was the only time he didn't treat me like a child. He told me it was not the time for literature. He also warned me not to get involved in politics.

Once involved, you won't know north from south or east from west and you will have lost your head without even noticing. I told him I couldn't complete my studies at university. Then be an observer. He said he was now an observer. Before the Cultural Revolution, in what the newspapers call the Anti-Rightist period when people were starving to death in the countryside, he was singled out and investigated and for many years he has stood aside. No wonder at that time he and my father lost touch. He had just sent one message by word of mouth that he was burdened by military matters and was off to make investigations in faraway Hainan Island. At the time I didn't know there was a message within the message.

From that time on, I too became an observer. It was on this same Beijing–Shanghai line that I saw "Attack with Writing and Defend with Military Might" fighters standing in a long single row along the railway platform. They were clutching iron spears and were wearing helmets of woven willow branches and red armbands. As soon as the train stopped, they blocked every carriage door. A person who was about to alight turned and squeezed his way back inside. They immediately surged in after him. The person screamed for help but no-one in the carriage dared to move and watched as he was dragged off the train. The group on the platform immediately surrounded him and began to kick and beat him. The train sounded the whistle and slowly moved off. I don't know if the person died or got away with his life.

At the time every city along the way had gone mad. Walls, factories, high voltage poles, water towers, man-made constructions of any kind, were all covered in slogans swearing to defend with one's life, to overthrow, to smash, and to fight a bloody war to the end. As the train roared along, there was the singing of battle songs on the broadcast system on board and on the loudspeakers outside in every place the train passed. North of the Yangtze at a station called Clear Brilliance – I don't know how it was possible for such a place name at that time – the platform and the tracks were crammed with refugees. The train's doors didn't open so people scrambled to climb through open windows into the carriages which were already packed like sardine cans. In response to this the people in the suffocating carriages quickly shut the windows. The glass became boundaries and the people inside and outside who were all refugees alike suddenly became enemies. Oddly enough, once separated by this transparent glass, the faces on the other side changed and became angry and hostile.

The train moved off and a barrage of stones hailed down along with a cacophony of swearing, smashing and screaming. This is probably what people see on the way down to hell while still believing they are suffering for their faith.

It was also during those years and also on this same railway track that I saw part of the naked corpse of a woman which had been cut neatly by the wheels of the train, like a section of fish cut through with a sharp knife. At first there was a violent jolt followed by a blast of the train whistle and the rattle of metal and glass. I thought it was an earthquake. Those times were really uncanny. It was as if heaven was responding to human beings, and the earth had also gone crazy and was shaking endlessly.

The train lurched ahead a couple of hundred metres before it came to a halt and the attendants, police and passengers all jumped off. Bloody strips of flesh were strewn all over the place on the stalks of the dry grass along the tracks and the air was thick with the stench of blood ... human blood is more rancid than fish blood. On the slope by the tracks lay this complete section of a woman's corpse, without the head, neck, arms or legs. The blood must have all spurted out, and it was starkly white, like a broken alabaster statue with the lustre of skin. The healthy young woman's body still bore traces of life and sensuousness. An old woman amongst the passengers brought back a shredded fragment of clothing from a withered branch some distance away and covered the lower part of the body. The driver, mopping at his sweat with his cap, frantically explained how he saw this woman walking on the tracks and sounded the whistle. When she didn't get out of the way, he immediately braked. He couldn't brake any harder because he had a trainload of passengers on board. The instant before the impact, she suddenly jumped up, and as she jumped ... Ai, she wanted to commit suicide, she clearly wanted to kill herself. Was she a student who had been sent to the countryside? A peasant woman? She hadn't had any children. Why talk about things like that? The passengers had all joined in the discussion. She definitely couldn't have wanted to suicide, otherwise why did she try to jump out of the way? Could dying be as simple as that? You have to be quite callous to die! Probably she was preoccupied. This isn't crossing a road, it is broad daylight and there was a train coming at her! Unless she was deaf, her heart would already have been dead, so being alive wasn't any better than being dead. The person who said this quickly walked away.

I'm just fighting to survive, no, I'm not fighting for anything, I'm just protecting myself. I don't have the courage of that woman and I have not reached a state of utter despair, I am still seduced by the human world, I still haven't lived enough.

76

He is all alone. He has been drifting around for a long time and eventually encounters an elderly man wearing a long gown and carrying a staff. He goes up and politely asks, "Venerable elder, can you tell me the location of Lingshan?"

"Where have you come from?" the old man asks instead.

He says from Wuyizhen.

"Wuyizhen?" The old man ruminates for a while. "It's on the other side of the river."

He says he has just come from that side of the river. Can he have taken the wrong road? The old man cocks an eyebrow and says, "The road is not wrong, it is the traveller who is wrong."

"Venerable elder, what you are saying is absolutely correct." But what he is asking is whether Lingshan is on this side of the river.

"If I say it's on that side of the river then it's on that side of the river." The old man is annoyed.

He says he has already come to this side of the river from that side of the river.

"You're moving further and further away," the old man insists.

"Then I'll have to go back again?" he asks, but can't help saying to himself, I really don't understand.

"I've already put it very clearly," the old man says coldly.

"Venerable elder, you are quite correct, you have put it quite clearly..." The problem is that it isn't clear to him.

"What is it that you still don't understand?" The old man scrutinizes him from under his eyebrows.

He says he still doesn't understand how to get to Lingshan.

The old man closes his eyes to concentrate.

"Venerable elder, didn't you say it is on the other side of the river?" he has to ask again. "But I've already come to this side of the river–"

"Then it's on that side of the river," the old man crossly interjects.

"And if I use Wuyizhen to get my bearings?"

"Then it's still on that side of the river."

"But I have already come to this side of the river from Wuyizhen, so when you say that side of the river, shouldn't it be this side of the river?"

"Don't you want to go to Lingshan?"

"Precisely."

"Then it's on that side of the river."

"Venerable elder, surely you're talking metaphysics?"

The old man says in all earnestness, "Aren't you asking the way?"

He says he is.

"Then I've already told you." The old man raises his staff, dismisses him, and walks along the river-bank into the distance.

He stays alone on this side of the river, the other side of the river from Wuyizhen. The problem now is on which side of the river is Wuyizhen? He really can't make up his mind and can only think of an old proverb dating back a thousand years:

"Existence is returning, non-existence is returning, so don't stay by the river getting blown about by the cold wind."

77

I don't understand the meaning of these reflections. It isn't a large stretch of water, the leaves of the trees have all fallen and the branches and trunks are grey-black. The one closest seems to be a willow, the two further off but closer to the water could be elms. The slender branches of the willow in front are loosely tangled and the bare branches of the two at the back have only small twigs on them. I can't tell if the water with the reflections in it is iced over, in cold weather sometimes there is a layer of ice. The sky is grey and gloomy and it looks as if it is about to rain, but there is no rain, no movement, the branches do not sway, there is no wind. Everything is frozen as if dead. There is only this faint trace of music, wafting and intangible. The trees all have a slight slant. The two elms slant, one to the right and the other to the left. The trunk of the slightly larger willow slants to the right and three branches of virtually the same thickness growing from it all slant to the left, so there is a sort of balance. Thereafter, it is fixed and unmoving, like a stretch of dead water, a finished painting which will not be further changed, devoid of any wish for change, devoid of disturbance, devoid of impulse, devoid of desire. Land and water and trees and the branches of the trees. Dark brown streaks in the water, neither sandbars, islets nor peninsulas and only amounting to a few small patches of earth poking out of the water are slightly interesting, otherwise the surface of the water is unnaturally monotonous. At the edge of the water at the extreme right is a small and insignificant tree. It is not very high and has many branches which grow out in all directions like withered fingers. The metaphor might not be quite right but they stretch out anyway and have no intention of coming together whereas fingers can retract. All uninteresting. Below the closest willow is a rock. Is it for people to sit on to cool off? Or is it for people to stand on so as not to get their shoes wet when the water rises? Maybe it is not for any particular purpose, maybe it is not a rock but just a couple of clumps of earth. There could be a road there, or something like a road, leading to the water. When the water rises, all of this would be submerged. Level to where the first branch of the willow forks, parallel to this branch, there seems to be an embankment. When the water rises it would become the shore, but there are many gaps and the water would still flood in. Where there seems to be an embankment it is not completely still, a bird flies up and dives into the net-like branches of the willow. If I didn't see it fly down there, it would be quite hard to see it. Its existence or non-existence lies solely in its having flown down there. The bird is in fact quite alive and on closer inspection there is more than one, hopping about on the ground under the tree and flying up and down. They are all smaller than the one which has just flown down and are not as dark either. They are probably sparrows, so the one hidden in the branches of the willow should be a myna, if it hasn't flown off. What is essential is whether it is perceived and not whether it exists. To exist and yet not to be perceived is the same as not to exist. Something is moving on the opposite shore, on the other side of the water there is a cart above the grey-brown clumps of bushes. Someone is behind pushing it and the person bent over at the front would be pulling it. A cart with rubber tyres on the wheels could be carrying a half-ton load. It is moving slowly, unlike the sparrows, and its movement can barely be detected. It is only after identifying it as a cart that its movement is noticed. All this is determined by thought. If a road is identified then it is a road, a proper road, one that is not obliterated even after rain and flooding. Following the broken line above the grey-brown bushes then going back to look for the cart, it can be seen that it has moved quite some distance and entered the branches of the willow. At a glance, it could be taken for a bird's nest but because it was identified as a cart before entering the branches of the tree, when one looks it is of course still a cart, moving slowly and moreover carrying a heavy load, a load of bricks or a load of soil. Do the trees, birds and cart of this scene also think of their own meaning? And what associations does the grey sky have with the reflections on the water, the trees, the birds and the cart? Grey ... sky ... water ... leaves all shed ... not a trace of green ... mounds of earth ... all black ... cart ... birds ... straining to push ... don't disturb ... billowing waves ... sparrows noisily chirping ... transparent ... treetops ... hungry and thirsty skin ... anything will do ... rain ... tail feathers of the golden pheasant ... feathers are light ... rose colour ... endless night ... not bad ... there's a bit of wind ... good ... I'm very grateful to you ... a vacuous formlessness ... some ribbons ... curling ... cold ... warm ... wind ... tottering ... spiralling ... sounds now intermingled ... huge ... insects ... no skeletons ... in an abyss ... a button ... black wings ... night unfurling ... everywhere are ... panic ... fire illuminates ... finely painted designs ... joined to black silk gauze ... insects in a straw sandal ... nuclei swirling in cytoplasm ... eyes form first ... he decides the style ... innate potential exists ... an earring ... nameless imprints ... I didn't notice that it had snowed but there is a thin layer of pure white which has not had time to pile up on the branches. The willow branches growing in the opposite direction of the slanting trunk have turned black. Above the branches of the two spreading elms, one leaning to the left and the other to the right, there was originally a stretch of shining white water, like snow which had fallen on a flat cement surface, the water must have been frozen. The mounds of earth which are neither sandbars, islets or peninsulas have become black shadows. If one didn't know they were mounds of earth one wouldn't know why they are black shadows. Even if one knew they were mounds of earth one would still not understand why snow hasn't piled on them. Further off, the bushes are still bushes which are still grey-brown. Above the bushes there appears to be the hint of a road, but it can't be seen clearly. In the upper part of the outstretched branches of the little tree is a winding white line crawling upwards, the cart must have been pushed up the slope there. At this moment, there is no cart on the road and no-one walking on it. If there were people walking on the snowy road they would be quite distinct. The rock under the willow, or the couple of clumps of earth which look like a rock, has vanished. The snow has covered all the small details but the tracks which have been walked on after the snow look like veins. An inconsequential snow scene like this creates images in my mind, induces in me a desire to enter it. By entering the snow scene I would become the back of someone. This back of course would not have any particular meaning if I were not at this window looking at it. Gloomy sky, snow-covered ground brighter than the sky, no mynas and sparrows. Snow absorbing thought and meaning.

78

A dead village, sealed by a heavy snowfall. The large silent mountain behind is also blanketed in thick snow. The grey-black is the bent branches of trees, the grey loose tangles are the needles of fir trees, the dark shadows can only be cliffs where the snow can't pile up. There is an absence of colour, it's impossible to tell if it's day or night for there is light in the darkness. Snow seems to be falling so that footprints appearing are immediately blurred.

It's a leper village.

Maybe.

There are no dogs barking?

They're all dead.

Call out.

No need to. There used to be houses here. A broken wall, crushed by the snow, heavy snow. They were all pressed into sleep.

Did they all die in their sleep?

That would have been better but unfortunately it was a massacre, a slaughter, a display of manliness by being utterly ruthless. First meat buns were thrown to the dogs, they were laced with arsenic.

Wouldn't the dogs have wailed when they were dying?

An expert only had to hit the dogs once on the nose.

Why not hit them somewhere else?

It is only when a dog is hit on the nose that it will die instantly.

Didn't the people fight back at all?

They were all killed inside their houses, they didn't take a step outside.

Couldn't the young girls and babies escape?

Broadaxes were used.

Weren't the women spared?

When the women were raped it was even more brutal–

Enough.

Are you frightened?

The village couldn't have had just the one family, could it?

One family with three brothers.

They all died?

People say it was a sworn enemy of the family or else an epidemic. Maybe they suddenly got rich, found gold in the riverbed.

And were killed by outsiders?

They occupied the riverbed and wouldn't let outsiders pan for gold.

Where's the riverbed?

Right under your feet and mine.

Why can't I see it?

All that can be seen are vapours rising from hell but that is just a feeling. This is a dead river.

You and I are on this dead river?

Yes, let me show the way.

Where to?

The other side of the river, to that stark white snow-covered land. There are three trees at the edge of the snow and further on is the mountain, the houses covered by the snow have collapsed under the weight. Only this section of broken wall is standing and behind it broken earthenware pots and fragments of celadon bowls can be picked up. You can't resist kicking at them and are startled by the flapping wings of a nocturnal bird taking flight. You can't see the sky and only see snow drifting down. There is fine snow on a fence and behind it is a vegetable plot. You know that hardy winter potherb mustard and *piaorcai* like the crinkled skin of an old woman's face are all buried under the snow. You know this vegetable plot well and know the location of the back door leading onto this garden. You have eaten hairy little chestnuts sitting on the threshold. You can't work out if this is a dream you had in childhood or a dream about your childhood, it would take a lot of effort to work this out. Right now, with great stealth, you are careful not to tread on the cat's tail. That animal's eyes glow in the dark, you know it is looking at you and you pretend not to be looking at it. You must quietly make your way around the well, there is an upright chopstick propping up a woven bamboo basket and you and she are hiding behind the door holding a piece of string and waiting for sparrows to come along. The grown-ups are inside playing cards. They are all wearing glasses with round brass rims and have bulging eyes like goldfish. Their eyeballs stick out from their sockets but they can't see a thing and are holding the cards right up to their glasses. The two of you crawl under the table and all you can see are legs. There is a horse's hoof. And there is also a fat and very long tail, you know it is a fox, it swishes from side to side, turns hard, and becomes a striped tiger crouched in the armchair. It will pounce on you any time. You can't sneak past, you know if there's a fight it will be a fierce one, and it is about to pounce on you!

What's up?

Nothing, I seem to have had a dream. In the dream it was snowing on the village. The night sky was lit by the snow, this night was unreal, the air was bitterly cold and my head was light and empty. Anyway, I was dreaming of snow and winter and my footprints left in the snow in winter, I was thinking of you,

Don't talk to me about this, I don't want to grow up, I miss my father, only he truly loves me, you only want to sleep with me, I can't make love without love,

I love you,

Nonsense, with you it's only a momentary need,

What are you talking about? I love you!

Yes, rolling about in the snow, like dogs, go away, I only want myself,

The wolf will take you away in its mouth and eat up all your insides and the brown bear will take you to its cave and mate with you!

You only think about that, think about me, think about my feelings,

What feelings?

Take a guess, oh you are so stupid, I want to fly–

What?

I see a flower in the darkness,

What flower?

A camellia,

I'll pluck it for you to wear,

Don't destroy it, you wouldn't die for my sake,

Why would I want to die?

Relax, I won't ask you to die for me, I am really lonely, there are no echoes, I shout out at the top of my voice but there is only silence all around, there isn't even the gurgling of a spring, even the air is so heavy, where is the river where they panned for gold?

Below the snow under your feet,

Rubbish,

It's a secret underground river, they are all bending, scrubbing, and washing,

There's a burr here,

What?

There's nothing here at all,

You're really wicked,

Who told you to ask, hey, hey, there seem to be echoes, up there, take me there,

If you want to go, then go,

. . .

I can see, you and her, in the snow, on a grey hazy night, I can't see clearly but I can still see, you are in the snow, barefoot.

Aren't you cold?

I don't feel the cold.

You are walking with her just like this in the snow, all around are forests with dark blue trees.

Aren't there any stars?

No, and there's no moon.

And no houses?

No.

And no lights?

There's nothing at all, only you and her, walking together, walking in the snow, she is wearing a woollen scarf and you are barefooted. It's a bit cold but not too cold. You can't see yourself and only feel you are walking barefoot in the snow, she is at your side, holding your hand. You are holding her hand tightly, leading the way.

Is it far away?

Far, far away, aren't you afraid?

There's something odd about this night, it's inky-blue but bright. But I'm not really afraid with you by my side.

Do you feel secure?

Yes.

Are you in my arms?

Yes, I am leaning against you and you are holding me gently.

Do I kiss you?

No.

Do you want me to kiss you?

Yes, but I can't make up my mind. It's wonderful just like this, walking along. I also see a dog.

Where?

Up ahead, it seems to be sitting on its haunches, I know it's a dog. I also see you breathing out and the steam curling up into the air.

Do you feel the warmth?

No, but I know the air you breathe out is warm, you are simply breathing out air but don't say anything.

Do you have your eyes open?

No, they're shut but I can see everything. I can't open my eyes, I know if I open my eyes you will vanish, so I just keep looking like this and you just keep holding me in your arms like this. Not so tight, I can't breathe, I want to go on looking, want to keep you. Oh, they've separated, and are walking on ahead.

Still in the snow?

Yes, the snow stings my feet but it feels good, my feet are a bit cold but I need this and keep walking on like this.

Can you see what you look like?

I don't need to see, as long as I feel slightly cold and there is a slight stinging on my feet, and I can feel the snow and can feel you by my side, I feel secure and can relax and keep walking. My darling, can you hear me calling you?

Yes.

Kiss me, kiss my palms. Where are you? Don't leave me!

I'm right here by your side.

No, I'm calling your spirit, I'm calling you, you must come, don't abandon me.

Silly child, I wouldn't do that.

I'm frightened, frightened about you leaving. Don't leave me, I can't bear the loneliness.

Aren't you in my arms right now?

Yes, I know, I'm grateful to you, my love.

Sleep, sleep peacefully.

I'm not sleepy at all, my mind is crystal clear, I see the transparent night, the blue forest laden with snow. There is no starlight and no moonlight but all this can be seen clearly. It is a very strange night. I want to stay forever with you on this snowy night. Don't go away, don't abandon me. I want to cry. I don't know why. Don't abandon me, don't go so far from me, don't go kissing other women!

79

It is also in this winter after a snowfall that a friend comes to talk about the time he was on a labour reform farm. He looks at the snow-covered landscape outside my window and squints as if the glare of the snow is too strong and also as if he is immersed in his memories.

There was a huge derrick, he says, on the prison farm. Glancing out the window to a tall building, he estimates that it would have been at least fifty or sixty metres high, not less than the height of the very building we are in. A big flock of crows kept flying around the pointed top, they flew off and came back, circling endlessly and cawing all the time. The brigade leader in charge of this band of prisoners was an old soldier demobilized from the Korean War. He had a grade two award for meritorious action but having been wounded, one leg was longer than the other and he walked with a limp. He had some bad luck and wasn't promoted any higher than company commander and ended up being sent to look after these prisoners so he was forever cursing and swearing.

Cunt of someone's mother, what the fucking hell is going on? Just bloody won't ever let me get any sleep! He swore in Northern Jiangsu dialect as he walked around the derrick with his army overcoat draped over his shoulders.

Climb up and have a look! he ordered me. What else could I do but take off my padded jacket and climb? Halfway up, in the strong wind, my calves started trembling, I looked down and these legs just gave up and wouldn't stop shaking. It was during a year of famine and people were starving to death on the surrounding farms. We were a bit better off in the labour prison and the taro and peanuts we grew were stored in the granary after the company commander had taken his cut; we didn't have to turn it all over. Each person's grain rations were guaranteed and while we were a bit puffy we weren't constipated. However, I was just too weak to climb up high.

Brigade leader! All I could do was to yell down to him.

I told you to have a look at what's up there, he yelled from below.

I looked up.

There seemed to be a cloth bag hanging there, I said. I was starting to black out and all I could do was to shout down to him, I can't climb up any further!

If you can't then we'll get someone else! He used a lot of invectives, but he wasn't such a bad person.

I came down.

Get Thief for me! he said.

Thief was also a prisoner, a young fellow about seventeen or eighteen. They caught him when he stole someone's wallet on a bus, so Thief became his nickname.

I found Thief for him. This young fellow took one look and refused to go up. The brigade leader was furious.

I didn't ask you to kill yourself, did I?

Thief said he was frightened of falling.

The brigade leader ordered someone to get him a piece of rope, then said if he didn't go up he'd be penalized three days' grain rations!

It was only then that Thief, with the length of rope tied at his waist, went up. All of us watching from below were sweating profusely on his account. When he still had a third of the way to go, each time he moved further up he secured the rope to the iron rack and eventually got to the top. Flocks of crows kept circling around him. He waved his arms to chase them off, then from above a hemp bag slowly floated down. We went over to look. The hemp bag, which was pecked full of holes, was half full of peanuts!

Mother's cunt! The brigade leader unleashed another round of invectives.

Assemble! He blew his whistle again. Everyone was assembled. He began with a reprimand then asked who was responsible.

No-one dared to make a sound.

It couldn't have flown up there by itself, could it? I thought it was rotting human flesh!

We all forced ourselves to hold back, no-one dared to laugh.

If no-one owns up, everyone's meals are stopped!

At this everyone became anxious and looked at one another. But we all knew in our hearts that only Thief was capable of climbing up. Our eyes naturally fell upon him. He cast his eyes to the ground, then unable to bear it fell on his haunches and admitted he had stolen up during the night and put it there. He said he was frightened of starving to death.

Did you use a rope? The brigade leader asked.

No.

Then why were you putting on that big act just now? Just penalize that son of a bitch one day without food! the brigade leader announced.

Everyone cheered.

Thief bawled.

The brigade leader limped off.

Another friend of mine tells me there is an important matter he wants to discuss with me.

I agree and say go ahead.

He says it will take a long time to tell it all.

I suggest that he shortens it.

He says even if he does, he'll still have to start at the beginning.

Then start telling it, I say.

He asks if I know a certain high-ranking imperial bodyguard of a certain emperor of the Manchu-Qing Dynasty. He tells me both the name and reign title of the emperor as well as the name and surname of this high-ranking bodyguard, and says he is the direct seventh-generation eldest grandson of this illustrious person of those times.

I accept his statement without reservation and don't find it at all surprising, but whether this ancestor is a criminal or a meritorious minister of the emperor is of little consequence to him at present.

He says, on the contrary, it is of great consequence. People from cultural relic bureaux, museums, archive bureaux, political associations and antique shops have all visited him, repeatedly questioning him and harassing him no end.

I ask if he has one or two precious relics.

He says that's an underestimation.

Is it worth a string of cities? I ask.

Whether it's worth a string of cities he can't say. In any case it's hard to put a value on it, even one million, ten million or several hundred million wouldn't be near the mark. He says it isn't one or two items, but ranges from ceremonial bronze vessels and flat jades dating back to the Shang Dynasty to precious swords of the Warring States period, not to mention rare antiques and Buddhist calligraphies and paintings from various periods, enough to fill a museum. Early string-bound editions of the catalogued items run into four volumes and can be found in rare editions libraries. You have to understand that this is a two-hundred-year-old collection which started with his ancestor seven generations ago and was added to over the generations right until the Tongzhi reign period of the Qing Dynasty!

I say he shouldn't let this get out and start worrying about his safety.

He says there isn't a problem with his safety. The main problem is that he can't get a moment's peace. Even in his family, which is a large one, the relatives of his grandfather, father and uncles have all come one after the other to see him about it, and make such an endless racket he thinks his head will explode.

Do they all want a share?

He says there isn't anything to share, the thousands of volumes of old books, gold and silver, ceramics and other household items were torched and looted countless times by the Taipings, the Japanese, and the various warlord factions. After that, his grandfather, father and mother handed over to the authorities and sold off items and then the house was ransacked several times, so he now has none of the relics at all.

Then what are they squabbling about? I can't understand.

So it has to be told from the beginning, he says, looking perplexed. Have you heard of the Pagoda of the Jade Screen and Gold Cabinet? He is of course giving by way of comparison the name of this pagoda which was a storehouse of old books and precious relics. There are references to it in historical books, local gazetteers, as well as the genealogies of his ancestors, and it is known to the people in all the cultural relic departments in his home town down in the south. He says when the Taipings entered the city, what they torched was in fact an empty pagoda. Most of the old books had been moved in utmost secrecy to their family estate, and as for the rare treasures listed in the catalogue, the family legend for successive generations was that these too had been secretly stored. It was not until last year, before his father got sick and died, that he told him they were buried somewhere in their old home. His father didn't know the exact location but said that a handwritten volume of poems by his great-grandfather, which had been passed on to him by his grandfather, contained an ink drawing of their old home with all the terraces, pavilions, gardens and artificial mountains. In the right upper corner were four lines of a Buddhist sutra which secretly indicated the location of this treasure. However this volume of poetry was taken away along with everything else when Red Guards ransacked their house. Later, when the family was subsequently exonerated, the book couldn't be found. The old man however could recite the four lines of the sutra and from memory drew a rough sketch of the old ancestral home for him. He committed these to memory and, at the beginning of the year, went for the first time to the old home to carry out an investigation at the actual site. However, the old ruins had changed into blocks of new office and residential buildings.

What more is there to it, it's buried under the buildings, I say.

He disagrees. If it had been under the buildings, then it would have been found when they were laying the foundations, especially with the buildings they put up nowadays. There are so many underground pipes to be installed so the foundations are dug quite deep. He looked up the builders and asked them but was told they hadn't unearthed any old relics. He says he carried out a great deal of research on the four lines of the sutra and, adding his analysis of the topography, was able to determine the approximate location as the nature area between two buildings.

What do you plan to do? Have it excavated? I ask him.

He says this is what he wants to ask me about.

I ask him whether he needs money.

He doesn't look at me and instead looks at the bare little trees in the snow outside the window.

How can I put it? Bringing up a son on my wife's salary and mine combined, we just have enough to eat, and that's not counting other expenses, but I can't sell off my ancestors like that. I would only get a certain amount as a reward for being a leader among leaders.

I say they will also issue a notice with the news that such and such a person who is the seventh-generation descendant of so and so donates cultural relics and is rewarded.

He gives a wry smile and says, won't he get his head smashed in fighting when he tries dividing up the reward amongst that big bunch of uncles and relatives? That alone makes it not worthwhile. Most importantly, however, is that he believes it will enrich the nation.

Surely there hasn't been a shortage of cultural relics unearthed? Have they enriched the nation? I retort.

That's just it, he nods, but having agreed he has second thoughts. What if he has a sudden illness or dies in a car accident? Then no-one will know.

Then hand on these lines of sutra to your son, I suggest.

He says it isn't that he hasn't thought about this, but what if his son grows up to be a good for nothing and sells it all? he asks himself.

Can't you first give him instructions? I interrupt.

The child is still young and should be allowed to study in peace. He says he shouldn't cause his son to become a nervous wreck over this puerile business when he grows up, as has been the case with him. He resolutely rules this out.

Then leave it for the archaeologists to work on in the future. What else can I say?

He thinks about it then slaps his thigh. I'll do as you suggest, let it stay buried! At this he gets up and leaves.

Another friend turns up in a brand new woollen overcoat and a pair of shiny black leather shoes with three scrolled bands. He looks like a cadre setting off on an overseas trip to carry out some important national mission.

Removing his overcoat, he says loudly he has made a fortune in business! The him of today is not the him of yesterday. With his overcoat removed, dressed in an immaculately pressed suit, a shirt with a stiff collar and a red floral necktie, he looks like the representative of a foreign company.

I say you mustn't feel the cold going outdoors wearing so little in this sort of weather.

He says he doesn't squeeze onto buses anymore, he came in a taxi, and this time he is staying in the Beijing Hotel! What, you don't believe me? Why should only foreigners stay in high-class hotels? He tosses down a set of keys with a brass ball and a brass tag with engraved English lettering.

I tell him the keys should have been handed in at the reception counter when he came out.

It's a habit from being poor in the past, I always take the keys with me, he says excusing himself. He looks around the room.

How is it that you are living in one room like this? Guess how many rooms I'm living in at present?

I say I have no way of guessing.

Three rooms and a lounge room. In your city of Beijing that would be the equivalent of what a bureau chief has!

I look at the ruddy glow of his clean-shaven face, he isn't thin and scruffy like when I met him on my travels.

How come you don't have colour television? he asks.

I tell him I don't watch television.

Even if you don't watch it, you've got to have one for show. We've got two at home, one in the lounge room and one in my daughter's room. My daughter and her mother watch their own programs. Do you want one? I can go with you right away to a department store and bring one back! I'm telling the truth. He stares wide-eyed at me.

I guess your money's not burning up fast enough, I say.

I'm in buying and selling, I make presents of these to all the officials, this is what they thrive on. Don't you need to get them to approve your proposals and give you your quotas? If you don't give presents doors won't open. But you're my friend! Are you short of spending money? If it's under ten thousand I can get it for you without any problem.

Don't go breaking the law, I warn him.

Break the law? I just give a few presents. It's not me who breaks the law, the ones they should catch are the big shots!

They can't catch the big shots, I say.

Of course you'd know better than me, you're in the capital, you'd get to know about everything that's going on! I tell you, catching me isn't all that easy. I pay all my taxes. I'm now an honoured guest in the homes of county dignitaries and regional heads of the bureau of commerce. It's not like when I was the town primary school teacher in Chengguan. At that time, to get transferred from the countryside to Chengguan, at least four months of my yearly salary was spent on meals for cadres in the education office.

His eyes narrow as he takes a step back and, with his hands on his hips, scrutinizes an ink painting of a winter landscape on my wall. He holds his breath for a while then turns and says, didn't you once praise my calligraphy? Even you thought it was good but when I tried at the time to put it into an exhibition at the county cultural centre, it was turned down. The calligraphy of some important officials and famous people is sub-standard but aren't they the honorary chairpersons and vice-chairpersons of calligraphy research associations and aren't they the ones shamelessly getting their work published in the newspapers?

I ask him if he still does calligraphy.

I can't make a living from calligraphy, it's just like with the books you write. But if one day I too become a famous person, people will come sniffing at my backside after my ink treasures. That's society, I've given up on it.

If you've given up on it then there's no point talking about it.

I'm cross about it!

Then you haven't given up on it. I ask if he has eaten.

Don't worry about it, in a while I'll get a car to take you to whatever restaurant you like, I know that your time is precious. I'll first get what I have to say out of the way, I've come to you for help.

How? Tell me about it.

Help get my daughter into a prestige university.

I say I'm not the president of any university.

And you wouldn't get appointed, he says, but surely you must have some contacts? I'm now considered wealthy but people still think of me as a speculator. I can't let my daughter's life be like mine, I want her to go to a prestige university so she can get into the upper stratum of society.

So she can find herself the son of a high-ranking cadre? I ask.

I have no control over that, she knows what she must do.

What if she won't look?

Stop interrupting, will you help or not?

It depends on her school results, I can't do anything to help.

She's got good results.

Then all she needs to do is sit for the examinations.

You're really pedantic. Do you think all those children of high-ranking cadres have passed examinations?

I haven't researched such matters.

You're a writer.

So what if I am a writer?

You're the conscience of society, you must speak for the people!

Stop joking, I say. Are you the people, or am I the people, or is it the so-called we who are the people? I speak only for myself.

What I like about you is that you always tell the truth!

The truth is, my good elder brother I'm starving, so put on your overcoat and let's find somewhere to eat.

Someone is knocking at the door again. I open the door but don't know the person holding a black plastic bag. I say I don't want to buy any eggs, I eat out.

He says he's not selling eggs and opens the bag to show me it doesn't contain a weapon and that he is not a criminal on the run. He carefully takes out a large bundle of paper and says he has come especially to seek my help. He has written a novel and wants me to have a look at it. I have no choice but to let him in and invite him to sit down.

He says he won't sit down but will leave the manuscript and call again at a later date.

I say there is no need to leave it for a later date, if he has something to say he can say it now.

He fumbles in his pockets with both hands and takes out a packet of cigarettes. I hand him matches and wait for him to light his cigarette so that he can quickly finish what he wants to say.

Stuttering, he says he has written a factual story—

I have to interrupt him and tell him I'm not a journalist and I'm not interested in facts.

Stuttering even worse, he says he knows literature isn't the same as newspaper reports and that this work of his is fiction. He has added an appropriate amount of fabrication to a factual basis. His purpose in getting me to look at it is to see if it is publishable.

I say I am not an editor.

He says he knows this but thought I might be able to recommend it, I could make any corrections I wanted. I could even add my name to it so that it could be considered a joint work. Of course his name would be put second and mine first.

I say that if I put my name to it, it will be even harder for it to get published.

Why?

Because it is very hard to get my works published.

He exclaims to indicate that he understands.

I am afraid he doesn't fully understand and explain that it would be best if he found an editor who was able to publish his work.

He stops talking and is obviously uneasy.

I make up my mind to help him, then tell him to take the novel back.

His eyes open wide and he asks instead whether I would forward it to the relevant editorial department.

It'd be better for you to send it directly rather than for me to forward it. It will certainly stir up less trouble, I say with a smile.

He also smiles, puts the manuscript back into his bag and mutters his thanks.

I say no, it is I who am grateful to him.

There is knocking on the door again. I don't want to open it.

80

You gasp for breath taking a step and then resting as you walk towards the mountain of ice. It is a struggle. The green river of ice is dark but transparent. Huge mineral veins, inky green like jade, lie beneath it.

You glide on the smooth ice and the biting cold stings your numb frozen cheeks. Barely visible snowflakes of all colours glisten before your eyes and the moist air you breathe out instantly forms a layer of white frost on your eyebrows. All around is frozen silence.

The riverbed suddenly rises and the glacier imperceptibly moves a few metres, ten or so metres or even much more in a year.

You are going against the flow of the glacier crawling like a partially frozen insect.

Up ahead, in the shadows where the sunlight doesn't reach, windswept flat slabs of ice soar up. When gale-force winds blow at a speed of over a hundred metres per second, these white walls of ice are polished to a high sheen.

You are in the midst of these ice crystal ruins and even while not moving you are gasping for air. There is a tearing pain in your lungs and your brain has already frozen so that you can't think, everything is almost blank, isn't this precisely the state you have been aspiring to reach? Like this world of ice and snow there are only some indefinite blurred images created by shadows – they don't tell anything, have no meaning, are a stretch of deathly loneliness.

You can fall over with every step, so you fall over, then struggle as you slide and crawl. Your hands and feet can no longer feel pain.

The snow piled on the ice gradually decreases and is left only in corners where the wind can't reach. The snow is solid, it gives the impression of being soft and fluffy but is in fact wrapped in a hard coating of ice.

A bald eagle is circling in the valley of ice below your feet, it is the only other form of life apart from you. You can't decide whether or not it is something you've imagined but what is important is that you do have visual images.

You spiral upwards. And while spiralling up between life and death, you are still struggling. You still exist, that is to say, blood is still circulating in your veins, your life still hasn't ended.

In the vast silence, there is a tinkling, a faint tinkling which is barely audible, like ice crystals colliding. You think you hear it.

A purple cloud haze appears on the mountain top, showing that the wind storm is swirling at high speed. Wisps of cloud on the edges show the force of the wind.

The tinkling becomes clearer and causes your heart to palpitate. You see a woman riding on a horse. The horse's head and the woman both appear above the snow line, against the background of the gloomy ice ravine. You seem also to hear singing accompanying the tinkling of the bells on the horse.

> Woman from Chang'an,
> Hair plaited with silk ribbons
> Jade earrings
> Silver bracelets
> Sash of many colours . . .

She seems to be a Tibetan woman you once saw on a horse next to a road-marker 5600 feet above sea level on a snow-covered mountain. She was looking back at you and smiling, enticing you to fall into an icy ravine. At the time you couldn't help walking towards her . . .

These are all memories, this tinkling which sticks in your mind seems to be a sound in your brain. There is an agonizing, searing pain in your lungs and stomach, your heart pulsates wildly, chaotically, and your brain is about to explode. When it explodes, the blood will clot, it will be a soundless explosion. Life is fragile, yet to obstinately struggle is natural.

You open your eyes, the light hurts, you can't see anything but you are aware that you are still crawling, the tinkling bells have become distant memories, indistinct longings, like sparkling ice flowers, fragmented, ephemeral, glistening on the retina of your eyes. You strive to discern the colours of the rainbow, you swirl around upside-down, float backwards, lose the ability to control yourself. It is all futile striving, vague hope, refusal to be extinguished, pitch-black cavern, skeleton's eye-sockets seeming to go deep inside, nothing there at all, a cacophony splits asunder with a blast!

... a never before experienced limpidity, a totality of purity and freshness. You perceive a barely discernible subtle, almost soundless sound, it turns transparent, is carded, filtered, clarified. You are falling and while falling you float up, so gently, and there is no wind, no physical burdens and no rashness in your emotions. Your whole body is cool, your body and mind listen intently, your whole body and mind hear this soundless, billowing music. In your conscious mind this thread of gossamer becomes smaller but increasingly clear, appears right before your eyes, delicate like a strand of hair, and also like a crack of light. The extremity of the crack fuses with the darkness, loses its form, expands, transforms into faint, minute points of light, then boundless countless particles, enveloping you in this cloud blanket of distinct particles. Minute points of light form clusters, drift into motion, turn into a mist-like nebula, keep slowly transforming, gradually solidifying into a dark moon tinged with blue. The moon within the sun turns grey-purple, instantly spreads out, but the centre further condenses, turns dark red, gives off bright purple rays. You close your eyes to cut the glare but can't. Trembling fear and hope rise from the depths of your heart, at the edge of the darkness you hear music, this solidified sound gradually expands, spreads and sparkling crystals of sound penetrate your body. You can't work out where you are. The particles of bright crystals of sound permeate your body and mind from all directions. As a mass of long notes take shape, there is a vigorous middle note, you can't catch the melody but can perceive the richness of the sounds. It links up with another mass of sounds, intermingles, unfolds, turns into a river which disappears and appears, appears and disappears. A dark blue sun circles within an even darker moon, you hold your breath enraptured, stop breathing, reach the extremity of life. But the force of the pulsating sounds becomes stronger and stronger, lifts you up, pushes you towards a high tide, a high tide of pure spirituality. Before your eyes, in your heart, in your body oblivious to time and space, in the continual surge of sustained noise, of reflected images in the dark sun within the dark moon, is a blast exploding exploding exploding exploding explo- explo- explo- explo- -ding -ding -ding -ding – then again absolute silence. You fall into an even deeper darkness and again feel your heart pulsating, discern physical pain. The fear of death of the living body is concrete like this, the physical body you failed to abandon recovers its sensitivity.

In the darkness, in the corner of the room, the line of bright red lights on your tape recorder is flashing.

81

In the snow outside my window I see a small green frog, one eye blinking and the other wide open, unmoving, looking at me. I know this is God.

He appears just like this before me and watches to see if I will understand.

He is talking to me with his eyes by opening and closing them. When God talks to humans he doesn't want humans to hear his voice.

And I don't think it at all strange, it is as if it should be like this. It is as if God is in fact a frog. The intelligent round eye doesn't so much as blink once. It is really kind that he should deign to gaze upon this wretched human being, me.

His other eye opens and closes as it speaks a language incomprehensible to humans. Whether I understand or not is not God's concern.

I could of course think maybe there is no meaning at all in this blinking eye, but its significance could lie precisely in its not having meaning.

There are no miracles. God is saying this, saying this to this insatiable human being, me.

Then what else is there to seek? I ask of him.

All around is silence, snow is falling soundlessly. I am surprised by this tranquillity. In Heaven it is peaceful like this.

And there is no joy. Joy is related to anxiety.

Snow is falling.

I don't know where I am at this moment, I don't know where this realm of Heaven comes from, I look all around.

I don't know that I don't understand anything and still think I know everything.

Things just happen behind me and there is always a mysterious eye, so it is best for me just to pretend that I understand even if I don't.

While pretending to understand, I still don't understand.

The fact of the matter is I comprehend nothing, I understand nothing.

This is how it is.

Written from 1982 to September 1989
Beijing and Paris

Appendix

Major Publications by Gao Xingjian

Xiandai xiaoshuo jiqiao chutan (A Preliminary Discussion of the Art of Modern Fiction). Guangzhou: Huacheng Chubanshe, 1981. [Literary criticism]

You zhi gezi jiao Hongchunr (A Pigeon Called Red Beak). Beijing Chubanshe, 1985. [A novella]

Gao Xingjian xiju ji (Collected Plays of Gao Xingjian). Beijing: Qunzhong Chubanshe, 1985. [Includes the plays *Juedui xinhao* (Absolute Signal), *Chezhan* (Bus Stop), *Yeren* (Wild Man), *Duibai* (Soliloquy), *Xiandai zhezixi sichu* (Four Modern Opera Excerpts)]

Dui yizhong xiandai xiju de zuiqiu (In Search of a Modern Form of Dramatic Representation). Beijing: Zhongguo Xiju Chubanshe, 1987. [Essays on theatre and dramatic representation]

Gei wo laoye mai yugan (Buying a Fishing Rod for My Grandfather). Taipei: Lianhe Wenxue Chubanshe, 1988. [A collection of short stories]

Lingshan (Soul Mountain). Taipei: Lianjing Chubanshe, 1990. [A novel]

Shanhaijing zhuan (Story of the *Classic of Mountains and Seas*). Hong Kong: Tiandi Tushu Youxian Gongsi, 1993. [A play based on myths and legends in the *Classic of Mountains and Seas*]

Dialoguer/Interloquer. Paris: MEET, 1994. [French version by Gao Xingjian]

Gao Xingjian xiju liuzhong (Six plays by Gao Xingjian). Taipei: Dijiao, 1995. [Includes the plays *Bi'an* (Other Shore), *Mingcheng* (Netherworld), *Sheng sheng man bianzou* (Variations on a Slow Tune), *Shanhaijing zhuan* (Story of the *Classic of Mountains and Seas*), *Taowang* (Absconding), *Sheng si jie* (Between Life and Death), *Duihua yu fanjie* (Dialogue and Rebuttal), *Yeyoushen* (Nocturnal Wanderer)]

Le Somnambule. Carni res-Morlanwelz (Belgium): Editions Lansman, 1995. [French version by Gao Xingjian]

Ink Paintings by Gao Xingjian. Taipei Fine Arts Museum, 1995.

Go t de l'encre. Paris: Editions voix Richard Meir, 1996.

Meiyou zhuyi (Without Isms). Hong Kong: Tiandi Tushu Youxian Gongsi, 1996. [Essays on literature and art]

Zhoumo sichongzou (Weekend Quartet). Hong Kong: Xin Shiji Chubanshe, 1996. [Includes the plays *Zhoumo sichongzou* (Weekend Quartet), *Shunjian* (One Instant), *Sheng sheng man bianzou* (Variations on a Slow Tune), *Wo shuo ciwei* (I Tell the Hedgehog)]

Au plus pr s du r el: Dialogues sur l' criture (1994–1997), co-author Denis Bourgeois. Paris: ditions de l'aube, 1997. [Recorded conversations on literature over three years between Gao Xingjian and Denis Bourgeois]

Quatre quatuors pour un week-end. Carni res-Morlanwelz (Belgium): Editions Lansman, 1998. [French version by Gao Xingjian]

L'Encre et la lumi re. Paris: Editions voix Richard Meir, 1998.

Yige ren de shengjing (One Man's Bible). Taipei: Lianjing Chubanshe, 1999. [A novel]

Une Autre esth tique. Paris: Editions Cercle d'art, 2000.

English Language Translations of Gao Xingjian's Works

Aspfors, Lena and Torbj rn Lod n, trans., "The Voice of the Individual", *The Stockholm Journal of East Asian Studies*, 3 (1993).

Besio, Kimberley, trans., "*Bus Stop*: A Lyrical Comedy on Life in One Act" in Haiping Yan, ed., *Theatre and Society: An Anthology of Contemporary Chinese Drama*, Armonk, New York and London: M. E. Sharpe, 1998.

Gilbert C. F. Fong, trans., *The Other Shore: Plays by Gao Xingjian*, Hong Kong: The Chinese University Press, 1999.

Lau, Winnie, Deborah Sauviat and Martin Williams, trans., "Without Isms", *The Journal of the Oriental Society of Australia*, 27 & 28 (1995–1996).

Lee, Mabel, trans., *Soul Mountain*, HarperCollins, Sydney, 2000.

Ng, Mau-sang, trans., "Contemporary Technique and National Character in Fiction", *Renditions*, 19 & 20 (1983).

Riley, Jo, trans., "The Other Side: A Contemporary Drama Without Acts" in Martha P. Y. Cheung and Jane C. C. Lai, *An Oxford Anthology of Contemporary Chinese Drama*, Oxford and New York: Hong Kong University Press, 1997.

Roubicek, Bruno, trans., "*Wild Man*: A Contemporary Chinese Spoken Drama", *Asian Theatre Journal*, 7. 2 (1990).

Critical Works in English on Gao Xingjian

Comprehensive listings of works on Gao Xingjian in Chinese, Swedish, French, German, Japanese and English are contained in Gilbert C. F. Fong (trans.), *The Other Shore: Plays by Gao Xingjian*, Hong Kong: The Chinese University Press, 1999, and in Henry Z. Y. Zhao, *Towards a Modern Zen Theatre: Gao Xingjian and Chinese Theatre Experimentalism*, London: SOAS Publications, 2000 (in print).

Barm , Geremie, "A Touch of the Absurd: Introducing Gao Xingjian, and His Play *The Bus Stop*", *Renditions*, 19 & 20 (1983).

Burckhardt, Olivier, "The Voice of One in the Wilderness", *Quadrant* (April 2000).

Chen Xiaomei, "A Wildman between Two Cultures: Some Paradigmatic Remarks on 'Influence Studies'", *Comparative Literature Studies*, 29. 4 (1992).

Lee, Mabel, "Without Politics: Gao Xingjian on Literary Creation", *The Stockholm Journal of East Asian Studies*, 6 (1995).

"Walking Out of Other People's Prisons: Liu Zaifu and Gao Xingjian on Chinese Literature in the 1990s", *Asian & African Studies*, 5. 1 (1996).

"Personal Freedom in Twentieth Century China: Reclaiming the Self in Yang Lian's *Yi* and Gao Xingjian's *Lingshan*", in Mabel Lee and Michael Wilding, eds, *History, Literature and Society: Essays in Honour of S. N. Mukherjee*, Sydney and New Delhi: Sydney Association for Studies in Culture and Society, 1997.

"Gao Xingjian's *Lingshan/Soul Mountain*: Modernism and the Chinese Writer", HEAT, 4 (1997).

"Gao Xingjian's Dialogue with Two Dead Poets from Shaoxing: Xu Wei and Lu Xun", in R. D. Findeisen and R. H. Gassman, eds, *Autumn Floods: Essays in Honour of M rian G lik*, Bern: Lang, 1998.

"Gao Xingjian on the Issue of Literary Creation for the Modern Writer", *Journal of Asian Pacific Communication*, 9. 1 & 2 (1999).

"Pronouns as Protagonists: Gao Xingjian's *Lingshan* as Autobiography", *China Studies*, 5 (1999).

Li Jianyi, "Gao Xingjian's *The Bus-Stop*: Chinese Traditional Theatre and Western Avant-garde", Masters thesis, University of Alberta, 1991.

Lod n, Torbj rn, "World Literature with Chinese Characteristics: On a Novel by Gao Xingjian", *The Stockholm Journal of East Asian Studies*, 4 (1993).

Ma Sen, "The Theatre of the Absurd in Mainland China: Gao Xingjian's *The Bus Stop*", *Issues and Studies: A Journal of China Studies and International Affairs*, 25. 8 (1989).

Quah Sy Ren, "Gao Xingjian and China's Alternative Theatre of the 1980s", M. Phil. thesis, University of Cambridge, 1997.
"The Theatre of Gao Xingjian: Experimentation Within the Chinese Context and Towards New Modes of Representation", PhD thesis, University of Cambridge, 1999.

Riley, Josephine, and Else Unterrieder, "The Myth of Gao Xingjian", in Josephine Riley and Else Unterrieder, eds, *Haishi Zou Hao: Chinese Poetry, Drama and Literature of the 1980s*, Bonn: Engelhard-Ng Verlag, 1989.

Sauviat, Deborah, "The Challenge to the 'Official Discourse' in Gao Xingjian's Early Fiction", BA Honours thesis, University of Sydney, 1996.

Tam Kwok-kan, "Drama of Dilemma: Waiting as Form and Motif in *The Bus Stop* and *Waiting for Godot*", in Yun-Tong Luk, ed., *Studies in Chinese–Western Comparative Drama*, Hong Kong: The Chinese University Press, 1990.

Tay, William, "Avant-garde Theatre in Post-Mao China: *The Bus Stop* by Gao Xingjian", in Howard Goldblatt ed., *Worlds Apart: Recent Chinese Writing and Its Audiences*, Armonk and New York: M.E. Sharpe, 1990.

Zhao, Henry Y. H., *Towards a Modern Zen Theatre: Gao Xingjian and Chinese Theatre Experimentalism*, London: SOAS Publications, 2000 (in print).

Zou Jiping, "Gao Xingjian and Chinese Experimental Theatre", PhD dissertation, University of Illinois, 1994.